MODERN LOVE

MODERN LOVE

LESLIE GLASS

St. Martin's Press
New York

Library of Congress Cataloging in Publication Data

Glass, Leslie.
  Modern love.

  I. Title.
PS3557.L34M6 1983   813'.54   83-2936
ISBN 0-312-54090-6

Design by Lee Wade

First Edition

10 9 8 7 6 5 4 3 2 1

*For the family in everyone
and for
Edmund
Alexander
Lindsey
in order of their appearance*

Thanks are due my good editor, Leslie Pockell, and J. Stephen Sheppard, my agent and friend.

MODERN
LOVE

1

ANNIE WAS on High Hopes, a dappled gray full of piss and vinegar. He plunged and snorted feverishly, tried to toss her off and had to be gated by two grooms. And then, restricted as he was, he still chewed metal and blew smoke and tattooed the ground with a fury Annie hadn't seen in him before. She gathered the reins in her hands while the trembling in the flanks of the horse rose through her thighs and up through her body until horse and rider alike quaked and shivered in the splintered morning air. Was this the way to ride a horse? She threaded the reins through her fingers the other way. "Shh," to the gray, High Hopes. He seemed an unfortunate color for a horse, not a color fated to win. But he had the spirit.

The sun was very bright, as sharp as the colors of autumn, and the air was needle cold. The helmet that should have been on her head was gone. It had flown off somewhere and now the cold bit into her ears. She was afraid that without the helmet she would be stuck at the starting gate with the horse in a rage of pink foam.

"Shh," to Hopes, "Shh." The other riders were in silks. Where were her silks, her reds and violets? Where was her protective helmet? They wouldn't let her ride without it. Splinters of ice seemed to rain from the sky and pierce her brain. She was in blue jeans and a blue sweater. How could she forget? The racing saddle was as nothing. Could she cling to the mane on the flat-out spaces, or were there fences she had to vault and streams she had to cross? "Shh," to the horse as she tried to remember the terrain.

There was something in her mouth, wads of gluey paste. Suddenly she was choking. Quickly, she had to clear her throat before the race began. She pulled with one gloved hand and two teeth loosened and dropped to the ground. The stuff stuck in her braces. Braces, why hadn't she gone back to have her braces removed? She only had a second to pull off the braces and save her teeth. Too late for that. The pliers were at home. Where were her silks? They were stuffed down her throat. Never mind the teeth, she had to pull out the silks soft as wallpaper paste. Too late. The bell rang and the horse freed at last charged down the track, releasing the silk in a long bloody stream and Annie's teeth one by one.

The bell rang again and Annie struggled for breath. Saturday, it was Saturday. Nate was sleeping with the covers thrown off even though it was cold in the room. She shivered and drew the sheet up to her neck. She was choking again, this time on a horse. She felt for her teeth with her tongue. All were there tight in her jaw. Just that dream again. It wasn't autumn it was summer, and the cold was the air conditioner blowing an icy stream on her face. But what was a horse doing in her old dream of suffocation?

The bell sounded a third time and this time the noise propelled Annie out of bed, but still before she had time to orient herself upward into reality where there were no horse races on a lazy Saturday in August, where she was thirty and not thirteen, where all her teeth were neatly arranged in her head, the wires gone for a good eighteen years now; and there was a lover still asleep in her bed.

She left the lover regretfully and opened the apartment door as far as the chain would let it go. Her sister Sara stood outside with her hands on her hips and a child on either side.

Sara was blond and tiny. Anyway, she was smaller than Annie, who was five feet four and three quarters in her stocking feet and always felt grotesquely large next to her dainty older sister. Sara also had the amazing good luck of violet eyes, masses of curls pale as beaten egg yolks, a cupid bow of a mouth and a husband who adored her. She was sweet looking and even now seemed somehow destined for greatness.

Annie, on the other hand, had serious gray eyes and straight hair more beige than yellow. In fact, it wasn't blond at all. Annie's nose was small, her cheekbones adequately defined, her mouth about the right size for a mouth, and she had a very winning dimple that jumped into the side of her face whenever she smiled. But it was tacitly agreed by those in her immediate family that Annie was no great beauty. She wore bangs and had the bad taste to be living with someone to whom she was not married.

Bad taste, as everyone knows, is one thing for a young girl who is new at love and curious, or poor. But it is quite another for a woman like Annie, who could easily support herself and was rapidly approaching that dangerous age when all the good men are gone and biological options begin to fade. Everyone who knew her worried that Annie's life was headed toward that great loveless void of independent middle age.

That August morning Sara helped push the void a whole lot closer by planting her desperate self on Annie's doorstep with the hazard Annie had never been able to refuse yet. Her children. The sort of thing lovers never like.

Annie regarded them doubtfully and whispered, "Nate's sleeping," through the crack in the door because she knew it wouldn't be a good idea for them to come in.

When Donald, the older child, poked his hand through, however, she knelt down and brought his grubby fingers to her lips.

"Get your hand out of there. Do you want it broken off?" Sara said. Then, "Open the door, Annie."

"I can't," Annie said sleepily. "The kids will come in and wake Nate."

"I can't imagine anybody being in bed at nine. I've been up since five-thirty. It's time he got up," Sara said firmly. "Good God, sleeping at nine. Annie, open the door."

Annie raked a hand through her straight, not-quite-blond hair. Nine o'clock? What could Sara be thinking of? Nine was practically dawn for Nate, who liked to miss morning altogether whenever he could. "Oh Sara, no," she cried. "Don't do this to me."

"I have to be in Connecticut in an hour. Please Annie, Martin is going to kill me."

"Connecticut?"

"Yes, we're going to Evergreen Hollow."

Annie nodded absently at the crack. "Have a good time."

"Open the door, Annie. This is important. We're going to see a house that's just going on the market today. I think it's perfect. It sounds perfect from the description."

"I'm sure, it's perfect." Annie paid no attention to Donald and his two-year-old sister Lucy, who were running up and down the hall knocking on doors and saying, "Hello, anybody home?"

"Annie, take the children inside before they wake up the whole floor," Sara demanded.

"The children? Aren't they going with you?" Annie was still mostly asleep and not at all sure what was going on.

"No, why do you think I'm here?"

"I don't know," Annie said blankly.

"You're taking the children. You said you would," Sara said indignantly.

"No." Annie shook her head. She was sure she hadn't said any such thing. "You told me you were going to get a sitter."

"A sitter for a whole day on Saturday! That would cost a fortune," Sara pointed out. She was being as reasonable as any person who was forced to talk through a door could be. And Martin was waiting in the car.

"Well, you're going to spend a fortune on a house, you must have a fortune to spend," Annie said. She ran her fingers nervously through her hair again. Wasn't this Saturday, her day off? Yes, Sara admitted it was. Wasn't she free today, and Nate asleep in the bedroom? What had she forgotten, she couldn't remember. "I think you should take them with you," Annie said. "And anyway, why didn't you call?"

"I didn't call because I didn't want to wake you up," Sara said self-righteously. Then she said, "You know I can't take them. You know how Martin is when he's house hunting. Oh, Annie, they run all over the place and knock things over. And Lucy gets tired so fast. Stop that, Donald," to Donald who had tripped Lucy with his foot.

Lucy began to cry.

"Sara, please take them with you. Nate is sleeping and we wanted a quiet day today."

Sara's eyes misted over. "How can you be so selfish? I haven't had a quiet day in five years."

"Are we coming or going?" Donald wanted to know. He came over and pulled on Sara's skirt. Sara took his hand and squeezed it.

"Oh Sara, I's sorry," Annie said weakly. "It's just that. . . ."

"Doesn't Annie want us?" Donald whimpered.

Lucy, abandoned on the floor by herself, began to take her clothes off with that extraordinary dexterity exhibited by two-year-olds only at the most awkward and embarrassing times. "Ha, ha," she giggled to herself.

"Of course she does—see the damage you do?" said Sara furiously. "They've been waiting all week to see you." A tear gathered in the corner of one eye and hung there dangerously. Her babies rejected. It was too much.

Annie wavered at the sight of the tear. "But Sara, Nate is sleeping. It isn't fair to wake him."

"Life isn't fair, Annie," Sara said. "Is he fair to you? My God, you can see through that thing. Donald, look the other way. Annie, Nate isn't fair. You shouldn't spend all your time thinking of him. Think of Donald and Lucy. You promised them."

"Did I?" Annie asked wonderingly. Did she? She honestly couldn't remember.

"And get dressed. I don't know what makes you think it's all right to run around like that."

"It's my house," Annie said feebly.

"Then what is that man doing there?"

No answer to that. Annie frowned uncomfortably, unsure what she ought to say. Sleeping didn't seem to cover the question. "None of your business" was beyond her. The two sisters were very close, except on the issues of love and marriage. Annie hung her head. It was the best she could do.

"Is Nate and Annie married?" Donald threw in the question as if he had been prompted at home. He had given up chasing Lucy down the hall and was waiting to see who would win him for the day.

"You know they're not," Sara snapped. She flung Annie another sisterly see-the-damage-you-do look so hostile and accusing that the tide was finally turned. Annie closed the door to release the chain. It was true she wasn't married, but she didn't want anyone to think she was an all-around beast.

When the door opened, Sara was revealed wearing a pink linen blouse with a ceramic bear pin on the collar, a Mother's Day present that May from her children, and a lime-green linen skirt that was new that day. It was a perfect outfit for house hunting in the suburbs. She tossed the strap of her shoulder bag over her shoulder in relief.

"Well, *thank* you," she said. "Goodbye, my babies," to two children who had already turned their attention elsewhere. And that was how she left.

Immediately, Donald rushed into the apartment in case Annie changed her mind about having them. Lucy was absorbed in trying to rid herself of her final bit of clothing, a wet diaper, in the middle of the hall.

"Lucy," Annie called. "Come in here."

"Too hot, Annie," Lucy cried. Her T-shirt lay on the floor along with two Miss Piggy sneakers, a pair of green shorts, two pink socks hardly bigger than a pair of match boxes. Also in the hall were a quilted diaper bag with yellow bears on it and a knapsack half opened, filled with games and balls and crayons now spilling out.

Annie ran into the hall and gathered up the baby things. "Come on, Lucy. No, don't do that."

"Wet, all wet."

"I know. Come on. I'll give you a dry one." Annie dropped the stuff inside her door and came out for the knapsack and Lucy, who was now naked and carrying the diaper down the hall in the direction her mother had gone.

Annie ran after her, caught her, swung her up in the air for a hug, and was hit smack in the face with the wet diaper. Lucy giggled.

"Very funny," Annie said. Oddly, her heart lifted with the weight of Lucy and she was not unaware of the comic nature of the picture she made—maiden aunt, businesswoman, in the hall of her building in a see-through nightgown, trying to carry a baby, who wasn't hers, into her apartment where her lover was trying to sleep, and would not be happy to see them.

She ran back to her apartment carrying the child awkwardly, plunged through the door and shut it quickly. It was funny, really it was. Too bad they wouldn't be able to laugh about it.

"My knapsack," Donald wailed. "You left my knapsack out there."

"Shh, Donald. You'll wake Nate."

"Not sleeping," Donald said triumphantly.

"Yes he is. He's sound asleep."

Donald shook his head.

"Oh, Donald, did you wake him up?" Annie cried.

"No, Annie. I just looked at him and his eyes opened. Get my knapsack."

"His eyes don't just open. You must have done something."

Donald was a sturdy child with a generally sunny disposition and sandy hair, who could disintegrate into tears in less than a second's notice. Now his lip puckered ominously. "If you don't get my knapsack, a robber will take it and I'll scream."

"Did you poke him?" Annie accused.

Donald shook his head. "I just looked at him."

"I bet you breathed on his face." She attempted a stern expression and failed. Donald breathing on the child-hating Nate was another funny thought.

"Please get my knapsack," he begged.

"All right, but don't go into the bedroom again. Don't move at all."

Lucy hung onto her like a koala bear with all four limbs gripped tightly around her.

"Let go, Lucy. I have to get the knapsack. Come on, I can't hold you both."

Lucy shook her head. "Tired," she said. She put her head on Annie's shoulder.

"What a sweet baby," Annie crooned. Lucy's golden hair smelled of baby shampoo. No other smell in the world was like it. Lucy's bare bottom was smoother than rose petals. "I love you," Annie whispered.

"What about me?" Donald demanded.

Annie sat down crosslegged on the wood floor. There was no rug inside the front door. The floor was clean and cool. Donald sat on one of her knees and Lucy sat on the other. For a second the three of them hugged and patted each other, and then the children began elbowing each other out of the way trying to get all of Annie.

"No, don't do that. I love you both. Shh, we have to be quiet Indians. Remember our games about Indians, how they tiptoe through the forests so quietly the animals aren't frightened? Shh, we have to be Indians now and not wake up poor Nate. He likes to sleep in the morning. Let's pretend he's a bear who will growl if we wake him up. Can you be Indians this morning?"

They nodded seriously.

"Good, we'll make a tent in a minute. But first Lucy has to get dressed. Lucy, I bought something for you. I was shopping and I saw some really big-girl underpants. I thought, 'Lucy is always taking her diapers off. Maybe she doesn't want diapers any more. Maybe she wants to be a big girl.'" Annie gently detached the children. "Let's look for them. They're around here somewhere." She went out for the knapsack.

Annie's apartment had a living room with a little alcove off of it. In the alcove was a dining table and four chairs, and a Dutch cupboard that had once been painted red. In a fever for purity one weekend soon after she bought it, she had covered it with paint-eating acid and stripped it down to its natural wood color. The bottom had wooden doors with carvings on them and the top had shelves and glass doors. Inside the top was Annie's collection of porcelain figures and candlesticks, the odd mug and plate, and the old china tea set that somehow had survived the childhood of her grandmother, her mother, her sister and herself. If she never had children, she planned to give the set to Lucy. The little bag with Lucy's underpants was squashed up next to the teapot in the cupboard.

Annie pretended she had forgotten where they were and began searching in the living room first. It had a large comfortable sofa, down-filled with a soft back and arms, covered with a chintz pattern from another century of the sort young men never like. It was the kind of chintz seen on wicker furniture in Victorian summer houses. Floppy cream and pink and maroon peonies lolled on a ground of forest green leaves. A double window faced east on Lexington Avenue, and the years of morning sun had faded the colors gently without wearing away the fabric. A club chair and footstool were covered in a discreet pink tweed; and the rug, which left bare half of the bleached white wood floor, was dark green and white wool woven to look like a simple rag rug with thick fringes on each end. There were two trunks in the room, one in front of the window with an elaborate stereo and tape system on it and one that sat in front of the sofa like a table. There were several old brass trivets set around in convenient places for drink stands, a row of healthy plants by the window, one tree that nearly touched the ceiling, and on the wall separating the living room from the narrow pullman kitchen was a floor-to-ceiling bookcase filled with books.

The two trunks and another one at the foot of the bed in the bedroom had arrived one evening nearly six years before when Nate, after a whirlwind courtship of some ten days, announced that he was coming to stay for a while if that was all right with Annie. In the ten days Nate had proved himself an affable easygoing sort of person, also a more experienced and enthusiastic lover than anybody she had known before. But even these attributes might not have swayed her if it hadn't been pouring rain outside and the trunks were not piled in the hall. Later, when questioned by her outraged sister, Annie had to admit that although she had been impressed by Nate's looks and his physical being, she let him in primarily because of the rain and the trunks in the hall. No one, least of all Annie herself, had expected him to stay on indefinitely like the man who came to dinner.

"Now where did I put that bag," she said.

"What do you have for me?" Donald demanded.

"The bag, the bag. It must be here somewhere." Annie picked up a pillow on the sofa and looked behind it. "Is it here?"

"What about me?" Donald said.

"Help me find it, Donald, and then we'll find something for you. You look in here and I'm going to close the door so Nate doesn't hear us and wake up."

Annie tiptoed down the short hall past the large closet she used for her clothes, and the bathroom. Without taking too careful a look inside the bedroom she closed the door, turning the handle so there would be no click. There were some chattering noises in the living room, not unlike the sounds of a bunch of chipmunks looking for trouble. Annie went into the bathroom and washed her face, then disappeared into the closet. All of her things were in the closet, even a small mirrored medicine chest where she kept her hair things and her makeup. She was thinking about what they would do that day. Go to the park, buy balloons. She ran a brush through her hair.

She nearly always dressed in the closet. Before she moved all of her things in there, she and Nate bumped into each other getting dressed. They jostled for space in front of the mirror over the sink. In the mornings she felt a certain distaste for his presence. He seemed to take up the most space then, snapping towels, splashing water everywhere and leaving wet towels on the floor, even singing with the stereo on when she wanted it quiet so she could think about the day ahead. She liked to come up to the surface quietly with a cup of black coffee and the newspapers propped up in front of her so she would know what was going on in the world. Before her shower she read every bit of the *Times* and the *Wall Street Journal*. Annie was a stockbroker.

After Nate had been there for a few months and playing house was still a novelty, Annie moved into the closet. It became the room of her own where she could paw through her underwear drawer in peace, and peer uneasily into the mirror without being observed. On the whole she felt lucky, but in the mornings a sense of discomfort, even unhappiness, hung over her as if something were not quite right. She never felt altogether safe until she swung through the door of her office in the Pan Am building.

Now having settled the program for the day, she chose a set of pink underwear and a pink summer dress, put on a pair of sandals and then took them off. She didn't want any tap, tap, tapping on the wooden floor. It only took a second to dress. By then she thought it was time to find the paper bag.

Donald, however, had found it already. He had helped Lucy into a pair and put some on himself over his shorts.

"Donald, where did you find those?"

"I know all your secrets," he grinned.

"I bet you do," she laughed. "Let me see you, Lucy. You look terrific. Don't they feel good? Much better than naked."

"Thank you, Annie. Like them."

"You take yours off, Donald. You have your own."

"She's just going to pee in them," Donald said.

"Waaa, will not pee!" Lucy wailed.

"Of course you won't. You can go to the toilet any time you want. You know how to do that, I know you do."

"She'll pee in her pants. She'll make a puddle on the floor. Mommy says."

"Don't say that, Donald. Come here, Lucy. Annie will help you. Remember how we taught Dolly to go in the toilet? Where's Dolly? Has she been good?" Annie rummaged in the knapsack looking for Dolly. Dolly's hair was badly matted and she had no clothes on.

"Poor Dolly, she's naked again."

"She wet her pants so we had to throw them away," Donald said. "If she wets again, we'll break her neck."

Lucy began to cry.

"Shh, Lucy. We're Indians, remember? Don't worry about Dolly. Here, let's put some pants on her." Annie put a pair of Lucy's new pants on the dolly. "There, a little big, but she's dressed now. Donald, give me a kiss. Oh, I love you. You're my big boy, my helper. Now, we're going to have juice—"

"She'll pee on the floor," Donald warned.

"Shh, Donald. Are you dry, Lucy? Look, Lucy's dry. We're going to have juice and then we'll go to the park and see the animals. And if you're very good I'll take you to a restaurant for lunch."

"Yay, McDonald's," Donald said.

"Burger King," Lucy cried.

"Shh, only if you're quiet. Donald, you help me pour. Lucy, you get the napkins. Look and see if there are crackers."

"McDonald's," Donald said, going into the kitchen.

"Burger King," Lucy wailed.

"Whichever is closer," Annie said. She put two plastic cups on the table and helped Donald pour juice. She gave each child a vitamin C tablet and went back into the kitchen to make herself a cup of coffee.

A minute or two later Nate stood in the doorway in his shorts with his very yellow hair sticking up. "There's a baby in there three-quarters in the toilet yelling 'Wipe me.' Can't you hear it?"

"Oh God, Lucy."

Annie ran into the bathroom where Lucy was desperately clinging to the edge of the toilet seat with two hands. Her bottom was so low it almost touched the water. "Good girl," Annie cried. "Nate, did you see that? Lucy's a big girl now. Lucy, I'm so proud of you. Look at that, she went by herself." Annie helped Lucy pull up her pants and showed her how to flush the toilet.

"Lucy, you're terrific. But next time tell me. I'll help you. Sweetheart, the toilet is too high for you. I don't want you to fall in. Will you remember to ask me next time? Nate, maybe we have something we could use as a stool. This toilet is really very high. Oh, I'm so proud."

Nate stood there scratching his head. "What's going on?"

"Lucy just went all by herself," Annie said. "Isn't that wonderful? Tell her you're proud."

Nate looked at the little girl in the flowered underpants who clung to Annie like a limpet. He blinked.

"We're going to McDonald's," Donald said helpfully. "Did we wake you up?"

"Burger King," Lucy said. "Didn't pee on the floor."

"I'm very proud of you," Annie said. "What a lovely girl. Nate, isn't she wonderful?"

"It's nine-thirty," Nate said.

"Oh, I'm sorry, Nate. They woke you up. Do you want to go back to sleep? We'll be quiet." Annie looked at him anxiously.

"You didn't tell me we were having company."

"What about a cup of coffee? I just made some. I could run around the corner and get some croissants. . . ."

Nate went into the bedroom and pulled on a pair of jeans that had been lying over the back of a chair. Annie followed him still holding Lucy. "Would you like some croissants?"

He muttered, "You didn't tell me."

"I didn't know."

"I thought we were going to have a quiet day."

"It was a surprise to me, too." Annie brushed the hair back from Lucy's forehead and hugged her tighter.

Nate frowned at the child. "Same old story."

"Really, I had no idea," Annie protested.

"That's what you always say. I thought we were going to the beach today. I told the Greers we were coming out."

"I know that, but you didn't get up early enough."

Nate pushed past her and went into the bathroom. He splashed water on his face, on his hair, on the floor. He brushed his hair with angry strokes. Donald watched him soberly. When Nate was finished brushing his hair, Donald held out a handful of animal crackers. "Nate, have a cracker," he offered in his most conciliatory manner.

Nate ignored him.

"He's talking to you," Annie said. "Thank you, Donald, that was very thoughtful of you." Annie took a cracker and looked at it. It was a lion. She put it in her pocket. She willed Nate to be sweet, to look at her, and at Donald who was so cute. She willed him to be broad-minded and not hate her sister. But he refused.

"I just don't believe this. You told me we were having a quiet weekend this weekend. You promised."

"Let's not talk about it now," Annie said quietly. "It's just one of those things. . . ."

"That happens every weekend." He wagged a finger in her face.

"Not every weekend," Annie said.

"It's like being run over by a train. I didn't hear the phone. What did she do, just ring the doorbell and run away?"

Annie shrugged unhappily because that was very close to what happened. "I'm sorry," she said meekly.

She took the children and settled them at the dining room table with glasses of juice and a plate of crackers. "Stay here for a while, will you?" They nodded seriously.

Annie walked back to the bedroom slowly, wondering what she could say to make it right. When she got there Nate was carefully examining his shirts. She stood in the doorway for a second watching him. He was completely preoccupied. He picked up one shirt after another, examined the collar and seams of each one and then put it back. He looked up, saw her watching him, and then went back to his inventory as if she weren't there.

At that moment a familiar feeling of hopelessness swept over Annie. Not because he wouldn't recognize her, but because he could hurt a child. She took the lion cracker out of her pocket and bit off its head. The dry cookie crumbled in her mouth. She wanted to close the bedroom door and walk away. But his stern survey of the shirts held her there. They were summer sport shirts, striped and solid-color knits. She had washed and folded each one herself. It was as if she had a stake in how he found them.

"I'm sorry," she said finally, through the dust in her mouth. She came into the room and closed the door behind her.

"Why do you let her run over you like that?" he said.

"It's very hard not having any break from them. You know Mother won't help, and Sara doesn't have any life at all. Not with Martin alone, I mean. I feel sorry for her, Nate."

"What about me?"

"I'm sorry."

"I'm really tired of it," Nate said. He chose a white shirt and put it on.

"I know you are. But it's just a few hours. We'll be alone tonight, and we can go out to the beach tomorrow early. We could even go late this afternoon.

"It's like a curse."

"Don't say that. They're wonderful children."

The door opened a crack. "Can we have more crackers?" Donald whispered.

"Did you eat them all?" Annie asked.

"Lucy doesn't like them when they're broken. She wants some other ones."

"Go and tell her I'll be there in a minute," Annie said.

"They don't leave you alone for a minute." Nate adjusted his collar and then adjusted it again, opened another button so more of his chest showed.

"It's only for a few hours."

"I want to go now. We can take them back."

"No, we can't, Sara and Martin are not home."

"Shit."

The door opened again and a little hand was waving in the crack. "Cookie?" Lucy said.

"Shit," Nate said again.

"No more cookies," Annie said. "Please, Lucy, go and color for a minute." Annie began making the bed. "Go ahead." She pounded the pillows and piled them on the trunk.

"I'm fed up. You can't stand up for yourself. You let everybody run all over you. The place is a zoo."

Annie finished the bed. "It's not good to think only of ourselves."

"Bullshit."

"I'm sorry." She hung her head. "It's only for a few hours. If it's too much for you, you can go to the beach by yourself." Annie regretted saying that instantly, for he shrugged.

"If that's what you want."

"I want to be together, you know that. I want us all to go for a walk. Kids can be fun. They're interesting and sweet. Come on, how much does it cost to be nice for a few hours? I'll give you a cup of coffee. You'll feel better. I'm sure you will."

"Not me, Baby. I won't go walking with any kids."

The door opened again. "Lucy went on the floor," Donald announced.

"Oh, poor Lucy," Annie sighed. Right in her new underpants.

"That's it. I'm leaving," Nate said. "Enjoy your day."

"Wait a minute. Have a cup of coffee." Annie reached for his elbow.

He pulled away. "I'm not eating where children pee."

"Oh, Christ, I'll clean it up. Big deal." To Lucy, "Don't cry, Angel. We'll catch it next time."

"Pants dry," Lucy cried. She held them up. She had been careful to take them off first. Annie smiled at her logic.

Nate tied the arms of his sweater around his neck and collected his keys and wallet while she was cuddling the child. She didn't see him walk out the door. She was by then mopping up the dining room floor with a handful of paper towels drenched in Joy. It was only the smallest drop, hardly an accident at all.

"Don't cry, Lucy. It was only a drop. All gone now." She took the child on her lap again and Donald patted her shoulder. I hate him, she thought, of Nate. At that moment she did.

She hugged the children and they hugged her. They were so loving that they calmed her. Whatever she gave them, they gave back tenfold. For a second she wished that Nate could walk in and see them sitting together so he could understand that there was something more important in the world than the freedom to flee at will. But she had heard the door close and knew he would not in an hour change his mind and return. She shook her head, then bit her lip to keep from crying.

"What's the matter, Annie?" Donald asked anxiously.

One can't equivocate with the love of children. "Nothing at all, Sweetheart," she said. "Let's go out and see what we can see."

Later, when they were in the park, Annie forgot how afraid the thought sometimes made her that her own sister was trying to mess up her life. The brightness of the sun and the children made her confident again. She could manage them all, she thought. She always managed. After a while she even stopped looking for Nate's face in the crowd. In the park everyone said how beautiful the children were with their balloons tied to their wrists, and everyone thought they were hers.

2

As soon as Sara left Annie, she raced through the lobby and dived into the car. She was shaking with indignation, but didn't have time to say a thing.

Martin was grumbling ahead of her. "What took you so long?"

"Oh, Martin. She wasn't up, can you believe that?"

"I guess you should have called her."

"I just can't understand her," Sara cried. She smoothed her

skirt out on her knee and tried to calm down by examining it critically. It was the kind of linen that was supposed to resist wrinkles. It said so on the tag. It had looked so good hanging on the rack that Sara took it against her better judgment. Now she waited for the skirt to fail her. She smoothed it down again and looked at it. No wrinkles yet. Well, maybe the tag told the truth. Still, Sara resisted brightening up.

Annie's situation depressed her and this house-hunting was getting harder every week. Sara was beginning to feel she couldn't stand it much longer. She was fed up with Annie and fed up to the teeth with Martin's dream of a house. He had this dream, this persistent wish, that he wouldn't let go of no matter what. All his life it had shimmered in the distance, an image he wouldn't give up. He saw himself with feet planted firmly on earth that was his. He saw himself pacing out the perimeters of his territory with hose in hand, making water fall in lazy arcs on lush lawns that cost an arm and a leg to regreen every spring. Lawns so even one could play golf on them if golf was what one wanted to play. Martin didn't. But he had the whole vision: himself coming home on the commuter train, his face hidden behind the evening paper or in the morning, lost in the *Times*.

In the midst of scores of other travelers even with knees bumping, he would be for an hour twice a day quite alone. And then he would emerge at the other end refreshed, prepared, purged somehow of whatever he had left behind. He got this dream from *Father Knows Best* in his childhood, when his own father brooded in their tiny back apartment on the fall of the country during his college days that never rose for him again.

Martin never got over feeling that he had a bad start. He was born in a home of poisoned dreams and didn't want to pass any residue on to the next generation. He wanted a home for his family. The lawn was gratuitous, Martin didn't need the lawn. But he needed to rid himself of his father, who had put his hopes on his older son, Bernie, who repaid the debt of his college years by leaping out of a window after graduation with his diploma in his hand. Martin needed a home. He wanted the plot of land with the trees left natural. He wanted to stand with the hose in his hand making water on his territory while the sun set casting his shadow huge on the house behind him. And for years Sara had been willing to let him have it.

Now she sighed bitterly. "Annie is really getting impossible," she said. "I don't know how we can trust her when she behaves like this. She knows how important this is to us. And it isn't as if she has anything else to do."

"You probably should have called her."

"She promised, Martin. She said she would. She just never thinks about how hard it is for anybody else. She and Mother are so selfish. . . . I can't believe she was in her nightgown. Donald could see through it. He was looking right at her. So thoughtless. He'll probably grow up warped. Christ, she wanted us to take them with us, and Donald was standing right there feeling rejected."

Sara sighed. "I hope she gets dressed."

Martin safely negotiated the car across the Willis Avenue Bridge and headed toward the New England Thruway.

"You should have taken the Triboro Bridge. It's faster," Sara said.

"It costs a dollar and a quarter and it's not faster," Martin sighed, too. "Maybe you should have called Annie and told her you were coming."

"Why are you always criticizing me? I try to think of everybody and nobody appreciates it. Do I warp Donald by running around naked? Do I forget all the things I'm supposed to do?"

"I wasn't criticizing you."

"You said I should have called her. Well, I didn't call her because I didn't want to wake her up. And do you think she could be thoughtful enough to get up on her own? Not her."

"Well, we're free." Martin said. He reached out for Sara's hand and she allowed him to take it.

"Free for a minute," she acknowledged.

"It feels good, doesn't it?" Martin said. He looked quickly at his wife, with her blond curls, violet eyes. Her slender legs were crossed demurely at the ankles.

"Doesn't it feel great to be alone? Listen to how quiet it is."

Sara's mouth considered a smile. The odds were against it two to one as she brooded on the morning. She had been up since five-thirty, torn out of bed and then ripped apart by three towering wills each charging in a different direction. No one wanted the breakfast offered. They each wanted something else from a store not yet open. Each refused to put on the clean clothes available. The noise level was decibels above the federally regulated maximums for steel and textile workers. Annie was naked and unmarried, selfish as usual. And then there was a sudden release into the hot wind of the highway going—where?

"I like the ride," she said finally. "I just wonder what it will be like when we get there and never come back."

"We'll love it," Martin promised. "You know the city is getting worse every day. Bag ladies all over the place even in midtown, and there's no money to clean the streets. The stink this year is worse than anything I can remember."

Sara thought of the bag lady in the park, stinking too, in her rotting clothes. She shuffled around muttering obscenities and curses that frightened the children. And suddenly the odds shifted and she smiled. "You're right," she said.

"Feeling better?"

Sara nodded and let the air streaming through the window soothe her, hot as it was. They'd find a house, sure they would, maybe even today. Annie would come for weekends, and then she'd get married and move next door. Then life would be perfect. For a second she was so cheered she forgot Annie was already thirty and unlikely ever to be a married lady next door.

The first house they saw was past the very fancy town of Evergreen Hollow. It was in one of those horseshoes builders develop where one house is right next to another. As they turned into the street they saw three colonials all alike except for the color of the front door. Across the street were three Tudors with bricks gleaming from cellar to roof. Then down at the end where the drive circled around, there were three modern houses so spare and angular they would look good only if no one cluttered them up by living there.

The one at the end with its lawn abutting the ninth hole of the Evergreen Hollow Town Golf Course was the one they saw. It was all glass and steps and wooden decks coming out at odd angles. It was only just being finished. The yard was a parched desert. The gray earth hadn't been watered in weeks, and the newly seeded lawn had turned brown. On the golf course past the chain-link fence that marked the boundary of the property, a foursome played through between the mist of a line of sprinklers. In contrast to the lawn, the golf course was the lushest of greens. Outside on the drive in front of the house an army of neighborhood children gathered on their Hot Wheels and tricycles and two-wheelers, pushing doll carriages and bouncing balls, checking them out.

"Plenty of friends for the children," Betty, the real estate lady, said enthusiastically of the children. "This is really the best buy in town. Such a friendly environment, and the golf course is right here so you know you'll never be developed."

Martin adjusted his glasses uneasily. Being an accountant he knew how to measure things. He counted fifteen children and twelve cars, not counting theirs and Betty's. One had a trailer supporting an altogether too fast-looking speedboat. The Tudor houses seemed to close in and the modern houses looked ready to take flight. He didn't like Sara in the setting. Sara stood on the deck sweating freely in her pink blouse, looking doubtfully through the window. They were both having the same thought, Annie wouldn't like it here.

Betty didn't seem to notice their frowns. She was blond, too. In Connecticut everyone who counted was blond. Betty struggled with the lock, which didn't seem to want to open. She talked as she struggled. The place was on sale at a hundred and eighty. It had been two twenty-five, but since the landscaper failed to water the lawn while the builder was on vacation in July, well, the place didn't look its best right now. Of course when the interest rates fell in the fall as they were predicted to do, the builder would raise the price again and there would be a stampede on the place. But since the price was lower now it was silly to worry about interest rates because they could always renegotiate the mortgage later. It was a marvelous place, wasn't it? Except that she couldn't get the door open.

She panted with the effort of working the key in the lock. Martin didn't offer to help and Sara sweated. Sara didn't like seeing people suffer. She had wanted to buy the first thirty houses they saw years ago just for the sake of the broker. Now she was tougher. Finally after walking around the place three times looking for an open window, with many children joining the parade, they left without getting in.

"What did you think?" Betty asked eagerly as they parked for a minute outside on the main road.

"I think it's much too suburban," Martin said quickly.

"Oh no. This is very modern. It has a two-story living room

with a balcony outside the master. I'm sure you'll feel differently about it when you see the inside."

"We're Democrats," Sara said suddenly. "We couldn't live in a house with a master, could we, Martin?"

"I don't know what the neighbors would say," Martin said fussily.

Betty's smile withered in the heat. What did that mean? She looked at Martin more closely. He was shorter than she, and wiry. He wore steel-rimmed glasses and looked like some sort of intellectual. "You're not a writer, are you?" she asked.

"No," Martin said.

"Well, we have lots of Democrats in the Hollow. We're very relaxed here about most things."

She got in her car and took them right over to the Finchley house. It was an old Tudor in an old neighborhood with some very tall trees on the streets and few bicycles. Martin cheered up immediately and started banging the pipes with enthusiasm. This was more like what they wanted: age, respectability. The owner of the house was blond, too. Her husband had choked recently on a piece of New York strip steak at a convention in San Diego where no one knew the Heimlich maneuver. And now she was eager to sell. Sara thought they ought to buy it so Mrs. Finchley could start a new life in Tampa.

The only problem with the Finchley house was that the bedrooms were all right next to each other and the bathrooms were not located anywhere near the bedrooms. They seemed to be scattered around the house at random, like potted plants for atmosphere. And all the plumbing was in shades of blue. Downstairs the entire kitchen including the sink was aquamarine. The powder room was pea green, the color of a public swimming pool. Still, it was a beautiful house.

Sara ran upstairs to take a second look. There didn't seem to be a master in this house. She poked her head into a baby-blue bathroom and Martin pushed in behind her and shut the door. "What a house," he said.

"It's beautiful, isn't it?" She looked at herself in the mirror and noticed that she looked blue in the light. She giggled. Martin joined her in front of the mirror and they stood there for a second considering the picture they made in the suburban bathroom with a blue plastic shower curtain behind them.

"This is the life," Martin said. "How do we like it?"

"We'd have to walk down the hall to go to the bathroom."

"We could knock down some walls," Martin suggested. "Let's try it out," he whispered. "I sent Betty down to pace out the acreage."

"Oh no, Martin. No. I'm soaking wet. It must be two hundred degrees today. Oh don't kiss me like that."

"Let's lock the door and take a shower." Martin unbuttoned her blouse and licked a salty drop from between her breasts.

"Take a shower?"

"Yes, and try it out."

"There's no time for that. We have to decide about the house—don't do that, this is Connecticut." She ran the water and splashed a few drops in his face.

"So what, they have a great school system here." He splashed her back.

"Oh, Martin."

They wrapped arms around each other and kissed in front of the window. But the glass was frosted blue and Betty, looking up at the house to gauge their progress, couldn't see them.

"I love the house," Sara said. "But I don't know if I like Connecticut."

Martin was wrinkling Sara's skirt right out of the performance promise of its tags. It looked like spring lettuce bunched in his hand. Martin let it go in alarm, but Sara didn't notice. She was cool and hot at the same time. There was silence everywhere; not even the birds made a sound. The water on her face and chest made her feel as unreal as a mermaid. It was as if the two blond ladies downstairs had faded away in the summer heat and they were alone.

Sara splashed Martin again. "Do we like Connecticut?"

"We like each other," he said. They both looked at the blue wall-to-wall carpet that no doubt covered baby-blue ceramic tiles. Martin reached over and locked the door. As he did, it suddenly occurred to Sara that there was nothing to do in Connecticut but this. It made her laugh as she sank to the floor.

Some minutes later, still breathing heavily, they pulled themselves back together again.

"Martin," Sara sighed. "You're really wonderful at that. You're a master craftsman, you really are. . . . Martin, angel do we love it here?" She reached for him and squeezed his penis.

"Oh don't do that. Ha, ha. Don't tickle me. Oh God, don't kiss it. Sara! Too late, think of a joke quick. Ha! This must be a Republican house. I'm not a master at home. Why don't you do this at home?"

"There's always something else to do at home. Martin, tuck your shirt in, you look sloppy."

"So do you," he muttered.

"Martin, did you notice that the bathroom is in the wrong place?" Sara went out in the hall with her blouse half untucked while he was still struggling with his zipper.

"Look what you did," he said. "Just look at that."

"You see, the bathroom should be here next to the master."

"Shut the door," he demanded.

"And Martin, look. The entire acre is pachysandra."

"I don't believe this."

"I don't either. A whole acre of ground cover is un-American," she said.

"They didn't want to mow the lawn; it's been naturalized."

"Martin, the kitchen should be in the back not the front, with the dining room looking out on the swimming pool. Martin, tuck your shirt in, you look so sloppy, Baby."

"What swimming pool?" Martin emerged from the bathroom with a vaguely disgruntled look. He'd washed himself up. He thought he looked fine. From master to baby in a second; he grimaced at the change in Sara, all business now.

"Ah, there you are." Betty charged up the last few stairs. "I've been looking all over for you. How do you like it?" She looked from one to the other with narrowed eyes.

"It has its charms," Sara said. "But the bathrooms are in the wrong place and the kitchen is green, there's no place for my sister, and the swimming pool needs a lot of work."

"The swimming pool? Your sister?" Betty looked puzzled. She had just paced out the boundaries as Martin had asked her to do and as far as she could tell there was no swimming pool on the property.

"Martin, angel, don't we need a separate wing for Annie? She can't be all squashed in like that and have to walk down the hall to go to the bathroom, can she? What do you think?" Sara asked. "You're the master."

"Oh well," he murmured modestly.

"No, Martin," she insisted. "You're the boss. You say." She winked past Betty's body that was frozen on the top step with suspense and tension, one foot raised to the last step and her face rigid with hope.

"A darling house. In move-in condition," she threw in as Martin paced the upstairs hall one more time.

"The swimming pool does need a lot of work," he said finally. "Do you have any land?"

"Land?" Betty said dully.

"Yes, plain land, preferably with a stream running through it, and a place to go hiking. I think we need a hike in it, don't you, Sara? For Annie."

"Oh, Martin," Sara beamed. "Land."

Martin knew immediately by her look that it was the right thing to say. Land, that's what they'd look for. Land of their own. Even Annie had to approve of land. They went right back to New York to tell her. They got there in time to have ice cream and cake at snack time. They babbled on about earth and brooks and trees and planting bulbs in the autumn. Annie sat there with a dull look in her eyes and they were annoyed that she didn't have the grace, the generosity, the sensitivity to seem the slightest bit pleased at their very successful day.

3

THAT WAS the day the house started. The day of the baby-blue bathroom, though Sara never admitted even to herself that the bathroom had anything to do with it. The next thing Annie knew, they had found an isolated piece of land and forced her to drive out to take a look at it. They told her they wouldn't dream of buying a thing without her approval.

When they returned Annie was so sick she had to lie on the sofa in Sara's living room with an ice pack on her head. On top of her Donald and Lucy had piled the baby quilts from their beds. When Annie closed her eyes, Lucy put a lettuce leaf on her forehead. It was a small piece of lettuce, still wet from its washing, and a few drops slid down over Annie's eyelids. She was covered up and full of aspirin, alone for a few minutes in the living room, and safe in New York again; but she could not avoid a barrage of images from the day in the country she had just endured. Visions of Pine Wood, New York fluttered down behind her eyes, like dead leaves falling at night. She had seen the place in a haze from the back of the seat of the station wagon while she tried to calm two restless children constantly thirsty, nauseated, and worried about their bladders. Yet the content of the place stuck with her.

She remembered the trees, already turning autumn colors, and the three churches. Two were large stone structures and one was wood with a red door. The library was the largest nonsectarian building in the town. It had been a three-story department store with a cupola on top, but had failed for some reason in the fifties. The small old-fashioned main street was cute and there was a cute railroad station at one end. At the other end of the main street was the shopping center that consisted of a huge A & P, a Rexall and a Woolworth's. Just out of town there was a strip of nurseries and garden-supply stores, each one situated curiously close to a fast-food joint. One of each: a Wendy's, a Burger King, a McDonald's, a Gino's, a Pizza Hut, a Dairy Queen, an International House of Pancakes. There was no Colonel Sander's, however; and on a whim of Martin's they had driven miles into the suburban wasteland to find the nearest Sears.

All they missed in the car was a drooling dog, the sisters' two complaining parents and Annie's recalcitrant lover. Martin would have liked them all, to give credence to the project. But they had no dog and the parents wouldn't come because they didn't like the idea of building a house. Wasn't one already built good enough for them? Nor did Nate want to spend Saturday stuffed in the car with four Bissels going to see a vacant lot. Only Annie could be persuaded to attend, and she was paying for it now with a particularly vicious headache.

She hated woods; and the building site Martin and Sara had chosen consisted of four scrubbily wooded acres with a stream. All she could think of was mosquitoes in summer. Martin really wanted to buy two plots for the four of them so they would have an eight-acre buffer between them and the world. The two plots together, however, cost more than he wanted to spend; so all the way there and all the way back he tried to convince Annie to buy the other four-acre plot available. He thought it might be nice for her to have a place to pack her roots if and when she ever managed to marry what's-his-name.

"Don't you see, Annie," he said, "if we don't cut down too many trees, we won't be able to see another house even in winter. We could be a little settlement and keep the family together."

Annie squeezed her eyes together tighter. It had begun to rain on the way home, and Annie had asked Martin to let her off outside her building. Sara wanted her to come home and be with them when they had their meeting with the architect.

"I have to get back to Nate," Annie protested. "I promised I'd be back by five. I think we're going out."

"Family is more important," Sara said. "Call him and tell him to come over for dinner."

"Good idea," Martin agreed. "We can all talk with Archie. Maybe Nate will be inspired." Martin turned around and winked at Annie.

"He's my family," Annie said.

"I made enough. If you don't stay, I'll just have to throw it out," Sara went on.

"Throw it out," Annie said. "I'm going home."

But they didn't drop her off. The children were so fussy they went right home and insisted that Annie come upstairs for some aspirin for her headache. She could call Nate before trying to get a taxi, they said. When she called, Nate wasn't there. Under the covers Annie felt a gnawing in her stomach that was a little like grief. It seemed as if they each worked to make things miserable for her.

Sara stood over Annie. "I called again. He's still not there. Maybe he went to the movies. Oh, Annie, please don't be upset. We love you."

Annie didn't answer.

"Well, Archie will be here in a few minutes. What do you want to do? You can't stay here. I have to clean up." Sara picked up the two quilts.

"Okay, I'm *sorry*," she said. She folded first one quilt and then the other. "I'm very sorry, but I thought you would just give the children their baths and settle them down for the night, and then have supper. I didn't think it was a big deal."

She took the quilts to the children's room and came back. "I don't know why you put up with him anyway. He never does anything for you. This isn't the first time he's disappointed you when he was supposed to be there, is it? Seven o'clock. Well, get up. I can't have a corpse lying here when Archie arrives."

"Oh, Sara, don't push me."

"Well, if you're not going to be useful, you might as well go home."

"What do you mean?"

"We had a wonderful day. I don't know why you have to end it like this. We walked in the woods and picked apples and kicked leaves. Oh Annie, it was so beautiful. And now you have to spoil it because of him."

"I have a headache," Annie said feebly.

"Is it a lot to ask to get them settled down? There's company coming in a few minutes. Annie, you're just so difficult lately."

"I'm not a maid. I did you a favor today. I came with you and saw your town, and your site, and I held Lucy's head when she threw up. You were kicking leaves, I was cleaning up your daughter. And you made me late. Every time I do something for you I get in trouble. I'm really fed up."

"We didn't make you late. We got home right on time."

"Not to my house, you didn't." Annie sat up. The ice pack and the piece of lettuce fell off. "You went to your house. I wasn't where I was supposed to be. Sometimes I could just kill you, Sara."

"I thought it was understood that you would help me with the children when Archie came. I can't plan a house with an architect and have two little children running around," Sara said pathetically. "How could I manage that?"

"It's not my problem." Annie held her head to stop it from pounding.

"You're getting to be just like Mother."

"I am not."

"Mother never does a damn thing for me. I can't believe it. She comes here to eat once a week, she pats them on the head and then she goes home. She doesn't even help me with the dishes."

"Well, she doesn't visit me at all," Annie said.

"And Daddy just sits there doing the crossword puzzle and I know he's already done it at home before he came. You're all so, so oblivious." Sara sat down and reached for the ice pack. She looked at it for a minute and then put it on her own head. "I don't know what I'd do without you, Annie."

"Sara, what do you want?" Annie said.

"I want some support. Do you think it's easy for me to leave New York? Annie, I want you to bathe the children. Is that too much to ask from my sister?"

Annie shook her head. "You messed up my day and got me home late so Nate had to go off by himself. You always do that. I have a life of my own, Sara, believe it or not. I can't always be here with you. I love you and I love the children. But you want too much."

"Annie, I understand that it's not me you're angry with. It's that jerk. Annie, please don't be mad at me. I just want something better for you."

"He's not a jerk."

"That unreliable jerk. I don't know why you stick up for him. I'm your sister. It's not like he's a blood relative who's here to stay. He's a traveler, Annie. He's not one of us. He'll never be one of us."

"Don't say that," Annie said sharply.

"Well, he's not one of us. If he were, he'd be here. You'd be married and we'd all get along." Sara said this quite reasonably. She picked up the piece of lettuce. "What's this?"

"Maybe I don't want to be married. Maybe I like it like this."

"He doesn't like us. You always come without him. The kids tell me he's never there. Why do you put up with it? He only makes you unhappy, why do you think you get headaches like this?"

"That's not true." Annie took back the ice pack and put it on her head.

"I know he doesn't like us. I can see by the way he looks at Martin."

"If Martin wouldn't send the wine back every time we went out to dinner, I'm sure Nate would love him."

"Well, Nate doesn't know a God-damned thing about wine."

"Neither does Martin." Annie stood up. "I'm going home."

"And leave me in the lurch?" Sara cried. "Please don't go. I need you."

"What are you going to do when you live in the suburbs, Sara? You'll have to work out more difficult problems than bathing the children alone."

"Annie, sit down a minute. Martin and I know this is going to be very hard for you. We want you to know that we expect you to stay with us a lot. We're going to build a room just for you, a whole wing if you want it. That's why we wanted you here with Archie tonight. We want you to be part of it. We're not leaving you behind."

"Oh, Sara, I know."

"Really, Annie. Martin feels you've helped him over the years. You never led him astray. Except for that oil-well drilling company. He lost some money on that."

"That wasn't my stock. I didn't want him to buy that."

"Well, except for that, you did very well for him."

"I told him not to buy that stock," Annie insisted.

"Okay, forget it. He's not mad."

"But I had nothing to do with it. That was his own idea."

"Annie, I'm telling you he's not mad. He's grateful."

"I'm glad."

Donald came running into the living room. "I ate everything, Annie. Will you give me my bath now?"

"No, Angel, I have to go home now."

"Do you feel sick?"

"Yes, Sweetheart, I have to go to bed."

"Oh, you can stay for a minute, can't you Annie? I have so much food," Sara said quickly. "You don't really feel bad, do you? Martin will be so upset."

"I'm sorry."

"You won't be able to see my bubbles," Donald said.

"Next time, Donald. I promise." Annie knelt down and gave him a hug.

"I don't think you should leave like this," Sara protested. "This is very important to us."

"I know it is, but I really don't feel well."

"He won't even be there," Sara said bitterly. She took the ice pack Annie handed her. She looked at it sadly. "I hate to see you hurt."

Annie shrugged. She went into the kitchen and kissed Lucy good-bye, and Martin, who was struggling to get some food into her.

"Didn't you love the property, Annie?" he said eagerly. "Doesn't it just spark your imagination?"

"It's very nice, Martin, very nice."

"Well, next weekend maybe we all can spend the night out there and get better acquainted with the neighborhood."

Annie ran out into the rain. It was like fleeing from a storm instead of into one. The rain was cold on her face and distracted her from her headache as she stood on the street hailing a taxi. The street lights, yellow in the early evening, seemed like beacons of freedom. Whenever she left Sara and Martin she felt the same, as if she had been granted a reprieve from prison. Even slogging home in the snow late one night the winter before when there were no taxis on the street, Annie felt the most wonderful exhilaration. She was free. She felt she could walk in the snow forever, heading away from the tentacles of her family. It was Sara who hurt her, not Nate.

Every time she saw them she knew she didn't want to be married like Martin and Sara, stuck for all time with a neurotic. Much better to have an easygoing relationship with a person like Nate, who was independent enough to go off by himself once in a while. Much better Nate, who didn't think every bottle of wine was spoiled or worry endlessly what her parents thought of him.

Annie paid off the taxi and hurried upstairs. She pulled off her raincoat and shook it in the hall before she opened the front door. She told herself she wouldn't be let down if he wasn't there. She wouldn't worry. She wouldn't. He was his own person. Independence was a good thing. It was better to be like him than like Martin, who fussed over Sara as if a frown from her would mean sudden death.

But still, Annie was disappointed when the lights were off. She got herself a drink and ate a stale roll left over from breakfast. As she sat on the sofa and waited, she kept reading the same piece of newspaper over and over. She had a headache; the headache came from her sister and the ride in the country and the fact that she was pretty sure that she had called on time and he hadn't been there anyway.

4

THAT YEAR
there wasn't the manic surge of energy the cool weather usually brought. Early snowstorms killed a lot of cattle in Montana, and then there were floods and mudslides in California. Two mine disasters followed, and a forest fire in Washington, which had already lost quite enough of its wood in the recent rages of Mount St. Helens. The market tiptoed through each day not quite sure what to do with itself in between devastations, rebellions in South America, coups led by former CIA agents in Africa, the slow falling away of NATO support of U.S. military strength in Europe, radiation leaks in nuclear power plants and terrorist attacks world wide. Every other day it seemed some world leader was struck down by the bullets of a Turkish, Palestinian, Lebanese, Moslem, right-wing, commie-trained, Libyan killer.

The market slowed, stock prices dipped. Interest rates hung in there very high. No one could predict what was going to happen next. In the office Annie tried to fend off a feeling of trepidation, as if the troubles of the outside world were beginning to close in on her own little territory. Each day it was more difficult to tell her clients how to protect themselves in such an uncertain economy. None of the signs was good. The foreboding followed her home, where sounds from the elaborate stereo system did not cover up the uneasiness there. For months a stubborn silence had hung in the air between Annie and Nate like dust visible only in sunshine.

In October Martin and Sara closed on their plot of land in Pine Wood. The day it happened Annie felt they had died. When they were children, whenever one of their school friends moved to the suburbs, it seemed to them that it was the new house itself, with space they couldn't even imagine, that swallowed her up.

Once they were gone, the girls were never seen again. Way back then, from the way her mother sneered, Annie developed the idea that the suburbs weren't safe. They were places in which people disappeared and became simple. After a few minutes they couldn't find their way back except in groups once a year for a matinee at Christmas time. Suburban people lived in the dark and forgot there were places lights stayed on all night, where people could go out for something to eat any time they wanted.

Every day, on their way home from school, Annie and Sara used to go to a coffee shop to be independent. For a quarter each they had hot chocolate and ate an elderly pickle, which used to be free in a bowl on the table. Even now, the coffee shop, one on every street, was an hour's refuge for them in any weather. A cheap sandwich, a moment of quiet if the bus didn't come, a place to sit and tell secrets no one else could share. How Sara would live without such a place to meet someone for fifteen minutes in the middle of a rotten day Annie didn't know. She supposed Sara would join the Y in the next town over and go to an exercise class on Wednesdays to break up the week. And she'd make friends with the mothers in her children's school whether she liked them or not. Well, Sara would break the ties of her own childhood and settle into the childhoods of Donald and Lucy, where Martin would feel safe from poverty.

Annie was very subdued in the office all day. She stared out at the ramp of the Pan Am Building, her view, and felt that she, too, ought to flee. Her father called her late in the day and told her how upset Brenda was. "You're our only chicken left," he mourned.

"Cluck, cluck," she said.

"Well, I suppose it had to happen some day."

"I guess so," Annie agreed.

"You better come over this weekend; Brenda will need the company."

Annie sighed. "I don't know if I can."

"You'll come. You don't want your mother to go into a depression, do you? I want you to come over and show her some support. You always seem too busy for her, Annie. It hurts her feelings."

"It takes a long time to build a house," Annie said. "They'll be around for quite a while." She sighed again. Her other phone was flashing its red light, but she didn't want to hang up on her father.

"I know, but it's different now. Your mother thinks they're doing this just to get away from her."

"You know that's not true."

"And what's his name, he doesn't help things either."

"Martin loves Mother, you know that. He wants to move to the country so he can take the train. The train is very important to him. He needs to travel."

"Not Martin," her father said impatiently.

The light on her phone glowed. Her secretary picked up. Now the intercom buzzed.

"Oh," Annie said.

"She thinks you should stop this rebellion of yours. You'll wake up one day and find you've made a mistake. You know what I mean. Well, don't tell her I said anything. I have another call."

Annie started to say good-bye, but the phone was dead. Her father never said hello or good-bye. He began his conversations in the middle and ended with the bottom line. She was just an egg that had hatched, a middle-aged chicken still in the yard. Her secretary stood in the door.

"Say I've gone home," Annie said.

She reached for her suit jacket and her raincoat and wandered out into the evening without saying good night. She began walking home up Lexington Avenue. Everywhere the stores were still open and people were hurrying. Annie found she couldn't hurry. She thought about stopping to pick up something to eat, but didn't feel like it. For October it was still very warm. Maybe they'd have a warm winter and the country would have a respite from the oil crisis. But that wouldn't help the airlines and related industries. Or Detroit. Annie shrugged and let the stock market go.

She liked the variety of faces in the crowd, even the small tingle of menace in the odd drunk, the possible pickpocket, the raving crazy lady on her corner by the 52nd Street Y. As always, she clutched her handbag tightly to her chest. She was a city person after all, who knew what it felt like to have a bicycle pulled out from under her just because she was small and weak and someone else wanted it. One had to watch out every second in the city, but Annie felt having to look out for oneself was not a bad thing. She was always trying to memorize faces in case she ever had to recall one.

As she walked slowly home, she felt very much on her toes. Lately there was a surge of people coming back from the suburbs. Even the *Wall Street Journal* noted that the flow was going the other way. It almost cheered Annie up to think of how much trouble Martin and Sara were making for themselves by giving up their apartment that didn't cost very much and plunging into a venture she didn't think they could really afford. There wasn't any better life in the country; they'd find that out soon enough. Maybe the pressures would even cause them to break up, and perfect Sara would have to face life on her own. The two children wouldn't seem such a miraculous achievement then.

Suddenly Annie started hurrying with the crowd. It was as if she had a premonition that a storm was coming up and she ought to get home before it began. She had a definite feeling of rain and lightning, though the sky was no dingier than it had been all day. A mild day it had been, quite clear even. But suddenly there was something in the air and Annie knew she had to get home right away so she wouldn't get caught in it.

She wanted to get home before Nate, to change her clothes and make drinks and be ready to tell him that things were going to change. Martin and Sara were going out of their life. No threats this time; the land was bought and there was no turning back. They'd be on their own again.

She burst through the door and found Nate on his knees by the window, carefully putting his stereo into a box.

"Hi," she said. "What are you doing?"

Then she looked around and saw that his trunks, which had been the coffee table and stereo shelf in the living room, had been removed.

"Well, I'm moving on," he said.

Annie walked into the bedroom. The foot locker at the bottom of the bed was gone, too. The closet in the bedroom Nate had used was empty except for the can of dead tennis balls they never got around to throwing out. She went back into the living room with a rush of blood threatening to explode in her head. She sat down on the sofa. Without the trunk there was no place to put up her feet.

"Don't get mad," he said. "I hate scenes."

"We certainly must think of you," she said.

"Don't be sarcastic either."

"Let's think of you, I want to think about you. When did you do all this?" She waved her hand at all the empty places.

"I didn't go to work today." He sat back on his heels and looked at her. "Are you okay?"

"I have a headache."

"I'm sorry. I was thinking of you. I didn't want you upset at the office. So I didn't tell you."

"I have a very bad headache."

"I'm sorry."

Annie put her head in her hands and held it as if it had been cut off. Nate came from California where everyone was divorced and no one got headaches. Her first thought was an unexpected one. Now she would never wear a white dress and for ten minutes be a bride.

He held out a handful of tapes and looked at the titles. He examined them critically the way he looked at all his possessions. "You bought these; would you consider them mine, or yours?"

"Martin and Sara bought their property today. I rushed home to tell you that."

"Good for them."

"I thought that would make you happy."

"I'm happy for them." He put all the tapes in a box. "I guess without the tape machine, you won't be needing them."

"Did you plan to sneak out before I got home?"

"No, I planned to talk to you. I'm not a jerk," Nate said. He picked up another handful of tapes. He examined them carefully.

"You let me walk out of here this morning without telling me."

"I thought you knew." He stacked the tapes in the box one by one.

"I would have stayed home if I had known. I didn't know."

"Well, you knew it would have to end some time. Would you like a drink?"

"We've been together six years." Annie looked at her feet. She had small feet but was hard on shoes. Her shoes looked old and she had only had them for a year. She could replace her shoes.

"Five years and a few months," Nate corrected her.

"A long time." Annie raised her voice. "A very long time."

"I'll get you a drink."

"If you do, I'll break the glass on your head."

"Don't get mad."

"Why not? I am mad. I think what you did stinks."

Nate clenched his California jaw with its white even teeth that he had never had braces on and never worried about losing. "I can't stand scenes. I'll tell you once. We made no promises. It was for as long as it worked. That was the arrangement." He threw the tapes in the box. "I didn't lie to you. We made no commitments; it wasn't any secret."

Annie was quiet. She had a sudden image of herself as a shabby creature, making the final sprint down her block for home, in her business suit with the bright raincoat cutting through the crowd like a slash of wet nail polish. She was on her toes, alert to thieves and pickpockets. She was racing to beat a storm, running to get home in time. It had seemed to her that there had been a history in her returns, in his, a history of Saturday nights and Tuesdays after work and all the days in between. She hadn't known it would have to end, not really. And it made her feel shabby and small to think their understanding had been so different. She realized that in the back of her mind she had always had that white dress waiting in the wings for the moment when the light was just right and Nate realized he wanted her forever.

The falseness of her own illusions hurt her more than he did. He was nothing more than himself. She could see his mind working, planning it all so carefully, choosing the day. She could see him going through their things and picking his out as if he were moving into a new office and taking his plants. He had cut her loose already. She could see it in his face, that she was nothing at all to him but the threat of an argument. No wonder she had never dared to raise her voice. One can only afford to fight with someone who won't go when it's over.

It was just as her mother had said, just as Brenda, the knife in her side, had warned so many times. Brenda said it cost him nothing to live there with her and cost her a lot to have him. Annie always thought of her as the prickles in a cactus whose painful splinters can be removed, but whose sting takes a long time to fade. Annie had insisted that her mother did not understand that vows did not insure happiness, or even a lifetime commitment any more. But, all the same, she had never believed in that philosophy Nate spouted about being free. It sounded silly and fake even as he said it. Nobody who loved was free.

"What did I do?" Annie said softly, looking around as if there might be some job she had forgotten, something important that she had missed between last night and this morning.

"You're a mother. You can't help it, you just are."

"A mother?" Annie said doubtfully. She was a stockbroker. She had a career; nobody could accuse her of being a mother.

"You deserve a family and all that stuff. I'm holding you back." This Nate said quickly, looking out of the window. The box was full now and ready to be shut.

"I don't want a family," Annie said wildly. "What makes you think I do? I'd hate a family. I have one I don't like already. I want you!" This last she cried out just as he shut the box.

"I never said I wanted a family. Never." Annie tore the raincoat off as if she meant to fight. Don't shut that box, she screamed, but only in her head because he couldn't stand the noise of people disagreeing.

"Yes, you do. You want to settle down and have a baby. I could see it in your eyes every time we went to bed, like a command to breed."

"Why didn't you tell me? We could have talked about it. It was all in your head, don't you see? I don't want a family. I don't. Don't turn away from me. It was your conflict, not mine."

"It went on too long. You can't keep these things going forever."

"Jesus Christ," Annie screamed. "Don't leave me!" She would have gotten down on her knees and caught at his legs as he passed with the first box on his way to the door if it would have made him stop and look at her. But he turned his head away and said the meter had run out and he had probably gotten a ticket already.

Then he shuffled, guilty now, there was no question about that, to the door, struggling with the heaviest box. When he got there he hesitated.

"I'm sorry, Annie." He stood there a second longer as if he expected her to kiss him good-bye or somehow ease him on his way. Or just say something that didn't sound like a curse. But she didn't. She watched him balancing his boxes without blinking.

At last he said, "I know you'll find somebody else. You're a wonderful person."

Then he left. He really did, like some creep in a movie one doesn't believe. Annie walked around the apartment twice to keep from running after him and screaming in the hall. It was only a three-room apartment; it didn't take long to make the tour, to see that the trunks were still gone and he'd taken everything in the medicine cabinet, even the aspirin.

It was very very quiet. Nate didn't like noise, but he didn't like quiet either. He had music going all the time. Now the quiet seemed the loudest noise Annie had ever heard. She watched herself looking out of the twelfth-floor window onto the street that had looked like a war zone ever since she moved there. They had dug up the street for a subway that never got finished. They bombed and drilled and covered the street over with boards and there was congestion and confusion there on that corner every minute of the day, even on weekends. She had always meant to move away from the chaos but never had. Now she considered her condition. How much did she know? How responsible was she for Nate's not marrying her? Did it even matter now that he never had?

It occurred to her that if they had been married, he would have paid for the cupboard in the dining room and the rug on the floor. He would have considered them his, and they would no doubt be gone now, too. But unmarried, Nate had paid only for half of the rent and the food and their evenings out, and those things could not now be taken back. She looked out at the lights of the city she loved so much and watched herself idly consider jumping out just for the novelty of it.

As she examined the unsatisfactory pieces of her life, the lights outside and the pigeon droppings on the window sill that she never cleaned, she had the same feeling she had had years ago when her mother sent her to camp for the first time. She was six. She was taken to a place deep in the woods where she had never been before. Eight little girls were expected to sleep in a cabin with only screens for windows. If it rained, shutters boarded them in. There was a lake where she was told they would go swimming every day even when it rained. The toilet was outside in a shack. Her father and mother left very soon, angry at her for begging them not to leave her there and for crying in front of the counselors.

Later, when Annie went to bed, she was full of so many ter-
rors she couldn't sleep for the first time in her life. The noises in
the woods were deafening roars. The breathing children were like
monsters. She was afraid she would burst with fear, her bladder
going first and filling the room with urine. She was alone without
her sister to show her what to do. She had a flashlight under her
pillow to help her find her way to the outhouse, but she knew she
couldn't go out of the cabin in the dark. If she let go of her bladder she would wet her bed and be disgraced. And if she didn't
drown in disgrace, she would drown in the lake and never get
home again. And while the hours swam around her in that lonely
place and desperation was a thing she could feel swallowing her
up, she knew that, awful as she felt, tomorrow the sun would
come up as always and somehow she would adjust.

Now, some twenty-odd years later, she stood looking out of
her window at a broken street that would never come right again,
thinking that maybe it would be best to get past the filthy window
ledge and add herself to the wreckage of the street. And as she
thought it, she also knew that the next day would still be Saturday. Monday there was work; and even though she was all grown
up now, alone and set adrift again, nothing in twenty years really
had changed.

5

SARA STRUG-
gled to let herself quietly into the apartment. She wanted to sneak
in and arrange her parcels without disturbing her mother. From
outside in the hall she heard the soft tinkle of the piano. Brenda
was doing her voice exercises. Sara had a plant under her arm,
two shopping bags, her canvas bag that held her knitting and her
handbag that she clutched against her breast to discourage thieves
even here in the hallway outside her mother's apartment. She
thought she could get the door open without having to put anything down, and finally she did.

She stepped into the apartment with a sigh of relief. Brenda had not heard her. She was still working on her scales. First Sara slipped into the kitchen that was still pretty much a mess, even though most of the work was finished. The new cupboards and new counters and new appliances were already in, and there was only the little eating nook in the corner to be completed. Sara shook her head with delight. It was hard to imagine how small and cluttered the kitchen had looked before. Now everything was sharp and compact, all white and green. It seemed much bigger, even with the carpenter's tools all laid out on the floor. It was three o'clock and he was gone already. No wonder the job was taking so long.

Pasted up on the fronts of cabinets and soffiting were a dozen or more wallpaper samples that Brenda had collected. Tiny flowered prints, cute vegetable mixes, as well as just carrots and radishes, also sprigs of herbs, eggplants, a couple of plaids and two different ones of vegetable people, which Annie thought were going too far. It was very dusty in the kitchen and Sara tiptoed back into the square entry hall.

"Aha." Brenda jumped out from behind the living-room doors with the fireplace poker raised above her head. "I thought I heard the front door."

"Mommy," Sara squealed. Brenda put the poker down and the two women hugged delightedly as if they hadn't seen each other only two days before at Sara's apartment.

"Poppet, how good to see you," Brenda said. "Let's have a look at you." She backed off and took a good look at Sara. Brenda was very trim in a suede skirt and hand-knit sweater of a delicate peach mohair with a ruffle around the neck and a thin suede belt nipping it at the waist.

Sara was wearing a similar outfit: a suede cowboy skirt, suede boots, a thick sweater jacket with a thin sweater underneath. She was wearing makeup, even lipstick, and giggled as her mother looked at her.

"Sara, you look adorable. I love that skirt."

"You bought it," Sara said. "I heard you singing just now. What good voice you're in. Really, I think you're sounding better than you ever have. Darling, have you lost weight?"

"Do you think so? I'm so worried. You know the whole acoustics of the place have changed since they tore out the old kitchen. I sound different to myself."

"Oh, Mother, the living room is still the same."

"I know, but there's dust everywhere. I'm afraid it's getting into my lungs. And I know the sound doesn't flow the same."

Sara put her arm around her mother's shoulder and gave her a squeeze. "Mother, you're a riot. You sound great. You really do."

"Well, what are you doing here anyway? Who's with the children?" Brenda asked. She ducked over to the mirror in the hall to check her face. She patted her hair.

"I got a sitter. That's what I did. I wanted to do some shopping and sneak in on you. So I did it. I wanted to see how you're bearing up under this kitchen thing."

Sara wandered back into the kitchen. "It's gorgeous. When they've gone you'll be thrilled you did it."

Actually, Annie was providing the new kitchen, but Brenda saw no need to mention it.

"What's all this?" She pointed at the bags on the floor and the plant.

"Oh I got you a *gardenia*. Look, there's one flower on it already. It's to get rid of the smell of new formica."

"Sara, you're a lovely child. You really are. You've always been the most delightful child. What are you really here for?" Brenda looked at the plant and sniffed it, and then took it into the living room where she put it in the place of honor on the coffee table. "I hope it won't die," she muttered.

"I'm here to see you," Sara called to her. "We never get a good talk with the children around." Sara started moving around the kitchen. She carefully stepped over the loose boards and tools lying about. "Let's have some tea. . . . Oh, I just love the new stove. I think I'm going to get one just like it."

"It was expensive," Brenda said thoughtfully. "But your father liked it."

Well, it's always worth it to get the top of the line; it holds up better in the end. Where do you keep the tea now?"

"Oh Sara, what would I do without you? Right there, next to the stove. See, the teapot is there, too."

Sara put on the kettle and moved back to her shopping bags. "Here, I have a little something for you."

"What is it?"

Sara gave her mother the package, beautifully wrapped. Brenda looked at it for a second and then eagerly tore it open.

"You shouldn't have, really." She opened the box and took out a white porcelain bunny mold with a pink nose.

"It's from your little bunnies Donald, Lucy and me," Sara said. "I was looking for something for you to hang on the peg-board and I just fell in love with him. You can hang him right here."

"He doesn't go with the wallpaper," Brenda said, gazing up at the array of papers.

"Sure, he goes with any of them. They're great. Which one have you chosen?"

"Oh, God. Well, those awful plaids got put in my bag by mistake and your father just loves them. I'm having the most terrible trouble with him."

"They're very fresh." Sara pulled off her sweater and took it out in the hall. Brenda stood there, still considering the papers.

Sara came back and made the tea. "Let's go in the other room, shall we? It's terribly dusty in here. Doesn't he clean up when he goes?"

"Fresh? Do you think they're fresh?" Brenda said doubtfully. The two women stood side by side. They had the same tiny frames and delicate coloring; both were very fair with lovely pink cheeks and small perky features. They looked more like sisters than mother and daughter. But Brenda had had some help keeping nature at bay. "I don't know about fresh."

"The colors are very pure," Sara said.

"All the papers I chose have pure colors," Brenda retorted.

"Of course they do. Any of them would be perfect."

"I did see one with bunnies and carrots on it," Brenda said thoughtfully. "I could get that one. That one would go with the bunny. I love the bunny, Sara. Thank you."

"Oh, you don't have to do that." Sara was horrified. "Don't put bunnies on the wall whatever you do. Look, the bunny goes with the parsley, and the radishes are really delightful—and look at the carrots. They're perfectly cunning. Any of these would do beautifully."

"But you bought me the *bunny*, Sara. And here in the nook where we'll have our breakfast we should be surrounded by bunnies to think of you and the babies every day when you're gone. Is that why you came over here today, because you're leaving me?"

"Oh, Mama!" Sara turned her back just a second in frustration. And then she quickly turned back and gave Brenda a hug. "Don't get upset, please. I didn't come for that, you *know* I didn't. Let's have the tea. That's what we need."

Sara made up a tea tray quickly and carried it into the little den that was Jack's whenever he was at home. There was a tufted leather chesterfield in there, purchased at a time when they weren't so expensive, an old butler's tray table, an armchair so comfortable they used to fight over it when they all lived together, and all the books from a long marriage and two sets of secondary and primary education. Also a good desk, English, that needed to be refinished. Annie had scratched the telephone number of her best friend from fifth grade in the top and there were tear stains next to it from the day when Annie found out she had been jilted for another girl.

"I've always loved this room," Sara said, sinking down on the sofa with a sigh. "It's so charming and restful."

"It's urban," Brenda agreed.

"Yes, it looks like it belongs in a town house."

"We like the city," Brenda pinched her delicate mouth.

"Mama, I'm making you a new sweater. Do you want to see it?"

"Really, Sara? Yes." Then Brenda checked her enthusiasm. "Well, sit down first. Pour the tea and relax. Really, you never get a moment's rest. All you do is run around and think about other people. You're going to run yourself into the ground if you don't watch out."

Sara sighed. It was true she did work very hard. She poured the tea and there was silence for a minute as they both had some, and one of the plain biscuits Brenda liked with her tea.

"What does it look like?" Brenda said suddenly.

"What?" Sara stiffened. She had been prepared for a grilling about the house, but couldn't help clutching up at the thought of describing it.

"The sweater. Sara, you're so clever I think you should go into business. Your sweaters are so much more beautiful than any I've seen in the stores for just hundreds. You have such wonderful ideas, such a sense of color. No wonder you respond to the wallpapers. Whenever I wear one of your sweaters, everybody compliments me. I always say my daughter made it." Brenda poured herself another cup of tea and held out the cup for Sara to add milk.

"I always wanted you to be a star, Sara. You have so much talent. I have to admit I was disappointed when you didn't want to sing."

Sara laughed, relieved at the comfortable old theme of singing, singing, singing. Brenda couldn't stay off the subject for more than ten minutes at a time. "You know I can't sing a note."

"Oh yes, I think you could have if you'd but your mind to it. You're so pretty, Sara. Well, have a biscuit. You look so thin. But I don't know, you really have a knack for designing things, and your children are adorable. And Martin, of course. He's a wonderful husband. I think you really did the right thing, when I think of it."

Sara sighed. Brenda studied her and pinched her mouth.

"You're very lucky, Sara. Not everybody has a devoted husband and two beautiful children and all the talents you have."

They both grew silent thinking of Annie. Then Sara spoke. "I couldn't have been a singer, Mama. There's only one star in this family. You're the star. You're getting better every week. I can hear it. I really can."

Brenda shrugged. "I gave my youth to my children."

"I know you did, Mama."

"I don't want you to feel guilty for leaving me now," she added decisively. "You're too good to suffer. I know that's why you got a sitter and came over here today. And I want you to know I hate guilt."

"I do, too, Mama."

"You have to do what your wonderful husband wants you to do. And if it means leaving your mother—your whole family. I don't want to count your sister out either. I know how much she means to you—well, if it means leaving us and making yourself miserable, I guess you have to do it." Brenda folded her hands stoically in her lap.

"I think you'll like the house. You'll come out for weekends."

"Is that what you came to tell me, that I'll like a house way out in the country, somewhere that isn't even Connecticut."

"Here, I'll get the sweater. I want to make one for Annie, too. But I thought I'd talk it out with you first." Sara went to get the bag of knitting. Her hand shook as she reached for the bag. Why the hell did she always have to bring Connecticut up when she knew they hated Connecticut.

"Let's see it," Brenda sighed.

"Oh, I just stood there for hours choosing these yarns. They have the most beautiful new yarns," Sara said brightly. "They've gotten so expensive, but when you consider how much they would cost if one bought them in a store, I guess they're almost worth it." She smiled coyly. "No, no. Close your eyes. I want to lay them out so you can see them properly."

Brenda had reached for the bag, but Sara pulled it away laughing. "You're going to be so beautiful in this."

"I'll pay for it," Brenda said.

"No, I want to pay for this one. You always pay."

"What's a mother for?" Brenda said. "I'm paying. I insist. It's not every mother who has a daughter as talented and generous as you."

"No, I won't hear of it. You buy me beautiful things all the time. Honestly, Mama, I think every time you buy something for yourself you buy something for me, too."

"Well, I have to have some pleasure in life, don't I? Your sister won't let me buy a thing for her."

Sara laid out the yarns on the sofa between them. Annie was in fact the subject on her mind that day. But with Brenda it was always important to be as indirect as possible. She hated getting to the point of anything. Sara finished arranging the yarns.

"I wanted to use all your favorite colors. Look, here's the winter heather and the pale misty green. And there's some pink angora for a circle around the yoke and at the cuffs. I'm going to sew some amethyst beads around the neck.

Brenda sucked in her breath with rapture. "Oh!" she said.

"The body of the sweater will be a mixture of these two, see. And there will be a very luxurious yoke with this and this, which will be repeated down on the arms. Here's the sketch. What do you think?"

"I think it's gorgeous, Sara. Really ravishing."

Sara beamed. "I really designed it with Annie in mind, but I wanted to work yours out first. I'm really quite worried about Annie."

"I agree, she's very shabby." Brenda touched the yarns. "Maybe you should give this one to her. Do you think this will itch, Sara?"

"I never make itchy sweaters, Brenda. These are your colors. You come first always."

"I don't know. This one looks like it might itch. I have very delicate skin you know." Brenda held the sketch up to the light. Sara had used colored pencils and it looked very professional indeed. "What's wrong with Annie, now?" she said finally. "Tell me. I won't tell her you said a word."

"Well," Sara hesitated. "I think there's something going on."

"Don't tell me they're going to get married," Brenda said rolling her eyes."

"No." Sara was silent for a minute.

"Your father says he'll commit hara-kari if they get married. That boy has caused nothing but trouble for poor Annie. Can you imagine being tied to him for life? I just don't understand how she could be involved all this time with someone who's so— careless."

"Mother, I think Annie's very unhappy."

"I'm not surprised. She's very self-destructive."

"She has headaches all the time. Every time I see her she's suffering. Mama, I do my best to try and help her. But I get angry with her."

"You're an angel, Sara."

"No, I'm not. I lose my patience. She's like a child; the minute I see her I get mad. She's always got that draggy dull hair and those sad eyes. Most of the time she looks like a, I don't know, shabby. A girl like her can't afford to go without makeup at her age. And everybody looks so good. There's a lot of competition out there." Sara paused.

"She only cheers up for the children. It breaks my heart. I try to get her involved with the children. I want her to see what she's missing living with a jerk like that. I want her to *see* what she's doing to herself. But she just won't budge and I get so . . . Mama, I get so *cross* with her." Sara blew her nose on a napkin and then reached in her bag for her compact.

"Don't blame yourself, Sara."

"But I want to *help*. She's getting worse and worse."

"I know, you're an angel. Everyone should have a sister like you."

"But I don't help. I just make it worse. She goes away so mad at me and I feel guilty. But what am I supposed to do, tell her she's all right when she isn't?"

Brenda reached over and squeezed Sara's arm. "Baby, Annie's

very difficult. We both know that. You know we would do anything for her. I would dress her like a princess if she'd let me. I'd give anything to have her married to someone like Martin. But Annie just isn't like you. We can't expect as much from her. I guess it's too much to hope for two daughters as successful as you."

"I'm not successful. How can you say that? I'm just a mother."

"Sara, you have a husband who adores you. That's successful, believe me. . . ." Brenda sighed. "I know Annie isn't as pretty as you. She doesn't have the personality that's attractive to men. She never did. But this! This is just destructive."

"He's awful," Sara sniffed. "I feel so rotten about it."

"Shh, it isn't your fault."

"But she just won't face up to it."

"Have a cup of tea, Sara. I hate to see you upsetting yourself, especially with all the things you have on your mind."

Brenda poured Sara some more tea, and Sara took a sip to please her, even though by now it was quite cold.

"I'm not upset. I'm just a little worried."

"It's important to have a man who's loving. I guess if you act like a piece of shit, you're treated like one," Brenda said bitterly.

"Oh, Mother!" Sara said, shocked.

"I don't know why she acts like that. We've always been so careful to point out her good points, to encourage her even when she's messing up."

"So have we—Martin and I," Sara said eagerly. "She's not—"

"Is it so wrong to want her to be happy?" Brenda interrupted. "All we want is for her to find some nice man, like Martin. I don't mean as good as Martin," Brenda said hastily. "Nobody could live up to Martin's standard. But she ought to be able to find some *nice* man who could appreciate her for what she is. There's someone for everyone. Just look at all the really ugly girls who get married and are happy."

"That's what I tell her."

"What do you suggest?" Brenda said.

Sara sighed. "I like the plaids."

"What?"

"If Daddy likes the plaids, maybe you should consider them," Sara said.

"I mean about *Annie*," Brenda said, suddenly cross. "Don't push me into plaids if I don't want plaids. Jack doesn't know a damn thing about decorating. You know that."

"But he likes them, and they are very cheerful."

"Poor Annie," Brenda said. "Maybe I should talk to her."

"I don't know. She just doesn't seem up to telling him to fish or cut bait. I feel so rotten about it."

"Well stop feeling rotten right now! You've done your best." Brenda patted her shoulder again. "You're unusual, get that into your head. You can't live your sister's life for her. If she wants to withdraw from the support of her mother and her sister who love her, that's her problem. Not ours."

"Oh, Mother, do you really think so?" Sara said doubtfully.

"I love you, Sara, don't feel guilty."

"If you think I shouldn't, I'll try not to." Sara touched her yarns.

Brenda considered her for a second. "And don't feel guilty because of me either. I know I'll adjust. And Annie will have to, too." Brenda's eyes filled up and she dabbed them very carefully so that her mascara wouldn't run and make a mess of her face.

Sara turned her head so she wouldn't have to see the tears.

"Such beautiful things you do, Sara." Brenda, too, touched the yarns.

Sara pulled her hand away. Brenda had a way of turning everything into pain. Now she was deserting her, and Annie was a piece of shit. The next thing she'd do would be to tell Annie Sara had said it.

"Oh come on now, I *told* you not to feel guilty. Brenda will adjust. I won't be happy, but I'll adjust. Now, show me the amethysts."

Sara reached into her handbag and pulled out a little envelope. She emptied the contents into Brenda's open hand.

"Oh; they're lovely. Are they real?" Brenda said. "See, I'm fine."

"They weren't expensive," Sara said with less spirit than she had shown before. "I have a source."

"I'll pay for them," Brenda said firmly. She rolled them around in her hand, examining them one by one. They looked like gumdrops.

"So many things to remind me of you when you're gone, Sara," Brenda said mournfully. "And now I'll have to cope with Annie all alone. I'll have to think about what to do with her." She sighed. "Isn't it terrible how much we have to suffer because of men?" She handed the stones back to Sara, shaking her head.

Then she gathered up the tea things and took them back to the kitchen.

Sara sat paralyzed on the sofa for a minute. Suddenly she was terribly depressed, as if the whole happiness of the day she had spent on her own had been wiped away in a minute. Which one of them did her mother really mean? Finally she went into the kitchen to cheer up Brenda so she could go home without a fight.

6

THE LESSER brokers at Howard and Plunket sat in the boardroom, a large square space surrounded by a shoulder-high wall of opaque glass. In the old days the boardroom in brokerage houses had a big board on one end with stock prices ticking across it all day. In the back of the room usually there was a row or two of chairs where clients could park themselves for a while and see how they were doing. But there are no extra chairs in boardrooms any more, and no big boards. Now spaces called boardrooms are crammed with secretaries and typewriters in addition to brokers with desks and chairs and typewriters and automated quotation systems. Every broker starts life with a telephone and an automated quotation system that projects information on what looks like a small television screen. Whether he can rise out of the boardroom into an office of his own depends on his ability to use those two instruments.

There were only four private offices across the windowed wall in the main midtown office of Howard and Plunket in the Pan Am building. They were supposed to belong to the managing partner, John Carlton, and the three top-selling brokers. Annie had become a top-selling broker two years before. But she lost the next chance at a private office because of Carl, who was very fat.

Carl hadn't fit in his space in the boardroom very well even when he started there. But he got fatter every year. Finally in the small cluttered space that was chaos at peak traffic times anyway,

Carl began causing a gridlock every time he tried to get in or out. There were complaints about missed calls because he prevented people from getting back to their desks. One day a broker lost a fifty-thousand share sale from a client because Carl was stuck between him and his desk. By the time he got free, the client had given up and called someone else. There was such bad feeling in the boardroom about this and other incidents that Carl was moved to a private office as a temporary measure. After a few months of Carl the other man in the office couldn't stand it any more. He transferred to the Stamford office and Annie was given his place. Since the move meant a promotion in status as well as a window that was almost hers alone, Annie did not complain.

Mostly Annie and Carl ignored each other; that is, they tried to ignore each other. They sat only five feet apart and couldn't help knowing all there was to know about each other's lives. Carl was not a top-selling broker. He had a wife who made a great deal more money than he and worked in a building a few blocks away on Park Avenue. He spent most of his time trying to reach her on the phone, and agonizing when she didn't return his calls. Since he was interested only in the arms market, he did not have as many clients as he might have.

He was crazy about the war effort. His desk was littered with *Aviation Week and Space Technology, Aviation Daily, Air Force,* Defense Marketing Service newsletters, *Proceedings of the Naval Institute* and every book Jane's ever published: *The World's Air Forces, World Arms,* a catalog of amphibians, and so on. He wanted to get into strife and was always looking at companies that made exploding bullets, whistling bombs, heat-seeking rockets, laser-guided missiles, anything that was launched, shot, propelled and, on reaching its target, obliterated it.

Annie tried hard not to listen to Carl's sales pitches when he roused himself enough to make them. His researches included detailed studies of the world's war zones and what companies were profiting from the destruction. This information, and the killing capacity of each device, he took pleasure in describing in a loud voice. Every day she sighed with relief when Carl went out for a quick three dozen oysters at the Oyster Bar in Grand Central Station, or a number seventeen at the local deli. He then lumbered over to the building where his wife worked on Park Avenue and paced up and down in front of it, in hopes of catching a

glimpse of her going out or coming in surrounded by worship-
ping henchmen he could sometimes bump out of the way for a
second with a slight movement of one hip.

Every broker tries to have an angle. Annie started out being
the house expert in bonds. She sold bonds to old ladies and rich
people who wanted a tax-exempt income and didn't care that inflation would hurt their nest egg in the long run. Then the bond
market sagged and Annie became interested in stocks because
stocks could increase in value and make money, while bonds were
good only for people who could afford to lose it. Annie's method
differed from those of the other two top-selling brokers, Ben Custer and Sylvia Combe, and that of John Carlton, the managing
partner.

Sylvia's method was to go out to lunch with clients every day,
tell each client how much money she had recently made for all
her other clients and push whatever stocks looked good that
week. She did not mind if her clients bought high when it seemed
that the stock might go a point or two higher. She did not have a
favorite industry either. She preferred the high-priced glamour
stocks that she sold with the glamour of her person. She made
Annie feel poor and unresourceful.

From September to June, Sylvia sallied forth every day in a
mink coat studded with mink tails. The coat flounced her message
at 21, at The Four Seasons, at Sea Fare of the Aegean and sometimes Orsini's. Wherever she went, an extra chair was pulled up to
the table just so the coat would never have to leave her. She had a
chiming pocket watch around her neck and large diamond studs
plugged into her ears. At two, when her watch chimed, she picked
up the coat and plunged through the restaurant greeting anybody
she thought she ought to know. And she left the check to whomever she had invited to eat with her. Sylvia hadn't been with her
husband for years and was terrifyingly successful.

Ben, on the other hand, was deeply committed to natural re-
sources, very high quality stocks indeed. He liked metals and oils
and other things that were pulled out of the ground. It was Ben
who had gotten Martin involved in the company that made drilling rigs imperfectly and lost all those men in a storm in the North
Sea. Ben was thirty-five, the age that can't help galloping full tilt
toward forty. And he was desperate to get married. He had been
resolutely planning his domestic life for the last dozen years. He

had known when to sell gold, but he couldn't make a decision about a wife. Every year more varieties of possible wife offered themselves. Every month or so he fell in love with one of them. He would present her to Annie and Nate over dinner for their approval. He would go over her qualities while perched on Annie's desk, and then in a few weeks he would discover a fatal flaw and call everything off.

What Annie looked for was quite different. She watched those tiny up-and-coming two- to twenty-dollar stocks, those little companies that sometimes hit sixteen and split two for one, rise up like a phoenix out of ashes and make a killing when everybody else is out to lunch. So she didn't like to go out to lunch. She had always liked the feeling of having a little extra air to breathe when the others were gone. Then she punched out numbers on her automated quotation system with quite an intense feeling of relief. Carl made her feel as if there were no love left in the world. He made her feel that marriage was like a troubled country that dragged its neighbors into war. Sylvia was nearing fifty; she went at money twenty-four hours a day.

Not going out to lunch also gave Annie's clients a certain extra confidence of knowing there was hardly ever a time when she couldn't be reached. She had extensive telephone correspondence with people all over the country. She spoke to her sources, other brokers, clients in Florida, people in Washington who knew what was coming up. She liked to hang around in case something came up in Chicago or New Orleans or somewhere and somebody wanted to tell her about it.

The week Nate left her, Annie closed up to everyone around her. She cut them off as if they didn't exist for her anymore, looked through them if they spoke to her about anything but business. That week the bottom showed signs of dropping right out of the market. A plane crashed in Washington and there was another mine explosion in Kentucky. These things didn't affect the market, but the mood was grim. When all the lines in the office were jammed with panicked clients calling to find out what to do, Annie advised her clients to sell, sell, sell. Several of them sold everything they had in their portfolios and put their money into money market funds that paid fourteen percent. In the next weeks these were the only clients in the whole house who failed to lose anything at all.

Every day as the picture worsened and stock prices fell, brokers encouraged clients to hedge by buying more stocks as the prices fell. Annie held fast, saying don't buy a thing, and everybody talked about her. She had made what seemed to be a lucky choice and nobody who listened to her lost money. Suddenly she became the lucky stone everybody wanted to touch every morning at five to ten before the market opened. It was one thing when stock prices began to fall steadily to tell a client to sell a stock or two and buy one or two others that looked as if they had gone down as far as they were going. But to know the cusp when it came and dare not to sit quietly upon it, that was real daring.

"Sell, sell, sell." Annie's word came out of her depression, like throwing the furniture out of the window in a fire to keep it from burning, even though the drop from the window was great. But her word came just at the cusp. And while other brokers sat on the point of diminishing returns, shifting and hedging about with a few favorite stocks, Annie, strafed and wounded from shocks of her own, was ruthless.

After her lucky strike with the word "sell," a lot of people called her the new sage. In the mornings the lesser brokers would stop by the office and stick their heads in one by one.

"What about today?"

Was the country going to turn around? Was General Motors going to go the way of Chrysler or was Chrysler going to go the way of General Motors? Was Conoco going to pull off the du Pont merger, or would du Pont fall to Exxon? And what about it, could Interferon cure cancer? And if it could, who was making it outside of Czechoslovakia?

Annie, leaning on her elbow with a world-weary look, would mutter something mysterious like, "I'd look at Poland."

Ah, look at Poland. And the lesser brokers would run back to their desks and look at Poland, scratch their heads and worry. Poland, Poland, Poland. Did she mean the water, the ham or the country? Somehow it wasn't as clear a command as sell, sell, sell. But Annie wasn't in a good mood.

Every day Ben stopped by Annie's office, hooked one thigh over the edge of her desk and perched there for a while.

"What's up?"

Annie showed her enthusiasm for that question by turning her head to the window and the view of the ramp of the Pan Am

building where plump limousines disgorged their well-dressed oc-
cupants and gobbled them up at frequent intervals throughout
the day.

Lately Ben had lost interest in Ellie because of the promi-
nence of her teeth and was warming up to the idea of Clara, who
liked to fish.

"I want you to meet Clara," he said one day when Annie was
feeling even less inspired by her fellow man than usual.

"That blonde?" she said. She had a marked dislike for blondes.

"No, the readhead. The blonde is her cousin Suzy. Suzy
wants me to invest her money. Clara doesn't have any money."

"I didn't see the redhead," Annie said. "Only the blonde."

"I haven't brought her in yet. She doesn't have any money."

"I'd drop her, then," Annie said.

"Why? I'm not concerned about money. When you're choosing a partner for the rest of your life, you can't think about
money. She reads *Field and Stream.* Now that's important. Why
don't we go out one night? I think you'll like her."

"Oh, God. Not another *Field and Stream* lover. Really, you're
very naive."

"That's not fair, Annie. Lot's of girls like the outdoors."

"I'm sure they do."

"This is a special girl. She really is."

Annie yawned.

"She *is* special. Why aren't you interested in her? Usually
you're interested in my friends."

"You'll only get tired of her in a few weeks, why bother?"

"Annie, how can you say that? She might be the right one."

Annie punched out Personal Harmonics on her automated
quotation system to see how it was doing. It had gone up a half a
point since morning, but hadn't moved since.

"What are you looking at?"

"Personal Harmonics has gone up another half a point since
it opened this morning. I think you should buy some."

"You're kidding."

"It's gone from seven to twelve in two weeks. I really think
you should look at it. I have the prospectus right here." She shuffled through the papers on her desk and pulled it to the top of
the pile.

"That dinky operation," Ben shook his head. "No thanks."

"That dinky operation," Annie said in her sage voice, "is going to go up to sixteen and split."

"How do you know?"

"I just thought you'd like to know," she said loftily.

Ben laughed. "That kind of thing is not really in my line."

"Maybe it should be. It's the first breakthrough of biofeedback in the home. Think about it."

"I've got all the biofeedback I can handle."

"I know. Your life is very stressful. If you don't watch out, some day it's going to get you." Annie swiveled away from him and punched out a few of her favorite stocks.

"What's the matter with you, Annie?"

"Nothing. Just your closed mind. I think this thing is going to be very big."

Ben looked at her anxiously. He was an intense-looking person, dark, with a strong jaw and blue eyes. He used to be fat, but now he was thin and looked hungry most of the time because he didn't like to eat much until dinner.

"Did you think the blonde was cute? Suzy, I mean. Maybe I've been underrating Suzy. Her mother died and left her a lot of money. And I wouldn't have a mother-in-law. That's something to consider."

Annie shook her head in disgust. "When Roche buys out Personal Harmonics, don't say I didn't tell you about it."

"Does it vibrate?" Ben asked suddenly.

"What?"

"This biofeedback thing."

"Vibrate?"

"You know—can it turn you on? It could get very big if it vibrated."

"Jesus, You're disgusting. Only you would think of that. Go away, I'm busy." Annie made a brushing-away gesture to get him off her desk.

"It would be kind of interesting to be done by a machine," he mused. "Don't you think so? How does it attach?"

"It's for *stress*." Annie banged the desk with her fist and made the pencils jump. "Stress, like when life is too much and your head hurts and you want to jump out of the window." Annie held her head that was beginning to hurt again, right above her right eye. "I think it attaches to the brain."

"I don't know about electrodes in the brain," he said doubtfully. "Certainly not in a depressed state. Doesn't it attach anywhere else?"

"How should I know? I only have a prospectus. I don't have a sample. I wish I did."

"What's the matter?"

"Go away. I have a headache."

"I'm sorry. You're probably right. There must be a huge market in stress." He reached in his pocket and pulled out two Gelusil tablets in paper and a tiny tin of aspirin. He put the Gelusil back in his pocket and handed Annie the aspirin.

"You bet there is. I just know it's going to be big." She looked at the aspirin, and considered taking two.

"Let's go out to dinner. I want to hear more about this vibrator of yours. And I want you to meet Clara."

Annie handed back the tin without taking any. "It doesn't vibrate and it doesn't turn you on. It turns you off; that's the whole point of it. In fact, I don't see why you couldn't attach it on any stress point at all."

"That's more like it. Annie, take the aspirin. I want you to feel better. Listen we could go to El Chico and drink margaritas."

"I don't want to meet Clara."

"You like El Chico," Ben said encouragingly.

"Oh yeah. El Chico is where Linda Lou got on the table and did the Flamenco. Remember Linda Lou?"

"I'm sorry about your blouse. I forgot that she kicked the chili sauce on your blouse. But Clara is a singer. She won't get on the table, I promise. Annie, there's something the matter, isn't there?"

Annie took two aspirin with the remains of the cold coffee on her desk. She shook her head.

"Okay, we'll go somewhere else. Where do you want to go? I'll get my car out. We can go to Chinatown if you want."

Annie shook her head again.

"Tell me what's the matter."

Annie sighed. This conversation came after a very difficult several weeks for her. She had been trying to think of a good time to tell everyone that Nate had died while on a short business trip to Miami. After giving it a lot of thought, she decided he had been stabbed by a Cuban who mistakenly thought he was with the

CIA. Nate was a very nondescript kind of person who could flatten his features at will into a perfect mask of indifference that could easily be confused with the face of a hit man or spy. News of such a death would be certain not to make it into *The New York Times,* and possibly not even the *Miami Herald,* which, rumor had it, was no longer in English anyway. It was a poor end for Nate but no worse than the real one. Death was a no-fault separation and the only rebuke she need suffer would be that of failing to recover any insurance. But then it was typical of Nate to forget to make any provision for her in case of his loss.

Annie studied Ben's knee where it rested on the corner of her desk. For a second she was tempted to tell him the truth. He of all people should understand how a lover might not really love. She raised her chin and thought she saw a flicker of real concern in his blue eyes. His face, after all, wasn't a bad one and was well practiced in inviting intimacies. She kind of liked the moonscape look of his skin that came from the scars of an unusually severe case of adolescent acne. The scars made him look as if even he had been flailed once or twice in his life. Then her eyes lowered and she saw a small bright stain on the smooth front of his shirt. The smudge was in a funny place: third button down behind his tie.

"Go on, tell me," he urged.

Annie looked away, burned by the evidence of his kissing Suzy at lunch. "I'll tell you," she said angrily. "Everybody in the place is dying for a tip from me and I give one to you, you of all people. And what do you do?"

"I say let's talk about it over dinner."

"No, you want to know if it vibrates. You're disgusting."

"Oh come on, if it's electric it must vibrate, mustn't it? That's how electricity works. Little vibrations travel through the wire and send messages and impulses and power and things. I think you're right. There's definitely something to this electricity thing. I have a feeling it's going to change the whole world."

"Go away," Annie said sadly. His all-pervasive interest in sex depressed her.

"What's the matter? I can usually make you smile."

"Well, I happen to think there's something *to* Personal Harmonics. I think it may even be a valuable *thing,* quite apart from anything else."

"I don't know. I guess it just makes me think of the little boy who uses electrical impulses to make a dead frog's legs jump," Ben said. "I don't know how I'd feel about a machine soothing my troubled brow. Machines make me lonely. Please, Annie, I want you to meet Clara. I think Clara might be the right one, I really do."

"No," Annie said, more loudly and sharply than she meant to. "No, no, no!" No more of Ben's girl friends, no more double dates. Nobody at all. She saw emptiness stretching out in front of her and glared at Ben as if he were the source of all her pain.

Carl, coming back just that second from a late lunch and no luck in finding his wife, wedged himself between them. Before he moved on, he noted and indeed prided himself on noting, the acute distress plainly displayed on Annie's face.

In the most surly of tones he said, "If you molest her, too, I swear I'll break your neck."

"What do you mean, too?" Ben retorted. But he had to retreat hastily as Carl moved forward an inch and bumped him out of the way.

Was this a good time to say that Nate was dead? Annie looked from one man to the other. Carl had the look of wanting nothing more than to beat to death a rapist. Ben stepped back with an expression of utter amazement that began turning to outrage as Carl bent his knees and did a tiny dance step toward him. All the color had drained from Carl's face. He turned to Annie.

"What did he do, Annie?" he said softly. You can tell me. Did he touch you. . . ? One word from you and I'll kill him. I swear it. A sweet kid like you." He raised his fist as if he might actually strike.

Annie suppressed a giggle.

"Oh shut up," Ben said quickly.

"Don't tell me to shut up," Carl said ominously. "If you touched this girl, I want to know it. She's very close to me," he warned.

"God damn it, shut up," Ben said. "I wouldn't touch her. I wouldn't dream of touching her."

Annie drew in her breath sharply. Everybody in the boardroom had turned around and was watching the scene. Everybody in the whole office could see Ben's bristling indignation. Even now he was still babbling on.

"He must be crazy."

A wave of nausea swept over Annie. Ben was the worst skirt chaser she'd ever met, a man who, romancing one cousin, couldn't help stringing the other one along for later. He was the very lowest form of humanity, a lover so promiscuous no female with all her parts had yet been safe from his advances. He couldn't have a simple conversation without innuendo. His whole being was tied up in the hunt. His eyes glittered with it whenever he went out in a crowd.

Annie had seen him in action for a long time. She knew just how he worked and just what he thought. But she never thought when he looked at her that he saw the one person who didn't rate the effort. She shriveled in her cashmere sweater and business suit. If she could have been hung right then by the small cultured pearls around her neck, she would have welcomed hanging. A small tear, the first she'd shed, gathered at the corner of her eye and quivered there. She knew she wasn't pretty, but this was too much.

It had never occurred to her that he placed her outside the realm of possibility, that he admired her so little he wouldn't dream of touching her. Did he think she was *that* plain every day when he sat on her desk, when they used to go out to dinner, the four of them? So plain he couldn't bear to touch her? Worse even than a sister for whom a hug would be natural? Her lip trembled at the enormity of the insult.

"Well, God damn it, if you didn't touch her, then what the hell's the matter with her?" Carl shouted, looking from Annie to Ben and back again.

Ben shook his head. The two men regarded each other for a long minute while everybody in the boardroom looked at them.

Finally Ben broke the quiet. "Damned if I know," he said and slunk quickly away.

Annie found a tissue and dabbed her eye. Next door Sylvia's watch chimed three. Carl looked at his watch to confirm the time. Then he dialed his wife. She was in a meeting. Annie blew her nose and looked out the window. That night she was unable to walk into the grocery store to buy herself something to eat. She felt unworthy not only of love, but of life itself.

7

BRENDA FLOOD
was suffering from a terrible cold when she found out that Nate
had left her baby. For several days she sat forlornly at the piano
punching out solfège exercises she knew she ought not to try.

"So, do, do, do, so do so," she whispered to herself.

"Re re so la, re re so la." It was a sad tinkly sound without her
hearty, competent voice to accompany it.

She gargled tea with lemon while the humidifier whirred in
the background, misting her troubled spirit. It was not enough to
have this wretched cold that threatened to cancel her Thursday
lesson. No, now she had to find out that a thirty-year-old daughter of hers, who hadn't had the decency to get married, had been
avoiding her for weeks because she was now divorced, left,
thwarted, ruined in mid life and locked in her little apartment.
She refused to go out except to go to work; that was the case of
her baby.

It was not enough that this should happen, but to have to get
this shabby bit of news second hand from Sara, that was almost
the worst. But Sara had always been the thoughtful child, the caring one who bothered now and then about her mother. Brenda
went over and over in her mind what Sara had told her. Very
little. Sara said that Annie claimed she and Nate had a fight and
afterward they had broken up. And Sara found this out by going
over to Annie's apartment after Annie hadn't shown up for several weeks, which hurt the children and wasn't like her at all.

Sara discovered Annie alone in her apartment reading a
book. Sara thought that was a pretty sad activity when compared
with the alternatives available, like having dinner with her and
Martin and the children or going out with someone else. The very
lonely occupation seemed to indicate to Sara a deep depression.

Brenda brooded over this information for some time. It was true on the one hand that she didn't much like Nate. In fact, she thought he was a simpleminded sap. An account executive for an advertising agency didn't have much going for him in any case. But even among account executives in general, Nate was in a class by himself. He was the middleman between such clients as Happy Clam Chowder and the creators of television atrocities on the level of happy, clapping clam commercials that crept up on you and slapped you in the gut whenever you were happily watching M*A*S*H and least expected it.

Nate came to dinner and explained how they got the happy clams to clap. He lounged around in other people's favorite chairs, ate other people's favorite parts of the chicken, never said thank you for their Christmas presents. He drank the last of the Bristol Cream without asking if anyone else wanted it. When Donald was first learning to walk and kept crashing to the floor, Nate was the only one who thought of saying he hoped gravity would win. He had the most atrocious taste in music (he didn't like her singing at all) and wore his bleached streaky yellow hair a bit too long. He wore his shirts too tight. When he sat down bits of flesh popped out from collarbone to belt. In addition to all that, he pawed Annie in public with an enthusiasm that would lead any moderately optimistic person to assume that he would succumb eventually and marry her in the end. Brenda had assumed that he would marry her. That was on the other hand. She didn't much like him, but he was a blister she had come to expect to see.

"So so do, do do so," she whispered to herself. What hopes had Annie now? A job wouldn't keep her warm at night or take out the garbage. Brenda could not even console herself with a hearty rendition of "Some Day Her Prince Will Come," because her voice was as broken as her hopes for Annie's future. She had a picture of Annie having to resort to an old man, someone as old as her father, who would take her to Florida where it was warm.

"So la re me, do do." Brenda sighed. Annie was a tough nut, hiding in her apartment in shame, not wanting to come even to her mother who loved her and forgave all. A tear slid down Brenda's cheek as she thought of it, and splashed down on an ivory key. Her own baby lost and despairing, too proud to come to her mother. She couldn't stand it. She considered having her over for dinner and then afterward having a heart-to-heart as they used to in Annie's old room that was now the TV room. But she didn't want Jack to know and start screaming in case there was a chance that the two young lovers could be reunited. Jack would be angry and might say something to hurt Annie, and Brenda didn't want that. Jack got so emotional when it came to his daughters. Brenda sighed; he was too rough on them. No wonder Annie was afraid to tell them. Well, six years was a long time. Maybe he would find he couldn't live without her and come back.

Brenda hesitated. She didn't want to interfere. On the other hand, she couldn't let her baby suffer alone. She called her up and told her she was meeting her for lunch.

"I don't go out for lunch," Annie reminded her. "You sound awful. What's the matter?"

"I have the most stinking cold. I haven't been able to sing for days. I'm afraid I'm going to miss my Thursday lesson."

"Poor thing," Annie murmured.

"I want to see you. I haven't seen you in so long."

"Just a week."

"Weeks," Brenda said severely. "Several weeks. I'm very upset."

"What about?" Annie asked suddenly alarmed. Sara must have told her, and she had promised she wouldn't.

"You've been neglecting me. I don't understand how you can treat me this way. Your sister calls me every day." Brenda began to sniffle.

"But you've been so busy with your lessons and your kitchen. And with the market plunging this way, well, you know how tense things get."

"Don't make excuses to me. I want to talk to you. I think this may be a bit more serious than a simple cold. I've. . . ," Brenda paused, "I've spit blood."

"Oh no," Annie said.

"Yes, I did. Last night, and then again this morning."

"You better go to a doctor."

"It's not me I'm worried about," Brenda said. "I can take it. It's you. A girl with your looks, your talents shouldn't get tense because of the market. You're going to get lines. You're going to get a nervous stomach like your father. My God, when I think of your hair. Annie, I have to tell you I'm very worried. You neglect me when I'm sick. If I should die, who would take care of you, tell me that?" Another tear charged down Brenda's cheek.

"Oh, Mother, don't talk like that."

"I can't help it. You used to be the sweetest child. When you were about seven. We danced together, remember, and you sang like an angel."

"Mother, I hate to get tense before the market opens. Please, let's talk about this some other time."

"Of course. How thoughtless of me. We'll go to the Trattoria at twelve-thirty and you won't even have to leave the building. See you later, my angel, and don't worry too much about the blood. It wasn't much blood, just a little blood. A few drops to remind us all of my mortality."

Annie suffered all morning over the blood. She completely forgot the strategy she had planned so carefully in the shower that morning after reading the *Journal*. There was an article that gave her an idea and then one of her clients, who was going to be in meetings all day, called, and asked her about something he wanted her to buy the moment the market opened. And her idea and his idea jibed and she thought she might try a few things. . . .

After her conversation with her mother, however, Annie made the one buy and couldn't make the others. How shallow stock prices seemed in comparison with her mother's feelings. She was paralyzed by the thought that she had once again unwittingly caused Brenda pain, when Brenda was so loving, so tender, so caring about her. Even now Annie could remember Brenda holding her in her arms when she was sick and promising her the world if only she would recover. As if Annie could have control over her own fevers. Annie neglected her mother, it was true. And it seemed so unreasonable and cruel that most of the time she wished Brenda didn't exist at all, or else lived somewhere so far away not even telephone wires could bring them together.

Annie rushed downstairs, and Brenda, who had gotten there first, rose from the table and went to meet her.

"My darling, my darling, my darling." Brenda wrapped Annie in an embrace so voluminous, so forgiving, so full of love and sympathy that Annie was moved to cry out, "Mommy," as if they had been parted for years and were at last reunited.

At the sound of her title, Brenda drew back. "Annie, please!"

The Trattoria was a restaurant not of the dark and intimate variety. In fact it was quite open and airy, quite white in feeling. With plants around for greenery. A waiter tried to push past with a tray of fettucine Alfredo on his shoulder.

"Annie, you're blocking the way," said Brenda, who was in fact blocking the way herself.

Annie slid into her seat with another guilty feeling of having done wrong. Her mother hated to be reminded of their biological relationship and Annie's doing it in public, where there was so much light, was an unpardonable gaff. Brenda had red hair now, what used to be called strawberry blonde, a jaded carrot color somewhere between pink and beige and orange. Her face had been moved upward a bit, not so much that her small even features were frozen solid in parchment-smooth skin, but enough so that it was impossible to tell her age. She had a small frame not overloaded with flesh and, beside her daughter, she did not make a poor showing. Her outfit was several layers of coordinating challis prints, a skirt of one print, small close-fitting jacket over a blouse of another print, and over it all was a fringed square of quite another feeling. Dainty shoes and a handbag of snake. Even with her nostrils distinctly reddened, she had the look of a lovely person whose fortieth birthday had slid gently past not so very long ago. On the other side of the table the I-mean-business of Annie's blue serge suit was relieved by only the vaguest suggestion of frivolity in the red ribbon around her neck.

"Have a drink," Brenda said. She raised her own glass of something she had ordered earlier.

"Oh, I don't think I will. It makes me sleepy all afternoon. What did the doctor say?" Annie asked.

"What doctor?"

"I thought you were going to the doctor."

"Oh my poor baby," Brenda said. She took a hanky out of the snakeskin handbag and blew her nose. "My poor lamb." She struggled with her mucous membranes for a second.

"Mother, what's the matter?"

"Oh nothing," Brenda said miserably. "Brenda."

"Brenda." Annie said. It had never been easy for her to say it. She had once had a little friend, Brenda Fiukes, who liked to lock herself in the bathroom with Annie. Brenda, who was bigger and therefore the leader of the two, insisted that they take their

Lollipop underpants off and contort in front of the mirror on the bathroom door so they could get a good look at where their wee wees came from. Eventually Brenda worked out the more satisfactory arrangement of performing their examinations whilst sitting cross-legged in front of each other. Brenda Fiukes' older sister, who no doubt had installed the whole idea in Brenda's mind that babies would come out with her wee wee one day when she wasn't looking (thereby making it important for her to keep an eye on the situation every day), caught the two little girls checking each other out and probing each other in a most ominous way. She made such a stink about it, and the two mothers, too, that the name Brenda ever since had caused in Annie a feeling of tremendous unease, shame and sometimes even panic.

"Oh no," Annie said. "It isn't—" She faltered over the possible illnesses her mother might have.

"I can't stand to see you like this."

"Me. . . ?"

"I gave you everything. Your father and I. We tried our best, you know that you never wanted for anything. We fixed your teeth and sent you to college. There were always magazines in the house. There was no reason for you to end up like this." She looked at Annie with distaste. "Where did you get that awful suit?"

"My suit?" Annie said blankly.

"I thought I raised you better than that. No wonder, no wonder you have such an empty life."

"Mother, what are you talking about?"

"You come out to have lunch with your sick old mother and you look like an undertaker's daughter. Whoever told you you could wear a navy blouse with a navy suit? You look like a gangster. You won't have a drink . . . I know, I know. You want to be sharp for the market." Brenda sniffed. "I don't know what this obsession of yours is with money. You don't need money. We have enough money. Where is money going to get you anyway if you mix blue with blue?"

"It came that way," Annie said.

"What?" Brenda took a sip of her drink to clear her throat.

"The suit. It came with the blue blouse. It's the look. It even had a blue tie. But I took it off, I thought a red one would look better."

"Whose look? Not anybody I ever heard of. This year color is in, this is not a blue year, Annie. You're supposed to be splashy and bold. Look at me."

Annie looked at her.

"Well?" Brenda demanded.

"You look beautiful, Mother," Annie said, thinking that she might give the money back for the teeth and the schooling so she wouldn't ever have to hear about it again.

"Brenda."

"I love the dress, Brenda".

"Did that hurt? Did it hurt to say you love a pretty dress? Why don't you go shopping with me, Annie? I'll buy you a dress prettier than this one. It was expensive—"

"Don't tell me," Annie said quickly.

"But you should have it. Your father would be thrilled to buy you a few things. You shouldn't have to scrimp, a girl in your position. You need to look your best. You never know when looking your best might lead to something. We'll go on Saturday. Have a drink."

"Please mother, why are you carrying on like this? I don't need any clothes. I have everything I want."

"Why won't you have a drink to please your mother? I don't know what's come over you. You have everything, Annie: an adoring father, a loving mother, your sister and the children. And you won't dress well, you won't even have a drink and calm down."

"All right, Mother, I'll have a drink."

"Brenda."

"Brenda," Annie said sullenly.

"Good! Waiter." Brenda ordered Annie a Bloody Mary. Annie set her jaw.

"—Now," Brenda said, setting her own little jaw, and thinking that Annie was a tough nut, there was no getting around that. She resisted all loving impulses, look at her, blue on blue, her little mouth tucked in like a rosebud that wouldn't bloom. Annie resisted happiness, that's what she did. Brenda wanted to cry for her and sniffed experimentally, or else crack her on the head with a blunt instrument. Money. It was disgusting to see a girl dressing to make money, a young thing with all her life in front of her who thought all day about pennies and nickels. What man could stick with that? What Annie needed was to be tenderized with a meat cleaver. All this Brenda thought as she said "Now," and waited for Annie to take a sip from her Bloody Mary.

Annie took a sip and saw someone from her office. She waved.

"What happened with Nate?" Brenda asked. She broke a breadstick in half and stabbed a pat of butter with it.

"She told you," Annie said, the light dawning at last. She shook her head. Sara told. A lifetime of resentment washed over her. Sara had told again. It occurred to her, not for the first time, that she ought to leave town. If her leg were caught in a bear trap she couldn't be more imprisoned.

"Well?" Brenda said.

"We had a fight. We broke up," Annie said quickly. She blinked the beginnings of a tear out of her eye. "It doesn't matter."

"What do you mean it doesn't matter. Of course it matters. What did you do?"

"I didn't do anything."

"When a man leaves you after six years, believe me you must have done something."

"I didn't. It just didn't work out. It was an affair. It ended that's all."

"Annie!"

"Well, it was an affair."

"If you love someone you don't have an affair. You get married. I told you that a long time ago. Didn't I tell you? Why would he marry you if he had everything he wanted? And then you let him go, I don't understand you." Brenda shook her head.

"First you let him move in with you—do you close the deal first? No! You experiment. Some experiment. I told you you can't experiment with love. You had all the disadvantages of being married and none of the benefits. And then you let him leave just like that. You have to work for this kind of thing, hold on."

"Mother, shut up," Annie said as gently as she could.

"Shut up. Is that what you tell me when I'm trying to help you? Annie you're an ungrateful girl. I don't know what's going to happen to you. You're going to end up old and alone. I just know it. I coughed blood this morning."

"You told me. Did you go to a doctor?"

"Why should I go to a doctor? I know what's wrong. I'm worried about you, that's what's wrong."

"We might have broken up anyway, even if we were married."

"Don't be silly, Annie. Men look around all the time. They get restless. I know marriage isn't all a hayride. You have to work all the time, you have to hang onto them. Your father is a handsome man. You think I haven't had to think about that every day of my life? I know what opportunities he's had over the years. You know how it is in business. But, Annie, in marriage you have that commitment."

Brenda leaned forward eagerly. "You have that promise. That's what I hung onto all these years, the promise. You don't hold yourself high enough, that's your problem. You didn't ask for the promise in the beginning. I know you'd trade. You'd trade with your sister any day. It's been work for her, but it's worth anything. But you won't do a thing for it. Of course he had to leave you."

"We broke up," Annie said hotly. "And I wouldn't trade with Sara. I think her life stinks."

"He left you, Annie, face it." Brenda said severely.

Annie clutched her napkin. The threat in Brenda's words hit her so hard she could hardly breathe. And it wasn't the first time. So many times in restaurants when she had gone with Brenda for lunch, or after shopping, where she thought she would get something to eat, she ended up deep in a heart to heart that slashed her to the bone. Always it came as a surprise in a place where she couldn't respond. A place where there were people around, where the world was being normal, eating, having a drink, laughing at each other's jokes. A place where it would be crazy to scream or break the plates, or rend her flesh, all of which she dearly wished to do. She clutched her napkin with a familiar sense of helplessness, the rage and hurt caught in her fingertips. She knew everything that was wrong with what her mother thought, knew every hole in every argument she made, and yet it was true she was alone now. It was true she hadn't known how to close. But how could she have closed on a lover who said all along he didn't want a deal?

"Have a salad," Brenda said, looking over the menu and putting it down quickly. "We'll have chef salads," she said to the waiter who appeared at her summons.

The menu was taken from Annie's place without her having glanced at it. Run, run, the message fluttered through her thoughts like a thousand flags in an Independence Day parade. Run away before the unwanted salad eats you up. Beat it back upstairs where the market is a sure thing in spite of its ups and downs. Annie looked around wildly as if there might be someone who could save her before the salad came.

"What did you do?" Brenda said, but more gently now. "I want to know. I want to help you."

"I didn't do anything."

"You must have done something. Men don't leave just for nothing. I bet he had another girl."

"Mother, I don't feel very well. I don't want to talk about it."

"Of course you don't feel well. You're very unhappy. Look at what's happened to you."

"I don't want to talk about it."

"That's right, Annie. Hide your feelings. That's going to fix you right up. Hide your feelings a few more years like this and God knows where you'll end up."

"I'm doing very well. I happen to be the only woman in this family who can support herself. I'm not doing badly."

"I wouldn't call letting a man walk out on you doing well."

"I happen to be very successful; maybe I don't want to end my life an old married woman, who has to look in her husband's eyes to see herself."

Brenda blew her nose into her handkerchief and then reached for her compact. "Oh God. I look like death. I don't know what I'm going to tell your father. I just don't know."

"Don't tell him anything. It isn't his business."

"How can you say that?" Brenda said, shocked into snapping her compact shut and looking once more at her impossible daughter. "We suffer over you, worry about you. Love you, look after you as well as we can. Do you think it's easy for him watching you screw around for seven years, having people ask when the happy event is going to take place? And have to defend you. Sure, it's his business. You're his daughter and you're in a jam. What should we do, turn our backs on you? Do you think we have no feelings, I won't even talk about being embarrassed."

"Well, I'm sorry you take everything so hard. I'm not embarrassed. We broke up, that's all. It happens to people all the time."

"You are too, I can see it in your eyes. You wouldn't even come and tell me about it. If that isn't embarrassed I don't know what is."

Annie slumped over the table as the salad arrived. The noise in the restaurant had reached its highest lunchtime pitch. Normalcy everywhere, and in front of Annie the Bloody Mary looked like blood. She couldn't drink it, couldn't plunge into the salad on her plate. Inside of her everything had become still as if she were at the end of a long frozen corridor with closed doors down its length. At the end was one last door, glass, and through it on the other side was nothing but a vast expanse of white.

"Why don't you get your hair fixed," Brenda was saying, feeling Annie's silence and thinking that she was finally ready to listen. She forked a bit of ham and cheese into her delicate mouth. "Put a bit of color into it. It could look real cute, you know, if you had it curled. Get a pretty dress and call Nate for dinner. I bet you could get him back if you tried. You have the advantage of having lived with him for years. You know what he likes. He must have loved you or he wouldn't have stayed so long. Nobody else could get him that entrenched in just a few weeks. So he got another girl, you could forgive that. Be a little vulnerable, Annie. Show that you're not so tough. Show him that you need him, not all at once. Just be sweet. Meet him somewhere neutral a few times. Show him you care. I bet he thinks you don't care. You didn't fight for him, didn't make any demands. You didn't let him be a man, Annie, didn't let him claim you the way a man has to claim a woman. That's what happened." Brenda shoveled her salad into her mouth. She felt better now, had said what she wanted to say. And she could see that somewhere inside of her, stubborn as she was, Annie had been listening. She could see how Annie had a chance if she took it. Even Brenda's nose felt better. The walk was good. The air going home would do her good, too.

With the air of having done a good deed, Brenda finished her salad. She thought on the way home she'd see if she could find a really nice dress for Annie. And maybe after an hour or so she would have a cup of tea and try to sing. Annie might still get him back. Who knew what lurked in the hearts of men? She might even be married by the first of the year. Why not?

8

BEN SAT AT his desk with his feet up, worrying. His office was a foot smaller than Annie's, but it was a crucial foot. There wasn't space for another desk to fit comfortably so Ben didn't have to share. He had two extra chairs in his office, bookshelves on one wall and pictures on the other. Trout flies mounted under glass, a few anatomically perfect fish prints and some hunting scenes from the nineteenth century were hung close together, along with photographs of Ben in various kinds of sporting gear. He came from a small college town in Vermont where sports had been very important, and Ben had never done any of them, being too fat and too pimply to participate in any social activity other than eating. He had eaten through his youth with a vengeance and now had tremendous sentimental feelings for all forms of countryside. Trout streams made him giddy with longing. White water called to him in his sleep. He learned scuba diving in the swimming pool of his health club and once spent a whole day in Barbados under water. There was a picture of him in a wet suit on his wall that he consulted whenever he was low.

A few minutes before, he had jumped up and gone next door to talk to Annie, but when she saw him she hitched the phone to her shoulder and turned away. Ben went back to his office and bought a thousand shares of assorted stocks for two of his discretionary accounts. He always called first to say what he was doing, but the two clients in this case didn't care as long as he didn't make mistakes. He worked hard not to make too many mistakes. Then he sat back and stared at the wall. He was not looking at his books, however.

On the other side of the wall where Ben had his desk, Annie had hers. But thin as the partition between them was, they couldn't hear each other's conversations. Now Ben was worried about who she might be talking to. He leaned closer to the wall in an effort to hear. He couldn't. A little while ago Ben had had a conversation that surprised him very much. At first he was just surprised, and then he felt his life was changing shape as he spoke.

Nate had called. He wanted to know how Annie was.

"She's fine," Ben said. "Why do you ask?"

"Well, I'm a little worried about her. Is she really all right? What's she doing?"

"She's probably on the phone."

"But what's she doing, you know, with herself?"

Ben was silent for a moment. "What do you mean?" he said finally.

And then Nate said that Annie had reacted so coldly to his departure he was a little concerned about it. Well, he expected her to do *something*. Throw plates, scream, call him up at work every day, make him feel rotten. But he hadn't heard a word from her, nothing. Silence. It was getting him down. After six years that was pretty cold blooded, didn't Ben think so? Ben was so surprised he didn't answer for a long time.

"What does she say about me? Is she very mad?"

"Well," Ben said, "well, well."

"Tell me. I feel kind of bad about it."

"Well," Ben said again. He felt his spirits rising like a rainbow after a heavy storm.

"I'm living with Rita," Nate added.

"Rita?"

"Well, you know how it is. You just get to a point where it's all or nothing. Rita has a much more relaxed life style."

Rita was a model Ben had gone out with a year before for a short time. She was someone Nate had used in a commercial and brought to dinner one night for Ben. A blonde so stunning it was hard to look at her for more than a second or two at a time. Rita was so thin she had no discernible fanny, and she had no eyelashes when she went to bed at night. She had to have dinner at five-thirty because she felt nothing metabolized after six. Several times he had taken her out to dinner where the price was fixed and Rita ate only one of six oysters and the watercress that garnished her main course.

"And she's away a lot of the time. Right now she's in California. Ben, what does Annie say about me? I kind of want to get together and talk about it, but I thought I'd find out how the land lies before I called."

"I don't know, Nate. I think it may be a little late for that."

"I wanted to take her to lunch somewhere nice. I thought I'd help her through it, talk it over, you know. I've been thinking about how it ended. What do you mean 'it's too late'? God, does she have someone else already?"

"I think she might."

"No wonder . . . God, I'm surprised. No, I'm not surprised. Who is it? Was it going on before? I bet it was. Jesus. Ben, what should I do?"

"Let it end, it had to end sometime," Ben said firmly.

"Why did it have to? I was hoping she and Rita would be . . . friends."

"I think you're an asshole," Ben said suddenly, quite forgetting that there had been a time or two in his own life when he had pressed friendships on past and present lovers, certain they would like each other simply because he liked both of them. Of course, Nate wanted both of them. Ben was disgusted with this childish selfishness.

"You do?" Nate replied incredulously. "You think Annie's better than Rita?"

"I've got another call. Listen, I think you ought to let it go with Annie. She's doing fine. Why stir things up? I've had a lot of experience with these things. Believe me, once it's over, it's better to let go. And Rita's really something."

Ben hung up quickly and looked at the picture of himself in a wet suit. His heart was beating very fast at the thought of Annie Flood standing beside him in a trout stream. Annie in bed with him in a country inn. In a duck blind at dawn in the spring, or was it fall? Wait, or in a bikini in the Virgin Islands. He got up and charged into her office. She was on the phone.

Fifteen minutes later he sat there terrified that Nate might have realized that indeed he was an asshole, had called Annie and now they were making up. Finally he could stand it no longer and went and sat on the edge of her desk prepared to wait until she hung up.

After a minute or two in which she showed no signs of finishing up, he stopped looking idly out at the boardroom and realized he had an excellent opportunity to examine her without being observed. He did this pretty thoroughly for a while, and his conclusion was that Nate *was* an asshole. He was particularly absorbed by Annie's very lovely, slender, agitated, bitten-looking fingers. He did not realize as he was examining her that Carl was watching him and not liking what he saw.

Carl saw that Annie was keeping a truly boring conversation about bonds in Idaho going far longer than strictly speaking she had to. She was intent on the scene out her window and looked as if she would never hang up.

It was clear to Carl, who kept an eye out for such things, that Ben had finally cast his eye upon Annie in spite of Annie's recent protestations to the contrary. He was outraged by the intrusion of such vileness into his territory. Annie was the person with whom he shared an office. She was, in fact, his office mate. Women in offices in general, and his office mate in particular, should be safe as well as immune from such grievous offenses as office lust. He trembled with anger on behalf of all women in offices. He seethed at Ben swinging his leg where it hung from the corner of Annie's desk. He wondered what he could do.

He looked down quickly as Annie hung up and swung around in his chair. He wouldn't look. Annie got mad when he interfered in her life. He dialed his wife but couldn't get through. When he put the phone down there was a pause perceptible to everyone.

Then Annie looked up at Ben expectantly. "Well?" she said.

That "well" spoke oceans to Ben. It was a "well" of recognition, a "well" of surrender to the inevitable. Her eyes were as dark as the smoke from a Con Edison stack in January. "Well," indeed. He felt an even greater surge of excitement from her eyes than he had from the bitten look of her tragic knuckles. All other women paled to nothing before Annie's fiery, dark-circled eyes. A woman who burned in private, now that was a woman a man could give his heart to.

"Well," Annie said. "You love things in the ground. How about a couple of hundred of the best from Idaho? I know where you can get a lot of potatoes at a discount, and you'll never gain an ounce." Carl winced, but Annie ignored him.

"Triple A bonds sponsored by a farmer's coop, you can't go wrong."

"Annie," Ben breathed.

"What?"

Carl looked up fiercely. He couldn't believe the insult he was being forced to endure.

Ben muttered and stopped. It was hard to imagine now how he had overlooked Annie for so long. There she was, right in his own office, the girl he had been looking for all this time. And she was free, alone in her bed and she hadn't even told him. What modesty, what style she had. He longed to take her in his arms right then and tell her he loved her. He might have been moved to do this if a sharp pain on his left temple hadn't made him turn his head. Carl had an arsenal of rubber bands out on his desk and was shooting paper clips at him.

Annie coughed into her knuckles.

"Cut that out."

"What's on your mind, Ben?" Annie asked innocently. She watched Carl aim another paper clip.

"Well, I was wondering if you were doing anything tonight. Shit." Ben turned around angrily. "What do you think you're doing?"

Carl dialed his wife again. Still in a meeting.

"Yes," Annie said, laughing.

"You will?" he said eagerly.

"Yes, I'm doing something."

"You are, what? Jesus Christ!" A paper clip flew over his head.

"He always does that," Annie said.

"How do you stand it? Oh Annie, have dinner with me tonight."

"He usually stops if I ignore it. Stop it, Carl, Ben doesn't like it." Annie giggled.

"Uh, I thought it would be nice if we just went out on our own. I have something I want to talk with you about, something personal."

Carl smiled to himself. Annie was as good as married. She wasn't going to take any of Ben's crap. Nice indeed, it was disgusting, even the thought of it. He aimed another paper clip and waited for Annie to tell Ben to piss off, Jerk.

Her phone rang, though, and she took the call. She chatted for a few seconds while Ben stolidly sat there. He had a red mark on his forehead and one on his neck. When Annie hung up she didn't say, "Piss off, Jerk." She said, "What did you say? I'm sorry, I forgot."

Ben's secretary stood in the door. "Mr. Allen for you. He says it's important."

"I'm taking you to dinner tomorrow night. That's a definite."

Annie hesitated for a second and then made a funny motion with her head. It was hard to tell whether it was a yes or a no motion. Annie didn't know what it was herself.

But Ben decided it was a yes. "Well, that's settled then." He slapped his knee. "Tomorrow night, that's great."

Carl aimed fast and shot a paper clip at his ear. Paper clips on the ear stung a great deal, though they were not as good as a beheading. But Ben got up to take his call and the paper clip hit the bookshelf instead.

9

ANNIE WAS in a T-shirt and jeans, and was rubbing at her wet head with a towel when Ben turned up at her door the next evening with one red rose in green tissue paper. He had gone home after work and showered and shaved for the second time that day and changed his clothes, humming all the time. He felt buoyed up and excited as he hadn't felt in a long time. He wore a new Italian blazer and an English shirt.

On the way up in the elevator he had hoped that she would move close to him when she opened the door, close enough to touch. He was sure she recognized his feelings, though she had pretended not to. He was sure he saw a glimmer in her eye that afternoon when he passed her office and waved two fingers through the window. All day since yesterday he had been consumed by thoughts of her and how she would be. In love. When she opened the door, she would move close to him and raise her lips for a soft kiss, or maybe not so soft a kiss and he would feel that slender body whose lines he knew so well, but didn't know at all. He was sure she'd be passionate.

"Oh hello, Ben, want a drink?" she said casually, stepping back and leaving the door for him to close.

He was unnerved for a minute. Usually when he came to collect women they were honed to a fine edge, their avidness displayed in bright spots on cheekbones, brilliant lips, murky eyes, hair like the froth on a wave. "Oh, it's *you*." They acted surprised to see him, but not for long. Women loved him, they had for years.

"Am I early?" He put the rose behind his back. She did say it was okay, didn't she? They had a date.

"I'm late. I had to do an errand for my sister. I felt so grubby I had to have a bath. You don't mind sitting for a minute, do you? My hair will be dry in a minute." Annie noted the Italian blazer.

"That's just like my suit jacket," she said. "I like them when they wrap around like that without any flaps." She laughed. "You can't have much of a fanny, though, or you look like a brick."

To one who once looked very much like a brick, even a stout bit of masonry wall, the comment struck a fearful note. Did Annie think he looked like a brick wall? She moved off, patting her head absently with the towel. From the back she didn't look like a brick. He had lost his chance for the kiss and now faltered with the rose. He knew he was really in love this time because she seemed so perfect in spite of being late and having wet hair. The T-shirt alone, just plain red and shrunk in the wash, was enough to send him spinning years back into the black hole of adolescent inadequacy. He couldn't think of a thing to say and was overcome with the primitive desire to grab her and squeeze a tit.

"What would you like to drink?" Annie patted the sofa for him to sit down.

"Do you have water?"

"Lots, is that what you want?"

"It's for this." He held out the green tissue paper and she turned around and frowned doubtfully.

"For me?"

He nodded, feeling like a jerk.

"Thanks," she said. "That was nice of you." She moved off again, tearing away the paper. "Fix yourself a drink, I'll be right back."

Annie put the rose in the water glass in the bathroom. It stuck out of the glass a long way, diagonally like a slash. She took it into her room and watched it while she dried her hair. It was a better-quality rose, tightly coiled. But it didn't show signs of opening while she dried her hair. After her hair was dry and straight as a pin except for a little comma at the end that she disliked because it was such a poor excuse for a curl, she looked in the mirror for a long time. It seemed to her that rarely had she ever seen such an ordinary, such a plain, such an altogether unpromising human being. Now she was sorry she had confirmed the date for dinner with Ben just because Carl wasn't there to jump to a conclusion. She wasn't hungry and Ben's idea of a good time was a girl in gold lamé. She hated his new jacket and his sincere blue eyes and the rose that she accepted like a grievance she'd hold against him. Finally, she threw a sweater over her head and put on quite an old jacket.

All this time in the living room Ben wondered what she could be doing for so long. Several times he had to remind himself that Annie was the one true love of his life to avoid being rather annoyed. Then he was annoyed when she reappeared unchanged.

"I'm ready," she said.

"Well, what do you want to eat?" he said, quite piqued that he was expected to go out with someone who looked as if she had just that afternoon been stolen from one of the better girls' schools. No eye shadow, no color on her mouth, a Shetland sweater the color of prunes. It seemed pretty clear that Annie didn't care, that she was leaving her face at home. This was a face he had never seen before.

"Oh, a hamburger would be fine. I'm not very hungry," she mumbled. "We could go over to Daly's and listen to the juke box."

"A hamburger? I got a table at Mr. Chow's," Ben said. His eyebrows beetled into a disappointed frown.

"I'm not dressed for Mr. Chow's. Let's have a hamburger."

"You could get dressed for Mr. Chow's," Ben said looking at his watch. "Or you could go like that."

"I don't want to," Annie said.

"I don't want a hamburger. I had a hamburger for lunch. It was awful."

"I'm sorry it was awful."

"I had heartburn all afternoon," Ben added.

He had gotten up to go, but hadn't moved to where Annie stood by the door. Neither felt this was turning out well. They faced each other from opposite sides of the room

"I'm sorry," Annie said again. In the past when they had gone out there had always been four of them all trying to talk at the same time. This was gloomy. Annie sighed.

"Oh well," Ben shrugged. "You couldn't have known."

"No," she agreed. Then she said "I'm sorry" a third time. "I guess I just don't feel very festive. I must be tired."

"I wanted to take you out for a good time, just the two of us. I thought it would be fun." He moved across the room and took both of her hands. He stood for a second holding the two of them in front of him. They seemed like limp little birds, dispirited, fluttering slightly.

"Well, it's not like our usual parties," Annie said. She looked at his hands holding hers and gave him such a wry rueful sort of smile that he was completely disarmed.

They compromised by going around the corner to an Italian restaurant where it was quite dark and they couldn't see each other. Annie talked a lot about the market and drank more red wine than she realized. Whenever she drank too much she wanted to take her clothes off and sing an aria. It wasn't very long before she felt like singing an aria even though she knew she was really very depressed.

When the plates were gone and there was nothing but an expanse of white cloth between them, Ben's fingers reached for hers across the table.

"Your place or mine?" he murmured.

"What?" Her hand skittered away to the safety of her wine glass.

"I said, your place or mine?"

"Oh, that's a joke, right?" Annie smiled. "Ha, ha."

"No, it isn't. I want to make love to you. I've been thinking about it since yesterday. I haven't done a thing all day. I love you."

Annie choked on a sip of wine.

"You can come to my place if you want to. I've just had it painted white. We could go to work together in the morning. Wouldn't that be fun?" He looked at her anxiously. "Are you all right? Here, have a sip of water."

Annie coughed herself red in the face, but it was so dark it didn't matter. Then she took out her compact and dusted her face so thickly with powder she was sure it would crack if she smiled. How did he know about Nate?

"I'm not dressed for work," she said. "Or love," she thought. Then asked, "Why white?" because the other wasn't a good subject.

"I got tired of all that brown everywhere. It made me feel I was living in a cave. What's the matter, don't you like white?"

"Sure, white's very light." She shrugged. "How many coats did it take to cover?"

"Three. What do you say?"

"It must look a lot bigger."

"I mean about coming home with me?"

"I'd like some coffee," she told the waiter who had appeared and was hovering, waiting to see what Annie would say. Was she going to go home with him or not?

"Espresso please," she said.

"Annie, I know you've broken up with Nate," Ben leaned over and lowered his voice. "I know it, and I can't tell you how happy it made me. Why didn't you tell me? I thought we were very close."

"How do you know?"

"I tell you everything. I thought you knew you could come to me any time. I had no idea, no idea at all you weren't happy. You should have told me ages ago. I was really very hurt when I heard it from somebody else."

"From whom?"

"Well, Nate told me yesterday. I was flabbergasted. I really was, but I can understand how you've had enough of him," he added quickly. "What I don't understand is why you didn't tell me. How long would you have kept it a secret?" He shook his head. "I'm really upset."

Annie thought of the lipstick on his shirt that day he went to lunch with Suzy. She would have told him then but for the lipstick, and the fact that the news would have made her just another one among hordes of women who get left by their lovers. To Ben she would have been remains, like the girls he left himself.

"Oh, forget it," she said lightly. "It's not important."

"How can you say that? There isn't anything more important."

"I guess I don't think it's important."

"Oh Annie, let's go home."

"What for? I haven't got my coffee yet."

"I told you. I want to make love to you. I've always wanted to." He took a deep breath and let it out. Yes, it was true. He'd always wanted her. Sometimes when he came into her office and she looked up at him, her smoky eyes and the tender arch of her neck made him slink back to his desk feeling that neither he, nor life, was worth very much. At those times he longed for a Mallomar but called some girl instead, his candy of adulthood.

Annie shook her head. "I'm not like that," she said after a long minute.

He looked puzzled. "Not like what?" He held out his hand for her to take, but she didn't take it. After a time he had to take it back.

"I'm not like you. I can't go to bed with somebody just like that, casually, because there's nothing else to do. I did that once, and it was a mistake."

"This isn't casual," he said quickly. "This is serious."

"Let's talk about something else. I need a new coffee table in my living room. What kind do you think would look best?"

"What don't you like about me?" Ben said stiffly. "Do you think I'm not attractive? Is it the way I dress? I'll change for you."

"Don't be silly."

"Well, what is it then?"

"I lived with someone for six years. Doesn't that bother you?"

"Oh, that."

"Yes, that."

"He was an asshole," Ben said staunchly. "I'm glad you dropped him."

"He left me," Annie said flatly. Every time she said it she got tears in her eyes. She had been practicing saying it in front of the mirror at home, that their little affair was over, just so she would look strong in front of other people. But so far practice hadn't helped. Her eyes filled up.

"Well, it's not something to fall apart over," Ben said firmly.

"You're right. I don't really care." Annie shrugged (she was a great shrugger) and blew her nose.

"I won't leave you," Ben said earnestly. "I'll stay with you forever."

"That's nice of you, Ben."

"I feel strongly about this. You have a male brain," he went on, feeling rather encouraged. "That's important, and I'm very— attracted to you. I always have been."

"What's a male brain?"

"I also think you'd be great in bed. What don't you like about me—is it my face?" He stuck out his chin so she could have a good look at it. Other girls had been willing to stake their whole lives on the jut of his chin. He had a good strong chin, no question about that.

"I do not have a male brain," Annie said indignantly. Whatever it was, she didn't want it. And she was very doubtful about being great in bed.

"You have a cowboys and Indians approach to the market. You're my sleeping beauty."

Sleeping beauty is a term in the market for a desirable and vulnerable company ripe for takeover.

"This sleeping beauty only wakes up once every hundred years. I've had my fling for this century." She had another sip of wine to cover her confusion. Just looking at him made her nervous. What did he think he was doing anyway?

"Annie, you don't understand. I love you."

"Oh, Ben, you bound from person to person without a second thought. You think you can take anybody you want and then just let go when you're finished. You don't know anything about love." She shivered. That was a harsh thing to say, especially considering his practical experience. She couldn't even begin to imagine what his hands on her would feel like, shook her head to banish the thought.

"You loved him," Ben said in horror.

"Who?"

"That jerk. He broke your heart."

"Oh really," Annie said. "Really." That was just silly.

Ben hunched down in his chair, suddenly burdened with this vile new thought. She loved him. "I'm sorry," he said.

"I am too, let's forget it." She sipped her espresso now.

"Well, I thought you could feel something for me," he said morosely.

"Oh Ben, I feel something for you."

"Yeah, disgust," he said. His voice was filled with self-pity.

"Well, I don't want to go to bed with you. But I *like* you. I've always liked you." She put her hand on his arm. But when he put his other hand on top of hers, she took hers away. "Can't I just like you?"

"Did you like him?"

"Who?"

"That asshole."

"Oh stop it. It doesn't matter any more."

"Or did you *love* him. It's important to me. I have to know."

The waiter returned and asked them if they wanted anything else. In one voice they said no thanks.

"Let's go," said Annie folding her napkin. "It was a lovely dinner."

"He said you wanted a family. You wanted to get married and have children, and all that. He said he wasn't ready for it."

"He was lying. I don't want to get married. I'd hate to have children. I'm really very glad it's over." But her stomach clutched as she said it, and for a second she thought she might throw up before she got to the street.

"I'd like children." Ben grabbed his American Express card and followed Annie out.

"No, you wouldn't. You'd have a dozen by now if you really did." She gulped at the air. He wanted to go to bed with her; why did it make her feel so queasy?

"I didn't have the right person to make them. Now I have the right person. You're the right person, Annie," he said persuasively.

They pushed out into the night. It was getting colder now. It was definitely getting on toward winter. Annie shivered in the air. Time to start thinking about a coat. Don't think about Ben making babies, she warned herself.

"I can feel it in my gut," Ben said. He put his arm around her shoulder and drew her close for a hug. And all these years she'd been right there, living with someone else. Funny how things happened.

"What?" Annie said.

"Love." He put his face in her hair and sniffed its freshness. Annie didn't smell of musk or mink oil. She smelled of Pantene, not a bad company. He squeezed her shoulder and felt a responsive tremble. It felt a lot like love.

The tremble, however, came from a sudden gust of wind up Lexington Avenue and a memory that suddenly popped into Annie's head. One night several years ago, Ben came to dinner with a bottle of Kwell in his pocket. He wanted to have a quick bath in the bathtub before they went out to dinner so he could shampoo the crab lice out of his pubic hair. He couldn't imagine where they had come from. Ben said he'd scrub the tub with Ajax afterward, and they'd all be dead anyway. But Annie said, "Hell, no." She didn't let him sit on the sofa, and didn't enjoy sitting next to him in the restaurant either.

"What shall we do now? Want to see a movie?"

"I'm very tired," Annie said. "I'm going home." She didn't like his touch. His breath in her hair, his arm around her shoulder. She didn't want to fall into something again. She wanted to run.

"I'll come with you," he was saying. "I hate to think of you sleeping alone."

"Or yourself. Forget it Ben, you're too busy for me. I wouldn't go to bed with you if you had a blood test and a certificate from the health department."

"So you do want to get married," he said triumphantly. "I knew it was that."

"Not that."

"But you don't have to worry about that. I'm ready. Touch me, this is the real thing." He came to a full stop in front of the Colonial Nut Shoppe in order to gaze into her eyes and so that she could gaze into his. So he could draw her into an embrace. "We can get a blood test later," he murmured

But Annie ducked and avoided his lips.

"Annie!" She had moved off so quickly he had to jig a little to catch up.

"Forget it. I mean it. Just forget it."

"Okay." He put his hands up in the air. "You win."

"Let's be friends," Annie said.

"Sure."

"That way nobody will be hurt," she added uneasily.

"Right."

They paced along in silence for a minute, came to a light and stopped on the curb. "I didn't mean to hurt you," Annie said after some deliberation. "I think you're terrific and everything. I really do."

"It's okay. Forget it."

"It's just that I'm really not interested in—any of it."

"You'll get over it."

"No, not this time. I like being alone. I really do."

"It's okay, Annie."

"Well, it was sweet of you to ask." As if his proposal to go to bed were like an invitation to a ball she couldn't attend. Sorry, health hazard in the kitchen, can't partake.

They got to her building and stopped under the awning. In a second as she looked at him she changed again, was sure he had herpes, and didn't think it was sweet of him to ask.

"Why do you always say you want to get married anyway?" she asked suddenly. "You know it's just a lie you tell everybody to work up some feeling. They all hate you afterward when you let them go. And what do you get out of it? Nothing. You ought to face it, you're like me. You wouldn't put yourself on the line for anybody. You're just rock bottom cold inside. Well, good night." She shook his hand quickly and then went inside without turning around.

Upstairs she saw that the rose had opened in the warmth of the room. It hurt to look at it so she put it away where she couldn't see it. What a mean and hurtful thing it was to talk that way, to give people roses and say he was in love. Even with the rose in the other room she could still feel the weight of his arm around her shoulder and the small kiss he placed beside her ear. And she could feel a strong pull like the tide, an undertow inside of her that wanted to succumb, and be adorable, even if it was only for a minute. Even though she knew that when he looked at her, he saw her naked, a piece of pastry on a tray, just another one he could have if he murmured the right words. He said he thought she would be good in bed. It gave her a knot of anxiety in her stomach thinking about it.

Suddenly she saw her mother sitting at lunch that day, demanding to know what she had done to make Nate run away. Why couldn't she just dress up and catch one unawares like her sister instead of ending up over thirty and fucking around. Well, she was a lifetime older than she had been at twenty-four when Nate moved in for a while just because. But nothing else seemed to have changed since then except her. Now Annie remembered what it felt like to feel rotten after a date. Somehow she was terribly embarrassed that she had let Ben take her out and pay for her dinner. And she knew that if this was dating, she was going to have to pass.

10

GORGE AVE-
nue ran northwest out of Pine Wood. All the finest houses were
set quite close to the road facing south or north and each other. It
was traditional in Pine Wood to set the houses facing each other
like that because of the striking show they made from the road.
The town was in a little valley called the gorge. For a hundred
and twenty years the houses stuck pretty much within the perimeters of the valley where the land was more uniform. Bit by bit one
town's north and south outskirts began to run into another until
there was no break between them. The whole of suburbia was
held together by a network of shopping centers exactly like shopping centers all over the country. If one were put down in the
shopping center between Pine Wood and the town below it, there
would be no way to tell what part of America one was in. It
looked like Cedarwood, New Jersey where there are no cedars, or
Marek, Long Island, or Northbrook, Illinois or Anaheim, California.

It took the last forty years to fill up the East Coast from
Boston to New York. And now with more and more companies
building their headquarters in huge industrial parks, suburbia
was heading west, too. There were no big companies in Pine
Wood yet, but the string of houses on Gorge Avenue had begun
to stretch northwest farther and farther away from the railroad
line and Route One, out toward what still resembled country
where the train didn't go. It was here that Sara and Martin chose
to build their house.

Martin's and Sara's site was quite far out on Gorge Avenue,
way out of town and west of the Merritt Parkway, too. But even so
far out, the houses were built on the road to be seen. Martin and
Sara were having an argument about this. They had gotten past
the French chateau Sara wanted, to look like a house down the

road with the curved red terra cotta tiled roof and the white stucco front. They had debated endlessly about having a Mexican compound, walled all around; a New England salt box, gray shingled; a builder's clapboard colonial painted white with green shutters. Sara wanted something to go with a picket fence if she couldn't have a chateau. Martin wanted a lawn.

Archie was one of Martin's clients. Archie said that he would design anything they wanted. They each described something different. Archie ignored them both and presented them with the plans of his specialty: a house he had built with some success in many resort areas. The house would be built on cement piers a foot or so above the ground. It would float like a flying saucer over the hilly land, going from one level to another without disturbing the surface of the ground at all.

The house would be unlike any other in the area. The basement wouldn't flood in the spring or fall because there would be no basement. There would be a two-story living room and the only stairs in the house would lead up to the main bedroom on a balcony over the living room. The living room would float through to the dining room, which would be a glassed hallway between the living-room building and the kitchen-studio-garage building. On the other side another float-through glass passage, this one a playroom or sitting room for children, would lead to a third building where there would be bedrooms for the children and the guest room.

Although it looked very big and had three buildings, this would not be expensive to build, Archie argued. But it fit with nobody's idea of a house. Sara pointed out that the dining room was a hallway. Archie said that a house should commune with nature. They should feel in all seasons as if they were outside, and nothing else but living in a window could achieve that effect. He planned to put solar reflectors in the roof, and wanted them to buy a windmill to make electricity so they could plug into the grid and have an all-electric house, free. Except, Martin said, that the windmill cost fifteen-thousand dollars. Archie agreed they could forego the windmill if they had to.

Sara and Martin dubiously studied the plans. Archie hurried them for approval because he wanted to sink the piers before the land froze. Without a large foundation, they would be able to start building before the spring. Sara and Martin faltered. They had something more—traditional in mind, something recognizable as a style. And Brenda and Jack thought the house looked atrocious.

Jack, who had never lived in a house except for one month a year in a moldy beach cottage on Cape Cod, particularly disliked the spread-out disorderly look of the place, and the fact that it would be made of wood that would turn gray with age. Sara dug her heels and asked for another plan. Archie insisted that he had met all their requirements in this design. Brenda thought they ought to get another architect who would do what they wanted. Martin didn't want to do that because another architect might lead them into basements and more expensive materials. Brenda asked Annie to knock some sense into them, and Martin, too, looked to Annie for support.

Since Annie's dining room was an alcove, she liked the idea of eating in a window. What was the point of living in a house that was as closed in as an apartment, she asked. She thought they ought to commune with nature, why the hell not? Annie did not exactly admire Archie Kurr who was a short, sloppy, plump person with a red nose and the shabbiest-looking clothes Annie had ever seen. But she suspected that Sara and her mother objected to his appearance more than his ideas, which were interesting, definitely peculiar. When Annie said, "Do it," Martin slapped her on the back with brotherly devotion. Annie was a peach, he'd always known it.

Now, dressed for hiking in the Arctic and armed with the plans, they stood first on one piece of land and then on another. They were arguing about where Archie had set this floating structure of his. It was Saturday. The leaves were gone from the trees, and the woods looked even more scrubby than before. The front of the property, the acres that faced the road, was lower than the land in the back. It was kind of marshy.

Archie was wearing a tweed jacket with patches on the elbows and a long scarf around his neck. He wore gloves and a knitted seaman's hat. He looked as if he had had a drink or two instead of his breakfast, but then Martin said his nose was always red, even in summer. Martin had chosen a hunting jacket from L.L.Bean, a heavy sweater underneath and Frye boots. Sara looked like a winter rabbit in a white curly lamb coat.

"Isn't it just bracing," she cooed, until she stepped into the marsh and got her leather boots wet.

Annie, who had come to see the leaves in their last stage and because she had nothing else to do, was bundled up in ski clothes she had never used for skiing. She quickly took charge of the children, who wanted to run off and find a deer for dinner.

Archie's plan called for building up a road through the marsh. On higher ground a flat side of the house, the garage actually, with no windows, would face the road and look like the side of a barn. The rest of the house would face northwest and southeast to catch the sun all day long. The house would be set up high and hidden in the woods. The dining room and living room would look out on the small plateau that sloped down to the gurgling brook for which they had paid extra.

For an hour or more, Sara and Martin and Archie paced over the four acres arguing bitterly about the view from the road. Sara wanted the gorgeous expanse of the three buildings to be visible from the road. She wanted a magnificent family compound. And Martin could not help but agree that such a placement would look impressive to cars passing by.

Archie refused to build in a marsh and that was that. They'd have sewage problems, he said, and the land was too low. His pudgy face was red with the cold, and he wheezed with impatience.

"Don't you understand that not one of these houses on the road gets any sun? I don't care how big or small the windows are, all they have is filtered light and all they see is road."

"But to drive into what looks like a barn," Sara lamented.

"That's the surprise of it. That's what makes it so witty and unusual," Martin said appeasingly.

"I don't want a witty house. Where did Annie go?"

"She's down there by the stream," Martin said.

"Oh, Martin, you don't suppose she's stupid enough to let one of the children fall in. I'm so nervous about that water. Oh, Love, would you be an angel and tell her to come back."

"And you could put the windmill right back here. Then you'd really be blending all the elements of nature," Archie went on.

"Forget the fucking windmill," Martin said.

"Oh, oh. My feet are so wet. Martin, tell Annie to bring those children back here. What are they doing down there?"

"Sara, more than your feet will be wet if you build down there," Archie said. "You don't want a damp house, do you?"

Down by the stream, Annie crouched with the children, look-

ing for a trout or a toad or something. Her stomach gurgled with
hunger. She had had a cup of coffee in the morning, but now
with no one else to feed she could never manage to make anything for herself. She would take a package of English muffins
out of the refrigerator and look at them. They always looked cold
and hard to her. She would imagine how they would taste toasted
with lumps of melting butter on them, but she couldn't make the
leap of putting one into the toaster. The eggs, too, looked inedi-
ble in their shells, and the bacon turned green in its cellophane
before she got around to eating it.

During the week it was better. She got a roll at the deli and ate
it in her office, savoring the crumbs while Carl watched her
wistfully. She got a certain pleasure from Carl's discomfort. But the
weekends were long. On weekends she had taken to going out
early. She took some clothes to the cleaner every Saturday whether
they needed cleaning or not and then walked around until eleven
when the museums opened. After an hour or so she broke down
and went over to Sara's to see what the children were doing. They
were always glad to see her.

"Is anybody hungry?" Annie asked after what seemed to be a
week of futile hunting for something alive. "I think everybody
went to Florida for the winter."

"Hungry, hungry," Lucy said.

"Me, too."

"Good. Let's go. Let's take the car and get a hamburger."
Annie stood up and stretched.

"Yay, McDonald's," Donald said.

They hiked up the hill to where Sara looked frozen against
the sky.

"Look up here on the hill, see what you can see," Archie said.

"I can see another house over there," Martin said.

"I mean, you can see the sky. You can see the brook. You
have a place to put the swimming pool right here. From the
dining room you'll see the swimming pool; on the other side you
can have a Japanese garden. This is very good land for a Japanese
garden."

"Nothing grows in a Japanese garden," Sara said. "Does it,
Martin?"

"This is the kind of land that cries out for a Japanese garden," Archie repeated. Martin nodded.

"There's always a tree in a Japanese garden," he said helpfully. He went and took Sara's hand. "I'm sure you'll love it."

"But Martin—" Sara broke off before she could protest further. First she'd lost her picket fence, then her red tiled roof, then her green shutters. She was losing the battle for a house facing the road like all the others in Pine Wood. Archie wanted the place to look like a farm with a barn and a windmill and now a Japanese garden that didn't seem to go with anything. For a minute she almost collapsed and cried.

"Martin, what about your lawn?" She snuffled, with a tissue to her nose.

"Never mind the lawn. We'll get some really wonderful rocks and set them carefully. And then we'll have a wonderful tree right in here and a few, very few, wildflower kind of flowers coming up here and there," he said enthusiastically. "I just know we'll love it."

"Oh, Martin, what about my roses?"

"There's serenity in rocks, Sara," Martin breathed. "Just think, we can put a bird feeder in here. There are supposed to be some great birds in this area, aren't there Archie? Look, Annie's coming back. Hey, Annie, did you find anything?"

"We dug in the ground," Annie laughed. "But not even the worms seem to be at home. Have you decided where to put the house?"

"They want to put a Japanese garden right where you're standing," Sara cried.

"How lovely."

"But I wanted a rose garden."

"That would be nice, too. Listen, the kids and I are hungry. Do you want to go out for lunch now?" Annie said. The kids hung on her hands, hopping from one foot to the other.

"Great," Sara said. "Let's go to lunch."

"I don't think we're finished yet," Archie broke in. "I want to pound some stakes."

"Pound stakes?" Sara cried. "What for?"

"Just to give an idea of where it will be. It won't take long. I want you to be able to walk around in it so you'll know how it will be."

"You don't have to, Sara," Martin said quickly. "I can do it with Archie, if your feet are wet."

Sara looked at them doubtfully.

"Go ahead. Have lunch with Annie and the children. That's a good idea."

"What are you going to do?"

"We're just going to pound a few sticks, that's all. Approximately where the house is set in the plans, and then you'll get a better idea of how it will look."

"I want to see it," Sara said firmly.

"You can come back and see it," Martin suggested. "You don't have to stand here in the cold."

"I want to stand here in the cold. We're planning my house."

"Angel, I thought your feet were wet."

"It's okay, now they've frozen."

"Oh, Sara," Martin said.

"Go ahead, Annie, take the children," Sara said. "I'll stay here."

"Do you want me to bring back food?" Annie asked. "How long do you think you'll be?"

"Yes, that's a great idea. Bring food," Sara said. "The thought of it will keep me going."

Annie took the children down the slope through the marsh to where the two cars were parked by the road. Then she had to go back through the marsh again because Martin had put the key to the car in his pocket and had forgotten to give it to her. Finally settled into the front seat, Annie turned and checked the children in the back. "All set?" she asked.

She revved the engine with a certain lack of expertise. The car eased out into the road and shot down the hill. Annie felt an unexpected thrill. She turned on the radio and fled down the winding hilly road with a wonderful sense of release, mixed with the suspense of not quite knowing whether she might fly off the road and hit a tree.

It took twenty minutes to get to the local McDonald's. Annie was feeling decidedly chipper and fond of the country by the time she got there. She was even able to place the car in a slot near the entrance without slicing the car on either side. As soon as she got inside the warm building and was surrounded by the smell of old oil and cooking hamburgers, she decided they would not buy food and hurry right back to the site where they would have to huddle miserably in the car with their hamburgers and french fries. They would sit there and eat in comfort.

Annie ordered two hamburgers and french fries and one Big Mac and one shake with two cups and coffee, while Donald wandered around looking for a table. Annie looked around. This was not like the McDonald's closest to her, where the clientele was every color of the human rainbow and as likely to steal one's handbag as one's table. It certainly looked the same inside, but the Pine Wood McDonald's was all parents and children and teenagers with their own cars.

She took the tray and went to the table Donald had chosen over in the corner by the window. He had taken his jacket off and Lucy's and had put them on the two extra chairs around the table, claiming it like an adult.

"Thank you, Donald," Annie said. "That was a good job. Lucy, do you want a high chair?"

Lucy nodded.

"I'll get you one. You stay here." Annie went across the crowded room and found a high chair. When she came back, Donald was deep in conversation with the man and the little girl at the next table. The little girl was about Donald's age. Her hair was the color of a new chamois cloth, straight and glossy. It hung down in the back and curled under at the bottom just like Annie's. She had bangs that covered her eyebrows and large dark eyes, also like Annie's, that held a very serious expression as she listened to Donald talk about his floating house, and his mommy and daddy.

Annie was touched right away by the face of the child listening to Donald. She looked sad and very small next to the father. Annie didn't notice the father except to register that he was large and had black curly hair and a closely cropped beard.

But he had been eyeing Annie from the moment she walked in. She cut a trim figure in her red ski pants and red-and-white parka. She had a jaunty red knitted cap with a white pom pom on the top and the definite air of being a visitor. He noted the well-defined features, her small nose, small mouth, large dark eyes, tawny complexion now pink from the cold. When she walked in from the outside and pulled her hat off, her sandy hair shook free with admirable springiness. Her face was a delicate oval and she had rounded cheeks and a dimple on one side by her mouth.

When the boy had come near, he invited him to take the table next to his and asked his name. Donald obliged by giving his life history, omitting most of the details that might be of interest to a grown-up. His name was Donald. That was Lucy, his sister who was dumb. She still needed a bottle to go to bed. And they were going to have a floating house if his mommy didn't go crazy from the noise. No, that wasn't his mommy. That was Annie. His mommy was on the hill with her feet frozen solid.

Annie appeared with the high chair.

"Come on, Lucy, your hamburger will get cold," she said. She turned her head and smiled at the little girl at the next table, and the dimple popped into her cheek by her mouth.

Annie hoisted Lucy into her chair and unwrapped a hamburger for her. "Come on, Donald. We don't have much time."

She sat down, opened her jacket and unwrapped her Big Mac. She took a hungry bite and then realized when her mouth was fuller than it should be that the man with the little girl was sipping his coffee and watching her chew. Usually when someone watched Annie eat she took smaller bites and tried to appear uninterested in her food. She poked at it delicately and pretended that she was taking it in merely to stay alive.

Now, however, in the McDonald's in Pine Wood it didn't seem vital to appear dignified. She didn't know anybody and nobody knew her, and anybody who went to a McDonald's wasn't worth knowing anyway. So she sighed and let Lucy take the meat out of the roll and eat it like a savage. She was only a child after all. And though Annie managed to keep most of the many ingredients inside her sesame-seeded bun, she ate her own with the same abandon.

Donald ate with a little more finesse. He was sitting in the chair closest to the people at the next table and when he had eaten about half of his hamburger, he turned to them and announced. "I'm seven."

The man smiled. "Are you?"

"Yes, I can read."

"Oh, Donald," Annie said.

"How old is she?" Donald pointed at the little girl.

The man turned to her. "How old are you, Vanessa?"

Vanessa put her napkin over her face.

"I'm seven," Donald said.

"You are not," Annie protested. "Tell how old you really are."

"Seven," Donald insisted.

"I bet you're really five," the man said. "Vanessa is four-and-a-half."

"I'm six," Vanessa said quickly. She looked at Annie. "I like your outfit," she said.

Annie broke into a huge grin. "Why thank you. I like your outfit, too. And you have a beautiful name."

"Vanetha," she said carefully.

"It's beautiful," Annie said.

"What's your name?" Vanessa asked.

Annie hesitated, not sure whether to give her first name or her last name or no name at all.

"Annie," Donald blurted. "She's our Annie."

"Luthy," Lucy said.

"Hurry up, kids," Annie said. "We have to go in a minute."

"Do you live here?" Vanessa asked.

"We live in New York," Donald said. "Seventy-eighth Street and Third Avenue. But not Annie."

"Daddy lives in New York," Vanessa said. "He a doctor."

Annie smiled.

"I live here," Vanessa added. "We're broken."

"Separated," the man corrected her quickly. "We're not broken."

"Oh," Annie murmured. She squashed up the box her hamburger had come in. How sad. She looked at the child. No wonder they looked so sad, the two of them sitting there alone on a Saturday. She crushed her napkin and her coffee cup. "Well, kids, are you finished?"

"No," they said in one voice.

"I'm Herb Mickle," the man said. "Are you alone?"

Annie was too taken aback to answer.

"No," Donald said sharply. "She's with us."

Herb Mickle smiled wryly. "I can see that. How old are you really, Donald? Are you sure you're not ten?"

"You know I'm not ten," Donald said.

"You're fourteen," Annie laughed.

Donald's mouth puckered. "Annie, you know I'm only four," he said tearfully.

"Oh Donald, I know you are. I was only kidding."

"Don't tease, Annie. It's not nice," Donald whimpered.

"You sound like your mother," Annie said.

"Well, you do tease," he said.

"Forget it, Precious. We have to go now." Annie looked quickly at Herb Mickle. "Their parents are building a house here," she explained, knowing she didn't have to explain. But she didn't want to be rude, and they seemed nice. Maybe Vanessa would be at school with Donald. She smiled at Vanessa. She was a sweet little girl.

"They're standing on a hill trying to decide where to put the house. It's very cold and they're waiting for hamburgers," Annie added.

"Where?" Herb asked.

"Way up on Gorge Avenue."

"Vanessa and her mother live on Gorge Avenue. About a half a mile out of town."

"Oh, you're deep in civilization," Annie said.

He laughed. "If you wanted to call it that." He raised his dark eyebrows. "Do you live in New York? You look like a New Yorker."

"What does a New Yorker look like?" Annie laughed too.

"It's an air," he said, "just a way of being, I guess."

"Well, we have to go," Annie said without moving.

"I know what it is. You look competent." He smiled.

"I'm a stockbroker," Annie said quickly. "That must be it."

"Really?" Herb said delightedly. "I've been very dissatisfied with my broker lately."

"I'm finished," Donald said. He squashed his things together. "Let's go."

"Finisssed," Lucy echoed.

"Who's your broker?" Annie propped her elbow on the table.

"Oh, just somebody at Kidder Peabody."

"Let's go!" Donald said impatiently.

"Who are you with?" Herb asked.

"Howard and Plunket in the Pan Am Building.

"I'm very dissatisfied with my broker." Herb looked at her with deep seriousness. "Maybe you could give me some advice."

"If you like," Annie shrugged.

Donald pulled on her arm. "You said we had to go."

"Oh!" Annie remembered her sister and her frozen feet. Sara would be so mad. Sara would complain and demand to know what the hell had kept them. Didn't Annie take into consideration that Sara was standing there in the frigid cold waiting for her? Annie's face sobered at the thought of Sara's anger. She shook her head slightly, thinking how mean Sara would be because her feet hurt.

Herb hesitated at the fall of Annie's face. She looked to him as if she might be attached. Of course almost everybody was attached to somebody. He was sure she was taken. On the other hand, he liked her looks, and the way she was with children. He made a quick decision.

"Um, maybe we could have lunch one day," he said.

The dimple popped into Annie's cheek. Oh, fuck Sara, she thought. She turned her attention to Herb Mickle, the doctor, who wanted her advice because she looked competent.

"I'd like that." She beamed at the child. He had a nice child. "But I don't stay out long at lunchtime."

"I'm not really allowed out at lunch either," he confessed.

They smiled at each other. Both too busy for lunch.

"Well." Annie shook herself out of the warm feeling she had for this nice man and his nice child. "We really do have to go." She gathered all the things and went to the garbage to dump them out. He watched her.

She came back and pulled Donald into his jacket, Lucy into hers. "Say good-bye, kids."

"Good-bye, Vanessa," Annie said. She looked at Herb. "Good-bye." She turned away and pulled on her jacket, then waved her hand.

"Wait." He leapt out of his chair and followed her to where she had gone to order more food. He was quite a large person, heavier than Nate. He looked substantial, with a serious expression and a most interesting beard. Annie looked him over. He was a doctor; that made him okay. Maybe his wife was an intolerable bitch who had trapped him when he was young and honorable.

"Three Big Macs, three coffees and some cookies," Annie said. She smiled up at Herb. He was wearing a yellow cashmere sweater and a tweed jacket.

"What's your name?" he said.

"Annie Flood," Annie said.

"Really?" He thought about it for a minute. Then he nodded. "It suits you."

Annie collected her food and her children and herded them out to the car. By the time she got them settled and the car started, Herb had come out with Vanessa. They got into a fine green sports model Mercedes with M.D. plates. As Annie pulled out of the parking lot, Herb tooted his horn.

Annie blushed all the way up Gorge Avenue. It was silly to feel so damn good, she told herself. God damn stupid. But she couldn't help it. The drive in the country was so healthy. "Don't you feel *great?*" she demanded of the children. "Breathe that air!"

She felt so terrific not even Sara could depress her now. She thought of Sara without trepidation. If Sara said one thing, even the tiniest thing, she was going to hit her over the head with the hamburgers. But when they got back, Sara took a look at Annie and wanted to know what had happened.

"Annie, you look—wonderful. Look at that color. What happened?" Sara said.

"We met a broken doctor," Donald said. "He's in love with Annie."

"What!" Sara said.

"Oh, nothing," Annie murmured. Then she said, "He's not broken, he's separated."

"He has a little girl, Vanetha," Donald added.

"Really," Sara whooped. She grabbed Annie and hugged her, almost knocking the bag of hamburgers out of her hand. "Oh, Annie, really?"

"It's nothing," Annie said modestly.

"Oh Annie, a doctor. How wonderful. I'm so happy. Is he cute?"

Annie shrugged. "He has a beard."

Sara hopped from one foot to the other. "I've never kissed anyone with a beard. Have you?"

"We just met," Annie said.

"I mean anybody else," Sara slung her arm around her sister. She did look kind of cute in that red suit. "Silly," Sara said.

"No, I don't think I have either." Annie laughed. They walked arm in arm through the marsh together, trying to hop over the wet parts. They marched giggling up the hill to where Archie and Martin were still driving stakes like maniacs.

"I waited and waited, Annie. I was afraid you weren't coming back. I was afraid that you had just taken off or had an accident. But I'm so glad now that you didn't hurry. Annie, I'm so happy you met someone."

Annie looked at the site. Suddenly it looked less forlorn. She could almost see the dining room glassed in, the passageway and the Japanese garden filled with daffodils in the spring. Maybe

Nate was the racehorse in her dream not fated to win. Maybe the silks stuffed down her throat were really the wrongness of him, choking the life out of her. Annie raised her face to the sky and puffed steam out of her mouth, thinking herself stupid to let such a little thing as a stranger's smile persuade her that she was not yet dead after all.

11

AFTER SHE met Herb, Annie went into a frenzy of housecleaning. Suddenly it seemed that everything in her apartment was old and shabby and charged with so many memories it was painful to come home. At first the emptiness of the bedroom without Nate's shirts in the drawers or suits in the bedroom closet had been a kind of suspension, like an oil slick on water too heavy to cut. Annie had to wait to see if it would dissipate, or he would return. For a while she almost thought he would. Return. She'd fixed life for him.

Nate hadn't liked the peonies on the sofa, so Annie had bought striped sheets of electric blue and brown and a coordinating quilt with a large herringbone pattern to make the bedroom seem his. The blind that went across the large double window was also blue, a thick woven thing deeply efficient at keeping out light. She had taken down the billowy white Swiss curtains that had been there before he came. Everything had been white then: white sheets, white shades, white dust ruffle around the bed, a white bedspread with more eyelet ruffle. It was as if she had been waiting for him to bring color to the place where she slept.

Or that was what she told herself when the room became blue and brown, with masculine prints on the walls, the whole thing a jangle of color and pattern that was never as restful for her as the white had been. For years after the change, she started out of her sleep, panicked by the darkness where she felt it should have been light. And she would have to piece together the present to make it right again. The blue, like blackout, on the window, the man asleep on the striped pillow, the comforter spiked with brown. In sleep she was nearly always afraid. Before Nate came she hadn't been afraid. But after he came, bit by bit, she had taken everything that was hers out of the room until there was nothing left except herself, anxious as a child being made to sleep without a nightlight. She was troubled by the way he had come to her, and other things. Every day she had a squirmy feeling that things were wrong. Yet the man was there, blonde as a beach boy; and, next to him, the uncomfortable things seemed so small and insignificant she had to be crazy to let them bother her.

So she had changed the room to be comfortable for Nate, to ward off a loss so enormous only the daily buying and selling, the balancing acts of a brokerage house, could calm the gnawing anxiety of being wiped out altogether. It never occurred to her that having him there weakened her, that she never feared losing or being alone until he came.

For Nate, however, the sheets hadn't mattered, nor had the cleanliness of his clothes, or even dinner every night. In spite of her income and their single state, Annie had been a traditional wife. Eventually he had fled anyway, leaving her with a color scheme only now she could admit she had never for a minute liked. Still, after he was gone, the room hung in suspension while she waited to see what would happen. She dreaded opening the drawers or the closet door where Nate had kept his suits. She half expected to find a message there, a note in a bottle or tucked in a corner. "Annie, you have bad breath." Or, "I can't help it, I've always preferred men." Or alternately, boys, girls with really blonde hair, cantaloupes. Pink sheets and beer with dinner. Another possibility was something tender like, "I have leukemia and I've decided to die alone. My number is 724-4935 in case you want to call me in New York Hospital. P.S. You're too good for me, really you are."

One day after Herb hadn't called for a while and Annie was so withdrawn Ben couldn't stand it, he told her about Rita. He thought he was doing her a favor, fixing it so she could focus her anger and flush Nate out of her system. He was sick of Nate and wanted him out of their lives forever. So they could think about each other and fall in love.

Annie took the news very quietly. So it was another woman, and not the children, who had done it. Nate had told her it was the children. This was very hard to bear. Now she had to think of Rita, whom she had always rather admired, insinuating herself into Nate's thoughts while he was living with her. And worse things than that. The lies. Their sleeping together when he was out late, when she was innocently babysitting for Sara.

After she thought about it for a minute, she told Ben that the whole thing was his fault for having an affair with Rita in the first place. "You have to try everybody out," she complained.

"What?" Ben's face fell. What did he have to do with it? He forgot that, after breaking up with Rita, he had told Annie all about it. Rita slept with a blindfold on. He told Annie it was like sleeping with a corpse. Rita kept old Coke bottles and shoe boxes and stacks of shopping bags. She didn't eat a single thing when they went out and was like a stone all night long.

"You shouldn't have shown an interest," Annie said. She glared at him.

"What are you talking about?"

"If you hadn't broken up with her, she wouldn't have turned to Nate. You hurt everybody."

The project backfired. Now Annie began probing Ben's memory for how they were, she and Nate and Rita, who hadn't seemed as if she had been with them for very long, or indeed had made much of an impact. That was how much she knew.

In the middle of a debate on interest rates, Annie flung out such questions as, did Ben think Nate had slept with any of his other girl friends—either at the time he was dating them or after they had parted? She loosed these queries at unexpected moments, hoping to catch Ben off guard. Neither Nate, nor his own girl friends were subjects he wanted to discuss. But each time Annie came into his office with a distracted air and sat down, he was caught off guard. He tried to prepare for her by remembering Susan Thoby, another treacherous woman.

In her short-sleeved cashmere sweater sets and pleated skirts, Annie suddenly bore an amazing resemblence to Susan Thoby from Ben's high school days. Susan (probably not Thoby by now) had been a sweet-faced girl, not quite quick enough to think without moving her lips. She also asked Ben difficult questions, things like—what does Richie Thomas say about me in the locker room? The last thing Ben did in the locker room was listen to what Richie Thomas had to say about anything. He was too worried about not seeming to be able to grow anywhere near enough hair to cover his plump pink flesh. He hadn't thought about any of it for years.

Remembrance of Susan Thoby came back to him when Annie rejected his embrace outside her building. Susan Thoby had been like that, so wholesome and clean she made him sick for years with prurient interest.

"Hey Bobby—" He was called Bobby then, short for Benjamin.

"Would you run over to the drug store and pick something up for me?"

He never recognized the sarcasm in her inviting giggle.

"Uh, sure. What do you want?" Ben had been proud of being able to get to the store and back in a good fifteen minutes on his bike. He got caught by her every time.

"I need some *Tam*-pax for next week." And she would dissolve into fits of hysteria of the sort girls reserve only for those they thought were truly awful: sub-ugly, something along the lines of a paraplegic toad. She laughed when his pimply face turned purple.

In the crucial years after his father died and before his fed-up stepfather decided he had to go, Ben suffered most consciously over Susan Thoby and her menstrual cycle.

"Hey, Ben." Annie flopped into the chair by Ben's desk and stuck her feet straight out in front of her. "What's the total float on Lasernetics?"

Ben looked quickly at the picture of himself in a wet suit. In it, he had the oxygen tanks held out like trophies and looked like a Greek god (no less than that) coming forth from the sea. His hair was longer then, very dark, and just vaguely curly; and his weight was the lowest it had been since he was twelve. He was very proud of that picture, had the apprehension that something painful was behind this question about Lasernetics.

"I don't know," he said.

"Oh come on, you know all about Lasernetics. We were talking about it only the other day. I bet it was you who took the prospectus off my desk," she said.

"I did not."

"You asked me about it. Somebody asked you, remember?"

"Lasers for medical use, is that the one?" Ben leaned back in his chair and looked at himself with a fly rod in his hand. He looked pretty good in that picture, too. He inclined his head toward it, but Annie didn't follow his gaze.

"You know that's the one."

"I don't know why you're interested in all those funny little medical companies," he said. "Look at what's happened to Personal Harmonics."

Annie sat up, suddenly alarmed. "What's happened to it?"

"It's down to ten."

"Oh that. It went down to ten yesterday." She smiled. "So you're following it."

"It went down to ten," Ben repeated.

"Well, I started buying it at four. It'll come back. I told you, Roche will buy it out and then it will go up to thirty. Watch and see."

"What's this obsession you have with medicine?"

Annie's response all through childhood when asked what she wanted to be when she grew up was invariably, "A man, or maybe a doctor." It had been a bitter disappointment to grow up neither. She shrugged and reached out for a leg, pulled on a wrinkle in her pantyhose. Ben leaned over for a better view.

"Sickness is a natural resource," she said finally. "So is garbage if we could only harness it."

"Well, I don't have it." A light flashed on Ben's telephone and he took the call. He looked at Annie, away from Annie, back at Annie, listened for a second or two and then asked if he could call back.

"Oh, pardon me," Annie said, rising to leave. "One of your women."

Ben hung up. "No, don't go."

"I don't want to interrupt a personal call."

"It wasn't anybody," Ben said irritably. "Sit down."

"It was, too, somebody."

"Let's see," he said quickly. "I think the float on Lasernetics was one million five, and I hear Bache has about two-hundred thousand."

"I knew it was going to be something. I just knew it." Annie sat down. "Where did you hear that about Bache?"

Ben shrugged.

"Well, if Bache has that much, then somebody must be trying to buy it out. Who is it?"

"I don't know."

"You do, you know all about it," Annie protested. "Tell me."

Annie's secretary popped in her head. "Phone for me?" Annie leaped up, color suddenly in her face. She jumped just as she had for more than a week now whenever the phone rang. She knew Herb would call. She knew it. That license plate was like a sliver of truth shot out into a world of shifting ambiguities. By now she couldn't exactly remember his face, but the M.D. on his license was as real and solid as the road going home. He said he saw competence in her, said he would call, and now after almost two weeks she still believed he would. She raced into her office and grabbed the phone.

"Hi, Baby," Brenda said. "What are you doing?"

Annie swallowed her disappointment. "Oh hello, Mother."

"What do you mean, 'Oh hello, Mother?' What kind of greeting is that?"

"Sorry. I thought you were someone else. How are you?"

"I just called to find out how you are," Brenda complained. "That's all. I'm not bothering you in your important work or anything. You won't lose ten-thouand dollars saying hello to your mother. Heaven knows I wouldn't want that."

"Oh, Mother."

"You earn enough money. Too much money already, and what good does it do you? Are you happy? Baby, tell me the truth does all that money make you happy?"

"It's good to hear from you, Mom. Are you feeling better?"

Brenda sighed loudly. "Oh, Annie." Annie never listened to her. She could say anything and it wouldn't register. "I wish you'd call me more often. Now that you're alone I really worry about you. What if you got sick in the night? What if someone broke in and caught you in your nightie?"

"I'm fine," Annie said.

"They don't always call up in your building, you know that. I've seen people just walk in. I don't think you're as safe as you think."

"Maybe they live there."

"Who?"

"The people who walk in. They don't ring up to announce people to themselves, you know."

"Don't get snappy to me, Madam, just because you're in a bind. It's not my fault."

"Oh Mother, please." Annie swung around in her chair and flushed at Carl's steady gaze.

"Okay, okay, let's not fight. I just want to know what's happening," Brenda said.

"Nothing's happening." Annie took a sip of cold coffee from the cup on her desk and made a face. It was as bitter as the arsenic she wouldn't mind taking right then. Nothing was new but another headache growing in her right eye.

"That's not strictly speaking true, Annie. I hear you've met someone."

"Who said that?" Annie turned away from Carl and looked out at a maroon Rolls Royce waiting downstairs, but not for her. What a life.

"A little bird told me. Who is it? What's his name? Has he called you? Is that why you're so disappointed it's me? I'll forgive you if that's it. I understand how a girl feels when she's waiting for a call."

"Listen, Brenda, I have another call. Can I call you later? It's hard for me to talk in the office."

There was a brittle silence as Brenda considered it, Annie had bought her a new kitchen, but what did she do with the rest of the money she made? You couldn't tell by looking at her or her apartment where it went. It was a crime to have such a shabby daughter when Annie could have anything she wanted, anything at all.

"You never do call me back, Annie. I wish you'd confide in me a bit more. It's not easy hearing everything secondhand."

"I hate it when you two talk about me, I really do." Annie clutched the phone so hard her fingers hurt.

"You should call me yourself. Then I wouldn't have to talk to Sara. I'm not judgmental. I don't get upset. I'm your mother; who's in a better position to help you?"

"But there's nothing to tell. Honestly, if there were I'd tell you."

"That's what you always say. But God knows what's really happening to you. You could be diseased or pregnant. You let people move in and out as if your place were a hotel. Do you ever say a word? Do you tell me you're having trouble? Six years, Annie, and I have to hear about it from your sister." Brenda paused for breath, so upset again that she lost her train of thought.

"I've got to go," Annie said. "I'll call you back."

"I'll see it when I believe it." That's what she always said when she was mad.

Annie said good-bye and hung up. "Shit," she muttered. She was going to have to murder her own sister. She closed her eyes. Why am I so depressed? she asked herself. Everything's fine.

"Did you read this article in *Barron's* about defense stocks?" Carl said. "I always knew defense stocks were underrated. Something good is going to come of this budget yet."

Annie didn't reply. I'm really depressed, she thought. She considered going out for a walk and trying to get mugged for some comic relief.

"This is the thing. Reagan wants a twenty percent increase in defense spending, but Congress is talking of a three-billion to ten-billion-dollar cut in defense spending. According to *Barron's* that means they're still expecting an eight percent increase even if the whole ten billion dollars is cut, which probably won't happen. Ultimately, there's going to be a thirty-seven percent increase in procurement funds in contracts that have already been signed."

"What are you talking? Are you talking airplanes?" Annie sighed. "I wish you'd forget airplanes and submarines. Submarines are dinosaurs, everybody knows that. And the airplane market has gone soft."

"I'm talking E-systems, Annie, not commercial. I'm talking GTE Sylvania, which is big, very big, in electronic warfare. If you look at subdivisions in Eaton, you'll find very large electronic countermeasures."

"Oh, God."

"If you follow your basic airframe companies, you can't go wrong. General Dynamics and McDonnell Douglas, they're your number one and two defense contractors, but the peripheral companies will do well, too. Annie, don't be upset. Our whole future depends on defense, really."

Ben stood in the door. Annie looked up blankly. "Who was that?" he asked.

"Who was what?" Annie asked.

"Do you want to see this article? Here, listen to this. General Dynamics will be manufacturing the F-16 and McDonnell Douglas will compete with new fighters, the F-16-L with the new delta wing, which will be flying against the F-15-E. One of them will be bought as a new type of fighter in addition to the F-16 and the F-15. GD has a four-year contract to build the F-16 at a 120-a-year rate, not counting foreign orders."

Ben interrupted. "The way you shot out of my office, I just thought it must have been somebody important. On the phone, I mean. We were in the middle of a conversation, remember?" He didn't know what it was leading up to, but he didn't want to miss it, either.

"It's also building attack submarines, and Trident missile submarines," Carl added.

"Forget submarines for a second, will you? I'm getting a headache."

"Well, it practically owns the submarine business."

"So what?" Annie asked sharply.

"All right, well, depending on which figures you look at, GD is either the first or the second largest manufacturer of tactical missiles. Hughes is the other one."

"We can't buy Hughes," Ben said mechanically.

"That's exactly what I'm saying. And GD has just bought Chrysler's tank business."

"Who called?" Ben asked.

"It wasn't anybody." Annie held a hand to her forehead. It hurt. It really hurt, all this lack of privacy.

Carl adjusted his weight in his chair. "Have you read this article, Ben? I think you might be interested in it."

Ben stood in the doorway, furious at Carl. He wished he could punch him in the nose. He hurt Annie. Every time he opened his mouth, Annie got a headache.

"These are the stocks that are going to quadruple over a four-year period, even if the commercial side of the companies sags a bit," Carl went on.

"Can everybody just be quiet for a minute?" Annie said. "Take the article away with you if you want to see it," to Ben who shook his head. Didn't want to see it.

"She went running out of my office so fast I thought it was something important," Ben said to Carl.

"Well it wasn't," Annie said. "Go away."

Go away? Wasn't it she who had come to him? "Was it Nate?" he asked anxiously, looking from one to the other.

"It was her mother," Carl said.

"Oh, damn." Annie got up and pushed past Ben. Down the

corridor she went, past Ben's office and the two secretaries with desks in the hall, and the office of John Carlton. At the end was a tiny bathroom only the top five people were allowed to use. For once it was free. Annie locked herself in and stood at the sink. Why am I so depressed? she asked herself. And then she looked up and saw her image in the mirror. That was why she was depressed.

Everywhere things were going crazy. In so many places the world was constantly at war. There was yellow rain in Afghanistan, unimaginable butchery in South America and Southeast Asia, planned lunacy in the Middle East, in Africa. There was the haphazard horror of flames licking up babies daily in tenements all over the tri-state area, maniacs stabbing their love objects in California, leaking missile silos only a chain fence away from playgrounds in Utah. People being starved and displaced everywhere. One couldn't even look at one's tampons without worrying about sudden death or insanity striking even there. Every day the deadly machinery of the twentieth century chugged on, bringing all the world's irreconcilable politics closer to their ultimate conflict. It seemed unlikely that life on earth would last another decade, and yet the face Annie saw in the mirror showed none of it.

It seemed impossible to her, with so many people suffering in so many places and all of their suffering so lovingly recorded in full color every day that she couldn't forget it even on weekends, that the issues in the lives of the people around her were so very small. Struggling for happiness was a twenty-four-hour-a-day job that occupied them even while they slept. And no one was successful. But they weren't successful because they cared what those Trident missiles were being built to do, or because they cared that another flood left ten thousand out-of-work people broke and homeless in Fort Wayne. They weren't successful because they *didn't* care.

Annie looked at herself in the mirror and felt miserable because her image in the glass was so ordinary and unscathed. It did not reflect a single significant human event. She was depressed because her mother had called and reminded her of her total worthlessness as a human being.

Finally she pulled herself together. She couldn't stop a war. She flushed the toilet in case somebody was standing impatiently outside waiting for such a signal. She washed her hands, put some lipstick on her lips and slowly opened the door. She couldn't stop research on chemical warfare, or electronic warfare. She headed back to her office. But at least she wouldn't profit by it. She couldn't go back in there. She hesitated; there was no place else to go. She inched into Ben's office and sat down.

Ben had his feet on the desk pointing away from her toward the window. He was in earnest conversation and didn't make any sign when she came in. He picked up his calculator and made a few calculations. As he talked, he watched the numbers change on his automated quotations system. He seemed to be arguing in favor of a certain stock while the client on the other side wanted bonds because the bond market was low right then. Ben was saying that the stock was going to do well enough so that the client could sell off a few to make the amount the bonds would have paid, but the client wasn't having any of that. Didn't want to pay capital gains on the stock. Finally, Ben said okay he'd buy the bonds and hung up. He looked at his watch. It was after four. Too late to buy anything.

"Spare me from old ladies," he said, making a note for tomorrow.

"Ben, why did you think it was Nate who called?" Annie asked after a minute. She stuck her feet straight out in front of her again and this time examined the scuffs on her shoes. The rug in Ben's office was the same as hers, brown with a pattern of black and turquoise triangles. In her office very little of it showed, and there was no place to put her feet except under her desk. She wore black patent leather shoes with small slanted heels. Even though she hadn't had them very long, there were a number of white scuff marks on them that looked as if they didn't plan to come off.

"Just the way you ran for it," Ben said sheepishly. "Sorry."

"Have you seen him?" Annie asked, turning her feet to one side for further scrutiny.

"No, why should I?"

"There aren't many loose men around. I thought for preservation of the species you'd stay buddies. We used to be such good friends."

"I hate him," Ben said. "I wouldn't think of seeing him." He watched the hair slide down over her cheek as she leaned over with a wet finger to scrub at her shoe.

"What does he see in her? I don't understand. Is she that pretty?"

This was a question Annie had asked before. Ben considered it again. Rita was pretty with her makeup on. Without it, she looked like a tired giraffe. "Not pretty, exactly. Maybe it's emotional. Maybe he likes the insecurity of her. She's out a lot."

"That's what he said he didn't like about me," Annie murmured.

"But he always knew where you were, Annie. You're straight."

Annie sniffed. Hanging out with her sister. That's where she was. The children were the only ones among them all who were really alive. She missed them every day she didn't see them, missed them now.

"Oh, Ben, I must be awfully boring," she lamented. She started with another finger on the other shoe. Yet it took him six years to tire of her.

"I don't think of myself as loose," Ben said thoughtfully.

"What, then?" Annie snorted. "Rita, God. That's what happens when you're single. You fall into bed with anybody."

"I can't help it if nobody has grown on me yet. You don't expect me to marry someone I don't love, do you?"

"What are women to you anyway, bits of mold? Grass that won't grow under dark trees?" Annie spit on her finger to try again on a prominent streak that seemed to be weakening.

"You know what I mean. Permanence is a long time."

"I didn't think he was the kind of man who needed more than one at a time," Annie went on. "I really didn't."

"Annie, you can't know what's in somebody else's mind. He's a very shoddy kind of person, a jerk." Ben turned away to show he had dismissed the subject.

"So there *was* more than one."

"Oh, forget it. What difference does it make now?"

"I'd like to know. I thought I was happy. If I wasn't happy, I ought to know it." She regarded him thoughtfully. "Shouldn't I know what happened?"

"Has he been calling you? I wouldn't speak to him if I were you. I know what happens. First the tentative phone calls, then a lunch or two. Dinner at a place you used to go together, and pretty soon you're hooked into a few nights a week while he promises to work it out." He slapped the desk with the flat of his hand. He couldn't stand it, Annie suffering so over a jerk.

"Is that what *you* do?"

"No, but I've seen it happen to other people. I mean, look what he's done to you already." Ben wanted to get up and shake her. Every time he said something about Nate, she changed the subject back to him. Why did she do that?

"He hasn't done anything," Annie said.

"Well, you're jumping for the phone. That isn't well behavior. I can see you wavering, reconsidering. Carl says so, too. It's not good."

"What the hell does he know?" It was Herb she was waiting for. They didn't know a thing about it.

"He knows you. And Marilyn does the same thing to him, only they have two children. He can't punch her in the nose."

"What are you talking about?" Annie gave up on her shoes, crossed her legs and looked up.

Ben was leaning forward stabbing the slender point of his pen into his blotter. There were damp spots under the arms of his blue shirt, and his tie was crooked. "Look at me," he said. Look at me, his blue eyes flashed.

She was a great shrugger. She shrugged them off. She didn't really enjoy looking at him. Even angry and with sweat stains, he was too attractive. It made her sick.

"Don't you see, you just can't torture yourself over someone who runs off all the time." He ended more weakly than he intended to because she refused to look at him. Well, he knew he wasn't a golden boy in cowboy boots, like Nate, but lots of women liked his looks. Anyway, they said they did. He wasn't exactly a two-headed dwarf who didn't bathe.

"He only ran off once in six years. That isn't too bad a record," Annie said evenly. "Anyway, there aren't many men around."

"What do you mean by that?" He sat up. Now there was an opening.

"Well men, you know, to go out with." Annie ducked her head from shame at having said that. "Oh, Ben."

"Oh, Annie, I can't stand to see you like this. What are you doing to yourself?" He looked at his watch suddenly. "Hey, it's five o'clock. Let's go."

Annie shook her head. "I haven't done a thing today."

"Come on, we'll have a drink and some dinner." He got up and over his light-blue shirt and dark-blue tie with its conservative white dot, he put his jacket. Dark-blue, double-breasted, with a thin white stripe.

He looked like a blue chip. The chip itself. His jaw was quite square. Other brokers wore plaid shirts with their plaid suits and sometimes highly patterned ties as well. But Ben sold only the most desirable stocks and never wore a brown suit. He tried to look as much like a banker as possible, and made much more money than one. He stood over Annie, looking down because she hadn't moved. Then he changed his mind about going out. It would be better if they were alone. He touched her arm.

"I'll come to your place, it's a shorter walk," he said.

Three days ago in a gray suit and a pink shirt, with a striped gray-and-white tie over it, Ben had said that the worst thing one could do after an affair ended was try to understand it. Annie thought about that as she washed down the chest of drawers in the bedroom and the whole of the bedroom closet with a strong ammonia solution. Nate had left a number of dustballs, but no other message behind him.

And only the night before—the very night before—Annie took down the dense blue shade, loosening the screws one by one until it fell on her head. She neatly folded the sheets and the blue down quilt and put them in a box for Goodwill to take away.

Then she didn't like the look of the stuff sitting there. She dragged it out to the back hall and left it there, the long shade balanced on the box. In her room the white sheets were on the bed again. She ironed them carefully, and the white bedspread, too. Then she found in the closet on the top shelf a small white neck pillow encrusted with bits of lace and ribbon that Sara had made during her Victorian period when she was still interested in romance. Annie put her face into it. The lavender sachet Sara had sewn into it still gave off the faint sickly aroma of old hope. Annie put it back on her bed along with the other four pillows again in white.

I've made him think I will, Annie thought as she and Ben walked home together. Already the season made it night at five. She thought of the damp patches on his blue shirt and his pen stabbing at the blotter.

When Nate and she were newly in love they used to meet on the street and Nate would embarrass her by pretending to pick her up again. It wasn't a nice game. He liked to tell her all the things he was going to do to give her a good time, to make him worth the effort.

It always reminded Annie of the time she was in Paris alone with her mother, for what reason she couldn't remember any more. They got sick from gluttony the first day. Stuck in their room the second night, groaning from the mixture of too many cream sauces, they heard life in the next room. First the muffled sound of a man on the telephone and then a knock on the door. A woman came in. He asked her name and if she had eaten. When she said no, he ordered dinner. Through the locked double door, on their side of the room, they heard the sounds of dinner and a discussion of the man's wife in Quebec. Brenda, who still pretended to be a girl, and Annie who hadn't yet had a lover, were transfixed by the revelation: the ordinariness with which strangers prepared for love. Brenda was greatly distressed that the walls in a first-class hotel were so thin and by the betrayal of the wife in Quebec, but insisted that Annie translate everything she could hear. After dinner the man began beating the woman with his belt and she squealed but did not express surprise or tell him to stop. Later when they were thrashing around on the bed, he slapped her loudly with his hand. Sometimes Annie still felt she could hear her crying. She wondered what made her think of it again. Ben was an old friend, not a stranger in a bar. He wouldn't hurt her as soon as they were alone.

He stopped at the liquor store on her corner. I've made him think I will, she thought, as he looked among the bottles of chilled champagne. Usually on Thursdays he went to his gym. She knew he planned to go today because the bag with his sweat clothes was parked by his desk. Today he had begun sweating early. He left the bag at the office, was buying champagne.

Champagne was for lovers, and Ben had passed over everything that was domestic. Why didn't she say no, quickly, before they got upstairs? She didn't have to, just because everybody else did. She wouldn't, she decided, no matter what. Then she thought of how Ben had slept with Rita, who was sleeping with Nate, who had once slept so soundly with her. What history they had between them. It made her feel sad and lonely. How many girls had he slept with whom he didn't really love? How many nights had she spent with Nate, who didn't really love her? What would she do when he touched her? Herb had never called her.

What was the answer? Would it be worse to be loved by Ben for a moment, or never loved by him at all?

On the corner a plain-looking girl pressed a leaflet into Annie's hand. She let it go. It flipped into the air and fell at her feet. On the front was the burning question, "WHAT ABOUT TEMPTATION?" Annie stepped on it as she passed.

12

BEN WANTED to cheer her up and get her mind off of Nate. That was his only plan, or so he told himself. He just wanted to be alone with Annie in a quiet place and make her laugh as he used to. To this end he bought a bottle of one of the better French champagnes. He cradled it in the crook of his arm as he followed her into her apartment.

"When I moved here the kitchen was terrible," she was saying. Suddenly she was talking a lot. "There was a tiny old sink and a World War I refrigerator that wouldn't freeze in the freezer but froze everything else."

She was remembering how Nate hadn't gone into the kitchen until he had been living there for a week. The first time he saw her apartment he went straight for the bedroom, without looking around first, without her even leading the way. She bit her lip.

"It looks terrific now, did you do it over?" Ben asked. He brushed past her to put the champagne in the refrigerator, a new one. He noticed that there wasn't much in it. A few yogurts, ketchup, some diet soda, tired-looking lettuce.

"The day I signed the lease I came back to the building and told the super to tear everything out. Then I went on vacation for two weeks. Here, we'll use these." She handed him two of the four stem champagne glasses she had bought at Tiffany on the occasion of Donald's birth when he came to dinner at three weeks old and they drank to his health. Ben put them in the freezer. He had to juggle four cartons of ice cream to make room for them.

"What happened then?"

"Well, I came back and found the kitchen stripped. Naturally I went to the landlord, or anyway the guy who handled the building. He was new and young. He had pimples on his chin. I told him there was nothing in my kitchen, nothing at all, and he had to give me new appliances."

"So they did," Ben finished.

Annie leaned against the counter. "They did. I had to pay for the dishwasher, of course."

"Very clever. You must have scared him to death. People with pimples will do anything." He waved his hand at the Cuisinart, the blender, the Kitchen-Aid mixer, the juicer, the toaster oven. "Do you use them much?"

Annie looked away. "Not any more. Let's go in the other room."

"So you live on ice cream."

"No, never eat the stuff. What gave you that idea?" She sat on the sofa and kicked off her shoes.

"You have a lot of it." He sat down next to her, pulling at the creases in his trousers.

"Oh, that's for my children. I mean, my sister's children. Donald is four-and-a-half and Lucy is two. They eat ice cream. Do you want to see their pictures?" She jumped up before he could answer. She padded into the bedroom and was startled by the white bed and the white walls, the Swiss curtains so carefully starched from spray in a can, and the pictures of her family in rows on the dresser. She picked up several of the children, started back and then returned for the picture of Sara and Martin. In it Sara had her head on Martin's shoulder and both of them were dutifully smiling into the sun. Annie held it in her hand looking at it for a long time.

The day she took that picture Martin's mother died. They had gone to visit some friends in a country house in Dutchess County and didn't hear about it until late in the day. They were so impressed by the grandeur of the house and the tennis court and the swimming pool, all belonging to an old girl friend of theirs who had married well, that they didn't know what to do first. Swim or play tennis. Ah, lunch on the terrace, of course, where the pictures were taken to commemorate the day. They almost agreed to stay the night. But Martin's mother had been complaining of chest pains again, and they decided they'd better go back. Martin was so upset when they got home that he punched his hand through the kitchen window and had to be stitched up in the same hospital where his mother lay in the morgue. Now he was going to have a house of his own.

Ben had arranged the glasses that were not quite frosted and the bottle on the biggest brass trivet and set it in front of the sofa. He stood looking out the window down Lexington Avenue where the traffic was still tied up.

"Here they are. Lucy's bigger than this now."

Ben turned around. "I remember Lucy. You brought her to the office last summer. She showed me her underpants."

"She must have liked you. She only does that with people she likes. Isn't she beautiful?" Annie sat down gazing at the picture. "I just love her."

"Have a glass of champagne," Ben said. He started peeling the foil off the cork. "Oh yes, she's beautiful," when Annie thrust the picture between him and his task.

"She probably won't stay blonde like that. I didn't."

Pop. The cork came off the bottle. Ben masterfully poured some in each glass. He still had his jacket on and looked impeccably proper, even grand. Annie missed it, though. She had switched her attention to Sara's picture.

"Of course Sara is still very fair. This is my sister. She's beautiful, too."

Ben raised his glass. "To your sister," he said gallantly.

"Martin is an accountant but you know Martin and Sara," Annie added. "They're building a house in Pine Wood."

"Let's see." Ben took the pictures from her and looked at them one at a time. "Very nice-looking family. I've always thought so," he said. He put them down way over on his side of the sofa out of Annie's reach. "Here." He handed her the other glass of champagne.

Annie looked at him piercingly. "Don't you think she's beautiful?"

"To you, Annie," he said and couldn't help smiling at the way she sat, with her skirt pulled down over knees held tightly together. Not his usual sort of girl at all.

She hesitated for a second, her glass held high. Then she murmured, "To you," and they bumped glasses.

They sipped silently for several minutes, inspecting the bubbles in their glasses, looking up from time to time and smiling at each other.

It was the silences Annie hated. There always seemed to be silence at the core of everything. When she was little and wanted something she couldn't have, the punishment for desire was the silent treatment. First a cold rebuke, then the cutoff; and then when she howled in fury, they locked her in the smallest enclosure they could find, the closet. Sara and Annie had made the second closet in their room into a kind of club house. It was big enough for a little table where they neatly stacked their drawing paper and tape and crayons and glue for projects. Along the bottom of the dress rack where they didn't yet hang their clothes, they put a pillow and some old quilts. Sara was the angel child. She would smack Annie with a hair brush and when Annie hit her back, Sara in tears ran to Brenda.

In the storm that followed Brenda and Sara got quieter and quieter until Annie was the only one making noise. They'd put her in the closet to scream herself to sleep. Then at dinner they pretended she wasn't there, umming and ahhing over the picture Sara had made in the interval. Families always do that. They make an agreement beforehand about who causes the trouble. Usually it's the one who caused the most trouble in the womb, stayed there a week too long, made a painful entry. Or it was the one who had colic and cried for a solid year. Right at birth they know who has no judgment, no consideration or restraint.

What *about* temptation? Annie wondered what Ben was thinking behind his smile. She had never been good when the conversation lagged. Whatever was in her mind fogged up there, the thoughts all jamming together in a cloud that filled her mouth with doubt. Alternately she thought that she was boring, that the plants needed watering. She always watered them on Thursday. She knew that Ben's girls were playful and suggestive. She ought to say she liked the champagne. Yesterday it had rained. There was a blind girl waiting for someone to help her across the street as Annie was walking home; but though she wanted to help, she was too embarrassed to take her arm. One didn't talk to strangers. Brenda said people were tricky. One couldn't really be sure those rolling eyes weren't on the lookout for a patsy's handbag. If someone took her handbag, would Annie take up the chase, screaming

"Thief, thief!" And what if no one came, and the girl stepped off the curb into oncoming traffic and was crushed to death? It would be Annie's fault, Annie's alone.

"It's wonderful champagne," Annie said carefully. Maybe she was wrong and he didn't mean to after all. She smiled, blinking uncertainly. The cashmere sweaters she wore were very soft, pale yellow, the color of Martin's weekend socks. Touch my breasts, she thought. Bite your tongue.

"What are you thinking?" Ben asked.

Annie shrugged. "Nothing much." She swilled down some more champagne. "It's good," she said. Touch my breasts, they're bigger than Rita's, she thought.

"Have some more." He poured more in her glass.

"There's no music. Nate took the stereo with him. . . . I have a record player in the closet. We could take it down, but there aren't any new records." She looked at his hands.

"I like the quiet."

"Quiet makes me nervous," Annie murmured.

"I never would have thought that about you."

"Only when I'm with other people, I mean. I don't mind it when I'm alone."

"Shall I talk more? I was just thinking how nice it is to be with someone who doesn't have to chatter incessantly. You never find out anything you want to know."

"You find out everything when people talk. It's when they're silent that you have to be careful. People are so tricky," Annie murmured.

"What I mean is that most people talk a lot without having anything worthwhile to say. They inundate you with minutia."

"What's worthwhile to you?" The embrace of a stranger on the first date?

Ben smiled. "Go ahead, push me into a corner."

"I mean, what would be worthwhile for us to discuss? Nuclear disarmament, the Mideast? Corruption in India? How about the human rights of the insane not to be forcibly medicated?"

"I wonder what's really on your mind?" Ben got up and took his jacket off. He hung it over his coat on the front doorknob. He knew Annie was up to any of those subjects, and that was both daunting and exciting at the same time. Briefly, he looked at her books, then wandered into the dining alcove where the stripped

Dutch cupboard was. He noticed there was a thin layer of dust on the table.

Annie saw a glint of silver at the end of the sofa and reached over to where Ben had stuffed her family. Down between the arm and the soft bottom cushion. Lucy was on top. She picked up the picture of the child's smiling face. "Give me a kiss, Baby," she whispered and kissed the glass over her mouth. Lucy was the best person at love she had ever come across. The first thing she did every time was climb into Annie's lap and rest her cheek against Annie's. "Love you, Annie," she said. And if Annie got tears in her eyes, she wiped them with a tiny fist and reached over to pat her shoulder.

Annie poured the last of the champagne. They'd taken it very seriously right to the end, like medicine, or a heavy drama. And now that it was finished, he looked as if he meant to go. Funny, I don't feel drunk, she thought. But she didn't feel up to putting the pictures back on the dresser in her room. She slipped them under the sofa while Ben stood at the window. She leaned back over the plump rounded arm of the sofa, her pleated skirt rising high up her thighs. Her stockings were white and slippery, like the silk they imitated. She only bought the best.

She stretched again. Then with her back arched and her head upside down she had the cruel thought that he might really be a fraud under all the talk. Suppose in fact he was no more than a tease, his dirty mind just a wish of what he'd like himself to be. She righted herself and watched him taking in the view from her window. It would certainly account for his swift change of partners. No one could hold up well for long against real reluctance. Annie sighed. Go on touch me, I won't say no.

"What?" Ben swung around abruptly.

She grabbed at her skirt. "What?"

"I thought you said something."

"Give me a minute," she said, irritable now. "I'll try to come up with something worthwhile."

"You don't have to." He sat again. "Cheers." He drank the last of the champagne and looked at the empty glass.

"I've never known you to be so quiet," Annie complained.

"I'm not quiet," he said defensively. "I'm thoughtful."

He wasn't being sexy, that was the problem. With Ben's mind on something else, Annie didn't know where to put up a defense. It was disconcerting. How could she even think of giving in if he didn't make a move. Thoughtless was the norm, thoughtless was what was called for now. What did he think he was doing, thinking at a time like this? The whole idea was to drink the champagne and do it. For the exercise, for the warm feeling of skin on skin, for a breathtaking crescendo on clean white sheets. She'd already thought of the sheets; what else was there to consider?

"Well?" she said finally. The suspense was killing her.

"Well, what?"

"I thought you wanted to talk to me. Now you don't want to talk. What's the matter?"

"Nothing's the matter. I'm very happy just being with you."

"That's ridiculous. That's not like you at all."

"How do you know?"

"Where's your real self? It's terribly hot in here. Don't you want to—go in the other room?"

"Are you teasing me?" Ben didn't look at her.

"No, why would I do that?"

"You remind me of somebody." He turned the empty glass around and around in his hands.

"Oh," Annie said, taken aback.

"I don't want to fall into any traps."

"What trap? Do you think I want to catch you?" Annie laughed at the idea. She had never caught anything in her whole life. "Tie you up so you can't get away? Do you think I want to hold you prisoner here forever without hope of escape, rape you repeatedly and never give you dinner?"

Ben laughed, too, because it didn't sound bad. He said, "No, I think you don't want to."

"Then what's the problem?" She took his hand and drew it to her cheek. "I'll show you my room."

He stirred next to her. Ah, now he was going to fall on her and show her how good he was. She closed her eyes with the back of his hand against her face. A second later she opened them again. He hadn't moved.

She flushed and let his hand drop. "I wasn't going to trap you," she cried. "It's just so terribly hot in here, and, and you do it all the time. What's the difference?"

"I think in this case it would be a whole lot better if we were in love," he said seriously. "And you're drunk," he added. It wouldn't be fair if she were drunk.

"Well, that's just ridiculous." Annie jumped up and lurched

with the two glasses into the kitchen. "Coming from you that's the dumbest thing I've ever heard." She put the glasses down on the sink. Jesus Christ, what was the world coming to? she thought. Then, Be a good sport. Don't break the glasses. She considered the slender stems. Wasn't it his idea to come here? What did he think he was doing, spending thirty dollars on a bottle of champagne if he didn't mean to do it? Shit, the whole world was crazy. And the room spun around, too.

He appeared with the empty bottle. "Where should I put this?"

"Give it to me. I want to keep it as a souvenir."

"Annie, you're drunk." Ben laughed. "You really are."

Annie bumped into him and reached her arms around his neck. "Okay, then let's be in love for ten minutes. Go ahead, fake it if you have to."

"Oh, I don't have to fake it. You're the problem. I don't want you to be tough, I want you to mean it." He laughed again as she swayed against him. "You're cute when you're drunk, don't tempt me."

"Come on. I'll be silent the whole time and you can pretend I'm deep."

"No, don't do that."

She had slid her hands down his chest and was tugging at his shirt. "I want to feel your skin. You smell like raspberries. . . . Ben, I have to sit down."

"No, no. Not here. Hold onto me, I'll take you in the other room."

"I want to go to bed," Annie whispered.

"All right, all right. Hold on." He picked her up. No problem, he lifted weights every Thursday. She licked his neck. "Cute, very cute." He bumped his shoulder against a wall going down the hall. At the door to her room he hesitated. One look at her room and he knew he didn't want to fool with it. If she was teasing, that sweet white room was going to hang around in his memory for a long time. He just knew it. "Can't you walk from here?" he muttered.

"No, I'll faint." She kissed the corner of his mouth, nudged it with the tip of her tongue. Touched her lips squarely on his for a second then did it again. She giggled. His lips were as hot as hers. They nuzzled her back.

"Ooo, that's right don't think," she murmured. "Just lie down like that. Close your eyes, I'm a geisha taking off your shoes."

Ben tried to sit up. "You're very sexy. If I love you, will you marry me?"

"Close your eyes." She pushed him back against the pillows. He was all blues against the white. She explored his face with her lips. "I've always wondered what you taste like. Have you ever wondered that . . . about somebody? I like the way you taste."

"Annie, tell me. I can't take much more of this."

"Sweetheart, I can't either. I want to touch your skin. How do you get that thing off?" On her knees she fumbled with the knot in his tie. "You're not easy to undress."

"I usually do it myself."

"Okay. Forget it." Annie flopped down on the bed and shoved her face into a pillow. They lay like that for some time, side by side, he face up and she face down. He stared at the ceiling, which was also white. Somehow he hadn't expected her to be so sexy, so appealing. It made him afraid of how he would feel if she didn't really like him. Nate still couldn't get over how much she didn't care when he left. And this was different even from that since Annie made it no secret what she thought of Ben. A bum with women. He didn't want to be a bum. He wouldn't do it.

He turned his head to say that and couldn't help being diverted by Annie's back, quite a big patch of which was showing beneath her cashmere twinset. Guided by a rather sophisticated heat-sensing device, his hand homed in on the bare skin. Just a little massage on the lower back to put her gently to sleep, he assured himself. Nothing pushy.

After a while he turned on his side. In his face was a lacy little pillow that smelled of dry days in summer houses. Embroidered in pink was the slogan, "Esteem the Giver." Who the hell was that? He moved the pillow out of his view and leaned over to kiss Annie's back. He didn't mean to exactly, but it seemed more appealing than any front he could remember. And if her back was that good, her front had to be exceptional, too. Her skin smelled of spring flowers.

"Okay, you win," he whispered, overcome by an unexpected surge of longing that went quite a way beyond mere lust. "Whatever you want."

For that moment anyway, she had no doubt what she wanted. She turned over and pulled him into her arms.

13

THE NEXT
morning, however, Annie could not imagine why on earth she
had done such a stupid thing. She was full of remorse. She was
almost tearful as she surveyed her wardrobe and tried to decide
what to wear, or whether she should get dressed at all. It seemed
to her that she had already worn all of her clothes that week, or
they all looked the same. Nothing appealed. Maybe she ought to
stay home. Judging from the light charging through the window,
she knew it was a sunny day. A perfect day for not going to the
office. And she did feel awfully rotten. Maybe she was terminally
ill.

All the mystery was gone, a long friendship was ruined. And
not only that, she was just like everybody else. She liked him. No,
she didn't like him. She splashed her face repeatedly with cold
water. Didn't like him that way. She had to remember that—she
knew him better than he knew himself. So she couldn't believe a
word he said, even if he thought he meant it. God what a jerk she
was.

Sara called while Annie was telling herself what a jerk she
was. She was so serious about being a jerk she was almost ready to
call her mother, who would no doubt agree.

"Annie, are you there?" Sara said. "I want to know what
you're getting Donald for his birthday so we won't duplicate."

"Is it tomorrow already?" Annie asked.

"No, Annie, it's today all day. Where's your head?"

"I mean Donald's birthday."

"Yes, it's tomorrow, as you well know. Now, what do you say?
Mother is getting him a cowboy outfit, so that leaves a tepee that
he wants and that huge Tinker Toy set."

"I got him a puzzle of the United States and a globe," Annie
said. "At Rand-McNally a couple of weeks ago."

"Oh, really, Annie, that's too much."

"They didn't cost much."

"I mean for a five-year old."

"You don't want to stuff him up there in the suburbs and make him think Pine Wood is the whole world, do you? Next year I'm going to get him *National Geographic*. Should I get him the tepee, too?" she said doubtfully. "I don't know about the Tinker Toys."

"That's too much," Sara said, and sighed. "You confuse the issue."

"It can be from all of us. Where do you get it?"

"Well, I do have a lot to do today. Why don't you get both of them and we can work out who gives what tomorrow."

"Both of them?"

"Well, you might as well, as long as you're going to a toy store."

That decided Annie that she really belonged at the office. "I'm going to work," she protested. "I don't have time for this."

"You offered. Why offer if you're not going to carry through? Really, Annie, you always do that. I never know when I can count on you. You're not reliable."

"I'm reliable. When haven't I been reliable?" Annie cried. But she didn't feel very reliable. The night before she had fallen for a bottle of French champagne. "Okay, okay, I'll see what I can do," she said before Sara could say when.

"Don't say that. Promise so I can count on it. Don't tell me tomorrow what a busy day you had. We all know how important you are."

"I promise," Annie muttered.

"Good, now what's your favorite color these days?"

"I don't know. What in?" She wanted badly to tell Sara what she had done the night before, but restrained herself because Sara couldn't keep anything to herself.

"It's a surprise, I can't tell you," Sara teased.

"Then I don't know . . . pearl gray?" Annie said, her heart not in it. "Navy blue?"

"Red," Sara said. "How about red for a change?"

"I like red in flags," Annie said. "God, I'm late."

"Red, then." Sara paused. "The last time I wore red somebody asked me if I had my period."

"Must have been Mother."

Sara laughed. "You're right, damn it."

"It's funny that you would pick red for me," Annie said. Brenda had raised them to think red was the color of guilt, the color of a leaking wound. If you wore it, you showed that something was in your mind that shouldn't be there. A lady didn't have her vagina in her mind, no sir. Brenda didn't think fannies ought to jiggle in pants either. She still blamed Sara's early marriage on the red toreador pants Sara wore that year without a panty girdle underneath. Dis-gusting. No wonder Martin lost his head.

Those toreador pants." Brenda still referred to them now. "Bright red, you could see her coming for a mile. Thank God we didn't have a dog to walk or she'd have been strangled in an alley. Well, she sure got what she asked for." Except that there were absolutely no alleys at all on the East Side of New York.

"You were wearing red when we went to the country. You looked so cute. Did he ever call?" Sara asked.

"No, no," Annie said quickly, thinking of what Sara had asked for and gotten. "Don't waste your time on me. I don't need a thing, really."

"Don't be a martyr, Annie." Sara hung up without saying good-bye.

Annie took the bus. She always took the bus when she was late, and got there later than she would have if she had walked. The traffic seemed to have a way of timing its gridlocks to the worst days, almost as if it were echoing blockages of the mind.

"I didn't really do that," Annie told herself. What a jerk, and he wouldn't even have done it. She put two tokens in the change box instead of one. It was just like her not to want him to get away with being decent. She stared out of the window as the bus didn't move. Oh well, she was drunk at the time, as well as insane. If he smirked at her today, she would just not remember it. It happened in another dimension. Back in this dimension, she could deny it. Women have been doing that ever since the creation. Sometimes it made a lot of sense.

Still, she didn't feel easy as she walked the path through the boardroom with her head down. She told herself that even if she didn't deny it, there was still nothing to worry about. People do it every day. After a minute or two no one thinks a thing of it. He had probably forgotten it already. On the other hand, denying it seemed to be the best approach.

Her phone was ringing as Annie came into her office. She picked it up.

"Is this Annie Flood?"

"Yes, who is this?"

"It's Herb Mickle. We met recently in a Burger King. Do you remember?"

"I never go to Burger King," Annie said. But she felt as if someone had just given her a reprieve from her excesses of the night before, a new chance to be grown up, a real man to think about in a friendly way. All of those things in a single call.

"You were with two delightful children. And I was with my daughter, Vanessa. We made a perfect quintet."

"It was McDonald's," Annie said. "How nice to hear from you. How are you?"

"How are *you?*"

"I'm super," Annie said, in fact feeling a whole lot better.

"I've been thinking about that. Can we meet? Are you free for lunch today? I'm going to be in your neighborhood."

"Well, sure," Annie said, forgetting that she never went out to lunch.

"Shall I come to your office and collect you?"

"Um, no," she said quickly. She looked over at Carl, who was on the phone. There was always Carl to consider. One had to prepare people for Carl. And what if Ben was around and smirked. That would never do. She hesitated, not wanting to be pushy.

"Is the Trattoria all right? I could call for a table," she said tentatively.

"Fine. Twelve-thirty?"

"I'll see you there then. It's in the Pan Am Building."

Annie was too relieved to buy that day, so she sold. Some days she liked only to sell. Selling put her in a good mood and she went downstairs early. She got a table on the other side of the bar, around the corner. It was against the wall where he wouldn't be able to see her when he came in. But she was only there for a minute, peering into her compact, when he found her.

"Hello, there," he said.

She jumped. "Oh, hello." She shoved the compact under her napkin. "You're early."

"So are you."

They smiled.

He was certainly acceptable looking, rather thicker than she remembered him, though. In a brown plain suit and light brown tattersall shirt. He still had the beard and dark eyes, small mouth. His curly hair was thinning a bit on top, a funny muddy color. He looked older than he had in the country. Perhaps it was the brown he covered himself in. Annie found herself making him over. What did he look like without the beard? Probably fatter. But looks didn't matter. He had a nice smile.

He sat down and looked around. "Do you come here often?" He looked her up and down, too. But couldn't see much, just a gray sweater and white lace collar, her pearls.

Annie repressed a laugh because they were so like a blind date. If they could hand over each other's life histories, neatly typed, it would be a lot faster. Or, as they did in the new dating services, study each other's tapes. Alone, each could sit in a dark room and watch the other talking on a television screen. That way they wouldn't have to make the commitment of spending a single minute together until each was sure the other was worthy of the effort.

"I don't like to go too far, and this place is not bad, do you think?" she said.

"I've never been here before."

"I come here every few weeks." Usually with a family member, or once in a while with a client, she didn't add. She kind of liked the plants and the noise.

"How about a drink?"

"I'd like one. What about you?"

He ordered Campari and soda for himself. Careful. That was a good sign in a doctor. A Bloody Mary for Annie. So, what was his story? She smiled as they waited for the drinks. How long had he been married, separated? What was his wife like? Where did he live, have his practice? What did he do? He looked at her so forlornly, Annie thought for a minute that he might be seeing in her some sign of disease whose symptoms she didn't yet feel. After last night she did feel pretty seedy. Maybe she looked over thirty.

The drinks came. "Cheers," she said.

"Cheers. How is the house coming?"

"I don't know. I guess they've started it. Their architect already had a construction company in mind. So they must be ready to break ground. They expect to have it finished by summer."

Annie told him about how Archie and Martin pounded stakes to convince Sara the placement was good, and even tied strings around them. And then when they were finished, pulled them all out again.

He laughed and said it was easier to buy.

"Then you never get what you want," Annie said. "And it costs so much to change it. I wouldn't want to live in a house."

"Really? That's unusual. Most women want a home of their own."

"I have a home of my own. It's three and a-half rooms. I can leave it whenever I want. The roof never leaks, the basement never floods, and there's a guard at the front door to announce my visitors. I can't think of anything more homey than that."

"Well, sorry," Herb said. "I didn't know you were that kind of woman."

"I think a house is a prison anybody can get in and nobody can get out of . . . unless you walk out, of course." Suddenly she looked down at her drink ashamed. Maybe he hadn't walked out.

"I guess you want to know why I'm separated," he said reading her mind. "She had someone else."

"Oh, I'm so sorry." Annie's heart dropped into her feet. She almost blurted out that she had lived with a man for many years who had somebody else, too. So she knew what it was like. She almost took his hand to show her sympathy, but luckily she was prevented from doing so by the waiter who appeared just then.

"The mussels are good," she murmured.

He ordered mussels.

"Sorry, we're out of mussels."

"What? It's not even one o'clock," Annie said indignantly.

The waiter shrugged. "What can I do?"

Herb ordered canneloni and a salad. Annie smiled. She looked around, ordered a chef's salad.

"So. You're a stockbroker," he said. "Do you like it?"

"Yes, of course. Do you like being a doctor?"

"It's a funny thing for a girl to do."

"Oh really," Annie laughed. "You don't have to have a head for numbers. It's all automated, you know. My calculator does it all," she joked.

But he nodded seriously. "Are you any good at it?"

"I like to think so."

"Then tell me. What should I do with my money?"

"Okay," she said, serious for a moment, too. "What are your objectives? Are you interested in preserving your capital, generating income, or capital appreciation? If you're interested in preserving your capital, you might put your money in a money fund. If you're not as concerned about inflation and want a steady income, you would put your money into bonds. There's more return on lower-rated discount bonds, but a slightly greater risk." She looked around the room, then grinned. "I bet you're interested in speculating."

He nodded. "Of course. I've been speculating about you for two weeks. I was afraid to call. I thought you might have a husband or a boyfriend, or someone lurking in the wings. Was I right?"

"Not at the moment," Annie said. "I'm absolutely unencumbered."

"That's just terrific, really. Can I get you another drink?"

"No, thanks."

He didn't have one either. "I feel so much better," he said. "Now you can tell me all about stocks."

"I can?"

"Sure. Tell me anything." He put his chin in his hand and prepared to listen. "It isn't often that one gets to hear depressing news from such an adorable source."

"Oh well, the economy *is* very depressed," she agreed, blushing a little.

"And stocks are down."

"Well, the market is undervaluing a lot of stocks based on traditional formulas. But I think they'll come back."

"Why are they undervalued?"

"Why?" she giggled. "Well, three factors. One—Corporate earnings are down. Two—Inflation is receding only very slowly, if at all. Three—Interest rates are not coming down far or fast enough. Plus, the perceptions of institutions and the buying public, and uncertain times, make people behave more conservatively with their money."

"Are you suffering?"

"Right now?" Annie asked, "or in general?"

"Well, if people are being conservative with their money, they must be buying fewer stocks."

"That's true. Many brokers are in trouble. Times are bad.

But, you know, there are some very attractive bargains around for the aggressive investor. If you're looking at undervalued stock that is selling below book value, then you stand a reasonable chance of doing well when the economy recovers. And when the share price is below book value, the downside risk is low."

"I bet you're an aggressive investor," he said admiringly. "It takes nerve for that."

"I'm number four in my office of thirty-two brokers." She lowered her eyes modestly. "Of course, I don't make as much as the President of the United States, the man in the next office does that." She frowned at the mention of Ben. "But I do very well. Now tell me, what's your specialty?"

"I'm an allergist."

"Oh." Annie laughed in spite of herself.

"Is that funny?" Herb looked annoyed.

"No, not at all. You just looked like a—I don't know, someone with saws and things. I knew an orthopedic surgeon once. He always went around in bloody sneakers."

"Really?"

"Yes, he was married to a friend of mine. I had a pain in my leg once, and he wanted to take me in the bedroom and give me cocaine for it. Up the nose." She laughed again, thinking of it.

"Did you go?'" Herb asked, alarmed.

"God, no. His wife had a fit," she sighed. "They're divorced now. He married his nurse . . . did you marry your nurse?"

"No, I'm still separated."

"I mean your wife."

"No, she's just a woman. She wouldn't know how to make as much as the President. I wish she did, then I wouldn't be having so much trouble now."

"That's too bad," Annie said. "I'm sorry. Maybe it would have been better if you hadn't lived in a house."

"She wanted the house."

"A home of her own."

Herb nodded.

"But you had to commute, and that took a lot of time. She was lonely."

"You make it sound like a soap opera."

"Where do you think they get them from?"

"Do you want to taste this?" Herb changed the subject.

"Um, no thanks. I'm allergic to cream sauces."

"Really?" Herb said so hopefully that Annie giggled.

"No, I just feel sick after eating them," she murmured.

"Maybe there's a slight allergy there."

"I don't know. I just don't eat them. I get sick just passing a French restaurant."

"I love French food," Herb said.

"All that cream and butter, so fattening."

"I could stand to lose a few pounds."

Annie felt she was meant to say no, no, right then. But she wasn't like that; and anyway at that moment she was distracted by the shape of a head and springy dark hair she knew well. He was on the other side of the room and had his back to her. For a minute she wasn't absolutely certain it was he. Then he turned his head to talk to a waiter. He was laughing and looked awfully roguish, as he did when he was out with girls other than her. She strained to see whom he was with.

She hadn't meant to have any feeling about him, none at all. She even hoped this morning that he would focus his attention right away on someone else and forget it ever happened. But this was too fast even for her. She blushed with shame. Oh yes, it was another blonde. A real blonde she hadn't seen before. The kind of girl with almost white straight hair and china blue eyes who works for SAS. She had her cute little chin in her fist and was gazing at Ben as if he was the answer to a stewardess' dream.

"I don't know anybody else like you," Herb was saying. "Vanessa noticed it right away. She was very attracted to you immediately, and I was too," he added.

"She's adorable," Annie said distractedly.

"She's all I have in the world," Herb said. "That child is everything to me."

Annie smiled. "That's nice."

"I want to keep her with me."

"I don't blame you. She's just adorable."

"Would you like to see her again? Maybe we could do something together. Vanessa would like that. You like children, don't you?"

Annie was busy wanting to murder all people with yellow and red hair. She looked over and saw the blonde playfully slap the hands that had caressed her only last night. She had known that would happen. Why be surprised? He had to have everything he saw. It was a flaw in his character. She tried to listen as Herb talked, but it was difficult with homicide on her mind.

"We could go out to lunch; how about tomorrow?"

"Oh, I can't do it tomorrow. I have an important birthday party . . . Donald's," she admitted when he looked so crestfallen.

"She likes you so much," he said.

"I don't see how she could; she just met me," Annie said modestly.

"Oh no, this child has a very discerning eye. She has such a hard time at home—"

"It must be tough on her to have parents in two places."

"It's her mother. Her mother is hard on her . . . so when she sees a warm and loving person like you she wants to reach out. It breaks my heart."

"I'm so sorry," Annie murmured.

"I was at my lawyer's today."

"Were you," Annie said. She had finished her salad and her coffee by now, and was suddenly ready to go. The sight of Ben flirting with another girl disheartened her more than she ever thought it would. She couldn't bear to be in the same room with it. She had to go.

"Yes, his office is a block up on Park. He thinks there's a good chance."

"For what?" Annie said blankly.

"For getting custody of Vanessa, of course. Considering the circumstances. Would you like some dessert?"

"Um, no thanks. I've really got to be going. Lunch was lovely. Thank you."

Herb looked disappointed. "I was hoping you could do something with us tomorrow."

Annie thought for a minute without thinking. "Well, maybe I could meet you for a little while."

"What time is your party?"

"Well, actually, maybe it would be fun for Vanessa to come."

"That would be wonderful."

"Yes, I'm sure it would be all right. In fact, I think it would be very nice. There are a few children coming over at three."

"Oh dear, that's not a good time for me. I have an errand I have to do."

"That's too bad."

"But Nessy wouldn't have to go with me. I could leave her with you. Would that be too much trouble for you?"

"No, that's fine. I have to be there anyway. I don't mind a bit." Annie put her napkin on the table, and smiled at Herb as she stood, just in case Ben was looking in her direction.

"Great then." Herb grinned back.

She walked him to the outside door and gave him Sara's address. He wrote it down carefully in a notebook. And when Annie offered her hand for a good-bye handshake, he raised it to his lips and told her he couldn't wait to see her again.

$$14$$

SARA SAT AT the kitchen table with her head in her hands. "I can't imagine what you're thinking. You must be out of your mind."

All around her were birthday preparations, piles of balloons to be blow up, Superfriends paper cake plates, matching Superfriends cups. Streamers and dime-story party favors. The cake was a wonder of blue and yellow and green over chocolate with plastic cowboys and Indians frozen in a mock battle. Annie sat next to her, toying with an empty cup of tea.

"You could have asked me, you know. It's Donald's birthday."

"What's the difference, one kid more or less?"

"This isn't just one kid. This is an issue. This is several issues."

"Oh, really. I think this is just a question of one more kid coming to a party. That's all. Let's put up the stuff and not argue about it."

"Just a second." Sara put her hand on Annie's arm.

"Oh, Sara."

"The first issue is that this is my house. And you didn't ask me. That's just like you, charging ahead doing whatever you want and never mind what anybody else feels about it. And the second issue is the child. We don't even know her."

"How bad can a five-year-old kid be?"

"You're dabbling in a divorce. That's very messy, Annie."

"Oh, so that's what's bothering you. Let's put up the streamers."

"I'm telling you you're crazy."

Annie started opening the packages of party favors. "Martin is going to bring those children back here in a minute, and I think we ought to set up before they get back."

"Annie!" Sara whined.

"Sara, do you want another cup of tea?" She poured her some. "Look, you're getting yourself all upset over nothing."

"You always make things more difficult."

"Stop that. The child lives in the same town where you're moving. She may even be in Donald's class at school next year. It can't hurt for him to know someone."

"You're meddling. You're getting involved in somebody else's life. Somebody else's child. Can't you see that's trouble?"

"There," Annie said. She finished arranging all the favors in little piles. "Now, where are the loot bags?"

"They're here somewhere."

"I don't see them." Annie rummaged through the pile. "Boy, in a few hours all this stuff will be in the garbage. Too bad kid birthday parties are wasted on children."

"Who is this man, anyway?"

"You know everything I know. Last week you were thrilled about him. . . . Are you sure you bought loot bags?"

"God damn it, Annie, you know I did! They're here if only you'll look."

"Sara, if you scream at me, I swear I'm going to get up and leave. I can't take this today."

"I'm sorry, but your judgment is lacking. A married man now. God, Mother will have kittens. First Nate, now this."

"Look, you wanted me to have a boyfriend. That's all you seem to care about. You were all for it a few weeks ago."

"Well, maybe. But the child. You have no right to get involved with somebody else's child."

"It's his child," Annie pointed out.

"Well, can't you see what it means? Why can't you find a decent man who doesn't have any children, and have some of your own? There must be *somebody*."

"I don't know why," Annie said. "I really don't."

"Maybe you make too much money."

"Don't start that!" Annie screamed. "You're identifying too much, you don't know a thing about it."

"I want you to be happy!" Sara screamed back. "Mother wants you to be happy."

Annie threw a pile of stuff up in the air. It came crashing down and some of it rolled off the table onto the floor. "You're driving me crazy. How can you listen to her every day? How can you go over this and over this? Maybe I don't want to get married. Maybe I don't want to be tied down by a couple of demanding children. Did either of you ever think of that? I'm happy doing what I'm doing. And I'm not going to listen to you and your complacence any more." Annie's voice rose louder and louder until she was screaming and pounding her fists on the table. "I'm going home."

She got up from her chair and kicked it. The package of missing loot bags fell to the floor.

During this fit of temper, Sara got smaller and smaller until she ended up cowering in her chair and weeping quietly. "God, oh God," she cried. "You must be terribly unhappy."

"I'm going home. You can take your birthday party and your seventeen children and your husband and your precious mother and you can shove them up your ass."

Annie went into the other room to look for her coat. That was it. No more. She was leaving. Her coat and handbag were where she had left them slung over the bench by the front door. The whole apartment was clean. No toys anywhere, and the dining-room table had been moved so a children's table, with a Superfriends tablecloth, could be set up flat on the floor. They had planned to hang balloons and streamers from the chandelier. Fuck 'em.

"Ann—ee." Sara wailed from the kitchen. "Annnn—ee."

"Annie, I can't do it alone."

"Oh, Sara, shut up."

"I can't. I just can't. All those children running around." She sobbed into her hands. "I can't. I can't handle it."

Annie looked at her curiously, as if she were a creature from another planet. An airhead, a bubble brain. "Why did you plan it then?"

"I don't *know*," she wept. "Children need birthday parties. They talk about them at school. They think about them for months. Annie, they hire clowns and take fifteen of them to a Broadway show. Or, or, they go to a magic show. It's incredible."

"Oh, stop crying."

"I wanted him to have one. We never did. Don't you remember? Mother used to take us out to Hicks for lunch, with one girl friend. She'd take us to Saks and buy us a dress. We never had any parties. And now Hicks has been torn down. I saw it being wrecked just the other day."

Annie stood on one foot, and then the other. When they got older they were taken to a show and dinner at a grown-up restaurant. Brenda thought it was such fun. She would have liked nothing better than to do away with friends altogether. They were always not right somehow, had an accent from one of the boroughs, or lived in a house where Pepsi and potato chips were available. Other girls had television sets in their rooms and could use the telephone whenever they wanted. Brenda wanted her girls to grow up different. And they did. Sara couldn't even give a children's party without breaking down.

"Forget about Mother. Can't you forget about her, Sara? You're thirty-two."

"She told me not to do it. She wanted us all to have a dinner party, all of us together tonight and no children. She said I'd get tired and they'd break the furniture and it would be a disaster. Now I have to do both, one for him and one for her."

Annie sat down again. "Why do you listen to her, Sara? She doesn't have all the answers. Look at her. She's a fifty-one-year-old lady who still wants to be a singer. She doesn't have a God-damned thing to do in life but hang onto you and criticize and find fault. Why do you put up with it? Look at the trouble she's giving you about the house."

"Oh God, Annie. What if she's right? What if it's a disaster? What if we get there and hate it?"

Annie laughed. "You'll sell it and move back, big deal."

"What if he doesn't tell me he hates it and just finds somebody more interesting in the city and comes home later and later? Some secretary or some stockbroker."

"I'm his stockbroker. No threat there. Come on, Sara. Look at all this stuff you bought. You want it to be sitting here when the hordes arrive?"

"God, Annie, they're breaking ground this week. When they

tore down Hicks, I just felt like a piece of me was being crushed, like my past was over. Don't you see? In another minute it's going to be too late. Suppose Mother gets really depressed and has a heart attack or gets cancer or something. It will be all my fault, I could have stopped it."

"Sara, I'm glad Hicks is gone, it was overpriced. Come on, Mother will find something else to worry about. Maybe she'll get involved with Daddy for a change."

"You're never serious, are you? No wonder it's harder for me. I think about it. Sometimes I think I can't stand another day. I just want to get out there and buy a loom or something." She lifted her tear-streaked face. "I can't be like you. I'm not tough and competent. It's hard to live in New York and be nothing."

"You're not nothing. What a stupid thing to say."

"Don't look away. You know perfectly well I'm nothing. You tell me all the time that what I do stinks. All I do is babysit, if not for them—for *her.*"

"You have children. That's special," Annie said softly. "You make things. I can't make anything. As for Mother, why don't you just say 'no'? I do it all the time."

"I don't have anything else to do," Sara wailed. "I have no excuses, and she makes me feel so *bad.* She sits there and tells me what she did for me when I was little. And I just feel like I'm letting her down somehow. Being grown up."

"She's virulent; you've let her get to you."

"And I have all the burden of her. You don't help at all. She's like some voracious Aztec god. But instead of asking for new victims to pacify her, she recycles the same old ones over and over. I wish I could be like you. I do. I'd have lots of lovers all at the same time and I'd spend all your money."

"Don't talk like that."

"What do you do with your money? I've always wondered."

"Hey ho, we're home," Martin called from the other room. "Hey, what have you been doing? Nothing's done."

He came into the kitchen with the two children trailing after him. "What's going on?" He stopped when he saw them.

"Mommy's crying," Donald cried.

"No!" Sara said sharply. "I'm not."

"She is. Daddy, why's Mommy crying?"

"Go in the other room," Martin said.

"No, I won't. Mommy, Mommy."

"Damn it, don't hang on me," Sara cried. "All of you!"

Martin stood there blankly. "What happened?"

"I said don't hang on me."

Donald started to cry. "Mommy's mad at me. What'd I do?"

"Nothing, Donald," Annie said. "Mommy and I started telling each other sad stories, and she got sad for a minute. Come and tell me what you did. You, too, Lucy." She took them both by the hand and led them into the other room. "No, your coats won't walk to the closet. Pick them up."

"What's the matter?" Martin said when they were gone.

Sara scrubbed at her eyes with a used tissue. "Nothing," she said sheepishly. "Annie's new boyfriend."

"Baby, why do you worry so about Annie all the time? She's all right." Martin stood there in his raincoat, rubbing at the bridge of his nose where his glasses made a mark. "Annie always lands on her feet."

"Why don't you get new glasses? You're getting disfigured," Sara said irritably. "Why don't you get contacts? You'd look a hundred percent better."

"My eyeballs are the wrong shape. Honey, you've gotten yourself into a snit. Come on, perk up, we have people coming in a little while."

"Not people, children."

"Little people, and there are all these balloons to blow up."

"Stop rubbing your nose, for Christ's sake. It's driving me crazy. You know perfectly well they have a new kind of lens. They put them in all kinds of eyeballs. The least you could do is check them out—*try* them. Why are you so stubborn?"

"Are you desperate for a fight?"

"Martin, don't push me."

"Well, is this a good time?"

"I'm not fighting. I just hate to see you making holes in your face."

Martin threw his coat on the chair Annie had been using. He picked up a balloon, stretched it a few times and blew it up. Tied a knot in it and handed it to Sara.

"Damn it," she muttered.

"I bought film," he said, working on another.

She watched him morosely.

"And flashbulbs," he added. He tossed another balloon at her and she ignored it.

"What are you really upset about?"

"Nothing."

"Then get up and help me."

She stared at the piles of colored paper products and the cheap toys, wondering how anybody could be fooled by them.

"All this was your idea. You do it," she said finally. "I hate parties."

"It'll be easier next year. We'll have a treasure hunt outside. They'll love it."

This reminded Sara of Annie's extra child from Pine Wood. "I hope I don't hate it."

"You'll love it, too. Is that what you're worried about?" He batted another balloon. "I love you. It's all for you, don't forget that."

It's all for him, she thought, frowning. It was too far to go to say it. "Do you know what she does? She gets herself mixed up with all the wrong kind of people, and then she forces them on us. Is that right?"

His balloon rose in the air and fell to the floor. "I said I love you. Didn't you hear me?"

"Well, she does. She makes life impossible for everybody," Sara said defensively.

"Damn it, Sara, can't you think about anything else? You've got children coming, the place isn't ready. And what are you thinking about—Annie, Annie, Annie and her eternal boyfriend problems. My *God* it's getting me down!"

"All right. You don't have to scream at me. God, everybody pushes." She picked up a balloon and tried to blow it up. She couldn't get it started and threw it down with disgust. "I can't do it."

"Not like that. You have to stretch it first, like this." Martin stretched Sara's discarded balloon elaborately. "Now try it."

She took it from him. It was a particularly garish green, not quite evenly dyed. She blew. The balloon faltered and then blossomed. She held it up to him in triumph and let it go, letting its peculiarly human-sounding collapse splash noisily in his face.

"That's not trying." Martin tried to laugh, but failed. "Do it again." He handed her the balloon.

She got up. "I'll get Annie in here to blow. She's an expert."

"No, I want you to help me." He had the balloon in his hand.

She turned away, and his hand snaked out and grabbed her arm. "I love you, Sara."

"Let go."

"Sara, it's your child's birthday, not Annie's."

"You're hurting me."

"I'm hardly touching you. Sara, look at me."

"Don't push me," Sara warned. He let go and she pulled away. "It'll be quicker with three of us. There's a lot to do."

She went through to the other room, calling Annie to come and help. Martin sat down where Sara had been. First he rubbed the bridge of his nose where it was always so sore, and then remembering how idiotic the gesture made him look, he dropped his hand. And sat there waiting for someone to come back and help him.

15

THERE WAS a huge crowd of people, and she was trying to get through. All around was the smell of fish. Fresh fish and rotting fish, too. She was on the street. There were baskets of them, snails and clams and crabs, some still alive and scuttling over each other. People were pushing, and there was the sound of gun shots. Annie was looking for someone, but she wasn't sure who. It was someone little who had gotten away, was lost. Something squelched under her foot and she slid into the person in front of her. The slippery thing was still under her shoe. There was a hole in the sole and the wet soaked through. Annie dragged her foot along the sidewalk to get it off. She pushed toward the street with the crowd. Bang. Bang.

She couldn't find whomever she had lost. She was going to be punished for it. Everybody in the crowd was dark, dark hair, was pushing. Oh, she was in Chinatown. That was it. And they weren't crying, trying to get away. They were going toward the sound. Annie pushed out into the street. The dragon was there, undulating all its colors. Firecrackers popped in smoke all around it on the pavement. Suddenly the head of the dragon lifted and underneath was a tiny, gnarled old lady. She called out to Annie, wordless sounds that Annie didn't understand. She opened her mouth and traced with a crooked finger the smooth toothless ridges of her enflamed gums. Bang. Bang. There was a white spot, a canker, in the middle of her mouth that she wanted Annie to see. Suddenly it was in Annie's mouth, a wad of cotton getting bigger and bigger. She pushed it away with her tongue, but it grew and grew. The little lady pulled her underneath the dragon as the crowd surged closer and began ripping apart the form that covered them.

Annie tossed from side to side, stifled by the smell of fish and rotting garbage. Ugh, a piece of slime on her shoe. She struggled to get it off, panted for air and rose up to consciousness. Tightly swaddled in her sheets. White walls, white sheets, and someone knocking at the door. She shook her head as if it were a blanket she could free of foreign particles. Why did she have dreams like that? They scared her terribly; did they mean she was going to die? She got out of bed and pulled up the shade. Another sunny day.

Now the bell rang. Annie pattered to the door and looked through the spyhole. It was Ben, dressed for work.

"Oh, God, I thought you were dead," he said. "What's the matter?" He came into the apartment and gave it a searching look as if for some sign of foul play. He had put the lining in his raincoat and had his briefcase in one hand. His otherwise perfect face, pocked like a moonscape, was dented with concern.

"I had a terrible dream," Annie said. She stood at the door in her cotton nightie. "Do come in," she didn't remember saying.

"I'm sorry to hear that." He checked out the kitchen. There was no sign of any activity in the coffee pot. "Is there—," he pointed to the bedroom, "anybody in there?"

"What's the matter with you? What are you doing here?" Annie said.

"I called you all weekend, and you weren't here. I got worried, so I thought I'd come over to see if you were all right."

"I was having a terrible dream. I was in Chinatown, and I lost something," she murmured.

"It's Monday, Annie. Aren't you going to work?"

"And there were all these people around me. At first I thought I was in the middle of a revolution in the Far East somewhere, and people were screaming and getting shot. And there was this terrible smell, like dead flesh. Or anyway I thought it was. Have you ever smelled dead flesh?"

"Yes, the dog used to roll in it."

Annie looked at him with new interest. "You had a dog?"

"Are you all right?"

"Oh sure, sure, I must have overslept. What time is it?"

He looked at his watch. "Eight-thirty."

She was shocked for the first time. "Eight-thirty? What are you doing here at eight-thirty?" She looked down at the nightgown, gathered a bunch of it in front of her in a fist. She could feel the sleep poking at the corners of her eyes. Eight-thirty; no wonder she wasn't ready.

"I was walking to work. I thought I'd look in to see if you're all right. Are you alone?"

"No, I'm with you." Annie padded into her bedroom and quickly pulled the bed together. First dress the bed, then dress yourself. That's what a good little girl does in the morning. Annie went into the bathroom and looked in the mirror. Her hair was tangled and she looked like a ghost. She turned on the hot water and let the steam rise. Maybe he was a dream, too. If he had been real, he would have brought the papers in.

She wasn't quite awake. She felt her teeth with her tongue. All present in her mouth. In a second she turned on the shower and got into it. As she stood there, washing off the slimy discomfort of her dream, she remembered the weekend. Donald's hectic party, and Vanessa in a pink velvet party dress. Navy-blue coat with a velvet collar. And Sara wouldn't come to the door to meet Herb. Then, an hour over coffee with Herb who joked and laughed, in a high mood about something he wouldn't talk about. Back at Sara's apartment for another party, with Brenda and Jack this time. More present opening, all conflict put aside for a minute, except for Jack, morose over an early copy of the Sunday *Times*. And then on Sunday she went up to the Metropolitan Museum and listened to a string quartet playing in the Lehman wing.

While she dressed, Ben puttered in the kitchen, making coffee in his shirtsleeves. At first he was upset, almost devastated by her offhand attitude. No kiss, no look of recognition. No thrill of an unexpected meeting, on her part anyway. Then he took off his jacket and went into the kitchen where she had tackled him only—last Thursday. It was a lifetime ago. All weekend unconfirmed, it seemed like a movie he had seen alone. But back in her kitchen, he felt the walls remembered. He liked her kitchen, full of gadgets and things to play with, even though there were no oranges to run through the juicer. He felt contented, even relieved to be there. This was the way it should be, people looking out for each other, being together without having planned it. She looked cute in the morning, if a little daffier than he would have expected. Not as warm. It worried him.

He took his notecase from the living room and went back into the kitchen to make a list. Coffee, oranges, eggs, butter. He sniffed the milk. The milk was on its last day. Annie clearly didn't spend her money on sustenance. "Milk," he wrote.

"What are you doing?" She was dressed now, in an aubergine wool dress that made her hair look lighter. Now there were splashes of color on her cheeks and even some shadow on her eyelids. She narrowed her eyes at the list. What did he think he was doing?

"That was fast." His heart was pounding. She still didn't have any shoes on. Now she would stand on her toes and give him a kiss. That was what always happend with women.

What happened was they leaped out of bed. In the bathroom in a flash. A whole drawer full of makeup on the face, and then scantily clad, they came back to advertise their favorite part. Bosom, ass, legs, whatever they thought was the best feature. Tender underwear was the thing now. Waist cinchers and garters. Bloomers for thick thighs, camisoles for the shallow bosom. Tap pants for the hippy. Ben had seen it all. He thought with Annie it must be her toes she most admired, because they were the only parts of her covered in lacy material. She wore stockings with clocks, no shoes.

"You have lovely toes," he murmured.

"What are you doing here?" she asked suspiciously.

"Making coffee. You need some more." He poured some from the pot, stricken because she didn't kiss him. "Milk?"

"At eight-thirty in the morning?"

"I always take milk in my coffee. I get heartburn without it." He handed her a mug without milk.

She took it and burned her tongue, added milk herself. "But what are you really doing here?"

"Stop asking me. I didn't see you on Friday and couldn't reach you all weekend. Frankly, I missed you." He smiled. Now she would kiss him. She'd smile her sweet smile that made the dimple jump into her cheek, and she'd rise up on her toes to touch his lips. She had a gentle kiss, sweeter than any he'd known. That's what he thought. But she didn't kiss him.

"That's ridiculous," she said. "I can't imagine why."

"After Thursday, I think you ought to be able to imagine why." Ben was surprised. They fell into his arms when he said he missed them. That's what they always did. They stocked up their kitchens, or made lists for his. Once was a hopeful always. It always was.

"Well, I can't," Annie said seriously.

"What do you mean you can't? Can't what?" he insisted.

They had been leaning against counters in the kitchen, but now Annie moved into the dining alcove where the sun was streaming in.

"I love to sit here in the morning. It makes me think I'm getting a tan." Annie put her face in the sun and closed her eyes.

"Annie, don't you remember Thursday?" Ben asked, now truly anxious.

"Sure, the day before Friday."

"I mean it. Do you think I'd come barging in here if it weren't for Thursday?"

Annie did not even bother to open her eyes. "Look," she said coldly. "Don't put me on your list of housecalls because we had a glass of champagne together."

"It was a grocery list. Here, look, you don't have a thing in the house."

"I mean your other list."

"Listen, Annie," Ben said sternly. "We had a lot more than champagne together."

"I only remember the champagne; and frankly, I'm not interested. I'm really not."

"Who was that fat person I saw you with on Friday?" Ben said furiously. "Is he the reason for this? What happened?"

Annie sat up. "You know, you make a good cup of coffee."

"He looked like a dope. What could he offer you? Damn,"

Ben muttered. "I do better things than make coffee. You know I do."

"Oh, don't be so defensive."

"I'm a good cook, and I even wash up."

"I don't see you washing up," Annie said.

"Who was he?"

"Who?"

"That fat person. Don't deny it. It had to be something pretty shady or you wouldn't have run off right after lunch like that. You didn't even say good-bye to me. I wouldn't have thought you'd do something like that, not after Thursday. I wanted to make a date." Ben inched his chair over into the sun until they were sitting side by side with their faces tilted toward the little patch of sky in the south that hadn't yet been covered by building.

"I don't think he's fat," Annie said, considering it. Herb was large, but she didn't think he was really *fat*.

"He was fat," Ben insisted.

"So what?"

"So what? Fat is unacceptable. Fat is—it's disgusting." Ben flushed purple. He hadn't tortured himself for years to lose sixty pounds and keep it off to hear the great love of his life say, "So what?"

Annie laughed. For a second she almost leaned over and put her face into his shirt front. In the sun he smelled of laundry and soap, or maybe men's moisturizing lotion. He made grocery lists and housecalls. When he was upset, the firm-looking lines of his face collapsed. He looked not unlike a frightened five-year-old. Or a thwarted one. Or a spoiled playboy. She shook her head firmly.

"Carl is too fat," she said softly. "I think his body is disgusting. Sometimes I feel it's eating up all the space in the office, and one day I'll look up and find myself pinned against the wall."

"What a thought."

"Or splashed against it. I never see him eat. Where does he get it?" Annie closed her eyes and thought of Carl to avoid thinking of Ben, smooth, inventive, deep as midnight. Not at all like Nate's flurry of activity, a bearer, beating a short track to a clearing in the jungle. And always having something to complain about at the end, a cramp in the back, foot, thigh, shortness of breath, hunger, thirst. As if it hurt to make the effort, and the effort itself was no more than a temporary brownout of the soul.

"Gluttons have their ways," Ben said.

When Annie was curious about men, she used to think they were all the same, all bone and sharp edges. Knees, elbows, teeth, fingers all seemed to conspire to jar her, bruise her, pull her hair, distract her from the goal rather than encourage her toward it. It seemed that love was a wrestling match, even the kisses were hard. The excitement was in the anticipation, the imagination of what might happen. The reality was a bony thrust, too many limbs, and a crushed breastbone, or pelvis, or a piece of pinched skin. Pinned down for the count, she'd be all nerves except where it counted, where it was numb. Sara said she felt no pain at the moment of birth. It was worth the whole nine months of agony for those last ecstatic moments of absolute numbness. Annie had to work past the numbness, imagining her partner not a wheezing, churning clutter of bones, but a god from mythology, a swan, a bull, a flash of lightning striking her with fire where she hid at the end of the maze.

She'd had three partners, not counting Ben. He was the fourth, who had brought her beyond the pale of innocent speculation. The fourth made an army that had to be put down.

"They eat all night," he said, remembering; "secretly with a flashlight. Whole boxes of cookies, and a pie. Boston cream, with extra Cool Whip."

"Ugh," Annie said.

"Cookie flesh is disgusting. It travels, it moves even when you don't. It takes a secret eater to get really fat. They're the ones who won't eat a potato with dinner and say, 'I don't know why I'm so fat; I don't eat a thing.' But the family gets sensitized to the noise of chewing. They can hear it even when the doors are closed. Carl probably eats Dutch Pretzels with his nightly dozen jelly donuts just to drive his wife crazy in her sleep."

Annie laughed. "I bet you're right." But actually she'd had a glimpse of the possibilities of the flesh. Ben's flesh covered the edges. It was the muscles in his stomach that she was aware of, the tendons in his legs, the round smooth inside of his arms. The tip of his penis. He murmured in her ear. At the time she thought she could do without the murmuring. But she was enflamed, there was no question about that. And yet she thought the hunger was for something different. A permanent cure, maybe, a disillusion so complete she could smother her yearning in it.

"I know I'm right. Even I can hear him chewing at night."

"I think we better go," Annie said. "I'm awake now."

"I like this. It's nice here in the morning." He was remembering how Annie made him go even before he'd begun to think about clothes for the morning. He was dozing with a leg cradled between her thighs and his face in the curve of her neck, considering a midnight supper at the Brasserie or at least some soup from a can, when she shook him off suddenly and cast him into the night. He could not understand why she would do such a thing, and worried all weekend that he might have been drooling on her shoulder. She made no reply.

"Who was he, or was it someone else?"

"I don't know what you're talking about," Annie said.

"I want to be with you," he said earnestly.

"You are with me."

"I mean really. I want to see you when I wake up and have breakfast with you. I want to be part of your grocery list, and— everything."

Annie shook her head. And when he'd finished with the everything, she'd be the one with the leftovers. "It was just a client."

"Who?"

"Herb, he's an allergist."

"You spent the weekend with him, didn't you?"

"No!" Annie said indignantly. "Hell no, I was with my sister most of the time. Damn it, it's none of your business."

"Your sister?" Ben grinned. "Really? Sara with the children?"

"I only have the one." Annie collected the cups, furious that she had told him. She started for the kitchen.

"But he wants to play doctor with you, I could see it in the way he looked at you."

Annie turned back. "Christ, Ben, you had your back to him. You were playing with a stewardess with straw hair."

"Ha, you noticed!" He slapped the table with his hand. "Could I have another cup of coffee? I didn't have any at home."

"I didn't notice. I just happened to see you that's all," Annie said defensively. "I don't care."

"I had a date, I couldn't break it."

"I don't care. I'm not interested. I told you that."

"Can I have some more coffee? Please?" when she hesitated.

"All right, but drink it fast." Annie went and poured the coffee. She poured more for herself, too.

"Here." She put his down on the table in front of him.

"Why are you being so hard? You can't tell me you didn't like it," he said. She liked it, all right. She was a tiger, but she still hadn't kissed him.

"I'm not hard." She was silenced by the indictment. "That isn't fair."

"Well, you can't turn back now. This is something special. I know it is. I know about these things. You have to trust my judgment."

Annie laughed. She reached out to pat his hand, to show she wasn't mad at such self-deception. But she was mad. Something special to him was roast beef at $3.89 a pound. "Let's not fight about it, okay?"

"I'll fight, you turn me on," he said seriously. "I want you."

"Big deal. You want everybody."

Ben put his mug down. "Let's go."

"Well, don't be mad." She tugged her hair out of her face and hooked it behind an ear. "That's silly," when he didn't answer. She took the two mugs and rinsed them in the sink. Well, it was true he was a bum. It wasn't her fault he couldn't be trusted. So she tried it once. Men try it once all the time and don't come back for more. She turned off the water and heard him putting on his coat. What was he so mad about anyway? She didn't have to. She hadn't signed a contract saying she would until he got tired of her. The whole thing was absurd.

He was standing with his hand on the doorknob when she came out. "If I had a hat, I'd eat it."

"I have a hat, you can eat mine." Annie found her shoes and plunged her feet into them.

"You think I think sex is everything, don't you?" He put down his briefcase so he could help her into her coat. He pulled the hair out of her collar with one finger.

"Yes, you do."

"I think *love* is everything. Don't laugh, I do. I think if you let go and let it get you, I mean real passion for somebody so you can't think about anything else, I think it would be bigger than the scars you came with." Inadvertently he touched his face at the word scar. "Anyway, I think it would. Nobody comes to it empty, everybody's cluttered up with a past of some sort. Mine isn't what you think it is."

"I think if I let go, I'd spin right out into space. There would be nothing there to hold me."

"I'll go with you."

"Ben, how many girls have you slept with in the last six years?"

"Only one." He opened the door. "Here are your newspapers."

Annie leaned over to pick them up, the smile at his bit of gallantry wiped off her face. Wasn't it just like a man to promise the world and then fail at something so simple as remembering to pick up the papers!

16

PLAYING THE stock market is a very checks-and-balances affair, rather like a dubious romance. One plots and wheedles and plans so carefully, only to have some unforeseen, some unknowable factor (the whim of a President, a diplomatic gaffe) plunge everything into crisis. One couldn't be sure of anything from one twenty-four hour period to the next, except that there was no way to get away from it. The capricious nature of the beast was its allure. One day a broker could make a fortune for himself and his clients, right there on paper, and the next day lose it all. Just like love.

The only sure thing was that there was movement every day, a new chance to recoup, break even, get ahead. Every day some stocks made money, some stayed about even, and some lost. The idea was to move them around at the right moment for each one so that one's own favorites made more money than they lost. Movement was important also because a broker makes money not on a stock's success, but on the transaction itself. A broker has to buy and sell no matter how he feels or where the country is headed, recession or no recession.

In a slump the cost of hazarding guesses about what will do well hit everybody differently. Annie got headaches toward the end of the day; Ben, stomach aches. Carl ate secretly at night, as well as candy bars whenever he found himself for a minute alone. John, who hadn't been the best-selling broker in almost a year, seemed to be shrinking in adversity. Graying, balding, losing his nerve.

Ben began noticing John's decline in nerve just about the time he felt a jolt to his own. They were for different reasons, of course. John had passed the peak of his career, which was way back in the sixties. Now, with the seemingly endless economic crisis, his resilience was fading in exact proportion to the board's lack of satisfaction with his performance as a manager.

Ben, on the other hand, felt a weakening in his power because someone he liked didn't like him back. Two very different things, one might say. But John had been happily married for nearly thirty years, and he was the only one in the whole office whose anxiety about work really came from work. John was afraid the country was in a decline like Rome's, and would never come back to its post-war glory. Ben watched John shrink with loss of killer instinct and feared it was happening to him, too.

He didn't know how it ever occurred to him to become enamored of Annie, but now he couldn't think it had ever been any other way. He tried to remember what he really wanted to happen when he heard that Nate had run off. Did he mean to fall in love with her really, or did he just want her to fall in love with him? Or did he want to try it out, like a new pair of shoes, and see how love suited them both?

Now he thought of her on the other side of the wall from him, bent over her calculations, in earnest conversation on the phone, her shoes abandoned under her desk. He thought of her at night when he stir-fried his steak and vegetables in his electric wok, thought of her as he stood in line at the Chinese laundry with his sheets in a bag. His speculations about Annie slowed his life down to a shuffle. What did she do at night? What did she eat? What did she think about? He regretted not letting her tell him the end of her dream. She didn't tell him another. In fact, she hardly spoke to him at all. When he saw her at the office, she was cool, modulated down to a whisper. She acted as if she didn't care how he felt, as if their night together had never happened.

It made him crazy because other women liked him a lot, called him on the phone when he was too busy to call them. They told him he was great, the best. And for years he had believed it. Now he wondered if they had been lying to him all along.

He brooded, wondering what to do. He knew Annie was going out with a doctor who was truly disgusting in every respect. As long as Annie denied the serious nature of *their* relationship, however, he couldn't think of a single way to stop it. Sometimes he imagined her and her revolting doctor going to bed together, and he wanted to strangle her. What did she see in him, anyway? She must be radically deficient in taste. On other occasions, he found himself willing, even eager, to overlook the lapse with the doctor, if only she would love him instead.

What should he do, stop his whole life because Annie was being difficult? Every year Ben went skiing as soon as the snow came. He had learned to ski when he was four because his father wanted him to. He was thirteen when his father died with his skis on. Ben gave it up then, he thought forever. But, after he came to New York and made some money and started working out at a gym, his body tightened up. One year he had a girl friend briefly who liked to ski, so he took it up again for her. He was better at it than he remembered and continued the passion for the slope long after the passion for the girl had been forgotten.

He began practicing at the beginning of December behind the door in his office. He jumped with his knees bent, twisting from side to side with imaginary poles under his arms until his calves and thighs ached. This year he had planned to go to Vail before Christmas and stay past New Year's. He didn't like to be in town during the holidays and always made reservations in July of every year to be sure he would get away. For a single person the New Year was always a dreary event.

This year, as his calves ached, he brooded about how he would attempt to get Annie to go with him. Since the night of the champagne, as he would always ruefully remember it, Annie had become staunchly businesslike whenever she was with him. He couldn't find a way to broach the subject.

On December first, Annie began her year-end drive to determine the gains and losses of her clients so she could confuse the government accordingly. Every time Ben passed her office, her head was down and she was studying an account. She did this every year in December. But this year she was far more preoccupied with it than usual. For every client who made money when selling a stock, she looked for a loss to show the IRS. If there were not enough losses, she encouraged the sale of stocks that were in a losing position to create a loss. Because of her fall housecleaning, she had a better record that year than most brokers, which proved to her that acute despair is not always a bad thing.

Every time Ben came into her office, suddenly she was on the phone encouraging her clients to move quickly to take their tax loss. Ben noted that, in contrast to John's definite year-end sluggishness, there was nothing wrong with Annie's killer instinct. When in doubt, she cut her losses.

A few months before she had been very high on Springbok Pharmaceuticals, a company that had developed a new anti-arthritic. News of the drug had pushed the price of the stock way up. But the FDA had not gone ahead with its approval of the drug on schedule, and the stock price took a dive. Though Annie was sure the stock would recover by spring, it was in a definite losing position now.

The day Ben finally felt he could no longer delay forcing the issue of their relationship, Annie had been on the phone all day selling Springbok. He caught her with her coat under her arm, trying to sneak out while he was jumping on imaginary skis behind his door.

He grabbed his coat and caught up with her on the escalator. Their office was on the mezzanine of the Pan Am building, which meant that they never had to use an elevator.

"Hi," he said from two people away because there was a fat lady in front of him who wouldn't let him pass, and a thin man in front of her.

Annie pretended she didn't see him. When she got to the main floor, he lurched forward and grabbed her arm.

"Ow," she said indignantly.

"I have to talk to you. Sorry. I just didn't want you to get away."

She turned and fixed her serious gray eyes on him. "What's the matter, did something happen?"

"You've been avoiding me. I can't stand it any more," he said. They were blocking the door. They had to move. They drifted out of the building with the flow of traffic.

"No, I'm not." She walked on, though, making him think she was trying to avoid him.

"You don't talk to me any more."

"I'm just busy, that's all," Annie said. She swung her scarf around her neck and headed into the wind.

"With what?" he demanded.

Annie shrugged. "It's always busy this time of the year."

"Look, Annie, we're both grown up. Let's talk about it. We have to face up to the fact that something has happened between us."

Annie shivered a little in the cold. "Put your coat on," she commanded. "You'll catch a cold." He was still following her with his coat over his arm.

He obeyed and was silent for a moment. Then said firmly, "You can't do this to me. You turned me on, you can't just let me go."

She shook her head.

"You made me think you wanted me. You seduced *me*, Annie."

"Did I?" she said wonderingly.

"Yes," he said emphatically. "And now I love you." He flushed, cold as it was. "And you're ignoring me. Why?"

"It was an accident," Annie said suddenly.

"No, it wasn't. You were very definite about it." He took her arm again and made her stop against a store window. "Don't you like me? If you really don't like me, I'll go away. You know I will."

The abruptness of this promise produced a frown from Annie. "I like you," she said slowly.

"Then what's the matter?" The breath he let out made a cloud in the air. She almost reached for it.

She hesitated, then began walking again. "I don't feel very strong," she said in a small voice. "And you hurt everybody. I just—well, it's not for me that's all. You're not my type."

Not her type? He drew back hurt. "Then why did you start it? Why did you get me so excited?—If you think I'm so rotten. If I'm not your type."

Ben raised his voice. People turned around and looked. Nothing like a good fight in the street. Annie ducked into her scarf, so no one could see her.

"I don't remember," she mumbled. "I guess it was a one night-stand."

"You don't have a one-night stand with someone you see

every day," he said suddenly outraged. "I told you how I feel about you. It wasn't just *fun*. Oh, Annie, that's really bad form. That's really mean." He turned away humiliated, furious. He began to walk.

Annie had to skip a step to catch up. "Why don't you forget about it? It wasn't really anything. Just something that . . . happened. That's all."

"Not for me. I don't want to forget about it. I want you to go to Vail with me." It popped out, out of context while he was still walking away from her. Damn. He stopped.

"I can't," she said quickly before he could reorganize the blunder into a proper invitation.

"Okay. If you don't want to go to bed, we could just be together." He raised his hands appealing to her sense of fairness. "How's that? I'll amuse you. I'll prove that you're safe with me. I won't hurt you, I won't be pushy. Even if you want me to, I'll say no."

She laughed. "How long for?"

"As long as you want. How about a year? You want to be friends, we'll be friends."

"I don't trust you for a minute." She shook her head, still laughing. "You have no self-control. Even if you loved me, even if I loved you, you'd be in bed with somebody else the minute I was out of sight."

"What about you?" he protested. "Not even one day goes by and you're out to lunch with someone else. I could say the same thing about you."

"Oh, Herb's not somebody else."

"Yes, he is. What do you think he is?"

"I don't go to bed with him," Annie blurted. "If you must know."

"Yes, I must know. And I don't believe that. How can you expect me to believe that? You go out with him, don't you?"

"Oh come on. He's just a friend. I like him, that's all."

"You like me. You went to bed with me."

"Once! Why don't you forget it? We aren't even dating."

"Jesus, Annie, we'll date then." Ben rolled his eyes. Annie's logic was incredible, he didn't know what to do with it. "How can I forget it," he muttered. "It was a big thing to me. Now you like *him*. What am I supposed to think?"

"You're different," Annie said screwing up her face. "I *know* you."

"Well, of course you know me. That's the nice thing about it. You're supposed to know me. Look, we'll date if you want to. Then you'll know me even better. What are you doing Saturday?"

"I know you well enough already."

"Annie, you're making me crazy. What happens when you know *him* better—" He turned away. "I don't believe this. I don't believe you don't go to bed with him. I know *you*. And you've known him for weeks."

"Oh, Ben." She took his arm and squeezed it. "You're not grown up."

"I am." He looked at her tragically, then put his arms around her.

For a minute, in heavy coats in the wind, they hugged. Then briskly, Annie drew away.

Self-control, Ben told himself. If that was an example of self-control, it left a lot to be desired. They were getting dangerously near Annie's house by now. Ben wondered when he might be allowed to hug her again. Then he thought maybe she really liked that other guy. Maybe boring and fat to her was grown up. For a second he let that bit of bad news travel around in him. It felt like fat cells multiplying when he ate. Fat cells without the pleasure of eating.

Ben sighed. He had given up food to be hungry and thin. He had put love in its place. That seemed grown up. And he was good at love. Everyone said so. He was considerate, gentle, energetic. No one went home hungry. He wasn't ugly or overweight, not any more, and he could pay for anything she wanted. But so could she. What else could he give her? What else did she want? Self-control. What a bitter pill. Self-control was an impossible thing to prove. It wouldn't show no matter how much effort he put into it. He sighed again. Self-control wasn't in his line.

"Are you sure you won't go to Vail with me?" he said pitifully. "I could work on self-control there."

"No, I can't," Annie said firmly. "But you'll meet somebody, and by the time you come back, you won't remember that you ever gave me a thought."

"What if I save myself for you, Annie? If I demonstrated a lot of self-control, would you let me down?"

She made a funny motion with her head, a sort of yes, no, I don't know shrug, and one of her brilliant smiles that almost nailed him to the sidewalk.

"We could have a hamburger," she said, "if you don't have a better offer."

So, he gave her the hamburger and two weeks to think over going to Vail. But even though he took her to the opera, and twice to the movies, and each time exercised a great deal of restraint, she still wouldn't go to Vail with him. Which left him with the impossible dilemma of whether or not to continue working on her peculiar (and invisible) exercise of self-control two thousand miles away.

17

IT WAS VERY cold the last week of the year, and everybody was gone from the office. Even John Carlton, who went to Barbados every year at Christmas but didn't think he ought to go this year, went in the end. Sylvia was in Chicago with her sister. Ben was in Vail. There were some people in the boardroom, of course. But it was quiet. Carl was gone, too. He was in Disneyland with the kids because Marilyn had to be in L.A. to see someone.

This was the worst time of the year to live alone. Even with all the clients and their parties and a number of working women Annie knew who were available and eager for a dinner out, the season was tragic. It wasn't fun wrapping presents alone, going around and delivering them. Drinking egg nogs in other people's houses. Annie regretted everything: letting Nate move in in the first place, letting him stay there so long as if he were part of her forever and belonged there. And she regretted allowing him to go like that, with hardly a ripple. Once or twice she thought of calling him at the office, but didn't know what she might say. She hated him now.

She had Christmas dinner at Sara's so early that she was

home by nine. The phone rang about midnight waking her up, but there was no one there when she answered it. She said hello a dozen times, her heart beating so loudly it was frightening. She had a vision of herself suddenly old and talking to the walls.

Then at the very end of the week on the spur of the moment when they were out to dinner together, Herb told Annie that he was going to Palm Beach for a convention the following week and asked if she would go with him.

"It will probably be very boring for you, and Vanessa will be with me, but I'd like you to come," he said.

Annie knew that he was sad, too. She could tell by the way he walked, by the lack of spirit in his voice. He had hinted right away at the beginning of their friendship at a sexual problem, and she thought that must have something to do with it, too. It made her think again of herpes, also of impotence. Somehow it made her feel safe from abandonment. This time she couldn't be offered something that might be taken away.

She found it interesting and rather poignant not to be molested, to be looked at with a kind of grave reverence. He looked at her with a wonderful wistfulness, as if she had the key to something he couldn't open.

"I'm lonely," he admitted. "I'd like to get married."

"It's the season," Annie murmured. "It makes everyone feel like that." But there was a sudden increase in her heart rate under her cool. It occurred to her then that he might be a genuinely old-fashioned sort of person who wanted to really know her face before he became involved with her. Perhaps he thought reticence was a sexual problem. The idea gave him instant value in her eyes. Over the table she touched his hand.

It was a broad hand. Herb's fingers were thick, as if his ancestors had been hard laborers and he hadn't yet evolved beyond them. It was not a great hand, but it seemed to her that his less than perfect frame might be hiding a noble soul.

He shook his head gravely. "It's not the season." He told her she was sweet, a person of great quality. He'd known it the first moment he'd seen her. He could tell, he told her, by the gentle way she spoke to children, and by her smile. She had a remarkable smile, he said. He didn't think anyone like her could ever be interested in him.

Annie said no, no. He was a lovely person. Really. They held hands on the table for a minute, and it seemed true. After all, he could see that she was a person of quality and that made him a lovely person, too. In spite of his hands, which were not delicate, and his face, which was definitely rather too broad for her taste. She had the disconcerting thought that his head was much larger than hers and his body, too. And that in photographs (and also in bed) they would not go well together.

She looked at him critically. On the other hand, a noble soul was not a thing to be cavalier about, nor was someone who could see quality when he looked at her. When he told her once again how boring it would be, but how much Vanessa and he cared for her, how much it would mean to them if she went, she said very seriously that she would think it over.

The next day Annie walked over to Saks. There were always sales after Christmas, and she wanted to get something to go with the sweater Sara had given her. It was the kind of thing she didn't usually like. It was very fussy with designs in different colors, popcorns in pink, diamonds in silver, stripes of gold, and two layers of angora ruffle around the neck. But Annie had to admit it was sweet, and made her look as if she had a long and delicate neck.

She took the sweater with her in a bag. Halfway through her walk to the department store, it began to snow. First just a few gusts of white in the wind, and then within minutes the sky filled with it. What color would go with pink and gray? Annie's head whirled with thoughts of color and fabric, and also with the piles of paper on her desk. Something to go out in at night, or something to wear to relieve the endless boredom of office days? Then she thought she ought to sell the considerable number of Numodonics stock she had in several accounts. It was dropping even in this quiet week.

She almost turned around to return to her office, her mind on a company that made radio electronic tracers. Then suddenly the sting of the snow on her face made her look up. The sky was in a white fury as doesn't often happen in New York. Once a year now it snowed in earnest. The rest of the winter it was just bitter to the bone.

The last time it snowed like this the stock exchange closed, and Annie went up to Nate's office to get him to come out and play with her. He had gone for the day, nobody knew where, and didn't come home until long after dark. Annie rushed back to the apartment, thinking she would find him there. But after waiting for a while, she went out again and walked in the snow by herself. She remembered the feeling she had then of kicking the snow, licking the crystals as they melted on her lips. She wandered around the neighborhood, hoping to meet him on the street. He often went out for a drink with someone and let the hours pass around him.

He was free; his face said it clearly when she wondered aloud where he had been. His office closed at two for all those who lived in Hastings and had to go home on the train.

"If you don't like it, I'll go," he said. It was as simple as that, the limits made as clear as a line drawn against a ruler.

"Just asking," Annie murmured, backing off. Anybody would.

Now she lifted her face to the snow and thought of other losses. Sara's miscarriage before Donald and the six weeks she had spent in bed trying to save the baby. Annie used to sit with her after work, and they would talk about what defect would be too great to bear. Would they prefer the child to die rather than be born blind or deaf? Or to be missing a hand at the end of its arm? No. Eyes and ears don't make a person perfect. Annie and Sara would sit on the bed weeping, with a bottle of sherry between them, imagining defects they couldn't bear, and even more unbearable alternatives.

In this stark modern life with no superstitions, hardly any God to speak of, and all contact with the earth gone for many generations, the two sisters clung together with this one piece of primal mystery between them. And they decided that if this new life was granted Sara, and the baby was missing a hand or was blind or deaf, it would be a sign from the God they had been raised to ignore. The baby itself would be a call for love greater than any they had known, a demand from somewhere for a special effort beyond anything that had been required before.

They had decided how it would be, but Sara was very frightened anyway, and didn't move for a full week after the doctor finally told her she could. Then when she really thought she was out of danger, she went out to dinner across the street with Martin one night. And later, just before dawn, something split inside her and her blood flowed like a river.

Martin told Annie afterward that while they waited in the hospital for an operating room, he could hear the sound of Sara's blood pumping out of her with each heartbeat. No kidding, he heard the sound of the sea. It was like a flash flood uncontainable in a hospital room; it poured onto the floor. Sara grabbed his arm and told him she was dying. She said it in such a sweet way, so unlike herself, that her tone frightened him even more than the river of blood. He ran out of the room breaking all the rules of politeness in a hospital and screamed bloody murder until the doctor came and took her away.

Later someone said that Sara had made a mistake lying there for six weeks. With bad ones forty-eight hours was the limit. She should have gotten up and done a dance and been done with it before the trauma set in. Annie knew that if it had been her, no one would have made a fuss in a zone of quiet, and she would have died on the spot. No, the stuff would never have reached her to make her pregnant in the first place. It wasn't her destiny.

She let the snow swirl in her face. It was so beautiful that she never felt the cold. It was all in recognition, Annie thought, remembering that day in the snow when she had looked for Nate and couldn't find him. She knew that once she had let him move in, she could never have admitted he was a bad one, like Sara's first baby, and danced him off before the trauma set in. He seemed to have been sent her like an imperfect fetus, ovaries that didn't work, a package with no return address. He was her gift, and she had accepted him without question.

When she got to Saks, she walked around the building, looking at the windows, at mannequins prepared for the Caribbean in thin clothes of sand and orange and mocha. They made a nice contrast to the snow that was just beginning to stick on the street. They weren't Annie's colors. Earth colors made her look as if she had died last week. She felt she *had* died last week and worried about Ben in Vail not being as lonely as he had promised he would. If he really loved her he wouldn't have gone, she thought.

She was discouraged before she even got upstairs. Then she was more upset by skirts marked down from two hundred and fifty dollars to two hundred. Which didn't seem enough. Annie was not a woman who had to buy her clothes on sale, but she was a modest person, and old habits die hard. She knew the silk trousers that looked so glamorous on the rack would look like rags on the second wearing. She didn't like anything. She drifted upstairs to lingerie and was immediately engulfed in unbought fantasy.

Racks and racks of gowns and negligees remained from Christmas, the sort of pale nylon see-through things with butterflies and satin straps that Brenda still wore. And cotton shifts like Sara's. One could tell who a person was by the kind of underwear she chose. Brenda wore black, peach at night; Sara ecru, white at night. Rita? Annie wondered about Rita. Nate never bothered to tell her what he liked. He bought her a red nightgown once, with such a deep V-neck that when she turned over at night her breasts fell out. He slept in his shorts and a T-shirt like a schoolboy, never forgetting to put them back on.

Suddenly Annie found herself wanting a slip, something silky and smooth, the color of an icicle. Or the color an icicle should be, icy blue. She wanted lacy bikini pants to match and a garter belt slung low on the hips. Annie wore a garter belt years ago between the girdle of her extreme youth and the pantyhose of her twenties. She wore it for a year or two when panty hose seemed so ungainly and hot, and always ripped in her fingers when she tried to get them on. A garter belt was such exquisite sin. She was always aware of it; and her thighs, bare to the crotch, were always cold in winter.

Stalking the racks, Annie looked for such a thing now, that old dazzling first pleasure of being a woman. For a second she saw herself in stockings at the opera with Ben again. This time it's *La Bohème,* or better yet *The Marriage of Figaro.* After intermission as she sits, her dress slides up to reveal, for an instant, the ribbon over a garter, the band of Swiss lace on a blue slip, the flash of bare thigh. One doesn't get to see that so often any more. Or, she's at the office, carelessly crossing her legs with a legal pad on her knee. The slip shows while she asks questions about offshore oil. Ben was crazy about offshore oil, hidden away in shoals, drilled relentlessly by Exxon. She clacked the row of hangers impatiently. No doubt at that very moment, Ben was drilling himself a ski bunny, probably from California, a college girl with yellow hair and cotton panties. She let the operatic fantasy go.

She bought no garters, but a bathing suit, white and black, with a matching shirt, neither on sale. She bought a white suit that made her sweater look like a jewel. She bought sandals for the beach and crisp culottes to go with a lavender sweater Sara had made last year. And last, she bought a nightgown. It was blue and light as the froth on a wave. What the hell, she thought. And she bought the lacy negligee that went with it. What if she felt like it in Palm Beach and he felt like it, too? What the hell, she'd go, and try to figure out what it meant later.

18

THE FLIGHT from New York arrived at the Palm Beach International Airport at two-thirty on the day Ben was scheduled to fly back from Vail. By three he was hailing a taxi at La Guardia, and Annie and Vanessa were standing on the terrace of the Breakers Hotel looking out at the sea. Gunmetal gray even on this mostly sunny day. She was not thinking of him.

She was shading her eyes with one hand, not to protect them from the light, which was not that strong, but to stop the sting of the cold air. She was thinking about other people's marriages, how mysterious they were, and about her coat, which she had foolishly left at home. It was forty-five degrees in Palm Beach, and the beach was deserted. No white-coated boys with trays were delivering summer drinks to elegant people in bathing suits. The empty cabanas looked like part of a long abandoned movie set.

The Breakers was a grand hotel with a golf course in front of it and the beach on the other side. The cabanas were very chic and residents of the town often rented them for the season for more than they paid in taxes on their houses. The hotel was large and generous in the way that only very old hotels are now. And it had sunk, as old hotels have to, to the ignominy of conventions.

Herb made his way out to where they stood hand in hand on the terrace. He, too, had left his coat at home but didn't seem to be shivering as Annie was.

"Isn't this great?" He joined them and put a hand on Annie's shoulder. "They had us up on the fifth floor, but I got them to move us to two . . . in case of fire." He looked meaningfully at Annie, so she nodded seriously.

"Don't want to take any chances with my girls," he said heartily. "Let's go up and have a look."

In the elevator he said that his best friends, Morty and Ellen Cohn, were across the hall. "Isn't that great?" He smiled as if he thought it was great.

The rooms were not adjoining. There were two rooms between Annie's and Herb's, and he made a big deal of that for Annie's benefit. She didn't have any idea why. Her room had two beds with mock brocade bedspreads and curtains in cream and green. It smelled vaguely of mold and old cigarettes, and the carpet needed a shampoo. Her window faced the golf course. Right away, Herb took Vanessa with him so Annie could have her privacy.

"See, Annie is here, and we are here," he told Vanessa so she wouldn't forget.

Annie closed the door. If it had been warmer she would have opened the window to smell the sea air. Instead she opened the drawer of the desk and found some postcards of the hotel with the golf course in front of it. She wanted to make an X in red ink on her window and send it home. "I am here." But this room on the second floor looked squashed into the ground. And anyway there wasn't anyone she could send it to. No one who knew she had gone was glad she was here.

After a minute of contemplating why she had come just at the time when the holidays were over and life in the office was starting again, she walked over to the bed and peeled back the spread. She put it on a chair, then folded back the covers far enough so there was a patch of clean white sheet to sit on. She was depressed again.

In her white suit, she sat on the white patch of sheet and longed for a schedule. Anything to end the suspense of where she was going and where she would end up. It was terrifying to think that nothing was clear, that she traveled along with no real purpose, and that at the end of it all she might discover her whole life had been for nothing. She wanted to know what was going to happen; she didn't want to wait.

At her mother's house when she lived there, Annie remembered her father making an inspection of the house every night. If there was a toy or a workbook or a piece of furniture out of place, he insisted that whoever had left it that way get up and put it right, no matter what time it was. It made the girls think, life had to be like that, every night with every detail perfect. He made them think that order was an end in itself.

Annie used to worry that she would not grow up right because she wasn't orderly all the way through herself. So many things about her secret self were messy. At night she could not keep her nightgown down below her ankles when she slept, even when she weighted it with her feet. It always rose up and tangled somewhere around her chest as soon as she lost consciousness. Under the covers her underpants showed. This was a sign to Annie of lack of resolution. She could not keep her hair tidy on her pillow or her jaws shut tight. She could feel her breathing, ragged quite a bit of the time. A slack jaw did not bode well for the future. When she got the curse, she was certain she was the only girl in the whole world who couldn't keep her blood on the pad. It leaked around the edges sometimes when she slept and soiled the sheets. She was so anxious about this, she began wearing several pairs of underpants at night so nothing could get out. She would have stopped it altogether if only she had known a way.

She worried about her unruly thoughts, too. She seemed to wonder about other people's bodies and their sex lives more than other people did, and she was sure it was abnormal. Now she was speculating whether she would have been interested in Herb if he had been a dentist, with a child. Probably not. Still, if he had been a dentist she might have told him her dream of losing her teeth, and the canker sore on the red gums of the Chinese dragon lady. If he were a dentist, he might stop the dream and save her teeth. But he was an allergist, and she hardly ever sneezed. Perhaps she had been interested in Herb because she wanted to know what doctors thought of the flesh, since they knew what it looked like under the skin. But it wasn't easy to ask Herb about it when he seemed so uncertain about flesh himself.

"Hello? Are you there?"

There was a knock on the door. Annie jumped to answer it. Herb was dressed for golf, in powder-blue slacks and a matching Perry Como sweater.

"You haven't changed," he said. He looked at the bed, so carefully opened, and at Annie, who was still in her suit. "Are you tired?" he asked anxiously.

"You're going to get frostbite in that," she said. "Where are you going?"

Vanessa was in a pink sweat suit and pink sneakers. She was loaded down with beach toys.

"Maybe you and Vanessa would like a little nap," Herb said.

"No, no, no," Vanessa cried.

"Well, I was going to have a few holes. I was hoping you'd join me," he said, ignoring Vanessa.

"Holes?" Annie said cheerlessly.

"Yes, of golf. Don't you play?" Even Lydia, who didn't do anything, played golf.

"Oh," Annie said. "No." She'd never known anybody who played golf. She looked at him aghast. He had shoes with metal stakes coming out of the bottom.

"You don't mind then if I go without you. Of course, if you'd rather do something else, I won't go."

"Oh I wouldn't dream of stopping you. Please. Go. I'll take Vanessa and we'll play, won't we Vanessa?"

"If you're sure. . . ," he said. But she waved him off, didn't want to know anything about golf.

"Rapture," the five-year-old said.

"What's rapture?" Annie asked as she dug around in her suit-case looking for pants. She had only brought thin ones, had no socks to wear with her sandals. Annie sighed with dismay. She was going to freeze.

"Mommy says, 'What rapture, Nessa's going to Palm Beach with her daddy and a horse.' What's rapture, Annie?"

Annie didn't get it at first. She got it later when she sat with Vanessa while she had her supper downstairs. Herb was having his shower. He was having a drink in the bar when Annie was reading Vanessa her bedtime story. Herb's room was blue. Idly she looked around for his things. He'd put them all neatly away. Vanessa's were all over the place. The only things of Herb's that were visible were his toilet articles laid out in the steamy bath-room. He had a silver hairbrush with his initials on it, very shiny as if it had only just been polished. He also had a tiny leather manicure set, also with his initials on it, which Annie thought was interesting. An electric shaver. How funny, she thought, for what, his cheek bones? Nate and Martin used blades. And Ben—Annie didn't know about Ben. She had a stabbing desire to know what he used to scrape his scarred face, and to see the face. She considered this an unruly thought, as well as an unlucky one, and banished it.

Then an old woman whose name was Gracie came to sit with Vanessa so Annie could go out to dinner. Vanessa grabbed Annie and begged her not to go. And Annie debated, thinking maybe she ought to stay. She wavered. Was this what it was like to be married, every minute thinking of the child while the husband was talking business in the bar? And then late at night a bit of warmth for herself. Was a wife taken up like a silver hairbrush and then put aside before dawn?

On the plane Annie had envied them their husbands, the women with their mink jackets over their shoulders and probably a full-length coat at home. She had envied that possessive hand on the arm to make silence when a wife wanted to speak. She had never done that, nor had she been able to make that command in the night. "You're mine, I want you." She had waited for him to take her because he wasn't hers. She was only an option. She never forgot that.

Annie sat on Vanessa's bed and sang her a song. She made up some words the way her mother used to, the way she now did with Donald and Lucy when they hated to close their eyes in case the world ended before morning. And then she left her.

Six of them went out to dinner. They got a taxi and went up to Worth Avenue, where they strolled for a half an hour up and down the street before going to La Petite Marmite for dinner. Annie was in a silk dress that was like wearing nothing, and a sweater because she didn't want to wear the white jacket again when there were still three days to go.

"No, no, I'm all right," she told them. "I'm not a bit cold." And then suddenly she wasn't.

She was watching marriage again. Morty was annoyed at Ellen because she was late. And Ellen was annoyed at Morty because he fogged up the bathroom so she couldn't see in the mirror and because he already had three drinks so that his anger showed. "Slow down, my feet hurt," she said.

And then she told the story of how they had gone sailing and Morty grounded the boat. Ellen sprained her ankle and got hit on the head with the boom, and he wouldn't carry her to help. A doctor yet.

They went on arguing right up until they were seated at a table in the restaurant that looked like a garden. Nobody had time to notice the pool or the running water in the fountain.

"I carried you a fucking mile," he protested.

"You didn't. I hobbled. Sometimes it still hurts. I'll have a martini."

"You don't remember a thing. I carried you the length of that whole goddamned dock. I'll have a martini, too."

"You will not. You've already had three. Do you believe," without missing a beat, "that I had to crawl through the whole parking lot! It was miles. You know how they are in California. I almost got run over. And then we couldn't find the car. I had a goddamned concussion because he smashed the boom on my head. And then he can't find the car."

"Any idiot would know to duck when a boom comes at him."

The other wife was meeker, a little thing with hair like puffs of smoke, She was a child psychologist and so nervous her hands shook throughout dinner. Coquilles St. Jacques and turbot in a thick cream sauce.

"But Darling, you have to have it, it's the specialty of the house," Herb said, when Annie said she'd really prefer a steak.

"I don't really like fish," she said softly, because everybody's eyes were on her. Actually she didn't like cream sauces.

What? One of those difficult young girls who won't eat this and won't eat that and pretends to gag on garlic? She was the other woman. Other women always cause trouble.

"You don't like fish?" Ellen said, and they launched into a discussion about the kind of people who don't like fish. *Young* people, who weren't taught as children to eat what was on their plates. Ellen's children were all grown, and Martha's were in high school. Their children ate fish.

The women's eyes narrowed when the men forgave her right away and started to make a fuss over what she did. Herb said she was very efficient, very clever and was so good with children, which was rare, an unusual combination in a woman. It seemed that Herb's wife was not good with children, was a spendthrift and only after Vanessa was born had decided to go back to college. They had several bottles of wine, all white and none of them as dry as they should have been.

Later, in the ladies' room the child psychologist with the shaking hands, Martha, told Annie that Lydia, Herb's wife, had

an affair with a student fifteen years younger than she. And had
gone off with him for two weeks, eighteen months ago. Then expected Herb to let him live with them in the house until she made
up her mind between them.

"But you must know all this," she said.

Annie didn't know all this and was too shocked to reply.

"Now that he's divorcing her, of course she wants him back.
Not very nice," she sniffed, as if delighted that Lydia was getting
the mess she had asked for.

"How awful," Annie said. She had no idea that Lydia wanted
him back.

"In the same house, can you imagine?"

Annie couldn't imagine. Couldn't imagine any of it. She sat at
the table listening to them, three doctors talking for hours about
how much they made this year, and were likely to make next year.
It wasn't very pleasant to hear doctors talk this way. They seemed
to think they had the best business of all. None of their patients
died from their treatment and none ever quite recovered. They
told old jokes and revealed how much they spent for everything.

Finally they went up in the elevator and staggered down the
hall with the Cohns, now giggling and holding hands. Annie's
head was pounding from several whisky sours, the white wine,
Irish coffee (to keep her warm, Herb said), the squabbling cou-
ples, and suddenly the fear of a married man.

In the restaurant he put his hand on the back of her neck. In
the taxi, when she was forced to sit on his lap, he held her tightly.
She was afraid of what would happen when they were alone. Did
he want to try again with a woman really, after all he must have
suffered? She could feel a muscle twitching in her cheek.

Now, more than ever before, she could see what she had
missed in marriage. The tug of opposing wills year after year,
what it must have been like setting up house, sleeping together
the first time in a brand new bed, and fighting for space in it.
Juggling desire and anger and disappointment all at the same
time when things weren't going well. She had paid for her
mother's kitchen, but never shared in a joint venture. She had
played at it a little, a lot, she had thought. But all the time she had
been watching Martin and Sara struggle for balance, and she had
substituted their experience of marriage for her own. And now
she saw that the end of marriage, too, had stronger flavors of
despair than the mere bitterness that she tasted even now.

Herb stood close to her at the door as she fumbled for the key with shaking hands. "I'm sorry," she murmured, not exactly sure what she was sorry for. His wife, her desire to run from him rather than have him touch her?

"There's no need to be sorry." He brushed her forehead with his lips. "I should apologize to you for dragging you down here. They must have bored you. I know you're used to more excitement than this."

"No, no," Annie said. "They're nice. I liked them."

"They like you, I can tell."

Annie nodded, thinking that was not so. The two women didn't like her. She finally got the key into the lock. He looked at her with a peculiar expression she couldn't read. She didn't want to try to guess at it.

"I have to let the babysitter go," he said. It was after two.

She nodded again. "I'll see you in the morning. . . . I'm awfully tired."

"Yes, you're tired," he said. Again that look.

"I really am tired. I don't usually stay up this late."

He smiled. "I know."

She kissed him quickly on the cheek and he looked—relieved. Yes, Annie was sure he was grateful that she let him go. She went to bed feeling good. She was relieved, too. Now they wouldn't have to fight. She was certain they had settled something important between them without even having to say a word about it.

The next morning it was raining in Palm Beach, but something else was happening, too. The stock market was beginning its biggest rally in sixty years.

19

TWO DAYS later when the weekend came, Annie had been gone from the office only three days. Gold closed fifty dollars up; the Dow Jones was up sixty points, and interest rates had come down a point and

a half. It was an unheard-of situation, had never happened before. Annie was so busy wondering what was going on that she no
longer concerned herself with the weather in Palm Beach, the
allergists, or even whether she had made a mistake in coming. If
Friday had been a weekday, she would have flown back to be in
the office when the market opened the next day. As it was, there
wasn't a thing she could do until Monday. So she stayed on, the
way one stays on holliday when nothing is much fun but even less
would be going on at home.

She rushed into her office early Monday morning, desperate
to talk to someone, and then right away walked out of it because it
didn't look like hers. She counted the doors, then went back into
the room again. There was nothing on Carl's desk, no hundred-
weight defense books, no stack of empty shopping bags that he
kept for no reason that anyone could tell. There was no brass
paperweight in the shape of a heart with the word "Love" on one
side and "Hate" on the other that Marilyn had given him one
ambivalent Valentine's day years ago. No pencils in the Beck's
beer stein. In fact, no beer stein. Even the picture of missiles and
jets that had hung on the few available inches of wall were gone.

From time to time peculiar things happen in brokerage
houses beyond the fluctuation of stock prices. A broker will be
saying hello and good-bye to someone, and chewing the fat with
that person at odd moments of the day for five years; then he'll
come in one morning and there will be a hole where that someone
used to be. Without any signs, without a word of warning or a
whispered good bye, someone will just disappear.

The movement of brokers is a very secret thing. The loss of a
good one, who generates hundreds of thousands of shares sold,
means all those sales are taken elsewhere. To Kidder Peabody, to
Bache, to Merrill Lynch. It's a loss in income, a loss in prestige
and a blow to the back office where all the paperwork is done. So
if a good broker wants to leave, he's kicked out fast to prevent
speculation and dissension among the other brokers. A bad one
just disappears like a stone thrown in the ocean.

John wasn't there to consult—it was still very early—so Annie
went to see Ben. He was busy making notes on a legal pad and
didn't look up when she stood in his door.

"What's going on?" she said. Not hello, how are you, did you
have a good time with ski bunnies in Vail, or anything like that.

He grunted, because she was always like that, eager to talk

about anything else but him. She didn't acknowledge his tan. She stood in the doorway as if waiting for a bell to ring so she could be off. He looked at her out of the corner of his eye, and scowled because she looked so well.

"What's the matter?" she said suspiciously.

"What do you think?" he said after a long pause. He got back to New York after nearly two weeks away only to find her out of town. It seemed to him there was plenty the matter with that.

"The market's crazy. Carl is gone. What's been going on here?"

"Is that all you have to say?"

At that moment Gertie caught Annie's eye and waved from the end of the hall.

"I'll see you in a minute," Annie said. Whenever there was information needed, it was better to go to Gertie. Gertie sat in the back office and handled all the paperwork Annie still didn't quite understand. Annie did the buying and selling. She checked everybody's statements at the beginning of every month. Gertie executed the orders and entered the data into the computer. She helped with the difficult questions when new clients couldn't figure out what the columns meant and money seemed to appear and disappear at will. Gertie always knew where the money went.

Gertie was a thin dark girl, with a narrow face and large black-framed glasses. Though they were not at all the same sort of person or even at the same level in the office, Annie and Gertie were very good friends. Gertie's first and only boyfriend left town when she got pregnant a year before and Annie was the one who went with her to New York Hospital for her abortion. Gertie's mother and grandmother would not have let her come home again if they had known. So Gertie went to Annie because there wasn't anybody else she dared to tell. Then when Nate left, Gertie felt a great surge of satisfaction at the equality of rottenness in men. Not that she rejoiced in Annie's misfortune, but rather that treachery had not been reserved just for her. They had yogurt in Annie's office almost every day when Carl was out looking for his wife. And sometimes they had dinner together.

"How was it?" Gertie asked. She searched Annie's face for signs of sun and romance. There weren't any. Annie was frowning at the exchange with Ben.

"What?" The trip was pushed so far back in Annie's mind she had already forgotten she had been away.

"Your trip," Gertie said.

Annie made another face and sat on the corner of Gertie's desk. "Pretty rotten. Where's Carl?"

"Gone," Gertie said soberly.

"I know he's gone. I can see that he's gone. What happened is what I want to know."

"Marilyn got a job in White Plains. She wanted to be closer to the kids," Gertie announced with some relish. "So she said. We've had *some* excitement here."

"What happened?" Annie asked, impatient now.

"Well, there were meetings on Thursday and Friday. Everybody wanted to make a big push to buy while the market was going up. But John wanted to wait and see. He thought this surge was just an illusion and we could look forward to nothing more than a crash this week. It's very strange that gold is going up at the same rate as the market. What do you think, Annie?"

"I don't know. I just got here. What happened to Carl?"

"He went in to see John in the middle of everything and asked to be transferred to the White Plains office." Gertie lowered her voice. "Marilyn's old boss went to White Plains and took her with him. So Carl was right to be worried after all. How about that?"

Annie shook her head. Poor Carl. "So Carl went to White Plains," she finished.

"No," Gertie said sharply. "John must have been waiting for this. He said there was no room in the White Plains office. He kicked him out, Annie. We never even saw him pack up. He must have come back after five for his things. The next day everything was gone."

Annie went back to her office. For two years she had been waiting for Carl to leave and now that he was gone she felt as if she had been kicked a bit, too. Poor Carl. She could see him at home eating himself to death. She could see him driving the kids to school and then going home for a second breakfast, making a few half-hearted calls, looking for work. Annie sighed. That was the problem with this rally. How could the market be going up when all the other signs in the country showed a real recession? People were out of work, companies were failing right and left. John was right, it had to be an illusion. As soon as she decided this about the market, she put her shoes back on and went to look for John.

John was a mostly bald person in his late forties who looked a lot older. He wore gray suits, white shirts, blue-and-red striped ties, all of them from Brooks Brothers' boys' department because he had never gotten big enough to graduate, and didn't like to spend more than nine dollars for a tie. He had a too-small shiny nose and thin nervous lips, also gray eyes that darted around and wouldn't stay put anywhere. When he had to fire someone, they teared uncontrollably.

John had the biggest office. It was about twelve feet square and had no bookcases. It was a very tidy office at the end of the corridor just opposite the coat closet. He always knew who was late.

"Annie," he said when she came in. "Good to see you. How was Palm Beach?"

Annie shrugged. "Cold," she murmured. "And I missed all the excitement."

"Well, don't get excited, we're in for trouble," John said. He invited her to sit down with a wave of his hand.

"What makes you think so?" Annie asked.

But he didn't want to talk about it. "Just the feeling of an old work horse. This is definitely the time for caution."

He seemed to drift off so Annie changed the subject. "What happened to Carl?"

He waved his hand again. "Don't worry about him. His wife makes enough for both of them." He made a face, apparently thinking of Carl's wife. "That was his problem, you know. She made all the money and chopped his balls right off."

"He wasn't a great stockbroker," Annie said archly. But it seemed to her if anybody had done violence to Carl's manhood it was John. Marilyn was just working.

"But he could have been." Suddenly John rapped the desk with the flat of his hand, a very pale hand. But it made a loud noise in the quiet room. "A man has to make the money. You'd know that if you were married, Annie."

Annie stiffened.

"But you're not married, so you don't know." He slapped the desk one more time. And that was that.

"John, when are you having the desk taken out?" Annie said a bit more sharply than she meant to.

"What?" He looked at her again, as if surprised that she was still there.

"Carl's desk. I want to rearrange the office."

"Annie, you know I can't do that." John looked truly shocked. He sat back in his chair as if she had dealt him a blow.

"Yes, you can. It's not a double office. It never was. The desk was put in there temporarily just for Carl. And now Carl is gone."

"I'm surprised at you. You know this has been a bad year. It's a question of productivity. We need that space. We need the business generated by that space. I can't let it go empty."

"It's not empty. I'm in it, and I'll generate more business now that I have the quiet to think. I know I will."

He looked at her sternly. "This is what I hate," he said. "We have a two-day rally, and suddenly everybody thinks the world has changed. Well, nothing has changed. When the market plunges, there's going to be a terrific loss of confidence. There's going to be a stampede to sell. Prices will drop. Believe me, there's going to be trouble."

Annie was silent for a second, her cheeks bright red.

"I can't share that office any more," she said finally.

"We all have to sacrifice something, or we'll be out in the cold. I need another broker to take Carl's place. If I move someone in from the boardroom, I can take in someone new."

"I've been waiting for my own office for a long time," Annie said slowly. "I deserve it."

"Annie, do you know what goes up in this kind of market?" he said, just a little shyly now. She looked at him squarely. "The blue chips are moving, defense is moving. Chemicals, big industry, oil. Not your little speculative stocks."

"What are you telling me, John? Are you telling me you want to look for two new brokers and not one?"

"Now Annie, don't jump to conclusions. You know exactly what you mean to us here. You do well, very well, I don't deny that for a minute. But loyalty is very important, too. I don't want you to forget that you grew up here. We made you what you are. You don't want to make me unhappy, do you?"

Annie quivered with the temptation to tell him to go to hell. If she said it, she would go the same way Carl had, without another place to go. She hesitated, then said, "If you spent a day in there with someone, John, you'd understand it's too small for two people." It was as far as she could go right then.

John thought for a minute. "What if I put someone a lot thinner in there this time?"

She shook her head.

"Don't rock the boat, Annie," he said seriously now because she refused to laugh at his joke. "Let's see what the next six months bring before we plunge ahead with unreasonable demands, shall we?"

She continued shaking her head. If he brought someone else in there, it wouldn't matter what the next six months brought. There would still be no place to move him unless someone else left. And she couldn't see the likelihood of anybody going but herself.

"Tell me you won't make an issue of it," he said in his most conciliatory tone.

"I can't, John. It is an issue." She pulled herself together and left his office. It wasn't like her. Usually she was cheerful. She was upbeat. She liked to humor the boss. Now she felt that there really were a lot of things she hadn't liked about her office all along. She was very shaken up.

In this very uncertain frame of mind she went to Ben for comfort. She sat down without being invited. "How was your vacation?" she asked. That question was a sort of apology for being so short with him before.

"It was boring," he said. Not very forthcoming. "How was yours?"

"Cold. It rained." She shrugged.

"Who did you go with?" He made some scratches on his yellow pad.

She shrugged again. "It was a spur-of-the moment thing." She looked out of the window. Nothing worth talking about. She didn't want to talk about it.

"Shit!"

She started. "What's the matter?"

"I can't trust you for one minute, can I?" he said furiously. "I knew it. I told myself it was a mistake to go away for one minute. Then I said, well, you went with your mother, or, or Sara. But of course I knew all along I couldn't trust you. . . ." He changed his tone. "Annie, why? Why would you go with him and not me? What's wrong with me?"

"Ben—" Annie said sharply. She just didn't have the energy to go into what was wrong with him. "What's driving this market? Tell me, what's happening?"

"I'm very unhappy," he said, definitely looking sad. "I don't think I can go on like this. You want everything from me but won't give anything back." He had been away for two whole weeks and hadn't found anybody he liked either. It wasn't even a question of temptation.

"You should be happy, all your stocks are going up." Annie said this rather bitterly. Her stocks, as John pointed out, were not coming up at all, even in this extraordinary boom.

"Isn't it amazing?" Ben said in spite of himself. Last week while he considered suicide (not very seriously, though), he had the biggest sales rate of any three-day period of his whole career.

"Who's doing it? What's the psychology behind it? How can gold go up at the same time as the market? Gold goes up only when everything else is going to hell. This shouldn't be happening. Every rule says with this much unemployment there should be a recession. There is a recession. . . . Isn't there?"

"I guess some things can't be explained so easily."

"John didn't want to talk about it either," Annie said irritably. What was the matter with everybody?

"You don't care about me at all!" Ben said miserably.

"Oh, Ben. Please don't break my heart with dramatics. I care about you. If I cared about you any more, it wouldn't be good for me. You'd do something mean. You wouldn't care about *me* any more."

Now he was mean. He looked out of the window, wondered if she was right.

"Oh, come on, you're just doing this out of pride. I don't believe you even gave me a thought." She laughed nervously because it had to be true. "It's all a game, right?"

"How can you say that? I didn't think about anything else. I was so careless I almost broke my leg." He shook his head thinking about the leg he could have broken.

"But you didn't, did you?" She made a face at him, trying to be cute. "Come on, tell me about gold. You love gold. Everything you love is going up."

He pulled himself together because she wanted to talk. "I think it's the Europeans," he said grudgingly. "The Mexicans, too. No currency is strong right now but the dollar. Even the Eurodollar is shaky. I think it's foreign money buying gold. I think the institutions are buying the blue chips and pushing prices up.

That's what's making the private sector move so suddenly. It's kind of a panic from abroad in a way."

"John says this rally is an illusion. Are you telling your customers to get heavily into the market now?"

Ben dismissed John with a wave of the hand. "John is scared, Annie. When a man gets scared, he loses his judgment. I think this rally means we're headed for economic recovery. I really do."

Annie looked down at her hands. This was very worrying. Privately she thought John was right. So far Ben had been very lucky in his career. He'd had the magic touch. But now Annie doubted his optimism. The world was changing too fast for the old rules of economics to apply any more. There was no way to gauge probabilities any more. They would have to come up with a new way to look at things. Ben was still young and had the fearlessness of one who had never fallen. Annie was afraid that if he speculated too much and a sudden crash came after such a wild increase, Ben would be in serious trouble. She decided it was not a good time to tell him that she thought her time at Howard and Plunket had begun to run out.

20

BY THE END of January, however, there had been no crash. Everything seemed to be moving along as it should. Sara's apartment became littered with samples. She was absolutely awash with pieces of house. One couldn't go anywhere without tripping over a board, a piece of molding, chains loaded with formica chips that looked like marble, wood, aluminum, anything one could think of. Annie thought skin tones had to be next. Sara also had chunks of floor around the place—tiles and squares of wood. And pictures of sinks and sofas, little swatches of material.

Every time Annie came over with a wistful look on her face and wanted to talk about the market and gold (which only interested Sara if it could be worn), Sara piled her lap with samples and asked what Annie thought of them. Annie was very concerned about her office situation and wondered aloud if Martin thought she ought to leave *before* John put someone in her office with her, or after it was a fait accompli. It was a serious question.

Sara was forced to go off and play Sorry with Donald because Annie never made up her mind. Annie floated, always had, Sara thought. Why should she change now? But Sara couldn't make up her mind about the samples either. Annie floated on her decisions, but Sara wallowed in hers. She couldn't decide what color her bathroom fixtures should be, or about the cabinets in the kitchen. And everything had to be ordered months in advance. She didn't have much time if she wanted her kitchen to be installed in June.

Martin was euphoric because his stocks had gone up just when he had to make some payments on his house, and he found that he was going to have to borrow a bit less than he had planned. He was annoyed because he was selling his stock just when it was going up, but Annie assured him that the deterioration that had begun during the second week of the rally would continue and he shouldn't feel badly. So far nobody had been exactly right. The stampede to buy had slowed, and some deterioration had occurred, but they did not have either the through-the-roof boom Ben had been hoping for or the crash John had predicted. Everybody was taking it one day at a time and holding his breath.

In February Annie had her thirty-first birthday. Gertie bought her a cake in the office, and everybody sang "Happy Birthday to You." It was very depressing, especially since Carl was not there to finish it off. Then she had to have a birthday dinner with each of her friends and family. It took over a week to get past the humiliation of this new unwanted year heaped on her. February was not a cheerful month to have a birthday.

During her birthday dinner at Sara's when Sara could talk of nothing else but the desperation she was beginning to feel over not making a choice about the kitchen cabinets and the finish of the wood inside the house, Martin decided that Sara should visit the site on her own and maybe a feeling for the place would help her know what she wanted. Until then he had been watching the progress of the building himself because it was cold, and there really wasn't much to see. Before long it was settled that Annie and Sara would go together on a Saturday and Martin would look after the kids. Then Sara thought Brenda should come, too, and they would have their first outing together in many years.

After all this was planned, Sara felt guiltier as the day got closer. She hated to leave Martin alone with the children. He was likely to burn the apartment down. And she felt sorry for dragging Annie, who was only two years younger than she but unlikely ever to have such a wondrous thing as a house of her own. Brenda, too, now seemed a mistake. Brenda lately had taken to reliving her own parting with her mother thirty-five years before over and over to show Sara how deeply hurtful their good-byes would be.

Finally, as Sara dressed to go she could hear breakfast sounds in the kitchen. Martin was struggling with boiled eggs that nobody wanted to eat. All the night before Sara hadn't slept, worrying about the effect this house would really have on them all. Martin wanted to create new selves for them in Pine Wood, as if the place itself would clear him of his childhood. Four people in a small airless space, the hope of the future in the boy who would dive into the air shaft on his graduation day. Martin's brother had saved every penny he had made and left a thousand dollars for his funeral. At the time Martin had felt that only his own death might vindicate that of his brother. But somehow his own death had never quite come off.

Sara hadn't known the brother, but she suspected he was with Martin all the time. She didn't think they had been particularly close when he was alive. His death, though, had been so hostile, so deeply obscene it seemed to call out for a response even now. Some kind of retribution. An end to the family both brothers hated so much. Martin wanted to get out into the country where he could see frozen earth thaw and yield new life every year. Spring was very important to him. He told Sara he had never seen it, not really. Not day by day, damp, dark, with crocuses pushing their tiny blades through the half-frozen decayed leaves of last November. Sometimes over the last months, when it was finally clear that they were leaving New York, Sara was frightened when she thought they were leaving just for spring and to kill off a family that was already dead. Also it seemed hard on her that Martin's leaving his family meant her having to leave hers, too.

She went into the kitchen where Martin was smiling bravely over boiled eggs that were too hard. Lucy was crying over the eggs. And Sara saw that her nighttime Pamper, so sodden it hung to her knees, hadn't been removed.

"I can't go," she announced. "What do you want? Fried eggs? Hot cereal? French toast?" She had two packages with her: belts she had made for her mother and sister to commemorate their day together. They were braided leather and beads in different colors to match their Christmas sweaters. They were wrapped in tissue paper that looked as if it had been chewed by animals. The children had done the wrapping. She put the packages aside. Didn't want to go.

"Of course you'll go," Martin said heartily. "You're already late. They're waiting for you and probably mad already."

Sara whipped off Lucy's diaper and ran for underpants. She didn't want to be mad because he had forgotten underpants or couldn't boil eggs. She pulled Lucy into her clothes. She wanted to stay in New York and bake cookies. She'd let them be as messy as they wanted and wouldn't interfere. That was how children should learn.

"Go," Martin insisted.

Donald was pouring cereal into bowls. "We can manage," he said, a boy of barely five.

"I love you," she told them. Suddenly she didn't want to see what the site would look like with the house going up, or hear what her mother or sister would have to say about it. How would they manage without her? They had always been such a close family, the three women. Sara knew that she was what kept them together, kept the peace between Annie and Brenda. And the children provided a focus for them all. Already Brenda was bitter. Annie would probably have a breakdown when the children were gone.

"We know," Martin said. "Have a good day. Take your presents."

They took her to the door, got her coat. They all smiled at her. They liked the idea of grandmother, mother and aunt having a day off together. They were sweet, and Sara was afraid she would crash the car and not be able to return. Annie and Brenda, too. They'd all be dead or in comas and there would be no one to care for the children. Martin would be forced to marry again so there would be a mother for his children. Then she was out of the door and it was all right.

Brenda made such a fuss. "Oh," she cried when Sara arrived

at her apartment and presented the belt. "It's gorgeous. I saw some not as nice as this last week at Saks. They were over a hundred dollars." She glowed, but did not mention the price of the kitchen Annie had given her, where they were sitting not eating the coffee cake Brenda had bought for them.

"Oh, Sara, you're so talented, so generous. Let's see yours, Annie."

Annie tore her package open.

"I wanted you to have something to remember the day," Sara said. "How many years has it been since we've been together like this, alone just the three of us? Isn't it fun?"

Brenda had a few tears in her eyes that she quickly brushed away before her makeup could be damaged. "A long time," she said. "I don't know how long."

She gave Sara another hug.

Annie looked at her belt. Pink and gray, with beads in the middle that looked like coral and ivory, and thinner strings at the end so it could be easily tied. She examined the belt closely, not quite convinced that Sara had really made it, yet she knew Sara had. She must have done it at night when the children were sleeping. Or else they would have stolen the beads and made a mess.

"Sara, you're so generous," she said after a minute. "When do you have the time?"

"I don't really have anything to do," Sara said, pleased at the response, the admiration, the kisses.

And they both protested. She took care of two children, both of them very spirited, too, not to mention Martin. She was building a house in the country miles away, and she still had time to think of other people. "You're a wonder," Brenda said. "I hope you won't hate it."

"Don't say that, Mother," Annie said sharply. "She'll be fine."

"Have a piece of cake," Brenda said. "You need your strength."

"I don't think I want any," Sara murmured, knowing that her mother really did hope she'd hate it.

"You always wear gray, don't you?" Brenda said. "I think it reflects your state of mind." She had turned her attention to Annie. Annie was wearing gray flannel trousers and a gray sweater.

"I think it looks great," Sara said. She tied Annie's belt on and began adjusting the fringes. "I think you look terrific, really."

"I think it's because she's always thinking about money."

"I think she likes gray," Sara said. "You're very thin, Annie. Have you lost weight?"

"She wouldn't touch the cake, so I told her to eat a banana. Would she eat the banana?" Brenda complained. "I bet she has malnutrition. She'll only eat if she has a man to feed. And where's the man?"

"Let's go," Annie said. "Before I throw up."

"Why would a young woman with her whole life in front of her wear gray?" Brenda muttered in the elevator going down to the car.

Annie touched her arm and told her it was Sara's day. "Sara," she said. "Look at her. She's scared to death. For God's sake be nice, will you?"

Sara's hands trembled as she turned on the ignition, even though she had parked perfectly well in the middle of traffic only a few minutes before.

They were quiet on the way up. It had started to snow and Brenda and Annie decided it would be best to let Sara concentrate on the road. When they got to the house there was a powdering of snow on the ground. Nobody mentioned it. The countryside looked bleak. All the houses that hadn't showed in the summer showed now, isolated in the woods. Earth had been built up through the marshy area to make a driveway into the clearing, and some electrical lines had been brought in for the power tools. There was also a septic tank that hadn't been sunk yet. Sara was afraid of driving on the new road, so they parked on the side of the main road and trudged up the hill to the site. The floor had already been poured and the house framed in. The beams were set for the roof and a few outside walls were in. The floor was floating above the ground just the way Archie had said it would. Sara hadn't seen it before. The floor in the clearing, the house just framed in the snow. All of it was so magical Sara stood there awed. Suddenly it didn't seem to her like a lonely spot.

"Oh, Sara." Brenda broke the silence. She pulled her coat tightly around her.

"We ought to have a bottle of champagne," Annie said. She put her arm around her mother, who was shivering in her second-best coat.

"We ought to sit on the floor and have a picnic," she added. "Mother brought the cake."

"Oh," Brenda wailed. "I wish we had thought of coffee," and then to Annie when Sara rushed back to the car to get her camera. "It's all wood. Look, you couldn't make a house more cheaply than this. Isn't that plywood over there?" She pointed to great stacks of wood half covered by plastic sheets. "My God, it's a fire hazard already."

"It must be twenty degrees colder out here than in New York. Don't worry, Mother, all houses have wood in them somewhere."

"Annie, you couldn't stand it up here for five minutes." She squeezed Annie's arm. "Oh, Annie, I do believe you're bearing up well, considering. This is just terrible, do you think we can leave now?"

Sara came running back with the camera. "Get up there on the floor. I want to remember this always. Isn't it beautiful? Isn't it just incredible weather for the beginning of March? They'll have to get more people in if they don't hurry up a little. Brenda, dear, you're just going to love it. Look, there's going to be a swimming pool right over there, see?"

"No, I can't get up there; I'll rip my stockings."

"No, you won't, we'll help you."

"There's a step over there." Annie pointed to a box. "I wonder if this is the front door." She giggled. "Isn't it nice to have a householder in the family?"

"Smile." Sara snapped a picture: Brenda frowning in the snow; Annie clutching her arm. "Now, one in the house."

Annie scrambled across the frozen rutted ground, holding onto Brenda, who was threatening to break an ankle. Then up on the tippy box and into the house, or what would be the house. Sara took more pictures, of the bulldozer and the pile of wood and the two hills of earth that had been moved away when the land was leveled for the piers. She took a picture of the septic tank and her mother looking out at the stream that had a thin crust of ice on top.

"Can we go now?" Brenda asked. "I bet you're both starving."

"I love it," Sara said. "I'm going to have a studio over here, past the kitchen, see, a big room with windows."

"It's going to cost a fortune to heat this place," Brenda screamed at her where she stood with the camera. "It looks very big."

To Annie as they walked back to the car, "I feel my sinuses clogging up. I think it's dangerous out here. A burglar could break in and shoot them all in the head while they're sleeping. That's what happens all the time to people who live in houses. Out here, no one would know for days."

Annie laughed.

"Don't laugh, Annie, you never listen to the news. You don't know what goes on. But don't tell Sara I said that. I don't want to scare her. She'll know soon enough what it's like here. I bet she'll have to have an electric stove."

Sara ran up breathless and pink in the face. "I wish I could have put my foot in the cement when it was wet," she said. She grabbed her mother's gloved hand. "Aren't you glad you saw it like this?"

The kitchen would be natural wood, maybe stained a little, and the rest of the house, too. Now she didn't want anything too fancy. She didn't want it to look like California, or something out of *House Beautiful*. She wanted it natural, underdone, nothing in aquamarine. "I'm so happy," she sighed. She had gotten them there in the snow without crashing the car. All she had to do now was get them home again.

Soon they drove down Gorge Avenue toward the town. As they got closer, Annie started looking out for the number of Herb's house. It would be interesting to see what he had left behind. It would also be interesting to see the wife unloading the groceries.

"Doesn't your friend live along here?" Sara asked, confident now behind the wheel.

"What friend?" Brenda said quickly.

"Oh, Mother, you know, Annie's friend the doctor. Annie, should we look up the house number and check it out?" Sara was in an ecstatic mood. She bubbled with good will.

"One eighty-five," Annie said.

"How do you know?"

"I don't know," Annie shrugged. "Oh yes I do. Vanessa told me. She knows her phone number too. No, don't slow down."

They drove on for a few minutes, the three of them concentrating on the numbers. Down here, closer to town some of the houses had fences in front of them. Others had hedges.

"There it is," Sara squealed suddenly.

It had a stockade fence. Sara slowed down. "Shall I drive in the driveway? We can pretend we're lost."

"No," Annie said. "He comes up sometimes on Saturdays. I'd die if he saw us."

"We have a right to be here," Sara said.

"Drive on," Brenda ordered. "Annie's right."

"Stick-in-the-mud," Sara mumbled.

She drove on into the sweet town of Pine Wood, where very sweet little stores lined the main street. In the light snowfall, the town had a certain appeal. Sara parked in front of Ye Olde Soda Shoppe, and they piled out ready for lunch. They took a table by the window.

"If she comes along, you can point her out," Brenda said unexpectedly.

Sara said. "She doesn't know what she looks like." No one wondered who Brenda meant.

"She'll be with the child," Brenda said.

They all looked out the window, the house forgotten in the drama of divorce. No one passed right away with Vanessa.

"Did you meet him here?" Brenda asked. The place was light and neat, with old-fashioned iron chairs and round tables with marble tops.

"Not here," Sara said disgustedly, because she had already told her where it happened. "At McDonald's."

"What were you doing at a place like that?"

"The children like it."

Brenda made a sound as if McDonald's explained it. "Too bad we couldn't see the house."

Annie and Sara looked at her with surprise.

"Well, it would have been interesting. You can tell a lot about people by their houses."

They stopped talking for a minute to order and then Brenda continued. "So, Annie, what's happening?"

Annie shrugged, turning away from the window. She didn't really care to see Vanessa with a mother.

The drinks came and she proposed a toast to Sara's new house. They clicked glasses.

"What about your friend?" Brenda began delicately picking at her dry circle of individual undressed tuna. This question she asked several times a week, had in fact already asked it once that day.

Annie frowned because she kept asking even when Annie told her there was nothing to tell.

"You know, Annie. Don't pretend you don't know who she's talking about," Sara said.

"He's all right," Annie said dutifully.

"He must be more than all right if you went all the way to Florida with him." Brenda sniffed. She had managed to stay off the subject almost all morning and now she couldn't contain herself a minute longer.

"It wasn't like that," Annie said.

"You don't have to make up stories for your mother," Brenda said indignantly. "I know perfectly well what you're up to."

"What do you think of the town, Mother?" Sara broke in.

"Well, if she's involved with him, she's involved with him, Sara; why keep playing games about it? The question is when is he getting divorced? That's the question. It seems to me that if the mother gets the child, it doesn't have to be so bad an arrangement."

"I'm not going to marry him," Annie said in a little voice.

"If you married him, you wouldn't have to work. You wouldn't have to worry about silly stock prices all the time, or whether you'll have to share an office. It was absolutely unhealthy for you to have been squashed in with that fat man all that time. I always said so." Brenda paused for breath.

"Why do you want to work any more anyway? You've had your experience now, you know what it's like. You don't have to make a lifetime thing out of it, you know. Wouldn't it be better to be loved and cared for than insecure and alone? I mean, really." She looked at Sara for support. "I don't care how much money you make, Annie, *some time* you'll have to face up to being alone."

She looked at Annie sharply. "I know it doesn't seem that way now. But lovers don't hang around forever." She appealed to Sara again. "And how many will there be when she's forty?"

"That's nine years away," Sara said. "Leave her alone."

"Well, I'm not sleeping with him," Annie said. "He's a friend."

"I think we ought to meet him." Brenda ignored her. "Maybe he's all right. Maybe he's the right person for her. Some people make mistakes when they're young and then straighten out."

"I thought you hated the idea," Sara reminded her fiercely. Sara hated the idea.

"I can't turn my back on an established thing, can I? What kind of mother would I be? I won't be disloyal to Annie no matter what she does," Brenda said firmly. "I want her to be happy, don't you?"

"It's not an established thing. Why don't you believe me?" Annie protested.

Brenda looked up from her lettuce with a hard expression. "Are you asking me to believe that you go out with a grown man who's been married and had a child, that you've traveled together, and you're not sleeping with him?"

Annie looked from one to the other. "Yes," she said.

"I don't believe it," Brenda said.

"Not all men are bad," Annie said. "They don't all want just that."

"I didn't say they were all bad, just because you can't tell the difference. In fact I think it's my fault. I must have messed up somewhere."

"You don't sleep with him?" Sara said agog. "How do you avoid it?"

"I told you he's not like that. He happens to be interested in me for myself."

"Well, what do you do then?" Sara was alarmed. Annie didn't seem to know how to look after herself at all. Now she had a boyfriend who didn't make love. This was even more serious than having one who did.

"We go out to dinner. We talk. We do things together with Vanessa. He's very worried about his child." Annie smiled. They went to places like the Statue of Liberty.

"It doesn't sound good," Brenda remarked. She pushed her plate away.

"Why not? We're friends. I thought you'd be impressed with his character. The man loves his child. What could be more admirable than that?"

"You should be the first to know about men, Annie," Brenda said cryptically.

"Well, if the bad ones all want sex, how can you tell the good ones except by their indifference?"

"Oh, Annie," Brenda sighed. Annie did it on purpose, she just knew it.

"Maybe he sleeps with his wife," Sara mused.

"Oh, no." This was a thought that had not occurred to Annie. He was very bitter about the wife, said she was crazy. Annie thought it had more to do with his fear about not being good at it. Something deeply primitive, like terror.

"Or his nurse," Sara added.

"You really think the worst about everybody, don't you?"

Brenda and Sara exchanged significant looks. "He has to be putting it somewhere," Brenda said.

"Maybe it's his wife *and* the nurse." Sara wouldn't give up. "Have you seen the nurse?"

"Don't make me doubt him," Annie said unhappily. "It's hard enough to like someone as it is."

"Well, this is not a good basis for marriage at all," Brenda cried. "Really, you're impossible." She paused. "What's wrong with him?"

"They don't sleep together," Sara said. "That's something wrong already."

"Maybe it's her," Brenda said.

They both studied Annie seriously. She wasn't wearing any makeup again. And nobody was good enough not to need something at going on thirty-two. Her face was dead-of-winter pale and had an awfully sad look about it. Lack of sex, probably. Sara and Brenda exchanged looks again. A man's liking Annie for herself was not to them a good sign. Annie made a lot of money, and as far as they knew had spent very little of it. That might be attractive to a certain kind of man. They made a big show of finishing their drinks.

"I think we'd better have a look at him, Annie," Brenda said finally.

"I don't want to marry him," Annie said softly in her defense. She looked from one to the other for a glimmer of support. "I met him at a McDonald's. He has a nice kid. He doesn't push me, and I don't push him. It's comfortable to have somebody who doesn't want something. That's all there is to it."

"So now they'll put somebody else in your office with you. You'll be squashed and unhappy again. What kind of life is that? Let's meet the man. Maybe he's all right. Maybe he just needs some encouragement."

Annie shook her head. "Maybe the thing to do is move to another office."

They were quiet as they thought about that. Annie kept saying she was going to move to another office, but she kept not
doing it. They decided it was time to go. Brenda fumbled with
her handbag, but Annie had her money out first. They let her
pay.

"Maybe it's you, Annie," Brenda said.

Annie knew right away what she meant. She meant Annie
didn't know how to wear a pretty dress and capture them like a
butterfly in a jar. She considered the cold nights in Palm Beach
and how careful she had been to lock the door. All this time she
had been relieved that he didn't make a fuss. Now it seemed a
little strange that he didn't. She followed her mother and sister
into the car. Sara was perfectly confident now that she knew how
she was going to finish her house.

"Maybe it is me," Annie murmured. Inadvertently she
thought of Ben's furry stomach, sweet as a grassy meadow, and
his fingers where it still scared her a little to be touched. It hurt to
be touched through the skin, through the flesh and bone right to
the center, the source of life. It was scary to fall. She felt the
inside of herself was huge, was an abyss that she shouldn't get too
close to.

As the car started she closed her eyes. Nate used to say she
was the only person he had ever known who was so afraid to be
taken that she put her hands up like a shield whenever he
reached out to hug her. Maybe she really was just waiting to be
old so she could end up alone and past it.

21

ANNIE DIDN'T
know how, but somehow a routine had settled in. As spring
inched forward and then galloped in, over a matter of months as
the days got warmer, she became the second mother of yet
another child who wasn't hers. By degrees she found herself arranging her schedule to suit theirs, as if she didn't have to work

and had nothing else to do. In a way she allowed this to happen because she wasn't happy at work any more, but was too uncertain about why to do anything about it.

Carl was gone, but having the office to herself didn't provide the relief she had hoped for. She was kind of lonely without him, and she worried about what had happened to him. Every week she told herself that she would give him a call and find out how he was. And every week she didn't do it. Just as every week she didn't start looking for another job. John was spending time interviewing people to take Carl's place. But he couldn't seem to make up his mind about whether to push someone up from the boardroom and hire a beginner, or look for a big earner from some place else. John was hesitating because a big earner might pose a threat to his own position and quite frankly they didn't have the room for one anyway. The problem was no big earner in the world was going to share an office the way Annie had been doing for two years. And now she said she wouldn't do it any more. He wavered, unsure of what he ought to do. And she was left hanging, like the market, not sure which way to go.

Annie rationalized the time she spent with children, telling herself Sara would soon be gone, and Herb needed the support during this difficult time. Usually she left early on Fridays to be with Donald and Lucy. Saturdays she did her chores, went to a movie with Ben. Sundays she spent with Herb and Vanessa.

Then one Monday early in May Herb wanted her to take the morning off. Vanessa's mother was going to be away, and Herb had a meeting with his lawyer. He said he would take them to lunch afterward, if Annie would take care of her for an hour or so in the morning. And then she could go to work. Several times before Annie had taken a few hours here and there when Vanessa's school was off but the market was still on. Each time when Herb said he'd be back in an hour, he returned in two or three. She had, on and off, a niggling feeling that his requests weren't quite right. But she had been used to helping Sara when she was in trouble and could understand how a person could get caught without help. Herb didn't want to leave Vanessa with strangers. He was a working father and wanted his child. Annie couldn't help feeling flattered that she was trusted, that although they were only friends, he turned to her with his most precious treasure.

As a friend she felt she could do something that wouldn't be appropriate if they were lovers. After all, she wasn't taking another woman's child, or preparing for a long-term arrangement. Still, this time they had a bit of an argument about it. She said it was too much, and he wasn't reliable. He appealed to her feelings for the child, and reminded her of Vanessa's fear of strangers. And also, he promised to be back by noon.

So, Annie bought puzzles to pass the morning and called the office to say she'd be in later. Herb delivered the child and left for his meeting. Annie didn't feel so bad at first because Vanessa looked very cute in her best shoes and yet another velvet dress, her hair in two little braids tied with ribbons. She walked around the apartment in ecstasies, talking nonstop. She loved Annie's house. She loved Annie's purple dress with the white collar. She wanted one just like it.

She followed Annie into the kitchen where Annie went to pour herself another cup of coffee. The child was cute, of course, but now that she thought about it she did feel rather used. She hadn't really wanted to do this with her morning. Was any friendship worth this kind of strain? And what was this friendship anyway?

Her face was so solemn with these thoughts that Vanessa grabbed her hand. "Annie," she wailed. "Are we breaking up?"

Annie was so startled by the acuteness of Vanessa's perception—the child was voicing the question just as it was forming itself in Annie's mind—she gathered her in for a hug.

"I love you, Vanessa, remember that." She would have said more, about how grown-ups may change but the love for children stays the same. It was a hard concept to understand. In fact it was not understandable at all. Grown-ups' behavior was often inexcusable. Vanessa was afraid of losing everybody she cared for and she was right to worry.

For the first time Annie felt that she had been unfair. She had offered the child friendship with no intention of having it last forever. Without Vanessa really there was very little to Annie's and Herb's relationship at all. They had met with the child between them. When they were out alone, their conversation centered around her. If Vanessa hadn't been there, Annie now doubted that they ever would have become friends.

It was at this moment when the child guessed the truth and

Annie was at a loss for words that the phone rang. She jumped to pick it up.

"What are you doing there?" Sara sounded distraught. "I called your office and they said you hadn't come in. I'm worried. What's the matter?"

"I took the morning off," Annie said. "How are you, Sara?"

"Just out of my mind," Sara wailed. "Lucy has to go to the doctor, and Donald has to be picked up at noon, and God knows where Martin is."

"What's the matter with Lucy?" Immediately Annie was concerned.

"She's screaming and holding her head. God, I think it's meningitis or something. She's burning up. Can't you hear her?"

"Oh, Sara, I'm sorry. Yes, I do hear her."

"I don't know what to do."

"Don't get upset. Just think a minute."

"What are you doing at home? I was so worried. Did John hire somebody else after all this time? Did you quit?"

"No. What made you think it was that?"

"You never take a day off. Oh Annie, what will you do if you quit?"

"I'm not quitting, not today anyway."

"Well, I'm relieved you're there. I need you. Would you run over and pick Donald up and keep him there for a while?" Sara paused for a second to mumble something at Lucy. "Oh, Annie, I'm afraid she's really sick."

"Don't worry, I'm sure it's all right."

"Angel, please tell me you'll get Donald for me."

"I can't."

"Why not? What are you doing?"

"I have Vanessa here," Annie said as calmly as she could.

"You took the day off for that? Oh, Annie, are you becoming a mommy?" Now Sara was really upset.

"Her school was closed today or something, and I guess Herb wanted her in town for some reason. I don't know. Listen, why don't you call the school and tell them to put Donald in the afternoon session."

"I can't do that."

"Why not?"

"I just can't. It's not a flexible place."

"Oh, Sara, I'm sure you could."

"I can't," Sara wailed.

"Then call Mother. She'll pick him up."

"Mother's out. She went to her lesson. Oh, Annie, please. It's only a few blocks."

"Sara, what are you going to do when you move? You'll have to take care of things all by yourself, and not panic every time something happens. I'm sure she's all right," she added. But she could hear the child screaming.

"Annie, don't give me a lecture. Are you going to help me out, or not?"

"You know I will, of course I will. Call me when you get back from the doctor. I want to know how she is. And Sara—I have to go to work this afternoon."

"Okay," Sara promised. "I'll call you as soon as I get back."

"Shit," Annie muttered a little while later when she tried to get Vanessa ready to go out. Vanessa didn't want to be parted from her puzzles. She complained when Annie bundled her back into her raincoat because it looked like rain. Annie told herself that she would never get to work that day. She looked sternly at Vanessa, tugging at her hair, balking at putting on her shoes, almost tearful at having to go already. Annie gave her an umbrella to hold. She thought, Children are fine if you have nothing else to do. Then she thought, I hate this, I really do. It was almost noon and Herb had not returned.

22

DONALD'S SCHOOL was in a church on Park Avenue. There was a nursery school much closer to where Donald lived, but it looked too dirty and lived-in for Sara's taste. In the four-year-old room, a huge black rabbit was sometimes let out of its cage, and they had a lizard and some turtles. The day they visited, a large block structure fell down on a small boy and even though there was no blood, he screamed the whole time they were there. The director said it was just his natural expression and assured them he was fine.

The school Donald now attended was quite different. All the children had fair hair, many had blues eyes as well. The cubby holes with their names on them had no pictures of the children to show who belonged where. At three they were expected to be able to recognize their own names, or heaven knew they would never get into Harvard. As for the floor, their places in the circle were set at the beginning of the year. The children had to be just so many inches apart and their places were marked by strips of tape with their names carefully printed in magic marker.

Sara had chosen this fancy school because she wasn't sure then that they would be moving to the country, and she had heard that the better the nursery school a child attended the better chance he had for getting into one of the better prep schools and so on to Harvard, or even Yale, to which no one in either Sara's or Martin's family had ever gone.

Annie held Vanessa firmly by the hand as they went into the school building. She had taken the umbrella from Vanessa at the corner just so there would be no mishaps in this place where they kept so many children and tolerated so little from them. Annie had been here several times before and each time cowered in the sight of so many confident mothers all dressed up and most of them seeming even older than she was. Many of them, wheeling babies in strollers, seemed to be pregnant again. Downstairs in the hall, where the children were brought down, she pressed herself against the wall as if she could propel herself through it, and out into the air.

First, a group of bigger children came down. They were made to line up on the opposite wall and could only leave one by one as each mother was identified. Annie could see why Sara had been reluctant to call and ask them for a little extra time.

Finally Donald's class came out of the elevator. He recognized her immediately and waved and made signs at her, but the two women in charge kept him pinned in place until all the other children had gone.

"Miss Flood?" Donald's teacher came up to her. She looked at Vanessa and didn't smile.

"Yes," Annie said. "Did Mrs. Bissel call?"

"Yes, she did." She turned and beckoned to Donald. "We had a little trouble with Donald today."

"Oh?" Annie hunkered down to give Donald a hug.

"He pulled the paper off of the blue, red, and yellow crayons, didn't he?" She regarded him sternly.

"Oh my," Annie said.

"We all know that crayons are protected by their wrappers, don't we? What if all the children tore the wrappers off the crayons? We would have a Very Messy Room, wouldn't we?" she said ominously.

"Hi," Donald said to Vanessa.

Vanessa hid behind Annie's skirt.

"We certainly know what Donald's crayons at home must look like."

"I've never seen him do it at home," Annie said. "Maybe the ends were blunt."

"We don't have blunt ends on our crayons here."

Donald gave Vanessa a little punch to get her to say hello.

"Donald, don't do that."

Annie took Donald by the hand. "I think we'd better go."

"You tell his mother we have something to work on, won't you?"

"Yes, I will," Annie nodded seriously. "But I don't think he'll do it again. Donald, say you won't do it again."

Donald refused to answer, so Annie said good-bye for all of them.

Out on the street, they skipped a few steps to get past the somber atmosphere of the school's lobby where no children's pictures hung on the wall, only printed announcements of the church's activities.

Annie explained to Donald why she was there, and then why Vanessa was there. And then giggling and forgetting her altogether, the children broke away from her and ran to the corner, forcing her to charge after them in case they took it into their heads to try to cross the street on their own.

She caught up with them gasping for breath. They wanted to go out for lunch. "Don't run away from me again. I don't like to run after you."

"Lunch, lunch," they chanted on the street corner.

"You have to come back to my house. Vanessa's father is going to come for her."

"Aw shucks," Donald said. He punched Vanessa, she punched him back. They ran down Lexington to the next corner.

Annie watched them weave in and out of the pedestrians like maniacs and wished again that she had gone to the office. When she was two blocks from the school, she realized she had left her umbrella. She knew if she didn't go back for it now, it would be gone by tomorrow. But the thought of trying to turn the children around in the other direction and then get them back again without their crumpling on the sidewalk swearing they couldn't go another step without a taxi was too much for her. "Stop!" she yelled as they got to the corner.

Back in the lobby of her building, she asked the doorman if Dr. Mickle had come by.

"Nope," he said, and then launched into a lengthy speculation on how the iffy weather might resolve itself.

Annie debated taking the children to the coffee shop on the corner and decided home would be easiest. Too late she realized that she had bought presents only for Vanessa. They started squabbling the minute they got inside the door. Then Vanessa gave Donald the Smurf puzzle without a word, and they settled down to try it together.

The phone rang. Annie picked it up in the kitchen where she had begun to make tunafish sandwiches and cocoa, thinking it was Sara.

"Is Dr. Mickle there?" a lady's voice asked.

"Uh no," Annie said. "But I expect him very soon. Can I take a message? Annie thought it was the nurse in his office, or his answering service.

"This is Mrs. Mickle."

"Oh," Annie's voice caught and she couldn't say more. Suddenly her heart was beating too fast and she felt unreasonably afraid. What should she say? She held the receiver away from her, looked through the kitchen door at Vanessa playing on the floor. She was scratching at her head and pulling on her braids. Should she call her to the phone to talk to her mother? But maybe the mother didn't know she was there. On the other hand what was she calling for if she didn't know Vanessa was there?

"Can I do something for you?" she said firmly when no help was offered from the other end.

"Is this Miss Flood?"

"Yes," Annie said. "How did you know?"

"You're the woman who's trying to get my child to hate me. I know all about you."

"What? No, I'm not. You're mistaken." Annie gulped unhappily. "How did you get my number?"

"Isn't my husband enough for you? Do you have to turn my child against me, too?"

"No, wait a minute, you have the wrong person. I don't know what you're talking about." Annie looked wildly around. What did Herb tell her? What should she do? She faltered. "I think you ought to talk to him about this. He'll tell you."

"I know what he'll tell me. You have some nerve. First you turn my husband against me, and now you're trying to take my child. You can't get off so easily. You think I don't know what you're doing. I hear all about you. I know just what you're doing."

Annie turned the burner off under the milk. The voice terrified her. She wanted to take the receiver and hang it up, just put it back in its cradle and cut her off. But the woman sounded as frightened as she was. Her voice was not at all uncultured and crude as Annie imagined it would be. She had thought of Herb's wife as a monster. But the woman sounded desperate. Annie felt trapped and guilty. On the other hand, she hadn't done anything wrong. She was sure she hadn't. It wasn't as though she had caused their breakup. She didn't even know the woman, how could she turn either of them against her? Annie struggled with the feeling. She ought to say that, be straight and honest, maybe even tell her she caused her own downfall.

"Mrs. Mickle, I don't know what you're hearing, but I would never do anything to hurt you," she said. Strong, reliable, honest, forthright and true. She prepared to hang up, but was prevented from doing so by Lydia's determination to keep the confrontation going.

"You want to take my child from me. You think that won't hurt me?"

"No, I don't want to take her. I don't know what makes you think that. I don't want to talk about it. It's ridiculous."

"Is my daughter there?"

"Well, yes, she's here. But only for an hour." Annie swore under her breath.

"God damn you." The woman began to cry, and suddenly Annie felt like crying, too.

"Don't cry," she said furiously. "This is insane. Here, talk to her. She knows you're her mother."

"God damn it, you're all lying."

"I'm not lying." Annie said grimly. "The child knows who she belongs to. Just ask her."

"You think you can have her—and him, and I'll just sit here and take it."

"Calm down a minute. Who told you that? I'm getting tired of this. I have two children here and frankly, I'd rather be at work. My sister's another one. They both think I don't have anything better to do."

"He thinks he can do anything."

"I quite agree with you. What does he say?"

"The son of a bitch. What does he say about me? That I'm a bad mother, that I don't deserve to have her? Is that what he says?"

"He doesn't say anything about you." Annie paused. "What does he say about me?"

"Son of a bitch thinks he can do anything. He comes here, any time he wants, screws me, takes the child, tells me he's not coming back. My *God*," she broke off crying. "It's driving me crazy."

"What?" Annie said.

"Does he tell you I screw around? That's what he tells everybody. That's a laugh. The only screwing I do is with him. I bet he doesn't tell you that."

"No," Annie said, stunned.

"Well, he tells me about you, all right. He wants to make me crazy—"

"Is that true?" Annie said incredulously.

"No, I'm not crazy."

"I mean—he does that?"

"Yes, he says you're a better mother than I am any day, and better at everything else. He says you make more than a hundred thousand dollars a year and can take care of yourself. You're not just a bum. I bet you are. I bet you earn it on your back."

"Don't be a jerk. I'd be a rotten mother, and a worse whore. I think Herb is being cruel and stupid. I could never take care of a child full time, especially not yours."

"He says you will. He says you want to."

"Well, it's just not true. What else does he say?" Annie was outraged. "Some husband you picked."

"He thinks he can make me crazy. I got a job. He got a court injunction to take Vanessa away because I wasn't taking care of her. I had to quit. Now he says if I don't let him come and take her away any time he wants, he'll get custody because I'm uncooperative. Then he takes her, and when they're in the city, he calls and threatens me on the phone and says he won't bring her back."

"Do you want to talk to her?" Annie said. "She'd love to talk to you."

"Where is he?"

"I was just going to give her lunch, and then her father will pick her up and bring her home. I promise he will."

"I won't be put off."

"Listen," Annie said. "I don't have any part of this. Whatever is going on is happening between the two of you. I'm not in it."

"I don't believe you. He says he's going to marry you."

"He's not." Annie said furiously. "He has some nerve to tell you that."

"He says you won't wait any longer."

"That's just bullshit. It isn't true. I think he's just trying to upset you. Get a lawyer."

"I have one."

"Well, talk to him. It sounds like you're being abused." So said Annie Landers. She didn't know why, but she had a great sympathy for Lydia Mickle.

"Listen, I won't babysit again. I'd already decided this morning. Maybe you should call a marriage counselor. I don't think either of you want a divorce." Annie said good-bye and hung up quickly. She didn't want to be involved.

So Sara was right. Hysterical Sara, who couldn't manage a pickup and delivery in the same day, knew the shabby truth about what happened between husbands and wives. Ugh. Annie felt sick. She heated the milk for cocoa. It looked vile and disgusting. Why was she so depressed? She never even liked him. In five minutes the jerk would come and take the whole mess away. Then she'd run Donald up to Seventy-eighth Street and see what was happening with Lucy. She opened a can of tunafish. She was lucky, she told herself. What if she had really loved him, and he screwed her, too? See what happened when a person got involved. Annie prepared the story for Sara as she made the sandwiches. She was right not to have tried to get him. She was right, she was better off on her own. She was sure she would be in the office by two.

23

BUT IT DIDN'T
work out that way. When she went to serve the lunch, she discovered Vanessa with her hair all undone, crying because she couldn't put the rubber bands back in by herself.

"What's the matter, Angel?" Annie asked. By her watch it was now nearly one. Herb had been gone for two and a-half hours. Annie wanted Vanessa to hurry up and eat her lunch so she'd be ready to go when her daddy got back.

"I can't put it back," Vanessa cried. "I'm a mess."

"Don't worry about it, Sweetheart. Come and have your lunch." Annie looked at the puzzle. They had done about half of it and the rest of the pieces were scattered all over the floor.

Vanessa curled up in a ball and cried.

"Oh, come on. It's not important. We'll do it up later."

"No, now."

"Aren't you hungry? I made you cocoa. It will get cold if you don't sit down and have it now."

"Let's have it now." Donald wrapped Vanessa's ribbons around his wrist, then tied one around his head. This made Vanessa cry louder. She lunged for it, then collapsed in fury when Donald jerked it away.

Annie ran for a tissue to wipe up her tears. She was getting impatient now. She wanted the children to eat. She wanted to get rid of them, particularly Vanessa, whom she now thought of as a bomb in the middle of her living room. How had she gotten into this? She couldn't remember.

She swabbed Vanessa's face and begged her to come eat her lunch. But the child refused. She wouldn't sit down at the table with her hair in a mess.

"You have an obsession with neatness, Vanessa. It's unreasonable to worry about your hair now." But even as Annie said it she remembered that her own father made them wash up and comb their hair before they were allowed to sit down. What good had neatness done her?

"What's an obeon?" Donald asked.

"It's when you worry too much about something," Annie said. She stood in the living room above them with her hands on her hips. She had always thought that in a situation like this, *she* would never resort to screeching or threats. But now she was ready to scream, Sit down, or I'll break your neck. She didn't know what had ever made her think it would be all right to be involved with some other lady's child. She glared at Vanessa, huddled weeping on her floor, then softened, thinking maybe she knew her mother had called.

"Come on, Vanessa. There's nothing to cry about."

"I can't be messy," said Vanessa with a fist in her mouth.

"Okay, you win. I'll do your hair." Annie went into her bathroom and quickly washed her brush. She would rather have used Vanessa's own brush because it wasn't nice to use a grown-up's brush on a child's head. But Vanessa didn't have one with her, and Annie didn't have another. She shook it out quickly and dried it with a towel.

"Okay, come here." Annie sat on the sofa and pulled Vanessa between her knees.

One stroke and Vanessa began screaming because the brush was wet. Exasperated Annie said she could either have her hair done with a clean wet brush or eat with her hair down. There was no other choice. And big deal anyway. They fought over it for a few minutes. Vanessa didn't want her hair wet, and that was that.

"It won't get your hair wet, damn it," Annie cried at last.

"You swore," Donald said. "I'm going to tell on you."

"Come back here, Vanessa," Annie said suddenly with a curious note in her voice. Vanessa had pulled away and was scratching at her head again.

"What?"

"I want to look at your scalp. Do you have a sore?"

"Why?" The child stood a few feet away.

"Your head itches, doesn't it?"

"Yes."

"I want to see what's bothering you."

"Don't give me a shampoo." Vanessa inched away across the floor.

"Don't you like shampoos? I like shampoos. But I won't give you one. I just want to see you. Here, I'll just give you a ponytail without any brushing."

Annie put the brush down to prove her good will. "Donald, take that ribbon off your head, you're not a girl."

Annie caught Vanessa by the hand. "Come here one second and then we'll have the cocoa. How about it?"

Vanessa stood quietly between Annie's knees again, and Annie lifted her hair. It was quite tangled from the little braids she'd had, almost matted at the scalp. It looked as though it had dust in it, some gray-and-white fluff. Then Annie looked close and gasped. Vanessa's scalp was moving.

"Donald drop that ribbon," she screamed with all the shrill animal outrage of a double-crossed fishwife. God damn son of a bitch.

"What is it?" Donald asked. He came closer for a look.

Annie pushed him away. Her hand was shaking. She had hit the land mine in her living room and it exploded in a storm of fleas—or, or lice! She looked around wildly. How to save her home. Suddenly she itched all over. God, her sofa, down to the core. The woven rug. Donald with the ribbon in his hair. Sara would kill her. She'd never let him come home. A thousand thoughts ran through Annie's head. The implications spread, and she gasped with horror. Nobody washed Vanessa, neat as she pretended so hard to be.

"What is it?" Donald demanded. "I want to see."

"No, Donald," Annie said as calmly as she could. "Go sit on the floor."

Vanessa was strangely quiet now, too. Annie had her pinned with her knees. She wanted to spare her. A child who wasn't washed was a child no one cared about, no matter what hassles she caused. On the other hand, Annie didn't want her to touch anything either. "Um, Vanessa," she said softly.

"Is it lice?" Vanessa asked matter of factly.

"Have you had it before?" Annie let her go in surprise. Lice. God, it was lice. And they sent her out to other people's houses to breed with impunity.

"Or is it fleas?" Vanessa said. She stayed where she was, waiting for a diagnosis.

"Fleas?" Annie gasped once more.

"Fleas are black," Vanessa informed her. "Lice hang on, and they won't let go when you try to swoosh them out."

"Oh, God." Annie sank back on the sofa, then remembered and jumped up. They could go right through and breed in all her dear little feathers. She moaned. Then suddenly like a drill sergeant, "All right, everybody on the wood floor."

"Will I have to have a shampoo?" Vanessa wailed.

"You're damn right, you will."

"You said a bad word. You said two, Annie. I'm definitely going to tell."

"Oh, sit down."

Annie sat them both on the floor by the front door and gave them their tuna fish sandwiches, their cocoas. She told them to eat up and don't move no matter what. She retreated to the kitchen where she washed her hands; and then washed them again. She had noticed that Vanessa's neck had not known soap and water for some time either. She was on the road all the time. Probably each one thought the other washed her. Ugh. She sat on the kitchen stool and chewed her knuckles. It was a quarter to two. Why didn't that man come back and get his child? Annie almost wept with frustration. If he took her away, everything would be all right. Even now, it was all right. The children were quiet on the floor. They must be hungry. Then Annie realized that it wasn't all right. She couldn't return Donald home in good conscience the way he was. True, they had been together only for two hours. But in those two hours, she was sure they had touched. Donald had to be infected, too. She reached for the phone and dialed Ben's number.

"Ben," she cried. "I have lice."

"Annie?" he said.

"What should I do?"

"Is that why you stayed home?"

"No—I. Oh, God." With Ben on the phone, she felt free to break down. She broke down and cried.

"Okay, calm down. Hold on. No, don't go away. I just have to put you on hold for a second. Don't *cry*, Annie. It happens to everybody."

He came back on less than a second later.

"It doesn't happen to me," she wailed.

"You don't get crab lice from toilet seats," he said sarcastically.

"It isn't crab lice. It's *head* lice."

"Head lice. You must have had some weekend."

"Oh Ben, it's from a child," she said in a stage whisper. A child, as if it were a boa constrictor, or a gila monster with a poisonous bite. Or a pigeon with psittacosis.

"Which one?" he laughed.

"Don't laugh. I'm going to shoot myself. Where's that stuff of yours?"

"What stuff?" He was still guffawing with relief. A child with head lice, what could be funnier?

"That stuff, when you wanted to take a bath here, remember?"

"I don't know what you're talking about."

Oh yes, you do. You had crab lice in your—parts." She spit the last word out as if it were a hair in her mouth.

"I never did," he said indignantly. "You must be thinking of somebody else.

"No, I'm not. You were going out with that girl Odessa, or Odetta, and you came back here with a bottle of Kwell. I need it."

"What a memory you have," Ben said, all humor gone from his voice. "That was years ago."

"Well, I need the Kwell," Annie said snappishly.

"It was Adela," he said musingly. "She was French, or Algerian, or something."

"Ben, I need the *Kwell.* Sara will kill me." Annie whimpered just like Vanessa had only an hour before.

"You should kill *her,* this is an outrage."

"Don't make a joke of it; it's the other child."

"Lucy, that baby. Where would she get lice?"

"The *other* child," Annie said urgently.

Ben was silent for a long time. "Oh," he said finally.

"So, I've got to douse Donald before he goes home. Oh my *God,* and his clothes. His *sneakers.*"

"Put everything in the wash," Ben said. "I've got to go to a meeting in a minute."

"Ben!" Annie cried. "Don't go."

"I'm not going. I have a meeting."

"What about the Kwell?"

"I don't have it."

"What do you mean, you don't have it? You had it. Didn't you keep it in case of another attack?"

"This is not a good moment for jealousy."

"I'm not jealous. I just need the damn medicine," Annie said vehemently. "Christ, you have a one-track mind."

"No, Annie, you do. I forgot it and you remembered. . . . Now I remember. They gave me an ounce. I used a half an ounce twice, just to make sure. It's been gone for years," he added.

"What am I going to do?" Annie cried.

"Call the pediatrician."

"That's a good idea." She clapped her hands with relief and lost the phone for a moment.

"I'm glad to be good for something," he remarked.

"Oh my God, that's wonderful. Call the doctor. Oh, Ben, I love you." It just popped out of her mouth.

"What?"

"Thank you, I feel much better."

"Really? That was easy."

"Go to your meeting. I have to call the doctor."

"Is this thing over now?"

"Yes, it's over."

He seemed to nod over the phone. "I'll call you later."

The relief was enormous, extreme. It felt as if her heart was huge in her chest. She could feel it beating down in her stomach, as far even as her feet. It was over, all those months since the fall that she had struggled to like Herb because he was the last one left. Her last chance. All the worry if he liked her and how much. And if he liked her why he didn't show it. What he meant when he said this. What he meant when he said that. And then the big question. Why didn't he want to do it, when everybody else did?

Annie touched the phone with reverence. How did people begin and end affairs or have revelations in the old days without it? She picked up the receiver and called the children's pediatrician. She knew the number by heart. She knew how to lower fevers in infants, how to administer nose drops. In a few minutes she would know how to deal with lice. She wondered if Herb would show up before she finished, then realized that it didn't matter one way or another.

24

BRENDA WAS
on the phone the next morning early, demanding to know what
had happened. Sara was hysterical and wanted her to come over
to look after Lucy while she took Donald to the doctor. Annie was
still so shaken that at first she could hardly speak.

"What's going on?" Brenda asked. "She woke me up, Annie,
at seven o'clock and then wouldn't tell me anything. I asked her
what was the matter with Donald and she told me to ask you."

"There's nothing the matter with him." Annie had been
asleep. She grabbed the phone and took it into bed with her. At
first when it rang she was afraid it was Herb again and was prepared to hang up at the sound of his voice. But when it was only
Brenda, she piled up the pillows behind her.

"Oh, Mother!" she said. "You won't believe what happened,"
and then lapsed into silence.

"What happened?"

"Well," Annie hesitated. She had hardly slept all night because Herb was angry to find his daughter wrapped in a towel
while her clothes were being dried in the basement.

"What?" Brenda prompted. "Tell me."

Annie wasn't sure her mother was ready for a story like this,
but she told it anyway. She told her about Lucy's earache (it
turned out to be) and picking Donald up at school and finding the
lice in Vanessa's hair. And bundling the children up to go out to
the drug store in the rain, which finally decided at that moment to
fall, for the Kwell. When she got back Herb still hadn't turned up.
So she took all the clothes downstairs and put them in the washing machine so they would be drying when she gave the children
their treatment. She told her how one after another the three of
them had the five-minute dose of highly toxic chemical wash, and
how brittle it made her hair. And then Herb came back before the

clothes were dry and found the two children huddled in towels
having more cocoa, this time with marshmallows.

Throughout this recital, Brenda gasped and clicked. She'd
never heard of such a thing. It was outrageous. It was disgusting.
And then what happened?

"Well, I vacuumed the living room like crazy," Annie said.
"And washed the floors with ammonia, and then vacuumed the
sofa, too. It took me hours. I was going to shampoo the rug, but
the doctor told me if I vacuumed right away they wouldn't have
time to lay their eggs. Oh God, I didn't sleep all night."

"I mean! What did he say?"

Annie looked at the clock. "Oh my God. It's late. I've got to
get moving."

"What did he say, Annie?"

"He was furious that I touched his little flower without his
seeing her first."

"He's a doctor, he had a point."

"Mother, the child's head was alive. I could see them moving.
What was I supposed to do, sit here and let them breed on my
nephew? I had to treat Donald. I couldn't have sent him home if I
didn't. Dr. Mede said Donald could wait a few days. We could
check him out in three days and see if there was anything wrong.
Tell me, would you take the chance? Call Sara and tell her I did
the right thing."

"Did he look in her hair?"

"Herb?"

"Yes. Did you ever get a confirmation?"

"Look, do you know what Dr. Mede told me? He told me I
should sit there and pull every egg case out of every strand of her
hair with my fingernails. The fine-toothed comb is not fine
enough to do the job. Can you imagine my doing that? I told
Herb the easiest thing to do would be cut her hair. If it were my
child, I'd cut her hair."

"You haven't told me if he looked."

"He was too mad to look. He was furious. And I told him
she'd had it before. She knew just what was going on in her head.
She even told me what to look for. I almost died." Annie did not
tell her about Lydia's phone call. That was too much.

"She'd had it before?"

"Yes, and they sent her out with it."

"Well, Annie, you really pick them. And a doctor, too."

"He was mad at me because she might have gotten an allergic reaction. Believe me, *I* had an allergic reaction. I wouldn't see him again for anything."

"I've heard of people picking up things from their lovers, but this is the limit," Brenda said. "Do you want to have lunch, Baby? I'll buy you a new dress to cheer you up. I know, what if I got a professional cleaner to come in and do your apartment?"

"No, it's all right." Annie jumped up and began pulling on the covers. "I've got to go." Suddenly she remembered that she hadn't been at the office since Friday, and Ben hadn't called her the night before as he said he would.

"Lunch? I'll take you to the Plaza," Brenda wheedled.

Annie sighed. So that's the kind of day Brenda thought it was. The Plaza was where she used to take them when they were younger. Brenda used to know the head waiter in the Palm Court; he always greeted her effusively and led them right through the line of waiting ladies. Annie didn't know until she was all the way grown up that the hearty greetings he gave them were the direct result of the five-dollar bills Brenda occasionally pressed into his hand for the privilege.

The Plaza was where Sara was closely questioned about the state of her virginity in relation to that not very promising young man who was always hanging around on holidays. Small, with glasses, skinny, and with the mentality of a poor person. In tears behind a palm tree, Sara swore to God they hadn't done it, even though they had. And Brenda told her if she loved him, doing it was the Worst Thing she could do. If she did it, Martin would have no reason to marry her, if that was what Sara unwisely had in her mind. Such an ending had not yet occurred to Sara. But she resolved to marry him then, if for nothing more than to prove her mother wrong.

It was in the Palm Court that Brenda threatened Annie with being absolutely the only girl in her whole high school who wouldn't get into college. "It's not that I don't think you have what it takes," Brenda told her over practically the only chef's salad in New York that's cut fine enough. "But you're just not trying. If you don't perk up and do better, we'll have to get you a tutor. And you know how your father feels about dopes in his family." After this lunch Annie perked up and was rewarded with a telephone in her room, which never rang until she was away in college and not there to answer it.

It was also to the Plaza that Annie first brought Nate to meet her mother soon after he moved into her apartment. That lunch had taken many negotiations to arrange, and finally her father boycotted it, anyway. Brenda thought then that if Annie wasn't up to it, the power of her personality alone could make things right. She overestimated Nate's commitment and Annie's sense of right and wrong.

"What do you say?" Brenda pressed. Just lately she had started going to a new dentist. The man who had taken care of the family for thirty years had finally retired, and this new young man had taken over his practice. Right away he had the waiting room redecorated, and Brenda found out that it wasn't his wife who had done it. No wife yet, he told her, and Brenda said she had a daughter who was a stockbroker. "Interesting," the dentist had said. "Is she as pretty as you?"

Brenda hardly hesitated a second before she said, "Prettier," as staunchly as she could with a mirror in her mouth. He wore plaid pants, with his dentist's jacket over them, but these things were always adjustable in time.

"I can't, Mother. Maybe later in the week."

"Annie. I've been thinking. You really ought to get your teeth cleaned." Brenda said suddenly.

"What?" Annie now had plumped the pillow, had pulled the phone across the room and was struggling into her underwear with one hand, having bathed herself out the night before. "I can't hear you."

"Well, Sweetheart, we'll talk about it later. I have to call Sara. She's probably trying to get me now."

"Tell her not to worry. Donald's fine. I already went through this with Mede yesterday."

"I'll tell her," Brenda said.

"Mother," Annie said after a second.

"What, Dear?"

"He wasn't my lover."

"I know, Baby, try to keep your spirits up. We're all with you."

Upon hearing these sympathetic words, Annie lapsed immediately into a deep depression. She decided she needed a bath after all. She took a bath, then a shower, then changed her clothes three times. When she was finally ready to leave, Sara called.

"I'm sorry I got so upset yesterday. Lucy's much better, and Dr. Mede said he doesn't have to see Donald."

"That's good. I have to go. I'll talk to you later," Annie said. She stood in front of the mirror and combed her hair one last time. It was still very boring hair.

"Wait a minute. I really want you to know I'm sorry."

"Thank you, Sara."

"I'm sorry about Herb, too."

"It's okay," Annie said.

"It was a terrible thing to happen, especially after—"

"I have to go, Sara. I'll talk to you later."

"You aren't burned, are you? We're all sure you'll find some-body else. Do you want to come for dinner tonight? Martin was so disappointed when you ran off last night."

"I didn't run off. I had to vacuum the carpet," Annie said, "and if I don't go to the office today, I may not find my desk there tomorrow."

"Well, call me later and let me know."

"All right," Annie promised, though she knew she wouldn't call; and Sara would call her tomorrow and complain. "I'll try, but don't count on me. I may have to go out with a client." Or something.

"Who?" Sara demanded.

"Good-bye," Annie said. "Good-bye."

Sara sputtered in protest, but Annie fled anyway. She raced down to the office, where there was a mountain of paperwork on her desk. She had an ominous feeling, because Ben hadn't called her the night before as he said he would. Annie was a little later than usual, but still it was very quiet. Ben wasn't in yet, and that wasn't a good sign. It occurred to her that he might have gone in the night, because in a weak moment she said she loved him.

She went to see Gertie, who was working on her morning coffee, shaking two grains of sugar into the cup at a time so she shouldn't have to ingest one speck more of the poisonous sub-stance than she absolutely had to.

"Oh Annie," Gertie said when she saw her. "*Did* you miss a day yesterday."

"I didn't miss it, I had one of my own." Right away Annie noticed that Gertie had on new glasses. The frames tilted up at the edges and looked like two smiles under her eyebrows. The pins that held the temples on were in the shape of tiny hearts. But it was the color that was the most shocking of all. Ever since Annie had known Gertie, she wore frames that were as black as her hair, as severe as the set of her thin lips. They were round and made her look as old and unmovable as an owl, although two years ago the jilting boyfriend had not found her so. These new frames were orange, orange plastic with a thin stripe of clear running through it and the vaguest tint of bronze in the glass.

"Wow," Annie said. "What happened?"

"Lots of things have happened," Gertie said cryptically. With one finger she adjusted her new glasses on the bridge of her nose.

"You look like something out of a Fellini movie," Annie remarked. She perched on a corner of Gertie's desk. "Don't tell me you finally got up the nerve to move out." She didn't think Gertie's mother would ever allow glasses like that.

Gertie lived with her mother. Her grandmother lived upstairs. When Gertie had her abortion, they thought she had a cyst that ruptured. Afterward, they monitored her every move for evidence of further ill health. If she stayed in bed on a Saturday, they thought she was dying instead of merely depressed. If she went out with a girl friend and didn't come home until midnight, they huddled together downstairs and prayed. When she returned, they sniffed around her, silently rebuking her for worrying them. Secretly they were looking for signs of wear. Gertie and Annie always had a lot to talk about, even though Gertie's family was from Canarsie and had no education at all. Something about mothers and what they do.

"I met someone," Gertie said shyly.

"Oh no," Annie thought, but smiled encouragingly. "That's nice; is he—" "White," she was going to say as a joke, meaning American. As opposed to Puerto Rican, which was not. Or Arab. Arab was a dirty word in Canarsie. But then it occurred to her that the possibilities of even the most native-born American rainbow were very nearly infinite. He could be culturally from Buenos Aires and be most deeply disturbed. Or worse, white from South Africa, which is as alien in the soul as a human can get. Or Californian and terminally blond, soulless altogether. On the other hand, he could be Chinese, which would be a great improvement over the Italian she came from. "—single," she blurted. Sincere, she meant. Single didn't actually mean anything.

"Sure, he's single. Giovanni," she said reverently.

Annie laughed. "An Italian. That's too much. How did you manage that?"

"My mother's cousin's son. Don't laugh. He's beautiful."

"That's wonderful. Why is it so quiet around here? Has something happened?"

"He likes my mama," Gertie said wonderingly. "He brings her flowers."

"That's very thoughtful. What does he bring you?" Annie asked. She had her doubts about Johnny, as Gertie Americanized him. She didn't know why. Maybe it was the glasses. They were altogether too optimistic on such a serious face.

"The glasses!" Gertie said explosively. "He made them just for me. What do you think?"

"Wow," Annie murmured. That was love all right. "They're amazing. I said so right away."

"He's getting me contacts, too. He says there's a new kind of contacts that will work on my eyeballs. I have funny eyeballs, you know."

Annie slid impatiently off the desk, but paused to give her friend a hug. "I know you'll be very happy together." It was time to go to work. She turned away.

Gertie grabbed her arm. "Do you think so? Do you really think so?"

Annie nodded. "How can it miss?"

"If he found out," Gertie said gloomily.

"That's easy, don't tell him for a while. I've got to go."

"I can't tell him, ever."

"Oh come on. You'll have to tell him. These things happen to everybody You were only a baby yourself."

"It didn't happen to you."

"Well, Gertie, I'm not a Catholic. I've used every device known to man."

"How did you know?" Gertie looked shocked that Annie guessed.

"Honey, I know you would no more go to a doctor and announce your intentions than I would jump out of the window. It wasn't a hard question. Now what happened yesterday?"

"I'm not supposed to know."

"Gertie, did they hire someone else to be in my office? Oh God, I knew it. I just knew something terrible happened yesterday. I didn't sleep all night. Is that it?"

"I can't tell you," Gertie said, shutting her thin lips. "I told you the secrets of my life. That's as far as I go. Do you really think I have to tell him?"

"I don't know, Gertie," she said, anxious now. "Ask an authority. Ask Ann Landers." She turned away. Now she had to decide what to do.

"Where are you going?"

"I don't know. I think I'll take a walk."

"Go talk to Ben first. He has something to tell you."

"Is he leaving?" Annie gasped. So that's why he didn't call her. That was what happened in his meeting yesterday. Her face went pale.

"Ha, I knew it. You fell for him, too." She laughed, then said she wasn't laughing when Annie really looked distressed.

It seemed strange. One of her friends had been going to get married to one person and then a week before the wedding he changed his mind. He had dinner with a casual friend, someone who had been a chum for years, to tell her good-bye. It was to be their last dinner together and suddenly he realized what it would mean to him not to see her any more. At the very last minute, he left the lover and married the chum. Now Annie knew that she couldn't have left Howard and Plunket even for an office of her own, because the spirit of Howard and Plunket was Ben. If he left, there would be no reason except a paycheck for her to get dressed and come in every morning. It hit her like a brick falling unexpectedly from an old building.

"I'll see you later," Annie murmured.

She walked back through the boardroom. Now everybody was there. She passed her secretary. "I didn't know you were here," she said.

"I'm not."

"Here are your calls. Hey, you look tired."

Annie took the sheaf of pink slips and went into Ben's office.

"Hi," he said. "I thought you were going to spend the whole morning in there with Gertie. So now you know."

"I know," Annie said. She sat down and stared at the carpet to avoid looking at Ben. The carpet was still brown and blue, but it was cleaner than it had been on Friday. Must have been shampooed over the weekend. "I feel like shit," she announced.

"I thought you'd be happy for me," Ben said. "Hey, don't be depressed. Now you can have my office," he said exuberantly.

"I don't care."

"What do you mean you don't care? For three months you've been talking about nothing else. That's all you wanted in life, your own office. And now you have it. I thought you'd be happy. What's the matter?"

"Nothing," Annie said, rifling through her messages. Herb. Herb. Sara. Lydia? Annie tore them up and handed the pieces to Ben, who threw them in his wastebasket. The others she kept. What did Lydia want? She was too miserable to be curious.

"Are you mad because I didn't call you last night?" he asked. It was as if he had grown a few inches overnight. He was that pleased with himself. He was so happy he was wearing a pink shirt with his gray suit, and a red tie.

"You look like a lollypop," Annie said. She thought she might die if he left. She was that depressed.

"I thought you liked pink."

"On *me*."

"Oh come on, don't be mad. It was my turn. It had to be me or Sylvia. And I was really the logical choice. How would you have felt if it was Sylvia, huh?"

"I would have been delighted if it was Sylvia. I don't care about Sylvia."

"If you cared about me, you'd be happy for me. I'm happy." He grinned to show how happy he was. "Everybody else is happy. Are you mad because I didn't tell you last night?"

"It would have been nicer coming from you."

"It's not my fault she told you. She promised she wouldn't. The memo isn't going around until tomorrow."

"She didn't tell me. I guessed."

"How could you guess? *I* didn't even know until yesterday."

"I don't know. I just—guessed." Annie attempted a little smile. "Now I guess I won't see you any more."

"Why not?" Ben was alarmed. "What are you thinking?"

"Well, you won't think of me any more. You'll be in another office, I won't be convenient."

"Annie, I'm only going down the hall."

"You are? Where are you going? E.F. Hutton? Bache?"

"What are you talking about? I'm going to the corner office."

"The corner office here? But John is in the corner office."

Ben shook his head. "Not any more."

"Oh my God, are you the managing partner?"

He looked at her as if she were crazy. "I thought you knew."

She jumped up and hugged him so enthusiastically, she almost knocked over his tilt-and-swivel chair. "Oh that's wonderful. That's terrific. I love your shirt."

"It's not that big a deal. Hey, why aren't you like this in private?"

John poked his head in. "Hi, Annie. I see you heard the news."

Annie recovered herself very quickly. "Well, not exactly," she said. "I'm sorry."

"Well," John said. He snorted. He'd seen Annie very nearly sitting in Ben's lap. He could see what was coming to this office as soon as he left. He frowned. He didn't look at all happy.

Annie sat down as meekly as possible.

"Aren't you going to congratulate me?" John said. "Or do I deserve a wake?"

"I don't know what happened yet, John. Nobody's told me." She looked from one to the other. "What happened?"

When John wouldn't speak, Ben finally said. "John is going to be running New Jersey."

"Oh," Annie took a deep breath. "That's wonderful, John. But of course we'll miss you."

"Thank you Annie, even if you don't mean it."

"Oh, I mean it, John. We will miss you. When are you going?"

"Friday," he said gloomily. "Are you that eager to see me go?"

"No, no. I meant we'll have a party for you, won't we Ben? We'll have a big party for you."

"Of course we will," Ben chimed in. He almost said "dear." Their first party. He beamed.

John said no, no he'd be embarrassed. Then a moment or two later he came back into the office and asked Ben where they were thinking of having it.

"We'll have a meeting and discuss it, won't we, Annie?"

Annie nodded seriously.

"Good, good." John walked out.

Annie turned to Ben. She could see the sense of responsibility, and even a little fear, fight with pure joy in his face. "What happened?"

"Poor John got promoted. I thought he was going to have a

heart attack and die on the spot yesterday when he found out."

"Poor John," Annie said, grinning so hard her face hurt.

John shuffled back in. "Have you decided yet?"

"No, we're still thinking about it."

"Maybe you ought to include Sylvia. She has very good ideas," John suggested. "It would be nice to get everybody involved."

This was the sucker who for months was too worried about upsetting Annie to hire someone to take Carl's place. Annie and Ben nodded at each other.

"Fine," Ben said. "I'll ask her to come in."

John went out again.

They giggled uncontrollably until Sylvia arrived a few minutes later with a notebook, so she could take notes. She had a very serious expression on her face. It made Annie think she really might miss John, or maybe they had something going together. She examined Sylvia closely; on the other hand, she might have wanted the job herself. Of course that was it. Annie was so relieved she couldn't feel sorry for her. Ever since Ben had made it clear he was unavailable to Sylvia's advances, Sylvia had always referred to him as "the kid."

Annie's secretary popped her head in. "Annie, there's a call for you."

"Who is it?"

"Your mother. She says she's going out and wants to meet you later."

Annie frowned, crossed her legs the other way. The other two waited for her response. Finally she said, "Tell her you're sorry, you can't get me. I'm in meetings all day."

25

UNTIL THE day of his promotion, Ben spent a lot of time worrying about what to do with his apartment. He'd bought it almost fifteen years ago, when the real estate market was way down. He bought it with what was left of his father's life insurance. His mother had given him the money as a present when he left home. It wasn't very much, but it seemed a lot then. The money had been earmarked to get him through college. Harold Page, his stepfather, decided that it would not be good for Ben to stay home and go to the local college, where he was the head of the English department and Ben's mother was the dean of women. This question of what to do with Ben had plagued them for years.

Ben had been a sullen teenager, and even more so when his mother remarried so soon after his father died. His real father had been a jovial, outdoors sort of person. He slapped his overweight son on the back and gave him fishing rods and skis and things like that for his birthdays. He had hopes that Ben's bulk would make him a football player even though Ben liked being inside (near the refrigerator) and thought he wanted to be a jazz piano player.

His mother was a tall woman with dark hair in a bun and a serious expression. Ben always felt he was a surprise to her. Even when he was very little, she would come upon him somewhere in the house and say, "Oh, it's you," as if she didn't expect him still to be there. She never knew what to do with him. When he was small, she was interested in bigger children. And then when he went to school and could talk like a person, he turned out not to be her type.

She married the English professor, who was as morose and inward as Ben's father had been outgoing and flirtatious. Quiet was what they wanted in the house, not the noisy pounding on the piano that Ben liked to provide. At meals they drank wine and turned on dreary classical music. Ben ate with his head down, said almost nothing at the table, and dreamed for years about being a Marine.

He knew they gave him the money for silence. As he got older, he asked more and more questions about his father and mother when they were young, and what they did when they were older and going separate ways. His father didn't always come home for dinner. And when he did, his mother sometimes went out instead. Until he was in grade school he thought all families were like that, the parents taking turns with the child. Sometimes he was sure they had adopted him and later were sorry. Other times he felt he was the result of an indiscretion of theirs, before abortion was possible. They were the kind of people who would marry for honor and then stick it out no matter how miserable they were. His mother never told him how long she'd been sleeping with Harold before they were married, or anything else he wanted to know.

In college he found he could support himself playing the piano, and invested his bribe money in the stock market. After a few years of quiet agony, he discovered even pretty girls could be influenced by music and money. When he came to New York, he took the corner apartment with a terrace, a large living room, two bedrooms and two bathrooms. When it went coop a few years later, he bought it with the profits from his stocks and began an endless project of decoration and redecoration. He knocked down a wall and put one up. He had the place painted bordello red because he thought it would be cheerful. But he got tired of that after a year or so. He didn't have anybody he wanted to marry, so he had the walls lacquered brown and used mirrors to reflect the light from the windows. He was going out with a decorator then and wanted to give her some work. She had the floors bleached white (like Annie's), but they didn't last as long as it took for the carpet to come. Chocolate brown with a beige border.

The previous fall, when he couldn't stand the dark any more, he had the place painted white. Suddenly the rug looked too dark. The mirrors were startling; and the sofa, hard and slung very low, in the beige that matched the border of the rug, now seemed too severe a style and was upholstered in an ugly color. He wanted to take the terrace and make it into a greenhouse, an extra sitting room with plants, but didn't want to plan it alone.

All through the winter he brooded endlessly, feeling debilitated and old. When the girls on the street began attracting him less and less, he spent more time in front of the television worrying that he had a sexual problem. He was tormented by Annie, who said he was as cold inside as a fish fillet. She called him "the man who hurt women." He was intrigued by her lack of interest. Annie didn't think he was worthy of remembering. In all his experience no one had ever forgotten how he was in bed. This rejection of hers troubled him so much (because it was a daily event) that when other girls still found him attractive, he didn't believe them. He questioned their honesty. He didn't think they had any brains. Right away he found fatal flaws in their bodies that it would have taken him several weeks to notice in his earlier life. And all this time he was half convinced that he could no longer have any fun because the decor in his apartment had ceased being harmonious.

Annie said his personality had always showed in his apartment that had no heart. And Ben worried about this, too, because it was true that he had always thought of it more as a zone of seduction than any sort of home. His mother saw it only once, several years before, when she came to New York for a convention and left almost immediately because she didn't like the city. She liked the apartment, though, with its Mongolian grill on the terrace. She said she never thought Ben would do so well. This remark depressed him for weeks, even though he was having an affair at the time with the most ravishing Hungarian girl, who had lived for years in Hong Kong and could speak six languages. Even his mother had been impressed with her. But Ben was concerned because she had a European mentality. She spent a great deal on clothes and felt it was his responsibility to pay for them, and all of her other whims. She didn't last very long.

Although he was not altogether convinced that an apartment could have a heart, he was more than eager for Annie to have a go at giving his one. He discussed this possibility with her all spring, in lieu of sex. His argument was that he was helpless on his own and the project would give them something to do with their Saturdays. Secretly, he thought if Annie put her heart into his apartment, she might like it there and want to stay.

So far Annie had not said no, but she never seemed to have a Saturday free to get started. She was always busy. He didn't want to get started on his own in case she didn't like what he did. So he worried. He worried about how much he didn't like his sofa, how miserable he was alone, about the many mistakes he had made in the past. He worried about what Annie really did with Herb the doctor, who surely didn't deserve more than one wife at a time. And most of all he worried that Annie's fear about him was well founded and he really couldn't relate to a woman any better than a dead fish. It was true he was nearly thirty-six, and the only woman he was sure he wanted got a stomach ache every time he kissed her seriously. She had a mouth phobia. She didn't want his germs, or his sperm. Or his well-exercised body, or anything. It made him crazy just thinking about it. It took all his control to be calm, and smile, and listen to her talking about her mother and her sister and the other parts of her life he wasn't allowed to share.

And then the day of his promotion when Annie got lice, he knew she was free. A small child who wasn't hers, a fat slob, she might take. But bugs, he was certain, she could never tolerate. He was so excited he didn't want to call her back and spoil it with his concern. He sat that night in his apartment, euphoric, and yet afraid to lift the phone lest she run away again.

He planned it that night, after John was banished to New Jersey. He would take Annie out on Saturday night, somewhere special. And he would give her a really expensive present, something symbolic that wouldn't give her a headache. Like a Cartier watch to show that time was passing. And then they would go back to his place because, after Nate, she said she'd never let anyone spend the night at hers. And then . . . he didn't let the fantasy go any further than that because there was just no guessing at how Annie might react. He was convinced that Annie had a surrender problem, in which case *his* having a headache would be more productive than overcoming her with sheer force. On the other hand, she might be sufficiently softened up by the watch not to require any additional persuasion. But still, he was not ready to abandon the option of brute force should it become absolutely necessary.

"Annie, I want your help," he said after visiting Tiffany and Cartier twice and not being able to make a decision on the watch. The watch Annie had was a little circle, as traditional and boring as it could be. A Timex with a red leather strap.

She looked up from some notes she was taking for a new account that needed a pretty severe updating. "What for?"

"I want to buy a present for my mother," Ben said. "For Mother's Day."

"Buy her a scarf," Annie said, and returned to her work.

"I don't want to buy her a scarf," Ben said.

"Well then, buy her some perfume."

He sat down at Carl's empty desk. "I was thinking of something a little nicer than that."

"What?" She looked at him fondly. Saturday they were going out to celebrate his promotion. She was going to have her hair done and wear her best dress. She smiled. "A new car?"

"No, I was thinking of a—watch. What do you think?"

"Doesn't she have a watch?"

"Sure, she has a watch. I want to get her a *new* watch, a nicer one," Ben said.

"How do you know she wants a new one?"

"Christ, Annie, don't second guess me. I want to buy her a watch. Whether she wants one or not isn't the question."

"Bully," Annie said, but she laughed. She knew why he wanted to buy her a present. He was proud, he was managing partner; a success. She'd never heard him mention his mother before. She was almost surprised he had one. But if he wanted to show off to her now, it was understandable.

"Will you come with me or not?"

"Where?"

"To buy my mother a watch, where do you think?"

"I don't know your mother, I wouldn't be any help," Annie said.

"Well, Annie, pretend you're choosing one for yourself. That's always the best approach."

"You do it; it's your mother."

"Annie, I asked you to help me. If you asked me to help you, I'd help you."

"All right, some other day."

"Next week is too late. Next week we'll be moving our offices. Everything will be a mess. I'll be tense. You'll be irritable. And anyway, Mother's Day is Sunday."

Annie threw her pencil down with exasperation. "All right, we'll do it now. God!" she muttered. But secretly she was pleased he wanted her with him. Buying something for his mother, now that was intimacy. That was big-time stuff. Quickly she ran down the hall to powder her nose. And then by agreement they met downstairs. Now that he was managing partner, they were worried about suspicion.

"What's your mother like?" Annie asked as they hiked uptown.

"Dour, she's very dour," Ben said. "She never liked me very much."

"Oh, I'm sure that isn't true," Annie protested.

"I don't worry about it."

"But I'm sure it isn't true. How could she not like you?"

"She used to tell me she got me at Sears and if I didn't behave, she'd send me back."

"I came from Saks, but I'm a second."

They laughed. Ben said after him his mother was too daunted
for a second. He said if he really had come from Sears, she would
have sent him back.

"Where do you want to go?" Annie asked. It didn't seem at all
strange to her that Ben would want to buy a watch for a mother
who didn't like him.

"Where do you think, Tiffany, Cartier, or Tourneau?"

"It depends on how much you like her. If we go to Tourneau
you can look at all the varieties and then buy her a copy."

Ben looked shocked. "You mean something that says Cartier
and isn't?"

"No, something that looks like Cartier and says Longines."

"You're something else. That's the sort of thing my mother
would say."

"Good. We'll go to Tourneau then." Annie didn't like Tiffany. She didn't want to go there no matter what.

They walked up Madison. Suddenly it was very warm, a real
spring day with a million-and-a-half people on the street. They
almost had to push to make progress.

"I'm sure she likes you," Annie said after a pause.

"Don't worry about it."

"But if you think she doesn't like you, that accounts for your
hatred of women," she mused. "That's your source."

"I like women," he protested.

"No, you don't. You never like anybody."

"Don't do that. I don't want to start feeling defensive in the
middle of an adventure." Ben took her arm as somebody tried to
walk between them.

"All right," Annie said, chastened. "I won't spoil your day."

A block further on she said, "I think she'll be thrilled, even if
she doesn't like you."

"Jesus." Ben fell into a deep silence that Annie didn't dare
break.

They went into Tourneau, where there were so many different kinds of watches it was easy to get discouraged. An oily
salesperson asked if he could help. Ben looked helplessly at
Annie.

"We're looking for a lady's watch," Annie said after a pause.

The salesperson waved his hand. They were all over the place. "What sort of watch do you have in mind?"

"How about a Rolex?" Annie suggested. Nate wore a Rolex. She'd always disliked it. A lot of metal and numbers and dials she couldn't read. The perfect gift for an unloving mother.

"Do you like Rolexes?" Ben asked. He'd looked at them before and didn't think they were feminine.

Annie walked over to one of the cases that had Rolexes in it. She pointed to the gold Rolex with a circle of diamonds around the face. "How about that?" she said. Why not start from the top and see how much he cared.

Ben gulped. That was the sort of watch South Americans wore, the kind of South American who had so much money he didn't know which way to throw it.

The salesman took it out of the case. "It's a beautiful watch." He held it up for Annie to look at. "Would you like to try it on?"

Annie examined it for a minute. "It's very heavy. How much is it?"

"Seventy-eight hundred," he said. "It's all gold, of course."

"It should be, for the price." Annie looked inquiringly at Ben. "What do you think?"

"It's very flashy," he said doubtfully.

"You're right. She's old. Do you think she'd prefer a leather band?"

"What do you like?" Ben asked her.

"Oh, isn't it for you?" the salesman asked.

"No, it's for a mother," Annie said. "We need something more—"

"Why don't you tell me which one you like."

Annie walked around and looked in all the cases. Ben followed her.

"What do you say?" he said.

"It depends on whether she wants something for dress or every day." She shrugged. "And how much you want to spend." She took him in a corner. "Why don't you ask him to show you all the five-hundred-dollar watches?"

"Why don't you just pick out one you like? It would be so much more fun that way," Ben urged her.

"But she might not like what I like," Annie protested.

"Pretend she does," he insisted.

"I can't do that. She probably likes those over there with the tiny faces and the numbers so small you can't read them. And, and, the diamonds all over them and a gold bracelet. That's what my mother likes."

"I knew this was going to be complicated," he muttered.

"All right, why don't you get her a Gucci watch with the gold wire band? They're chic and not very expensive."

"Do you like those? Ben said doubtfully. They didn't have any numbers on them. You couldn't get cheaper than that.

"No," Annie said.

"Then why did you suggest it?"

They glared at each other for a minute while the salesman wandered off. "I didn't think you'd want to spend so very much if she doesn't like you," Annie mumbled.

"You're not being helpful," Ben said reproachfully. Now he was getting discouraged.

"Well, how can I choose if you don't tell me whether she's tailored or sporty? If she likes metal or leather bands, or won't be impressed if she doesn't get gold? And how much do you want to spend? Be reasonable. I don't know the lady."

"I don't know her either," Ben murmured.

"Well, now we're in trouble." Annie relented and squeezed his arm. "All right. Never mind."

"Never mind what?"

"I'll choose." She pointed at the Longines that was a copy of the most popular Cartier watch of the moment. Stainless steel with gold screws. She knew just how much it was. Almost reasonable, and in Vermont his mother wouldn't know the difference.

"Is that what you like?"

Annie walked around again. "You could buy her one of the plain gold Tiffany or Cartier Tank watches with the black lizard band. They're very classic. She might like that best. But I think they're common. They're copied everywhere and I'm tired of a soft band."

"You are?" he said perking up a little.

"Well, if I were choosing."

"You like these?" He went over to the counter with the gold link bands. He pointed at some and the salesman came back. "I'd like to see these."

The case was unlocked and several watches were presented. Ben asked Annie to hold out her wrist. He nodded as one after another was buckled on Annie's arm. "Very nice, but they're a little big."

"We can have them shortened," the salesman said. "About four links ought to do."

Annie screwed up her face. He was looking in the four-thousand-dollar range. No mother was worth that. She had only been kidding about the Rolex.

"What's the matter?"

"They're very flashy," Annie said.

"I thought you liked flashy."

"Let's think about it. Let's take a walk."

"I wasn't going to buy it now anyway," he said. "I'll come back," to the salesman.

Out on the street, she said, "You got me all the way out here, and you weren't going to buy anything anyway?"

"Did you like the gold ones?"

"No," Annie said. "I wouldn't be caught dead in one of those. I thought you were crazy. And I didn't like the salesman."

"I didn't either."

"Don't buy anything there."

"I won't."

"Good." They stood on the street corner. "What shall we do now?"

Ben shrugged. "Let's go to Tiffany."

Annie balked. She got depressed in Tiffany. Tiffany was where everybody registered for their china. Tiffany was for engagement rings. Tiffany meant other people's weddings. She looked at her watch. It was getting late and she still had a lot of things to do. "I've got to go back."

"Come on, we're almost there. It won't take long," Ben urged her.

"I don't want to."

"Please." He wanted to go to Tiffany. "Just for a minute."

Annie sighed. "I don't really like Tiffany," she said. But she started walking anyway. Why did he have to buy his mother a watch? He admitted he hardly ever saw her. He should buy himself a watch. He had a pretty unimpressive watch and the strap wasn't even leather. It was nylon. She knew the face of his watch well. It was a plain Omega, probably twenty years old, bought at the local jewelry store for his high school graduation. She sniffed. His graduation hadn't been honored with any more conviction than hers. Surely the mother didn't deserve anything more than a Timex.

"Isn't this fun?" Ben said. "I love to go shopping with you."

"That's a joke, right?" Annie said. They had been arguing for two days about the details for John's party. She saw the revolving doors of Tiffany and told herself not to start hyperventilating as soon as they got inside. She thought actually she ought to be amused; it was just her sort of luck for a man to want her to go to Tiffany to help him buy something for his mother.

She turned her head away from the ring counters, which, even in the middle of a weekday afternoon, were jammed. Happily, the watch department was empty. Annie went to the men's side of the watch counter. "What do you like?" She asked jauntily. "The present should be for you."

"Why me?"

"You got the promotion. I like that one." Annie pointed to an Audemar Piguet, with a gold and stainless band.

Right away the salesman took it out. "That's the Royal Oak," he said. "It's my favorite."

"You like that better than the Santos?" Ben obediently bared his wrist.

"Everybody's copying the Santos," the salesman said. "It's old hat now."

"You just say that because you don't carry it." Annie laughed.

"No, I really think this is the classier watch."

"Do you have the woman's version?" Ben asked, admiring his wrist.

"Of course." Instantly it was produced.

"Now, you're a matched set," the salesman said when it was affixed to Annie's wrist. "Very handsome."

Annie nodded. "I like it better than the Santos."

"Are you sure?" Ben took his off.

"Don't you like it?" Annie pouted.

He looked in the case. "I guess you're right, the gold is tacky."

"Put it back on. Let's buy it."

"Buy both of them, it's very chic to have matching watches."

The idea amused them, and they began to fool around, and try everything on as if they were really debating which ones they meant to buy. Annie kept coming back to the Royal Oak. She said she liked the name. They put them back on again.

The salesman nodded vigorously. "I agree, these really suit you. Are they wedding gifts?"

At the same moment they soured on the watches and peeled them off. "We'll think about it," Ben said as they stepped away.

"I don't like this place. It makes everybody so materialistic." Annie grumbled. "Look at all this stuff. It makes me sick."

"Me, too."

"Maybe there's some place that has a copy of the Audemars."

"Right," Ben agreed. "Let's get out of here."

They went outside and breathed the gusty spring air. "How do people do it?" Annie said after they had been standing blankly on the corner of Fifty-seventh Street and Fifth Avenue for some time. "I feel like I'm suffocating every time I go in there."

"I don't know," Ben said. But he knew what she meant. The institution had a way of making the unengaged feel failed some-how, as if real people got it together and bought each other things. Stocked up in a big way with a lot of stuff they'd never thought about before, and didn't need.

"Let's go back to the office," Annie said. "I have a headache."

"I'm sorry."

"What for?" She turned toward Madison. "Nothing hap-pened."

He thought he ought to go back and buy the watch right then to cheer her up, but she was muttering about how sick it was to think *things* were important. Evil even. When there was so much trouble in the world. Starving children. Tortured Salvadoreans, zillions of imprisoned Russians with not a single civil right among them. That was what they ought to be thinking about, didn't Ben think so? They ought to send more money to CARE, for Christ's sake, and not just at tax time either.

"We ought to join the Helsinki watch," she said.

"You're right," he said, not listening to a word because it was true that Tiffany made him feel like shit. Even worse than the wedding announcements every Sunday in the *Times:* Mr. and Mrs. George Appleby announce the engagement of their daughter Ashley, a broker with Sterling, Whirling, to Ardsley Finklebaum of High Heights, who will be graduating this June from Eastern Valley Podiatry school. Ben couldn't help studying every one.

"It's disgusting to spend so much money on a dumb watch," Annie said. She planted her feet firmly on the sidewalk one foot in front of the other. Shit. Who needs it, she asked herself. It was terrible. People going crazy over the picture on a plate, over a little chip of rock that was nothing more than a cleverly aged piece of coal. People were crazy, thinking marriage was everything. Look at Sara, an otherwise reasonable person, thrilled to the core at the installation of a kitchen sink.

Who wanted it anyway? Who wanted to be part of a matched set? Not them. They plodded on in silence. In a few blocks they were back in front of Tourneau where the salesman wasn't very nice. It was all very stupid, Annie thought. Let the mother wear her old watch. Then her fingers crept into Ben's hand for comfort. And they both felt a lot better.

26

JOHN'S PARTY was a very manic affair at Aperitivo. Everybody drank more than they should, and there was a great deal of food—Italian. And the office never quite got itself back together again. Annie didn't care to see John's final good-bye, so she went home instead of back to the office. She wanted to get a really good night's sleep so she would look good for her date with Ben. She planned to do nothing all the next day but stay in bed and then have her hair done and get dressed. But nothing ever happened the way it was supposed to. She fell asleep at five, soon after she got home, and was awakened an hour later by someone ringing the bell and banging on her door at the same time.

She ran through the living room pulling on a pair of jeans and a shirt. She was frightened and dazed by the noise and didn't scream "Who is it?" until she was in the kitchen with her hand on the downstairs intercom.

"It's Herb."

"Jesus." Annie buttoned her shirt. "What do you want?" through the door.

"I want to talk to you, what do you think?"

Annie looked out the peephole. He was dressed in a business suit. She opened the door.

"What are you doing here?" she asked curiously. At first she was merely curious, then she was alarmed, because he just pushed his way in even though she was blocking the door.

"Are you alone?" he asked.

"I can't see you now, Herb. Hey, please," as he went into the living room. "What do you want?"

He sat down on the sofa.

"Herb!"

"I've been in hell all week because of you," he said. He leaned forward and dropped his head in his hands.

Annie stood there with her hands on her hips. "You'll have to go."

"Annie, you can't throw me out like dirty dishwater. I'm in pain."

"I didn't ask you to come here, you'll have to go." She waved at the door. She did not feel pity. She did not care about his pain.

"I tried all week to call you. Why didn't you return my calls?" He raised his big head to look at her mournfully.

"You're a jerk," she wanted to say. "This is more attention than you've given me the whole time I've known you." But she said only, "I don't care."

"I know you talked to Lydia. Is that why you're treating me this way?"

"I don't care, Herb. That's the bottom line." Annie wouldn't move from the center of the room. She was angry. She was tired. She had had a lot of wine at John's going-away party.

"But she's a liar. She did that on purpose to chase you away."

"I don't care," Annie repeated. "I want you to go."

"I'm sorry I got so mad. I wanted to tell you that. Now, let's talk about it." He patted the sofa beside him as if it were his and she were the visitor come to try it out.

But Annie shook her head. She couldn't believe he wouldn't go. "You amaze me; I said I'm not interested."

"You're adorable. I don't think you mean that. You're not going to throw me out after all we've been through together."

Annie wanted to laugh until she realized that he was deadly serious. He really meant to stay whether she wanted him or not.

"Lydia is dangerous," he said. "It's her fault Vanessa wasn't treated."

"Herb, the child wasn't cared for. The only parts of her body that were clean were her hands and face. And she was with you. You were the one who brought her here to my house."

"Don't tell me that. Don't start that. It's not fair."

"Well, it's true. You left her here for the day. I don't even know where you went. She had lice. How do you think I feel about that? How do you think she feels about it?" She didn't wait for an answer. "I told you before you left that day it was finished, whatever it was. It wasn't even the lice," she added to be sure he understood.

But he didn't understand. He was flushed, and angry. "I told you I was sorry. I apologized. What else can I do? Kids get all kinds of things. I think it should be clear to you that she's not cared for by her mother."

"Or her father. Look, I don't really care, Herb. I just feel sorry for *her*. I don't care about you or Lydia, or what you're doing to each other."

Herb slapped the arm of the sofa. "So. You think a man can't take care of his child. Well, that's what I'm fighting for. I have the same sensibilities as any woman. I can take care of *my* child. A father is just as capable of mothering as any woman. Don't tell me you're prejudiced about men!"

"I don't want to talk about it." Annie walked to the door and stood by it. "Why don't you go?"

"But I'm in pain. I need you." He got up to come to her. "Look at what we were building together. Don't throw that away."

"Don't touch me," Annie cried as he approached.

"I want you." He held out his hands.

"Well, I don't want you. Don't come near me. I tried to say it as gently as I could. But I just don't want you. I'd like you to leave." She stood by the door. This was not fun. He was now following her around as she backed in a circle trying to think of something persuasive, but not dangerous, to say.

"I thought you understood. I really want to make a life with you. I want you to help me. Now we have evidence that the mother isn't competent. We can get her now. You're a witness."

"Get out of here, Herb," Annie cried with real fury. He had

reached out and taken one of her hands. Suddenly she felt trapped in her own apartment. For a minute she thought he was crazy, like the people who took shotguns and blasted whole families when their problems got too big. He even had that blunt look of a killer. She really thought he might wrap those strong fingers around her neck, and blow her away. Then she calmed herself. It was only her fingers he wanted, not the air in her windpipe. There was no pistol bulge of death in his pocket. He was just a selfish little boy who was mad at his wife. She was the one who was crazy for talking to him in the first place. Men weren't reliable, none of them. She should have known better.

"I want you to go." Her voice was so low he had to take a step closer to hear her.

"I can't, you're a witness," he said stubbornly. "I need you to tell what you know."

"Okay, I'll tell you what I know. I know you saw Vanessa every week and you didn't give her a bath either." Annie stood firm, even though she was afraid of him.

"That's not true." He shook his head. "You weren't there. You don't know."

Annie crossed the room, sat down in her armchair and looked at him hard. After a moment she said, "Herb, I think you're taking advantage of me."

"I don't think you really feel this way. I think you're just upset because I'm going through such a terrible ordeal. I think Lydia frightened you. I won't let her interfere with my life this way. I won't let her come between us."

"There is no us. There never for a moment was an us," Annie said coldly. "I don't want to have to say it again."

"Don't say it again."

"You wanted a new mommy for your child. Face it, you never looked at me for a minute. We have nothing between us but dead space."

"I don't feel that way. I feel good about our relationship. I know I've been busy, but I told you that would change. And Annie, it's bigger than you think. You're a witness. You heard her, you saw Vanessa. You're right, she was infested. I had to cut her hair myself. I won't let you go because of this."

Annie stood up in the middle of this. "You don't hear me. I'm not interested in you."

"Don't tell me that. I could have you subpoenaed, if I wanted to."

Now Annie laughed, in the middle of a rather vivid terror. It was a scared laugh, but it made him recoil with surprise. "Go ahead, I'll just say you left the child with me whenever you could. You brought her to me with lice in her hair. Try me as a witness, Herb, and see if I help your case."

His expression altered immediately. This was the one thing he heard, and suddenly Annie knew why she had never liked him. The bland and pleasant look he worked so hard to maintain, the one that kept her so effectively at arm's length, dropped now. Underneath the beard, under the restless movements, the hedging for space, was hostility so explicit Annie felt impaled on the spikes of it.

"You bitch. I should have known you'd let me down."

"Good-bye. I'm not very impressed with you either. You haven't behaved well to anybody, not even to the child you say you care about so much."

"You bitch. You God-damned bitch." His voice was a roar, like a tidal wave after an earthquake.

Annie thought she was felled by the noise alone as he loomed very large in her living room, his fist raised with judgment. She thought the moment for her punishment had come. She was deafened by the roar, defeated by it as she had been defeated by the screaming voice of her father coming after so much silence in the little closet.

In that second when he was so tall, so blood-red with anger, Annie could see herself in her mind's eye punished with that huge fist in her face. Her own kitchen knife rammed into her stomach. She'd heard of it, crazy people striking out for nothing. Stabbing women and letting their blood collect in bathtubs so it couldn't get away. That's the sort of careful work a doctor would do. Bitch. He called her a bitch, and yet he was not redeemable at all. She trembled at the enormity of his self-deception, at the same time knowing that women always got what they asked for. They rolled their own fate over them like turf over a grave.

Annie backed shakily toward the kitchen door—for what? Some weapon to use in defense. Some smallish place to hide. Deep inside where the ice pick of a headache went through her right eye, she was almost certain he meant to hurt her. The menace was there in his raised fist and in his face. And it was there in Annie's recognition that somehow she'd always known that some day someone would hurt her. Herb's banging on the door, pushing his way in, and calling her a bitch was only the whisper of the wheel turning in her own head. The only thing left for him to do was move forward like a bulldozer and knock her permanently down.

But apparently that was not a privilege meant for her. Annie was struck only with a very bitter look and her own door slammed in her face. Shakily she turned the three locks on the door and fastened the chain. When she had done that, she felt no safer. She had visions of his starting a fire outside her door like a crazy person burning down a hotel. Trembling all over, she did what she always did in times of stress; she called one of the people she always thought she was trying to get away from.

Sara said, "Call downstairs and see if he left. Frankly, I think your doorman should be sacked for this. Annie, do you want to stay here for the weekend?"

At the sound of Sara's voice, Annie calmed down right away. "I'm all right; I'm sorry I bothered you."

"Don't be ridiculous. I'd come over if Martin were here. Do you want me to come over when he gets home? Or should I come now with the kids?"

"Sara, don't tell Mother," Annie said. Her hands were still shaking, but the abject terror was gone now and she was merely ashamed. What was she so afraid of anyway? She hardly knew, and yet she had felt this way before.

Once years ago she went out with a man who bitterly damned her as a lesbian in a taxi after an expensive dinner because she didn't want to go to his apartment. And another night with someone else she almost gave in to a particularly nasty assault because she felt resisting only acknowledged the violence of the attack. She felt it again the day Nate left her when she thought she ought to jump out of the window. His departure was another kind of violence, a last-ditch strike at her soul. And now Brenda would only say once again that she was not up to the rigors of courtship. She couldn't manage love at all. Oh, she could stoke something up, get it going on a course somewhere, and then she'd botch the job with ambivalence and a fatal nagging suspicion that there wasn't a whole lot to it after all. Just another mask that eventually had to fall.

"Why should I tell Mother?" Sara said. "She'd only be upset."

"You always tell Mother," Annie pointed out. "You like to get me in trouble, you always did."

"Annie," Sara protested. "You know that isn't true."

"Never mind." Annie didn't want to talk about it then. Sara was deceitful, but as long as she didn't know it, what good did it do to tell her?

"I mind."

"Oh, forget it."

"Annie," Sara said meekly. "Come over. You can spend the night. You can stay all weekend. You'll be safe here."

"I'm all right now." Annie said. "I'm sorry I said anything. I just felt—violated for a minute. It was silly."

"He's a jerk. I always thought so." Sara punctuated this statement by banging the lid loudly on a pan.

"Thank you, Sara."

"Well, he is a jerk."

"That's what you always say about everybody I go out with."

"You just have to be careful, that's all. Not every man is of the same caliber." After a pause, "Annie, we're going out to the house to hang the shades tomorrow and do a few things. Do you want to come with us?"

"No thanks," Annie said. Suddenly she was eager to hang up because she wanted to talk to Ben. But a few minutes later when she dialed his number, she was disappointed because he wasn't there. He had left the office even earlier than she, and now she was suspicious because he hadn't gone home. She brooded for a while about that, and became even more downcast as she considered the possibilities. Son of a bitch, he really was.

During dinner, Sara and Martin discussed Annie's bad luck and when they were finished, Sara called her back.

"Annie, Martin and I have a great idea," she said rather breathlessly because Annie had let the phone ring so many times Sara couldn't help getting frightened thinking that while she had been enjoying a chop, something bad might have happened to her only sister.

Annie, however, having brooded herself out, had fallen asleep again and was lying in the dark on her white bedspread, dreaming of being shut in a cave. She seemed to have been in there for many years because her hair was very long, or maybe it was cobwebs hanging from her head. But she was not unhappy in there even with the sound of scurrying around her feet and flapping in her ears. It was pleasant, in an animal kind of way, in the cave. Annie was disgruntled to be dragged out of it before she knew how the dream ended. She said, "Jesus, Sara."

"Were you asleep? It's only nine o'clock."

"No, I was resting. What do you want?"

"Martin and I have a great idea. We thought we'd spend the night at the house tomorrow and let the kids have a sleepover with you. That way we could get a lot more work done. The kids would love it, and you'd have the company."

Annie wanted to go back to her cave and find out if the flapping in her ears was really bats and whether she was eating them to stay alive. Or whether, as with the bird man of Alcatraz, the bats were merely the friends of her incarceration. Somehow it seemed important to know.

"I dreamed I was in a cave," Annie said. "It was very strange."

"Did you hear me? I said you could have the kids for the weekend if you want."

"Do you think it's a death wish?" Annie asked.

"What, giving you the kids?" Sara said uneasily.

"No, my dream. I couldn't see any light at all, but there was air in it. Is there air in sealed caves?"

"I don't know," Sara said. "What does a cave stand for, your vagina? Did you ever get out?"

"No, you woke me up."

"Maybe it was Mother's vagina." Sara settled in an armchair. "Was it red?"

They both laughed. "I didn't think of that."

"Do you feel better now?" Sara asked. "I don't like to worry about you."

Annie thought about it for a minute. It was warm in her bed, warm in her room. The front door was locked so no one could get in. "Yes," she said finally. Maybe the cave was her mother's womb and she was still waiting to be born. She liked that idea. "I do feel better."

"What do you say about tomorrow?"

"Do you really want to sleep there? It must be filthy and there isn't any furniture." It seemed to Annie a poor idea. It didn't sound like Sara. Sara wouldn't sleep in motels because she didn't think they were clean enough. Once Sara and Martin got caught on the Cape, and after Martin fell asleep in the only motel room they could get, Sara went out and spent the night in the car. Martin almost went crazy in the morning when he woke up and couldn't find her.

"Well, Martin thinks it would be an adventure. A kind of baptism of fire, for the house, I mean. I'm taking the vacuum cleaner," Sara confessed. "What do you say? It would make the kids so happy. They're really quite apprehensive about leaving you, Annie. They want you to come with us."

"That's sweet," Annie murmured.

"So you'll do it?"

"Sure, I'll do it," Annie said. Something about it bothered her, a buzz in her ear that told her there was a conflict somewhere. But she couldn't get the conflict to the surface. "I think I can," she said. "Oh hell. I can." Fuck it, she thought. Whatever it was, it couldn't be very important. And then she went back to sleep.

27

ANNIE WAS just on her way to the park with Donald and Lucy, the knapsack of toys and some peanut butter sandwiches for lunch when the phone rang. She was in the outside hall and had to fumble with the locks and dash back into the apartment to catch the phone on the fourth ring. "Hello."

"What are you doing? You sound out of breath."

"Oh my God!"

"It's Ben."

"I know." The realization that it was Ben and he was calling about their date hit her so hard she collapsed on the kitchen stool. Sara and Martin had gone hours ago and didn't intend to come back until after lunch tomorrow.

"What's the matter? Did something happen?"

"I forgot." Annie heard the front door click shut, and suddenly the wails of two little people locked out. "Hold on a minute." She ran to the door to let them in. "Be quiet," she hissed, "or I won't take you to the park. I have to talk on the phone." Annie ran back to the phone with Donald calling after her.

"Oh no, don't talk on the phone all morning."

"That's right," Lucy echoed. "Don't talk on the phone all morning."

"Shut up," Annie said.

"What's going on?" Ben asked. "Is there someone there with you?"

"Oh, I have a headache," Annie cried. "I forgot. I must have been tired. Remember how tired I was? Well, I went to bed, and then I was awakened. That must have been it. Please don't be mad at me."

"What are you talking about? I'm not mad at you. I expected you to leave early." He was dressed only in his shorts. He had been sitting on his hard sofa reading the paper. Annie's tone of such agitation—and the threat of another headache—caused him to get up and pace around the living room carrying the phone with him. "Take some aspirin. Don't let it get started."

"I forgot our date," Annie said in such a tiny little girl voice that at first he thought she was joking.

"You didn't," he laughed.

"I did."

"You're teasing me." He paused. "Annie, I don't want you to tease me any more."

"I really did forget. I don't know how I did, but I did. Are you going to kill me?"

"Annie, are you telling me you made another date?" he said slowly.

"Not exactly."

"If you made another date, you'll just have to call up and break it. This is one thing I just won't tolerate." This last he said with something of a savage note and it struck a similar chord in Annie.

"I wouldn't do that. What do you think I am?"

He spoke bitterly back. "You had a date with me first. You have an obligation to go out with me. If you don't, then we won't make another one. That's it," he said furiously. On the coffee table in front of him was the watch he'd bought her the day before, all wrapped up in a red Cartier box. He looked at it, stricken.

"Who's that in your apartment?" he demanded when she didn't respond to this ultimatum. "I mean it. I can't take this any more."

She was frantically waving at Donald and Lucy, who were chanting, "We want to go, we want to go," and banging on the front door with their fists for harmony. They didn't pay any attention to her signals so finally she screamed, "Shut up," right in Ben's ear.

"You want me to shut up?" he said.

"Not you, the children," she said wildly.

"Oh, children again, is that it?"

"Yes," Annie said meekly. And then, "Sara's children," quickly, so he wouldn't get the wrong idea.

He sat down on the sofa and flung his feet out in front of him, silent now because he finally understood that his real rivals for Annie's attention, and her love, were not over four feet tall.

"They're my sister's children, Ben," Annie said. "They're *family*."

"What have you done, moved them in?"

"Just for the night," she said faintly.

"Shit."

"I forgot; please don't be mad."

"I'm mad," he said, too mad to think of something more appropriate to say. He'd never been jilted for a midget before. In this case, two. He had to breathe slowly to bring his heart rate down. He didn't want to strike out before he started his new job on Monday.

"Sara called me last night when I was sleeping. And I guess I just wasn't thinking. I said, yes, I'd take them for the night. They're so cute, and it's probably for the last time."

He looked at the Cartier box on the table. Now he couldn't give it to her. "You're too attached to your family," he said ominously.

"I'm not attached to them—they inflict themselves. Oh please don't be mad. Sara's moving away next week. There isn't much of them left now."

"You did it on purpose." He picked up the box and turned it

over and over in his hand. Annie had said the copy was good enough because it was only a third the price. He'd gone back to Tiffany and looked again at the Audemars Piguet. The Royal Oak they both thought they liked so much didn't look so terrific on second sighting. It was almost three times the price of the Santos, and didn't have any gold in it. They must have been crazy when they considered it. Surely it was more than any watch that wasn't gold ought to cost. On the way out, he stopped to look at the rings. He didn't care for anything fancy. Just one big stone was what he wanted, in a patriotic color. Red, white, or blue. He thought it would be much more sensible to buy the Cartier watch, and a ring, too, if it came to that.

So, just before five, he wandered down to Cartier and bought the watch. He'd never spent so much on a woman before; and he did it with a feeling of permanency, with an irrevocable flourish of the pen. He'd even been foolish and bought it with a personal check, so now he didn't think they'd give him his money back. They'd only give him credit. What could he do with a fifteen hundred dollar credit at Cartier?

Annie leaned over to Donald, who was stepping on her toe to get her attention quietly, and told him she'd break his arm if he didn't stop it.

"Ben, I'm sorry. I guess I wasn't thinking. Maybe we could do it tomorrow night. What would you say to that?" She twisted the phone cord around her finger. "I could cook you dinner, if you'd like."

"If I said yes, you'd probably forget and go out with your mother instead," he said, not without reason. "You're not reliable. You're always changing your mind."

"I'm not."

"You're always with your damn family."

"I told you they're like a disease. They're always spreading into my neighborhood. What should I do, give pictures to the doorman and tell him not to let them in?" She poked her little finger into the curl of the phone card. "What should I do?"

"You're doing it on purpose because I'm getting too close. That's it, you know. I'm not one of your make-believe children. I'm a real person."

"Children are real people," Annie protested.

"Yeah, but once they get out, they don't try to get back in again."

"What?" Annie started. Her finger was caught in the phone cord. He was talking about sex again, and she felt a little responsive vaginal throb. "Don't start that," she warned.

"You surround yourself with children because you don't want anybody to get in, Annie. You don't even remember the high point of my whole life," he said.

Annie wanted to cry, "I do, I do," but the responsibility was enormous. She couldn't take it. If she failed on the second round, she wouldn't have a friend in the world, no one wanting her at all. No one even to pretend with in a restaurant, over a whisky sour. She was sure if she showed him she loved him, he'd go.

She'd seen it happen a hundred times, some girl holding his arm or leaning over to whisper in his ear, and suddenly her voice would seem too cloying, her dress pretentious, or too tight, her eyes too glitteringly aglow. And his expression would change. He didn't want her after all. Annie could see it happening, Ben turning away like a reluctant virgin (previously ecstatic but now faced with the burgeoning cock). With every move he made, she could feel the machinery of his singleness clanking along with him. He simply couldn't be any other way. His every tumescence was based on the prospect of flight.

"I'm sorry," she said. But she just wasn't good at it. She didn't have the knack of holding on under pressure. She always let go. "I didn't mean to hurt you."

"I want to see you," he said plaintively.

"I have the children. It's my fault. Maybe it *is* Freudian."

"I think I'll come anyway."

"With the children?" she gulped anxiously.

"You could cook me dinner," Ben said, now warming to the idea. "I'll help you babysit. Everybody should do it, once every decade."

"I don't think you'll like it," Annie said, another throb hitting her with a splash, like the first heavy raindrop in a sudden downpour.

"I'm sure I'll like it. What time do they go to bed?" echoing her thought.

"I don't think you'll like it," she said even more doubtfully the second time.

"I'll like it," he said firmly. "I'll be there at six."

"Oh God," she murmured. "I know this won't work out."

With the hanging up of the phone, Annie picked up the pace

of the day and started rushing around like a mother, impatiently dragging two little children behind her. To fulfill her promise she took them to the park, then sat there with her eyes glazed thinking of dinner, mentally turning the pages of cookbooks, wondering what to serve, what to wear. Did she have any candles, a bottle of wine? She had to be reminded to give a push to the swing, to stand at the bottom of the slide so Lucy didn't break her head coming down.

She realized she hadn't cooked a dinner like this since Nate left. Now she would buy a dozen clams, spend the extra fifty cents to have them opened for her, and then eat them standing up in the kitchen without bothering to shift them from their unwholesome-looking bed of ice to a nice clean plate. She'd fry a chicken leg and gobble it up before the grease had time to drain off onto the paper towel. She'd wash a head of lettuce and stuff it into her mouth, the oil and vinegar so unevenly mixed that sometimes it didn't meet in the same bite at all. She ate naked, or in a pair of underpants, wandering around the apartment as if looking for a companion to settle down with, and finding not even a cockroach, not a dustball, with which to commune in her pristine environment.

At eight o'clock, she'd retire to her bed with the same dirty book over and over and masturbate, imagining herself a prostitute, turning on for the payment at the end. Never for a moment did Annie forget that she had met Nate while on a date with someone else, a friend of Martin's, who collected ceramic animals and was an authority on ice cream. Nate, wearing his cowboy boots, was sitting at the bar resplendent in his yellow hair, the color of old corn in grocery stores. She remembered that particularly, and how he bought them a drink. When Annie's date disappeared for a minute to take a leak, Nate acted quickly and squeezed her knee. He said she was cute and asked if she had a roommate. Headaches were useful to Annie even then. She feigned one for the animal fancier, not concerned until later what Martin would think. And as prearranged, Nate turned up at midnight to demonstrate the limitations of living alone.

Nate was a born mooch, the way Ben was a born bachelor, but he made love with an energy Annie had never before encountered. After he moved in, it seemed worthwhile, even an honor, to poach the eggs and grill the chops for such an athlete. Or so he said he was. Anyway, it didn't seem at all at the time as if she might be paying someone to love her. It seemed to Annie, then, only logical—since her sister had the last good man on earth by an accident of fate—that she should have to choose between a pudgy ice cream lover and a pick-up in a bar who was looking for a congenial place to live.

She dragged the children to the vegetable store where she bought the first cherries of the season and asparagus. An artichoke for Lucy because she thought she wanted one, bananas for Donald. Also some watermelon and loose carrots because they looked fresh, two endive and some watercress. Then on to Pain de Paris for a bread, and the meat market because the kids wanted steak. Annie bought filet mignon so they wouldn't have to chew too hard with their precious baby teeth. But all the time she was thinking of Ben and his precious big teeth, and how he liked the simplest things, asparagus with Hollandaise, a few ounces of perfect beef, a salad. They hurried home to make brownies to go with the cherries and watermelon.

He turned up at five-thirty because he knew children had to eat early. He had been shopping and brought presents with him. Annie was still in her shorts, though her hair was washed and her face was close to finished. She started when the bell rang and asked Donald to open the door to give her a minute to put on a dress. He wouldn't so she had to make Ben wait a minute.

He was splendid in his summer blazer. He was carrying a shopping bag full of presents, and had a brown paper bag cradled in his arm. But it was his expression that was the most shattering of all. He was grinning so hard it looked as if his face might split up the middle. It was the kind of look Martin had sometimes when they all tried to hug him at once and he felt so full of them he could burst.

He kissed her on the cheek and the smell of raspberries hit her again. She smelled it in the office sometimes and dreamed of it at night. There was a lot of pain in the feelings she had for him. His smell made her dizzy. His voice often made her want to cry. It was silly, the dilemma of wanting to grab him but knowing it would only hasten the end. The "Hi" she muttered now hardly covered the pleasure she felt at having him there, and the fear of seeing him go.

He saw all the confusion in her face and looked over her shoulder into the empty living room searching for the trouble. Then, like a cat, she brushed against him and moved away.

"Where are they?"

At the sound of the bell, the children had retreated into the bedroom, where they were hiding on their stomachs under the bed.

"They're a little nervous," she said. An understatement, since they had wanted to flee. "Maybe they'll come out in a minute."

"Where are those children," he said loudly. "I've brought them some presents."

"You did?" Annie was surprised that he would think of such a thing.

"It usually helps." He handed her the brown bag. It was cold. It was champagne.

A fair head showed itself down the hall around the half-opened bedroom door. Annie shook her head to indicate that he shouldn't see it yet.

"I'm dying to meet your children," he said. "Did they go home?"

Down the hall toward the living room, they crawled on their hands and knees.

"Greedy little buggers," Annie commented. "How did you know?"

"I thought they'd be a little disappointed, so I figured I'd bribe them. Is that a child?"

Donald stood up. "I'm Ben, how do you do?" Ben held out his hand. Donald looked at the hand.

"Shake his hand," Annie prompted.

"Hi," Donald said faintly. "Are you going to marry Annie?"

"I hope so," Ben said seriously.

"Shit," Annie said and stalked off to the kitchen with the champagne.

"You said a bad word," Donald cried after her.

"So did you," Annie said.

"Shit," Lucy repeated. She crept to Ben's side and took his hand. Now she stood gazing up at him. He was wearing a pink shirt; so was she. "See, pink, pink."

"Do you remember me?" he asked, immediately smitten.

She nodded. She had taken off her summer dress and was wearing one of Annie's T-shirts that came down to her ankles. She had seen it in the drawer glowing at her pinkly and pulled it out.

"I have something for you." He got his bag and began doling out presents. "Two for you and two for you." He left Annie's watch in the bag. Now didn't seem a good time to give it to her.

They sat on the floor and opened the toys. In a little while, Annie came back and Ben opened the champagne. He had a glass while helping Donald to put together the car he had bought him. The pieces snapped into place, but he had bought a tube of glue just in case.

"I used to like these when I was little," he said.

Annie sat on the sofa watching him. He put on the rabbit puppet he had bought Lucy and asked her for a carrot. She ran away, and he looked at Annie helplessly. But Lucy came back in a second with a carrot. Ben ate it while Lucy sat on his lap.

They had dinner, and Ben cut Lucy's meat in such tiny pieces Annie was awed. Not even Martin, who had been told over and over, could remember how dangerous a piece of steak could be. He showed her how to eat an artichoke and urged Donald to eat his asparagus.

"No way, José," Donald said. "It makes your pee smell."

"That's true," Ben said, surprised he knew such a sophisticated piece of information; "but I don't mind." He glanced at Annie and laughed. She had tears in her eyes and he was afraid she had drunk too much and was getting another headache.

Finally, after the brownies and the cherries and the watermelon and a game of Sorry in which Lucy counted "One, six, ten," and Donald screamed because they let her cheat, the children got into Annie's bed and promised not to come out until morning.

She sank down on the sofa.

He stood looking at her for a while. "Do you want me to go?"

"What?"

"You look tired. I'll take off if you want me to."

"Sit down, did they depress you?"

"No, I liked them. That little one is just like you." He sat down but looked away. The sparkle he had before was gone now. He seemed almost snuffed out.

Annie moved over and took his hand. "What is it?"

"I've never had an evening like this in my whole life," he said, staring at her hand in his. "I don't remember being little and sitting at the table making jokes."

"No brothers and sisters," Annie murmured.

"No father and mother," he said.

"You had a mother and father."

"One at a time. They weren't ever together. I was a miserable specimen of a kid." He glanced at her quickly to see if she was alarmed at this bit of bad news.

"Did you think that?" she asked sympathetically.

"I wet my bed until I was eleven years old. Sometimes I was so scared at school I would shit in my pants." He snorted. "They called my mother to come and get me at school once. She dragged me home by the ear."

"Because you wet your pants?" Annie asked incredulously.

"I shit in my pants. It got all over my legs." He covered his eyes as if that could stop him from remembering the feeling.

She clutched his hand tighter. "You must have had the flu."

"My mother was furious. She almost pulled my ear off." He paused. "I'm sorry. I shouldn't have told you. It's disgusting."

"No, it isn't. All kids do that. That's why they make them take extra clothes to school. Donald almost takes a suitcase with him. Funny the things you remember."

"I was in second grade."

"Oh, God." Annie looked at him with such concern, he shrugged.

"I don't know what made me think of it." He had long since taken off his sleek summer blazer. His pink shirt was open at the neck and she could see a few curls of black hairs on the chest she admired so much. She couldn't imagine him a little boy, so scared he couldn't control his bowels. "I'm sure you were sick. What happened when you got home?"

"She made me wash my pants. She watched me do it. She wouldn't touch my shit. I can still remember how it floated in the water." He swallowed. "And then she went back to her office so I could think about it alone. She thought thinking was good for kids."

"Annie?" Donald stood in the hall rubbing his eyes. "Are you going out?"

Annie jumped up. "You know I wouldn't do that."

He had a bleary look on his face. "I was almost asleep and then I was afraid you went out."

She gave him a hug. "I won't leave you."

"Is he staying, too?" He pointed at Ben.

"Yes, sweetheart. We'll both be here to guard you."

"Thank you for the car," Donald said. He held it under his arm protectively. "I like it very much."

Ben managed to say, "You're welcome," as Annie took him back to bed.

She returned in a minute to find him standing by the window, studying the street. "Nice kid," he said.

"Ben." Annie stopped. She didn't know what she was going to say or what prevented her from saying it. Maybe that look of his, of wanting to get out.

"I'm sorry I told you that. You must think I'm a freak."

"I don't. I think your mother wasn't very understanding." She stood in the middle of her rug, afraid to move in any direction.

He sloughed it off. "I was a mess . . . Annie, I think I'm going home now."

"No."

"No, what?"

"You're not going home. I want to hold you."

He laughed uneasily. "I'm not a child." He stood up to his full height to demonstrate how old he was now.

"I know, but my arms feel empty." She sat down on the sofa and held out her arms. See, how empty they were.

"Your arms feel empty?" He stared. He'd heard a lot of girls say a lot of things to him, but never this. It seemed an extraordinary thing to say. But it was true she always seemed kind of all alone to him, even when she was living with Nate. "You're going to make me cry."

He sat down a little awkwardly, feeling too big to serve her purpose. He knew he was meant to hold *her*, massage *her*, supply a few orgasms if she wanted them. But he wasn't up to it tonight, with so many memories and two children in the other room. He sat there stiffly, his hands on his knees. "How do you want to do it?"

She pulled him over so his head was resting on her shoulder and her arm was around his back. She sniffed his hair and ruffled it with her other hand. His hair always felt finer than it looked and was so shiny she used to have the creepy feeling he oiled it. But there was no grease on her fingers when she touched it, and the skin on his neck was softer even than Donald's.

"You're nice," she sighed. It didn't go any way at all toward expressing what she really thought.

"Don't say that. I'm not nice." He submitted to the caresses uneasily, feeling he had disgraced himself by telling her, by not having had a sunny childhood.

"You feel nice to me."

"I don't think I'm up to it," he said vaguely, not certain exactly what he meant. "I feel kind of grimy."

"Don't worry about it."

"Oh Annie, I would wake up and it would be *cold*. You can't imagine how cold. I've never told anybody this before, but I felt so disgusting. I would go into my parents' room to tell them and my father wouldn't be there. I'd say, 'Where's Daddy?' And she'd scream at me, 'Do you think he wants to come home to a boy who wets his bed?' It seems strange now, but it scared me to death."

"What a burden," she said. "If my father didn't like something he just made everybody get up and talk about it. I remember being pulled out of bed at eleven o'clock to discuss why Annie can't control her temper. Why Annie can't pick up her clothes, why she can't do well in math. I usually had a temper tantrum, so they all left me to scream myself to sleep. I still don't like being awakened."

"I was afraid to scream. Screaming was for mothers. I really thought I was the reason for everything bad that happened."

"You weren't. You were too little."

"Don't say that."

"Why not?"

"I don't know." He was silent while he thought about it. "I had to sleep in the wet bed. She wouldn't change it in the middle of the night. She told me to sleep in it. That was my punishment."

"Ugh, that's sadistic."

"I was disgusting. I was very fat and had acne. As soon as I stopped wetting the bed, my face started breaking out. My mother hated me. She wouldn't take me anywhere. I was that grotesque. If I hadn't had such a strong sex drive I wouldn't have lived to grow up. I must have gotten it from my father."

"Is that what he was doing when he was out at night?"

"I don't know. He died."

"And you thought you killed him."

Ben closed his eyes. "I was thirteen, like a blimp. He was

trying to teach me to be a great skier. He'd been trying for years. But I hated it. I hated everything about him. He was so jolly, so handsome and big."

Annie was quiet. They were both quiet, almost afraid to disturb each other by touching now. His eyes were still closed. He went on, "There was a new ski jump. He took me up there to show how easy it was. Anybody could do it. There was a bunch of high school kids. Girls and boys teasing each other. The girls were trying to get the boys to jump. I don't know. It was like I was this disgusting little slug, and my father was saying, 'You have to take risks in life. You have to fly.' And suddenly the girls were interested in *him,* this middle-aged man who wanted to soar. They crowded around him laughing and joking. He loved it. And all of a sudden—" He pressed his face into Annie's shoulder, "He jumped." Ben sobbed. "He just jumped."

He had broken into a sweat and was sobbing at the memory. "Jesus Christ. He was trying to make me a man, and *he* jumped."

Annie held him tight and was crying, too, because she loved him and the telling was so hard. "He might have done it anyway, some other time," she whispered. "Did he fall?"

"No. He made it. He landed on his feet." Ben gulped but couldn't stop the tears.

"Then, what happened?"

"He had a heart attack. He must have been so fucking scared, his heart just burst. He was dead by the time anyone got there." Ben shook his head to make it go away. "Shit, that's the kid I was. I had to take the lift down. I couldn't jump after him."

"You were thirteen. What do you expect?"

Ben blew his nose. "He wanted me to be unafraid, to be able to face life. And I had no guts. What a jerk. I'm sorry."

"You should have told me before," Annie said softly.

"It must have been the kids. I don't usually think about it."

"I'm glad you told me. You've been carrying that around a long time. Did your mother blame you?"

"Hell, no, she was thrilled. She married her boyfriend, the head of the English department. Well, I think he was anyway. They got married."

"No wonder you hate women." Annie thought of the watch he wanted to buy her after so many years. He was so fierce in Tiffany wanting to buy something, and she hadn't been able to understand it.

"Annie—" Now it was Lucy standing in the hall rubbing her eyes. "I feel sick." Annie leaped up again.

"Your tummy hurt from too much brownie?" She reached the child and picked her up.

"I'm going to throw up."

"No, no you're not. Take a deep breath. You're going to be fine."

"Throw up," Lucy wailed.

Annie moved quickly to the bathroom. "Oh, no!" but didn't get her to the toilet quite in time. She made a mess, retched three, four times. Jesus, Annie thought. Now he would go and she wouldn't blame him. It was too much, just too damned much.

"It's okay, Lucy. It's okay," she said over and over, because that's what you told kids. "I'm going to take care of you."

Ben came to the bathroom door. "Oh God," at the mess, and then, "What can I do?"

"Oh, Ben, I'm sorry. Do you want to go?"

"No, of course not. Now I'm in my element. All we need is a little diarrhea, and I'll be fine. Tell me what to do."

The child was groaning and hot. Annie wet a washcloth and wiped her face.

"There's a pail under the sink in the kitchen. Put some Joy in it and fill it half full with hot water. Do you mind?"

He shook his head. No.

Annie put Lucy in the tub then ran into the kitchen for the rubber gloves, telling Ben not to let Lucy drown. When she came back he was delicately soaping her.

"Well, well," Annie murmured as she washed the floor.

He had her bundled in a towel when Annie returned with new pajamas and a new pamper. Lucy was now snoring on his shoulder, limp as one of her rag dolls. He didn't want to let her go. When he moved her, instinctively she put her arms around his neck. He kissed the top of her head.

"Why did you do that?" Annie asked a minute later, after returning from putting Lucy to bed.

He was in her armchair now, staring at his knees. "What?"

"It's big-time stuff to kiss a child who's just thrown up. That takes years of practice."

"I told you. She reminds me of you. I can understand why you love them."

"You can?" She sat on the floor at his feet, leaned against his knee. "Nate didn't understand."

"Maybe he knew you loved them more than him."

Annie stirred. "I picked him up in a bar."

"I didn't know that."

He stroked her hair. "You confessed the worst to me," she said. "So I have to tell you I picked him up in a bar."

"Come here."

"No." Annie felt his hand on her shoulder and moved away to the middle of the room where the rug looked like an island. "I never thought I'd see him again. I don't know why I did it. And then when he came back I thought it was an omen that he was— well, meant for me. He looked like a surfer, and I've always been so plain. Remember those old Gidget movies? I just couldn't believe how that funny-looking girl could end up with the best guy on the whole beach. The thing is, they were so dopey in the movies I wasn't surprised when Nate turned out not to have much upstairs."

"Why didn't you throw him out?"

"It never occurred to me. At twenty-four, I got a surfer." She sighed. "I got the beach. . . . And he wanted to stay. Nobody else wanted to stay."

"Jesus, why didn't you tell me?" Ben said. He got down on the floor, too, and crawled around looking for a good place to settle.

"I never saw anybody as fickle as you. Compared to you, he was the Rock of Gibraltar."

Ben lay on his back. "I thought he must be some terrific guy. Whatever I did I could never get your attention."

"You were always screwing around. When did you have time to think of me?" She nudged him with one toe. "You know what I thought that night? I thought there was nothing I could do with you that you haven't done already."

"I thought you were the sexiest girl ever. You think you were plain. That's funny. I was the ugliest kid in high school. I really was." He laughed. "And the fattest. I didn't kiss anybody until I was twenty."

"But you made up for it. I bet you've done everything."

He shook his head. "I'm not as exotic as you think."

"I bet you are. Name a place you haven't done it?"

"Grand Central Station," he said promptly. "Don't be insecure."

"No, I mean a real place. I bet you've done it everywhere, in the bathtub, on the beach. In the kitchen standing up," her eyes widened, "In the office after hours, on an airplane."

"I haven't done it with two kids in the other room," he said thoughtfully. "I've never done it in a car."

"You mean you've done it in an airplane?" she gasped.

"I've never done it in a car. I've never *wanted* to do it in an airplane."

"I haven't either. I've done it with a surfer, but never in a car."

"I had a car, but nobody would get in it."

They laughed. In a second Annie got up and checked on Lucy. When she came back, she turned off the light. She sat down on the floor next to him. "I'll get in it," she said softly in the dark.

"But will you remember in the morning?"

"Depends on what kind of car it is."

They rolled around on the floor, gingerly at first, expecting interruption. And then they began wrestling more fiercely as if it were necessary to fight off everything that had come before, the fat boy, the skinny girl, visions of raging parents and the punishment of violent death. Martin suffered from it, too. Annie could see the terror in her brother-in-law's eyes, the same fear Ben had that someone else he loved might go at any time.

As Ben ground his hips against hers so hard it almost made her cry out, she could feel the speed of the slide, the force of the earth pushed away, the crazed pulsing of that heart breaking in the snow. She could see the bloodless death. She could see the wordless grief of the hurt child who was too afraid to take the final leap. Had his father wanted them both to die?

Once again, Annie felt the nausea of her own violent death rise in her throat. This was what she was afraid of, not the revenge of someone she had failed to love. She was afraid of her breath, her heart, her life itself stopped by the pressure of her loving someone else. She could feel it sucking at her lips, sucking at her breast, squeezing her bottom as if it were a ripe fruit. Then she felt herself opening up, asking for it, receiving it, thrusting back, crying out, throbbing, grabbing him harder, and holding on. Most of all holding on, in spite of her terror so real she could taste it on her tongue, terror that love was only death some time in an alley. Much later, some time near dawn, Ben gave her the watch.

28

IT RAINED THE whole week that Sara packed her household to move to Pine Wood. Brenda spent much of that week in Sara's apartment watching her put her things in cardboard boxes. Five, six, seven hours a day she sat there, moving her chair from one room to another as Sara worked. It seemed as if Brenda felt Sara was suffering from a terminal illness and it was necessary to sit there hour after hour in her final days. And like a patient exhausted by the responsibility of behaving well to the end, Sara tried to keep up a running conversation to distract herself from the feeling of doom. It was hard for Sara to remember that it was just an apartment being dismantled bit by bit, and not a life coming to an end.

As each picture came off the wall, as each book was stowed away in a box, Sara commented on where it had come from, what she had felt when she bought it, read it, hung it in the place it had been for ten years or more. Brenda reminded her that they had been through a lot together.

The rebuke in Brenda's presence was so heavy that Sara collapsed in bed every night drained to the point where no one could talk to her. "Are you afraid?" Martin wanted to know. She shook her head, dumbly remembering years ago that she used to dream of her mother falling out of the window, and how she would wake up bathed in sweat, terrified that the dream would come true and there would be no one to take care of her when she woke up.

Martin whispered in her ear, "All children have to leave home." Sara turned her body to him. "I'm so tired I could die," and put her head on his chest. Martin's mother pushed him out.

He took up too much space with his thinking. She used to tell Sara that the noise from Martin's thinking could make her scream. But he wouldn't have stayed long anyway. They thought he gave his brother Bernie the drug that made him crazy. They thought so much of him they couldn't believe he might have gotten it on his own. "Sara?"

"Hmm?"

"I know we're going to be happy."

She pressed her body to his side.

"What are you thinking?"

"We'll be happy," she said.

Every day it was harder to wait for the move. In the kitchen Brenda mourned each wedding present that had survived the marriage. She knew what was missing, what had been broken or thrown out. She knew the source of all the spots on the once-white linen. Sara wanted to throw it out, but Brenda thought if Sara really wanted to, she could get it clean.

"Go home, Mama," Sara begged her when the children got to be too much. "If you go home, you'll see nothing has changed."

"How can you tell me that?"

Brenda sat primly on the side of Sara's bed, watching her fold blankets and place them neatly in a box.

"All daughters have to leave home sometime." She forced a little laugh. "You've had enough of me. I've been married for twelve years."

"There's nothing like a daughter," Brenda said ominously. "No other relationship is the same."

"You married and left your mother," Sara reminded her, and then was sorry. She knew Brenda's leavetaking was different. Brenda had told her many times that her mother had been disappointed in her because Brenda refused to learn to sew. Her mother had a tiny dress shop and struggled to support her and her brother. The three of them lived in one room behind the store. Her mother had always hoped that Brenda would become a dressmaker so they would be able to expand, maybe even prosper. But Brenda wanted to sing. Brenda always said it was a terrible thing for a mother not to support her children.

The singing was certainly a terrible controversy between her and her mother when she was growing up. Her mother didn't think she had a voice; she thought performers were bums. She was afraid Brenda would end up unfit for anything and have to be supported forever. Brenda had her revenge. She married and moved to New York as soon as she could. She left just as her mother was beginning to do well. She left her and never became a singer (except in her own living room) anyway.

The revenge took a bitter turn, though. Brenda wasn't happy in New York at first and told her mother she wanted to come home. The honeymoon was like a vacation, and after it was over, she wanted to go home. Her mother laughed at her long distance, that was how Brenda told it. She laughed and said Brenda had made her bed, and now she would have to stay in it forever.

All the years of their growing up Annie and Sara were threatened with that rejection by their grandmother. The lesson seemed clear: It was a dangerous thing to cross a mother.

"And you know what happened," Brenda said coldly. She bitterly watched her favorite daughter packing up, leaving her.

"I just meant change is part of life," Sara said, sitting back on her heels and feeling the old threat, that her mother might turn on her, too.

Brenda's expression changed swiftly. "You were the most beautiful child I've ever seen, Sara. I loved you so much I couldn't keep my hands off you. I never wanted what happened to me to happen to you. A girl needs her mother even when she's grown up, don't forget that."

Sara moved to the bed and put an arm around her mother's shoulder. "I'll always love you, Mother. That won't change."

"I didn't want you to marry so soon." Brenda looked down at her hands. "I wanted you to have an exciting life. I wanted you to see things, but you didn't see it that way. I was mad at you, Sara, but I didn't reject you. I didn't push you away." Her eyes began to tear, and for once she forgot her makeup and the two children in the living room watching "Sesame Street."

"You've been a wonderful mother," Sara told her. And thought that they were different, very different. Sara hadn't wanted to go home after her honeymoon.

"No one could love you like I do." Brenda blew her nose. "You're a good mother. You know, I saw you the day you took Donald to school the first time."

Sara laughed, thinking of it. "He waved good-bye. He didn't look back."

"You suffered," Brenda insisted.

"But I let him go," Sara reminded her.

They sat on the bed, holding hands for a minute. Then Brenda reached for her handbag. "We'll see how you feel next year when it's Lucy's turn. What will you do up there all by yourself?"

"I'll probably open a dress shop," Sara laughed, "and close the circle."

"Don't say that. You don't know what you're saying."

"You always told me I have an eye for design. Maybe I'll take some courses, who knows?"

Brenda powdered her nose. "No one loves you like your mother," she repeated. "You'll see when it's Lucy's turn."

Sara went back to the box she hadn't finished. "I don't feel that way about my children," she murmured. "I want other people to love them. Annie loves them, maybe as much as I do. If something happened to me, she'd be a fine mother for them."

"I didn't have the support you do. I was alone, with two little kids." Brenda shook her head again. "Sometimes I just got in the bathtub and cried."

"I don't remember that," Sara said.

"You don't know everything. You think everything in life is easy."

Sara kicked the box. "Why do you do that?"

"What?" Brenda turned to her in surprise.

"You take everything away from me, Mother." Sara stalked into the other room.

"What? What did I do?" Brenda followed her. "Don't turn on me when I'm suffering."

"Damnit. You think you're the only one with feelings. You think you're the only one who ever had a baby. Look at me, I'm not your baby any more. I'm doing it myself just like you did. There's no difference." She went into the kitchen. It was time for dinner.

"Except that it's easier for you," Brenda snapped. "You're loved."

"So are you. Don't give me that."

"By your mother, I mean," Brenda interrupted. "You can afford to be flippant. You had the love in the beginning when it mattered. That's why you're so cavalier about it now."

Sara slammed what was left of the pans around. "I'm not cavalier. I'm thirty-three. I have to grow up now."

"Is growing up moving to the suburbs?" Brenda sat heavily on a kitchen chair.

"Maybe for me it is," Sara said. She turned to the window so her mother wouldn't see emotion hitting her so hard. She realized it now. The floating house wasn't only for Martin. It was for her, too.

"I have to go home now," Brenda said suddenly.

"Don't be mad." Sara softened. "You still have Annie down the street."

"Oh, Annie left me a long time ago. She's so grown up all she cares about is making more money than her father. Is that a decent goal for a girl to have?"

"Annie has a new boyfriend," Sara said slyly.

"Don't tell me about Annie's boyfriends. I don't want to know."

"All right."

Brenda went into the other room to say good-bye to the children. They were watching television; they didn't bother with her. She came back into the kitchen where Sara was working.

"How do you know?"

"How do I know what?"

"About Annie."

"The kids told me. There was someone there. He gave them presents. They were impressed." Sara broke two eggs neatly into a frying pan. "Apparently Lucy threw up on him."

"It wasn't the doctor, was it?" Doctors had people throw up on them all the time. Brenda blanched at the thought of the doctor. "Annie has no judgment."

"It wasn't the doctor. It was someone else."

"Don't get your hopes up," Brenda warned. "He's probably another jerk."

"That's what I thought," Sara admitted. "I didn't want to know."

"Very smart. Leave her alone. That's the best approach."

"He's probably married," Sara added.

"Or divorced."

They laughed. Sara turned off the fire and led her to the door to make it easier for her to go.

"What's his name?" Brenda asked.

"Ben." Sara responded immediately.

Brenda made another impatient gesture. "What kind of name is that? Is he a handyman?"

Sara shrugged. Would a handyman come bearing gifts? "They said he had a blazer like their daddy's, and he spent the night."

Brenda pursed her lips in dismay.

"Or anyway he was there for breakfast. They had pancakes." Sara and Martin had been busy taping brown paper to the floors to protect them during the move. They had instant coffee with Carnation Breakfast Squares and had no idea what was going on at Annie's. She pressed the button for the elevator.

"She has no judgment, no judgment at all. I'm disgusted." Brenda turned back one last time. "Ben what?" she asked.

"I don't know, Mother. The children called him Ben."

"Nate, Herb, Ben," Brenda reeled them off. The elevator came. She stepped into it, shaking her head. "Why can't she find someone with a real name?"

29

IT RAINED THE day Sara moved. Around the house was a sea of mud, except in the back where flagstones were set around the pool, and in the front where Martin had broken down at the last moment and decided to blacktop the little road and the circular drive. They were grateful for it when the moving van arrived, a giant that would have slipped right into the bog, Sara thought, and stayed there forever like a piece of found art with all their belongings inside.

They unloaded in the rain, a team of five movers who worked until late that night. Then they pulled away with what was left of the case of beer Martin had provided against Sara's better judgment, and their tips. Some time during the evening the rain stopped without anybody noticing. Then the truck lurched out on the road and there was silence.

It took several weeks to lay the rugs, to line every brand-new shelf with paper, to unpack the linens and the kitchen, to decide where the furniture should go. The kitchen had wall ovens and a GenAir electric broiler that Sara was a little nervous about using. The inside of the house was all wood, washed with white or pale stain, and distressed to look old. Also treated not to burn, Archie assured them. Sara screwed smoke alarms in all the ceilings because smoke rises. She was proud of her ability with a screwdriver. It took her a bit more time to learn how to turn on the filter system in the pool, how to heat the pool for only two hours in the morning and let the sun do the rest of the work.

With all the activity, driving Martin to the station, shopping in the town, working on the house, struggling to convince the children that it was all right to go outside, spending hours by the pool in the afternoon, going once again to get Martin, eating late dinner, Sara forgot Annie and her new office. She forgot Brenda and Jack simmering by the phone in New York. After several weeks, she woke up one morning with a strange feeling she couldn't at first define. It took her all day to decide what it was. When they got home and Martin changed into his bathing suit, having decided to plunge into the pool even though it was a little chilly and not quite summer, she watched him plunge. As he hit the water and the children cheered, she realized that for the first time since she could remember she was not afraid. She had lived a whole day without fear. She hadn't thought someone would lure a child away to some unspeakably vile death.

In New York there was no horror she could imagine that hadn't happened a hundred times. She had been afraid of everything: building sites with tall cranes, elevators with creaky motors, crazy bag ladies. She had been afraid of eleven-year-olds with switchblades. It had even occurred to her that the delivery boy from the grocery store might not be from the grocery store at all, even when he was carrying the box with her canned peaches. Only at night when the doors were locked and they were all there together did Sara feel safe in the city, and even then the sound of fire engines roaring up Third Avenue all night made her fear fire.

Martin climbed out of the pool and reached for a towel. "Your mother called me today."

"Why?" Sara asked. She handed him the beer she had been holding for him since he came out. Now he drank beer, and drank it from the bottle.

"She doesn't like your area code," he said. "It's long distance. She has a thing about long distance. She wants to know why you haven't called."

"I'm busy," Sara said. "I'm getting settled."

"That's what I told her. She didn't think that was much of a reason. She says it only takes a minute to make a call."

"But it takes a whole day to work up the energy. By the time I feel ready the day is over, and it's dinner time."

They went inside, locking the gate to the swimming pool behind them. "You'll have to call her, she's upset," Martin said.

"Telephone lines work both ways. Why doesn't she call me?"

"You're the one who left, and I'm the one who made you leave. You can imagine how she was on the phone. Why don't you invite them up for the Fourth of July? We'll have a cookout and they can go swimming."

Sara made a face. "Do you really want them up here?"

"Why not? It's a long weekend, it might be fun for a day." Martin padded upstairs in his bare feet. Sara followed him.

She was afraid to tell him how she felt about New York because he still had to go there every day. Maybe he hated it now. She wondered how long it would take in the country to make her a helpless hick, wrinkling her nose at peddlers and garbage on the street, at the price of restaurants, and a bunch of kids walking in a row.

"We could have Annie, too. Maybe she'd like to try out the guest room," Martin said. He threw his bathing suit on a chair and she picked it up. Behind the kitchen was a little room just for laundry. He went in to take a shower while she thought about it. She had a nagging feeling that she didn't want them to come when she had just so recently gotten rid of them. She didn't care what Brenda said to Annie. She was mad at her for having another man in her apartment, confusing the kids about relations between men and women. She didn't want Jack there calculating the cost of everything and wondering aloud how they were possibly going to pay for it; Brenda commenting on the proportion of bare floor to rug, which was very high.

Somehow to her apartment-bred eye, the place looked awfully empty to her. They had filled the house with so many storage areas that now she was a little disturbed by the effect of everything put away. Brenda would think they had run out of money and could not afford decent furnishings, which was half true.

"Well, what do you say?" Martin said, toweling himself enthusiastically. "What's the matter?" to her look of dismay.

"Does this room look awfully empty to you?" she asked.

It had Sara's old dressing table, the large bed, two picture windows and a little settee with a table in front of it. Martin sat naked on the settee and motioned for her to sit on his lap.

"No," he said. "What else could it have?" about the room.

Sara giggled. "You're cute." She sat on his lap.

"Do you like it here?" He tickled her, forgetting that it was way past seven and he hadn't had a thing to eat since noon.

"Need you ask? Ha, ha, don't do that." She made herself smaller on his lap, hunched over to get away from his lips, nuzzled his rib cage. "You're very bony. How come you haven't gotten more substantial since you've become a householder?"

"Where are the kids?" Martin whispered. "I'll show you how bony I am."

"Oh no."

"What about it, do we have a housewarming party?" He kissed the back of her neck, one hand under her shirt. "It's warm in there."

"Not now."

"On the Fourth of July," Martin said. "I want to show off."

"How can you think of two things at once. Don't—I don't think I want to."

"Sit the other way."

Sara obliged and covered his stomach with her skirt. It was a full skirt. It covered his knees, too. "Come on," he said. "What harm can it do?"

"I could get pregnant. The children could walk in."

"I mean having your family here. It would be a nice day for them. I'd like it, too."

Sara sighed. She liked his skinny body. Every bone was a turn-on. "I'll do it," she said decisively. She got up and went into the bathroom.

"You will? Are you going to call them?"

"Go and see what the children are doing."

He came back a few minutes later and was surprised not to see her on the phone. In New York she had always been on the phone. Now she was lying on their bed in nothing but a tank top. She asked if the doors were locked but otherwise was so enthusiastic she forgot about the children. Later he asked what she had done with them. He went down to their rooms not knowing what to expect and found them already asleep in their beds.

30

ANNIE STUCK her head in Ben's office. Everyone else had left hours before. But now that Ben had moved to the corner office, he liked to be the last one to go home.

"Come on, don't sit there any more," Annie said. "I'm going."

"Go ahead. I'm busy."

"Oh, Ben, don't be like that." She went in and sat down. Ben's desk was bigger now and the back of his visitor's chair was higher. He had gotten rid of all the pictures of himself in sporting gear and now only had pictures of the kind of landscapes where sporting activity was most attractive. Mountains, lakes, forests, fast-running rivers with rocks in them.

Annie's chair was black leather and swiveled. She swiveled in it experimentally. "Oh come on. We can have dinner together."

"I'm sorry. I'm working. Have a good weekend."

"It's not for the weekend, it's for the day. I'll be back by dinnertime."

"I don't care, go on without me." He lowered his head so Annie was out of his line of vision. "It's all right. Don't give me a thought," he said. He wrote something on a yellow pad.

"Baby, it's you I'm thinking about. You'd hate it."

"Will you hate it?"

"Well, sure I'll hate it. What do you think?"

"Then why are you doing it?" Ben tore off the page and folded it up.

"I have to, once."

"You want to go. Tell the truth."

"Well, I wouldn't mind seeing it for a few minutes, and it means a lot to them," Annie said. She blew him a kiss to get his attention.

"That's just great." He frowned at the kiss.

"Why are you so mad? It's just for a day?" Annie said.

"Look, we're either together, or not together." He sat back in his chair and put his hands on his stomach. "Which is it?"

"We're always together. They call us the Bobbsey Twins. Everybody *knows*." Annie said. "When they left today, they said, 'Have a good time this weekend, you two.'"

"They didn't say it to me."

"They wouldn't say it to you, I'm the patsy."

"It's your fault. You want to be independent. Don't complain to me. Go off by yourself." He swiveled so he could look out the window.

"I'm not going off by myself. I'm going to see my sister and eat a fucking hamburger. Be sensible. It's only for a few minutes," she said getting irritable now and not feeling good.

"Before you said it was a day," he muttered.

"Well, a day is just a few minutes in the long run."

"This is not together." He swiveled back and regarded her.

"We're always together."

"This is not always together. We don't live together. We meet places."

"We don't meet on weekends. We live together."

"Living together on weekends is not living together. We could part at any time. Just like this," he said, snapping his fingers, meaning Sara's barbecue.

Annie lowered her head and looked at her hands. "I'm very tired of this conversation. You just can't imagine how boring living together would be."

"I think we'd enjoy it. And we'd be committed. That would make all the difference. I think you're afraid of commitment. That's why you don't want me to meet your family."

"I don't want you to meet my family because they're not worth meeting."

"I think it has to do with your father," Ben said thoughtfully. "I've been thinking about it, and I thinks that's the key."

"My father?" Annie laughed.

"You're always talking about your mother. You never mention your father."

"That's because he's not there. Come on, Doctor, I'll buy you a drink."

"I don't want a drink," he said sulkily. "This is important."

"Don't be silly. You always want a drink."

"What do you mean, he isn't there?"

"He sits. He doesn't say anything. The only thing he cares about is neatness. He's very neat, even with coffee cake. When we were little and we used to have family discussions to define our faults—ours, not theirs—then he would talk. But now that we'd kill if he criticized, the joy has gone out of his life and he doesn't talk any more." Annie crossed her legs. "Do you know what time it is?" She looked at the watch he had given her. Every time she looked at it, she felt a thrill.

"Oh my God, it's six o'clock." Ten seconds later she looked at it again. It still thrilled her and was still six o'clock.

"You mean he's withdrawn?"

"Oh, I wouldn't say he's withdrawn. Catatonic would be closer." She slid down in her chair and stretched out her leg to see if she could touch his knee with her toe under his desk. She couldn't, her leg was too short.

"So maybe that's it," he said. He stuck his own foot out and their shoes touched.

"That's what?" Annie's heart lurched. Physical contact with him did that.

"You think I'll find fault with you, like your father did."

"No." Annie got up suddenly. It was true that she didn't think she'd ever be treated well by a man, but she didn't want to discuss this question with Ben, of all people. "Maybe you're right. We need a little space. I'll go on home and catch you—Sunday?" She turned and looked at him with that mixture of confusion and wistfulness that broke him up every time. He was up and blocking the door in less time than it took her to get there.

"I don't want space. That's what I'm telling you. I'm tired of space, of meeting places and forgetting my razor and my things. Or, worrying about where your diaphragm is. It's never where you are. I don't understand it. I want to be together all the time." He put his hands around her waist. "And make the commitment. That's why I want to meet your family. They come with you."

For a second she almost put her hands out to make a wedge between them, panicked by the thought of another encounter with her family. Every little contact with them left a bruise somewhere. Ben would get one too, she knew it. Their ambivalence was her ambivalence. Even now with Ben's arms around her, she could still see Brenda banging away on the piano singing, "I hate men. I can't abide them even now and then," while she and Sara crawled under the piano howling for attention, slapping each other hard, and sometimes holding their ears.

"If thou should wed a businessman be wary, oh be wary." They didn't know what bewary might be. Did they ever find out? Annie reached her arms around Ben's back, making an effort not to push him away while she thought it over.

"Am I blue," Brenda sang. "And me, too," echoed Sara thirty years later. Annie thought they were. What would she do if she really loved someone? Under her fingers she could feel each vertebra in Ben's spine. His back was hard with well-muscled flesh. She had seen him working for it, grunting out thirty-five push-ups every night before daring to sleep.

Ben had a secret fear that his body might revert at any time and he'd wake up one morning a marshmallow instead of a man. In the morning, naked, with the sheet half off him, he propped up one elbow and said, "How do I look to you?" Joking, but at the same time as if he didn't know. He really didn't know.

It made Annie's stomach hurt, wanting to make him happy with familial revelations, but fairly certain at the same time that they couldn't do anybody any good.

"Don't you want to meet my mother?" Ben pressed. "Mine is worse than yours."

"Oh, Ben, I'd love to meet her. I'm sure she's lovely." Annie couldn't help liking the feeling of his hands around her waist. They made her feel small, fragile even.

Whenever he touched her he gave her a different sense of herself. The images were in his hands, in his face sometimes when he told her things. He told her he had always wanted to have his face sanded down to get rid of his scars. But he was afraid. Sometimes he played the piano for her, pieces he'd made up a long time ago. Listening to him reminded Annie of how selfish her mother had been, playing with her elbows out so nobody else could get close enough to experiment with the keys.

Annie remembered how Brenda hoarded information, too. She kept the important things back, like what their bodies were really for. The first time Sara bled she thought she had been wounded somehow. It came as a surprise. Nobody had told her it would happen. Then Sara told Annie little girls were filled with eggs and every month one would fall out. But when she grew up and got married, in a few weeks her husband would stick his penis in there, some juice would squirt out and bring an egg to life. Annie was so upset by this appalling news she went to Brenda calling Sara a liar. Brenda's reaction to this hysteria was to punish Sara, for telling, and Annie, for listening.

Annie still had this image of a penis as a squirt gun filled with life juice that could shoot at will (as soon as it got married) and cause unwilling eggs to jump up in the womb. Brenda's only comment about the sex act was that it seemed terrible to think about, but once one got married one didn't mind the inconvenience. Love had something to do with it, but the notion was so vague, it never took form. Annie thought that love was something that existed outside of herself. Some time, if she wore the right clothes, it would swoop down on her like the winged monkeys in the *Wizard of Oz* and carry her away to the witch's castle where, drugged by a poppy field and quite senseless, she would pour water on her fears and quickly end up a bride in the Emerald City. Love took one over and made one do horrible things like wanting to get married and have a squirt gun pushed up where it was surely unclean to have anything go.

Sara's solution was to get married as soon as possible to get the matter over with, and Annie's was to attack it head-on to find out what the fuss was all about. She didn't know at the time why love didn't seem to find her.

"Annie, what do you say?"

"If you saw them, you'd know," she murmured.

"Know what, that I love you?"

"You'll look at my mother, and you'll know who I am." Annie leaned against the door frame. He'd see her through their eyes. Or she'd see him through theirs.

"I've seen your mother; she's a cute little lady."

"I'm the plain one. You'll see when you meet my sister. They feel sorry for me." She plucked at his hands that could play the piano so well, and handle her well, too. "I'm not supposed to know. I'm supposed to think colorful clothes and bleaching my hair will make the difference."

Ben pulled angrily away. "You're not plain. I hear you say that and it makes me furious. I think you're fishing. I don't like it." He got his jacket and put it on. "Furious," he repeated.

"I feel plain." She walked out of the office kicking the carpet.

He hit the light switch and followed her out. "It's sick. You'll have to get over it." He checked the coffee machine to make sure it was off.

"I'm sorry." She waited while he locked up.

"I already know who you are. Do you think if I don't like your mother I won't like you?" He put his hand on her shoulder. "There must be *something* good about her if she made you."

31

ANNIE SLEPT fitfully through the night. Once again she had her dream of the cotton in her mouth choking off her breath and her teeth falling out one by one. It seemed a bad omen for the day. In the morning Ben brought her coffee in bed and tried to cheer her up. Annie refused to revive.

They drove up to Sara's house in silence. Sara had seemed doubtful about having a stranger there on her day, another boyfriend to churn up old feelings and divide the family. But Annie didn't give her a choice. She said, "We are coming," in a way that didn't leave much room for negotiation. They got there late, around three in the afternoon, because Annie insisted on stopping for a cake, for a bottle of wine, for a book on Japanese gardens. She wanted to take something else, but Ben lost his patience driving around the city. Then when they were almost there, he remembered that they ought to get something for the children and stopped to buy a rubber raft for the pool.

Driving up Gorge Avenue, Annie pointed out the hedge behind which Herb was probably fighting with Lydia at that very moment. Ben asked her why she had gone out with him so long if there was really nothing between them. And she said, "I don't know."

When they got to the house Sara came running out, followed by Donald and Lucy, and finally Martin. Sara was wearing harem pants striped like a circus tent over the bottoms of her bikini. Her little breasts were inadequately wrapped in a skimpy bandeau. She grinned like an idiot from Annie to Ben, and her blonde curls bounced on her shoulders. Annie looked quickly at Ben for his reaction. But he was saying hello to Lucy, who had lunged into his arms asking what he had brought her.

Martin, a small person with wild hair and a towel around his waist so it was impossible to tell if he had anything under it, shot out his hand.

"Ben," he said. "Good to see you." Ha, *ha,* look who it was.

"Nice to see you again," Ben said. He shook hands with Sara, too. He put Lucy down and gave Donald the package with the raft.

Sara hustled them inside where Jack Flood was sitting in a corner with the crossword puzzle. "Dad," Sara said loudly as if he were hard of hearing, "here's Annie."

"Huh? Oh Annie." He lumbered to his feet. He was as tall as Ben and had as much hair, but his was grizzled now. Gray and black. He had a big handsome face, the only real blue eyes in the family, an uncompromising mouth that softened now for Annie's arrival.

"How's my baby?"

Sara bridled as Annie stepped forward for a hug. He had a big heavy body, and enveloped Annie in a vaguely sweaty embrace from which she feared she might never be released. "You're a smart girl," he said finally. "What's a nine-letter tributary of the Rhine."

"Daddy, I want you to meet Ben," Annie said. "We can work on the crossword puzzle later."

"Who's this?" He turned to Ben. Ben was deeply preppy that day with khaki trousers and a maroon alligator shirt. Annie had chosen the shirt herself because Brenda would be suspicious of his predilection for pink, orange and pale yellow. Bass Weejun loafers, the easy smile of a managing partner.

"Ben, Daddy. Ben Custer."

"How do you do? How's your little girl?"

"No, Daddy," Sara said sharply. "He doesn't have a little girl." She turned quickly to Ben, "Or do you?"

"You don't? What did you do with her?" Jack said.

"I never had one," Ben replied coolly, "I'm somebody else."

Sara shot a fast glance at Annie. So Annie had told Ben about Herb. What a dope! "What a nice name," she said quickly to cover her father's gaffe. "Is it short for Benjamin?" She smiled coyly.

Ben nodded. "But I never use it."

"Do you have a little boy, then?" Jack asked, vaguely confused because he hadn't been listening at lunch.

"No, I'm not married yet."

They stood in a tight little circle around Ben and Annie, the children jumping up and down, pulling on their hands to get them to go outside for another swim.

"How about a swim?" Martin suggested. "I'll show you where you can change."

Sara rushed off to tell Brenda, who was putting on her lipstick in the guest room. Ben admired the house and Martin was telling him about the uniqueness of the design when Brenda came out. She was dressed for a resort, with a bold print skirt and blouse. She had a kind of turban wrapped around her head to protect her hair from the sun.

"Oh, how do you do?" She swept into the living room and gave him a heavy once-over, then stopped disconcerted. "Haven't we met before?"

"You have a good memory," Ben said. "Yes, we have. It's nice to see you again." He put his hand out and Brenda shook it.

"You work in Annie's office," she said, shaken to the core. This was Annie's friend from the office. And she was sleeping with him? How foolish could a person get? "Oh Annie, where are you going? you haven't said hello to your mother."

"I have a headache," Annie mumbled.

"I'll get you some aspirin," Sara said, but didn't move. Who was this again?

"Give me a kiss, Sweetheart." Brenda held out her arms. Annie gave her a kiss. "You look lovely. What did you do to your pretty hair? It's all cut off."

"My head hurts," Annie said.

"It must have been the drive out. What a pretty dress. I think your hair looks very cute. Come on, I'll show you the house," Sara said brightly. "I'll give you some aspirin."

"Jack, do you want a drink?" Martin leaned over his father-in-law, who had retreated to the farthest corner of the living room with his puzzle.

"Not yet," he said.

"How about a swim?"

"What's a six-letter word for Nahautlan people."

"How about Aztecs?" Martin suggested.

"Very good, Martin."

That was a most satisfying exchange. Martin led Ben off, pleased. There were times when Jack spent whole evenings and didn't say anything at all. Now he called after them, "Did Annie say she had a headache again?"

"I think it was the ride out," Martin said. "Sara will take care of her."

"Good, good. What did you say your name was?"

"Ben Custer," Ben said.

"Any relation to the other Custer?"

Ben shook his head.

"Too bad," Jack said vaguely. "You look like a football player."

"Jack was All-American," Martin said.

"That was a long time ago." Jack looked down at his puzzle. "Aztecs, that was a good one, Martin."

In the guest room Sara gave Annie some aspirin. "What's the matter, Annie?"

Brenda came in. "Isn't this just the prettiest room?"

It was all green and white, down the hall from the kids' rooms. It had a queen-size bed and sliding doors that opened on the terrace. Annie could see Ben in a bathing suit standing by the side of the pool.

"It's a beautiful house, Sara. I'm so happy for you," Annie said, clutching her head.

"Daddy said something that upset Annie," Sara said to Brenda. "He thought Ben was Herb."

"Oh no. Poor Annie. Would a cup of coffee help?"

"Sometimes I think he does these things on purpose." Sara stood with her hands on her hips, "And he's so cute, Annie."

"Don't say that," Brenda said sharply. "Sometimes it's just hard to keep track."

"He's very cute. Look at him out there with the kids. Does he wear contacts or can he really see?"

"I feel sick." Annie sat on the side of the bed.

She looked at her mother and sister. They looked like two tropical birds to her, too vivid to bear. She lay back on the pillows and wished she had stayed home.

"Did Daddy upset you in front of your friend?" Brenda said.

Annie closed her eyes.

"Annie, please don't be sick, you haven't seen my house yet," Sara cried. "You haven't seen my kitchen."

"She doesn't want to see the kitchen," Brenda snapped. "That's the trouble with you, Sara. Put yourself in Annie's shoes. Why should she want to see your kitchen?"

"What?" Sara recoiled at her mother's tone. And all day she had been so sweet. What had gone wrong?

"Use your head. Get your sister some ice."

Sara looked stricken and turned away to get the ice without a word.

Brenda put a comforting hand on Annie's forehead. "Baby, your turn will come. I'm sure it will," she said as soon as Sara was out of the room. "Don't be upset by all this. It's just a house. I don't think it's safe anyway with all this wood. Who'd want to live here?"

"I'm not upset," Annie said.

But Brenda was sure she was. Look at what she had gotten herself into now. "Is that your old friend from your office. The one who—" Brenda just couldn't keep silent on the matter.

Annie turned over and put her face into the pillow. She had known it wouldn't work. She could just die. "He's the managing partner. He doesn't work in my office. I work in his," Annie muttered.

"Here's some ice." Sara had put some cubes in a plastic bag and tied a knot around the top. She dumped it in Brenda's hands.

"Your friend wants to know if you're all right," she said to Annie.

"I'm all right," Annie muttered.

"He's very nice. He's telling Martin all about gold. Martin's thrilled. You never tell him about gold, Annie. Annie, is this the one Nate used to find girls for?" Sara asked.

Annie didn't answer.

"The ladykiller?" Sara said. "You know, the one who has to have a different girl every week."

"Sara!" Brenda stopped her short. "Leave Annie alone. It's not that one, is it Annie?"

She leaned over and told her to close her eyes for a few minutes and get a good rest. In a minute the aspirin would start to work. "Don't worry about a thing," she said. "We'll take care of everything, won't we, Sara?"

Annie asked her not to close the curtains as they left. She shook her head thinking of what they would take care of, then closed her eyes. She expected to lie there for quite some time, mulling over the many stupid things she had done in her life— and the fact that her family had shared in every one of them.

She didn't remember telling Brenda and Sara about Ben. She must have used him as filler for her conversation a long time ago. They seemed to know all about him. Right away they knew. They grabbed onto his greatest weakness and pushed it in her face just as surely as if they had opened him up and seen bad luck for her in his wormy entrails. It occurred to her then that they wanted her a certain way, somewhere behind Sara, limping along just missing every time.

She turned on her other side to look out the window at the pool on the other side of the terrace. She could see Brenda under an umbrella talking animatedly to what looked like an empty deck chair because she could only see the back of it. Sara sat crosslegged on the flagstones in her harem pants with Lucy on her lap. Martin had his feet in the pool. She couldn't see Donald in the pool. For a long minute they froze in the frame, her family, with her on the outside looking in and her father off somewhere by himself. Then a bare foot came into focus on the end of the deck chair. Two feet, one crossed over the other. The feet were Ben's. She stared at them.

Those feet found the strangest parts of her body. They were like funny little foreign things covering the terrain of her body with a language all their own. Who else would think there were possibilities beyond torture in the feelings of feet? Who else would think that feet could find shelter in the lee of a knee, interest in the arrangement of ribs in a chest, a meaningful future in the particular aspects of a spine?

Annie watched those feet from afar looking for signs of restlessness, boredom, the itch to travel on. But his feet were still. They didn't rattle for freedom while she spied on them, waiting for betrayal. And as she concentrated on the serenity of those toes, her head cleared. Without her realizing it, the stifling pressure lifted, the nausea of being wrong, doing wrong, ending badly washed quietly away. No one could see the future in his entrails but her, and although she couldn't see it clearly yet, she knew she was safe with those feet. She watched them; the minutes ticked off on her watch. She didn't drift off to sleep and let them go for a few minutes as she planned. What she let go instead was the wish that love would come on the wings of monkeys. The wish was so obdurate it had to be pushed out of her like the dream of the wad of cotton lodged deep in her throat. Love for someone else, someone other than her mother and her sister—someone with an extra moving part—didn't come from the sky. It didn't come from the transformation of a handy frog or the whim of a passing prince. It wasn't a piece of luck handed one like the price of a favorite stock going up. Love was a choice from within.

Annie got up and combed her hair. It hugged her head like a tawny helmet. She took off her summer dress and pulled on her tank suit. She walked out to the pool where everyone was laughing.

"Here's Annie," Brenda cried. "Are you feeling better, Sweetheart?"

Annie rested her hand on Ben's knee. "How are you doing?" she asked. "They'll eat you alive if you let them."

Ben said that he was doing fine, and moved his feet so she could sit down. Then moved one foot sneakily back so she sat on it.

"Do you think you could take a drink?" Brenda asked, and paused, her thought changing course mid-sentence as it often did. "Where did you get that *watch*?" she cried.

Sara leaned forward to have a look, displacing Lucy, who had almost fallen asleep. Ben had raised his knees and Annie was resting her arm on them, so the watch was clearly displayed. He wiggled his toes.

"Ben gave it to me," Annie said. She turned to smile at him and caught an impish grin on his face that made her think they had been talking about her terrible affliction, her headaches, and how she might never return.

"He did?" Brenda said, looking at him with new respect. "From Cartier," she commented. "You have good taste."

"It works, too," Annie said. "If it holds up for the summer, I might buy him one, too." She pulled on his wrist. "What is this watchband made out of, anyway, nylon?"

"I thought it was chic to be shabby." He caught her hand and held it for them all to see.

Brenda looked meaningfully at Sara, who for once was silent.

Then he said, "You're in trouble, Annie. This watch is guaranteed for a lifetime. The saleslady told me if you have any trouble with it, they'll replace the movement."

"Or maybe you'd rather have a different one," Annie said lightly. "I'll get you whatever you want. We could go shopping. Ben is the only man I ever met who likes to go shopping."

"I'll hold you to it," he teased. "You can buy me the copy. It's only a third of the price."

"A promise is a promise," Brenda bridled. "Annie wouldn't buy a copy, would you, Annie?"

"Look at the three of them." Ben addressed this comment to Martin, who had yet to involve himself in the conversation. "What a beautiful family of women. Lucy, too." Lucy had her mouth agape and was snoring in Sara's arms.

Martin laughed. "Yes, they're very strong."

"Strong?" Brenda recoiled at the word. Strong was not a word she would have picked to describe herself.

"Of course, Brenda, you're strong. Strong and beautiful," Martin said.

"What a son-in-law. I couldn't have ordered a better one," Brenda said.

"How about a swim, Annie," Martin asked quickly. "You haven't had a chance for anything yet: a tour, a swim, a drink. What do you say?"

"Yes, to everything." She snapped off her watch. "It's supposed to be safe to sixty-five feet, but I don't think I want to test it." She passed it to Brenda, who held out her hand for it, then stepped to the side of the pool and executed a very snappy dive that took her halfway down the pool before she surfaced.

Later in the kitchen Sara said again that he was very nice. Did Annie want to stay the night? She basted the chicken because she was still afraid to use the grill. The grease dripped right onto the electric coil. Was that right? And anyway just everybody served steak in the summer. She was making something that smelled amazing after marinating in garlic and vinegar and white wine all night and cooking all day with prunes and olives and capers. She showed Annie the cold wheat salad with everything else she could think of in it: almonds and orange peel, and some other undefinable stuff. It looked good. Annie said the kitchen was beautiful, the plate of crudities, also.

"Please, Annie, will you stay?"

"Not this time, Sara." Annie smiled.

"He's very nice. I suppose he could stay, too."

Annie shook her head.

"I wouldn't make a fuss if you wanted to stay in the same room," Sara said. "This is important to me."

Annie took the placemats into the dining room that was glass on both sides just as Archie said it would be. She put out Sara's silver and the plates. Sara came out with a tray of glasses.

"Why won't you?"

"I can't," Annie said. "I'm with Ben now. Maybe later, in a few weeks, we'll come and be with you when Mother isn't here."

"Oh Annie, are you leaving me?"

Annie shook her head. "I have my own life now, and you do, too. Look, you have all this. You don't need me any more." She waved her hand in a big circle at the house and the swimming pool where Martin was pulling the two children riding on Ben's raft. Ben was standing nearby in case one fell in and needed to be saved.

"Your friend is very nice," Sara said looking out at them, not realizing that she had said it before. "He's better looking than Martin. Do you think he'll last?"

"I don't know, Sara. I hope so."

They looked at each other, and suddenly Sara gave her sister a hug. "I hope so, too, Annie. He's beautiful. Look at how he is with the children."

They stood side by side watching the men.

"I love you, Annie," Sara said at last.

"I love you, too, Sara." Annie kissed her smooth cheek. "I really do."

Suddenly, Jack roared from another house away. "Whose shoe is this?"

Annie and Sara both ran through the dining room into the living room where Jack pointed an accusing finger at one blue sneaker lying in the middle of the room.

He roared again. "Whose shoe?"

Since the offending article was a sneaker, blue, and no bigger than his hand, there was a limited number of people to whom it could belong. In fact there was only one.

"It's Donald's shoe," Sara said. "I'll just pick it up. I know where the other one is."

"No. Don't pick that up. Get that child in here. He left it. It's high time he learned how to clean up his own messes."

"He's in the pool," Sara said. "I'll pick it up."

"Don't you dare pick up that shoe. You didn't leave it there. When he's out of the pool, you just send him on in here." Jack had an amazing ability to shift his attention so quickly no one ever knew how to make their transitions. Now he turned his head abruptly and left them standing as if on one foot with no place to put the other.

When they realized they were not expected to stay and started back to the kitchen, Jack yelled after them. "He play ball? He looks like he might have been a ball player."

"Ben?" Annie said, not sure he wasn't still thinking of Donald.

"What's his name, Custard?"

"Custer, E R, Daddy."

"What kind of name is that? Is he related to that general in the Civil War?" Jack looked at Annie dimly.

"Indian Wars," Annie said.

"That's right, India."

"No, I think he comes from the Armenian branch of the family."

"Really, I've never known an Armenian." He swiveled his head and they were gone for him. Whether he had shifted his thoughts to Armenians or the name Custer or the last word he could fill in in the crosswood puzzle they couldn't begin to guess.

He certainly didn't hear Annie say, "Neither has he."

Sara said hysterically, "I can't take that. I just can't take it." She walked back into the middle of the room, waved her arms like a great bird and swooped to pick up the sneaker without his looking up or noticing.

Annie laughed. "Let's have dinner."

"Annie," Sara twirled the shoe on her finger. "If you don't stay here tonight, *they* will. I don't think I can take it. Mother promised me she would never have any interest in the place and would never interfere with my life. But now she says she likes the house and wouldn't mind staying here. Annie, I can't stand it." Sara grabbed the sleeve of her terrycloth robe that Annie had borrowed, as if that way she could hold onto her.

"I'm sorry," Annie said. "We can't stay. Listen. If you don't want them here, you have to say no. Contract a communicable disease. Believe me, they'll go." Annie laughed. "Or tell Martin to frown. They wouldn't want to make him mad."

"I can't," Sara whispered.

"You have to say it from time to time. Learn, Sara. After the first time it gets easier."

A little while later Annie went outside to say dinner was served. Many hours had passed since they arrived. It had cooled off. Everyone had had several drinks. The light had begun to gray. The children had long since eaten their hamburgers and now were winding down in their rooms. After the wheat pilaf and the chicken, Jack opened another bottle of wine and made a toast to Sara's new house, her swimming pool, Martin, the architect.

"We have a nice family." He lapsed heavily into silence. And then when everybody was about to drink, he added, "And to Annie's friend, our first Armenian."

Ben exploded into laughter, followed by Annie and Martin, Brenda and finally Sara, who wasn't sure what was so funny but didn't like being left out. They drank to themselves. A fine family.

Then Annie and Ben collected their things. They made a final tour of the house. They said good-bye to a very edgy Sara, who didn't know yet what she was going to do about her parents. They said good-bye to Jack and an effusive Brenda, to Martin, who kissed Annie on both cheeks and wished her good luck and a safe trip home. They all hugged and kissed, and there were even a few tears.

And then Annie and Ben set off in the Honda Accord. Not too flashy, big enough for a weekend trip, with a rack on top for skis in winter. They turned to wave, and everyone stood in a row on the drive until they were gone before trooping back into the house and closing the door.

At the edge of the main road, just outside Martin's and Sara's property, Ben stopped the car so they could touch before going on. They were both very excited in the humid summer night. They felt they had passed through a kind of trial by fire that left them hot, but unscathed; and now the ordeal was over. They would live.

They giggled hysterically over Jack and the sneaker and his final toast, which was "To Hungarians," because he had no memory for people. The next time he met Ben he would remember that some relative of his once came from Latvia. Or was it North Dakota? Something to do with Indians. And wasn't his skin rather dark?

They necked like teenagers set free after a long heavy dinner, and then not like teenagers (or anyway not like the teenagers they had been), sucking each other's lips, gasping for breath, soaking wet everywhere and all undone.

They got the idea in the same moment, in the same breath almost, that they would shift their clothes just a little bit more. Then squeeze themselves all the way around the gear shift to Annie's side where there were no pedals and the seat snapped back all the way. A little yelp of triumph as their slippery parts eased together on the sticky leather seat, Annie's white summer dress up around her armpits. But never mind that, or anything beyond the sensation, the extraordinary sensation of being free, being together. Awkward as it was just then, still there was no other sensation on earth that was like it.

When they were finished for the moment, they looked at each other, grinning with a mixture of relief and pleasure, even pride of accomplishment. Then Ben let the clutch out and allowed the car to coast down the hill a ways before turning on the motor and the lights, the way kids still do. He wanted to get away unseen, and he had some vague thought that it would be rude to disturb the people in the house as they left.

Glass

Modern love.